THICKER THAN BLOOD

Jade, You Rock! Big love Xxx C Riley

MADELINE SHEEHAN
and
CLAIRE C. RILEY

Thicker Than Blood
Copyright © 2015
by Madeline Sheehan and Claire C. Riley

ISBN-13: 978-1505972610
ISBN-10: 1505972612

Edited by Pam Berehulke
Cover by Okay Creations

This is a work of fiction. Names, characters, businesses, places, events, and incidents are either the products of the author's imagination or used in a fictitious manner. Any resemblance to actual persons, living or dead, or actual events is purely coincidental.

ABOUT THE BOOK

Leisel and Evelyn lost everything. Husbands. Families. Friends. Lives that made sense. All they had left was each other, and a friendship that could withstand anything…

Even an apocalypse.

Until one fateful night, the marginal safety they'd come to rely on comes to a vicious and brutal end. With the help of Alex and Jami, both unlikely allies, Leisel and Evelyn are able to escape their shattered sanctuary only to find themselves face-to-face with a much altered, much crueler life where they have to find the way—and the will—to stay alive in a world they no longer recognize.

Traveling across a broken and infection-ridden country, the road-weary group is pitted against endless violence, improbable circumstances, and the ultimate loss.

Everything comes at a price, especially safety, the cost of which could very well strip them of the one thing they've tried so hard to cling to—their humanity.

Yet along with all the trials they're forced to endure, there's also hope in the form of love. Having loved Leisel from afar, Alex attempts to put the pieces of her fractured heart back together.

But in such a savage world, is there room for love?

In a place of nightmares-made-reality, where the living should be feared far more than the dead, an unbreakable friendship and a love against all odds can mean the difference between life and death.

There are friends…

and then there are Leisel and Evelyn.

DEDICATION

To always having someone to rely on, a person in your corner to fight for you no matter the reason, no matter the cost.

To having more than a friend, more than a sister, but a soul mate.

To the hope they give us, the strength they provide us, and the unconditional love they empower us with.

To best friends.

PROLOGUE

THE ZOMBIE APOCALYPSE didn't happen like it does in the movies.

Disaster didn't strike when we weren't looking. No, we were all looking. We were all waiting. It was a slow trickle that began with a nightly news broadcast. Yet another disease, another epidemic, was sweeping through the third world with crippling effects, decimating entire villages within mere days. The Vaal Fever they'd called it, and it took no mercy on its victims. Men, women, and children alike were ravaged by the disease, and most perished as a result.

Only, they didn't stay dead.

They awoke and attacked the survivors, spreading the virus through both their saliva and blood. And what could we do? Like all the other pandemics we'd lived through, we could do nothing but hope that the Centers for Disease Control could put a stop to it, or that the armed forces would protect us and ensure it wouldn't spread. So we hoped and we waited, trying not to worry.

We went about our daily lives. Like usual, we woke up every morning, we went to work and to school, we continued talking, laughing, living. But in the back of our minds, we were waiting. Seven billion people were all waiting.

That slow trickle grew, becoming a flood as more reports streamed in from all over the world. As a nation, we stayed glued to our radios, to our televisions, to the Internet, watching helplessly as the pandemic continued to spread. After that, governments worldwide took aggressive action to stop the disease from entering their countries. Airports shut down, shipping companies refused to sail, importing and exporting were no more.

Then the floodgates broke, and we learned the truth.

There was no treatment. There was no cure.

Africa was the first to succumb, then China, and Russia quickly followed. Suddenly our usually busy, bustling lives came to a standstill. Supermarkets and drug stores began limiting bulk purchases, generators were suddenly in great demand, and people had begun wearing face masks. Others stopped going to work altogether, refusing to leave their homes in order to avoid any sort of contact with other people.

When we got word that the disease had found its way to Europe and South America, panic—birthed from fear and helplessness—turned to violence. The American army wasn't big enough, wasn't quick enough, wasn't prepared enough for the sheer magnitude of the public outcry. Because of their lack of planning, a civil war broke out between the army and the citizens they were meant to protect.

As a result, entire cities went down in flames before the disease had even reached American soil. But when it did, when the first American fell to his knees, the government was ill prepared for the fallout and the sickness spread like wildfire. Indiscriminate, it took the weak, the strong, the young, and the old.

Before long, news reports and radio broadcasts were no more. The airwaves were filled with nothing but static. Our neighborhoods, our cities and states, the entire country, the whole world—all went silent.

When the world awoke again, it awoke with a rattling groan that promised only misery and loss.

And eventually death.

CHAPTER ONE

Leisel

THERE WAS BLOOD everywhere—on the bed, on the walls, on the floor. Some had even managed to find its way to the ceiling.

I looked down at my red-stained hands, at my naked body. It was all over me, coating the pale freckled skin on my arms, torso, legs, and feet. It was everywhere.

I hadn't seen so much blood in one place in…well, not in the past four years since I'd been living in this sanctuary from the outside world.

A small, manic laugh escaped my dry and scratchy throat, bubbling past my lips. A sanctuary? Well, it might be for most, but that wasn't the case for everyone, and least of all for me.

This place, Fredericksville, a once small and quiet town, and my current home, was one of the last known functioning towns left in the country. And for all intents and purposes, it was a safe place to live. Families survived within, protected by fortified walls and guarded by armed men who kept us safe from the numerous threats from outside. We had a leader, one man, and a council of sorts composed of a small group of men who created our laws. Together they devised a system of checks and balances to keep the peace.

Everyone had a job to do, determined by whatever skills one possessed in the old world. Women who could sew were still sewing, and teachers like myself were still teaching. Men who could build were still building, chefs were still cooking, farmers were still farming, police were still policing, soldiers were still fighting, officials were still officiating.

And our leader...

I looked up, away from my bloodied skin and across the dimly lit room to where an equally naked and bloodied body lay still on the bed. My husband, Lawrence Whitney, the leader of our community... was now dead and no longer leading.

Another laugh bubbled up and my eyes began to water. I'd killed my husband, a man who wasn't just a man but was the man in charge, the most powerful man in my world. And no matter how broken this world might be, murder was still a crime, at least behind these walls, and subsequently punishable by death.

There would be no trial, no defense attorney to help me present my tale of woe to a jury of my peers, to showcase the bruises, new and old, that covered my body. No one would help me explain the real reason why my visits to the infirmary were more frequent than most, why I often had one arm in a sling, why sunglasses always hid my eyes, and why I could occasionally be seen hobbling on a pair of crutches.

When it came to committing murder in this new world, the only thing one had to look forward to was death. Without the resources or space to house a long-term prison, the people of Fredericksville had little choice but to quickly and efficiently end the lives of their violent offenders.

I'd known this, and still I'd allowed my emotions to get the better of me. Allowed my pain to cloud my judgment. Allowed my fear to take control, to rear its ugly head and end the source of my misery, my prison, once and for all.

Oh God, why? Why had I done this, and here in our home of all places? There was no escape, no running and hiding from this mess I'd made. Not within the confines of a walled town, surrounded by armed men. The very same men who would be at our door at the first sign of morning light, ready to escort my husband on his daily duties, only to find him brutally murdered. And me, the bloodstained and obvious culprit.

If they didn't kill me outright, I would be taken into custody immediately, not allowed to see or speak to anyone. Within an hour of my apprehension, my crime would be known to all. Word traveled fast in such a small community, especially one with little in the way of modern entertainment. There was no television to be watched, no cell phones to keep us busy, and what little electricity that was harnessed from the nearby river was used solely for communication purposes within Fredericksville, lighting the community buildings, and providing a small amount of refrigeration in the cookhouse. Face-to-face gossip was our only source of entertainment, because it was all we had left.

I had a day left, maybe two, until everyone would be gathered on the main drag, where justice would be swiftly meted out. A public execution, a single bullet to my head, would provide a warning to all who might at some point be inclined to take the law into their own hands as I had so stupidly done.

The infection had efficiently ended society as we'd known it. In the midst of the destruction, a new world had arisen with a survival-of-the-fittest, better-him-than-me philosophy, the sort of archaic thinking that asserted that men and women were not equals. As for justice, it too was a thing of the past. We simply survived.

I sank to the cold tile floor, dropping to my knees with my arms outstretched in supplication. But who my pleading was for, I didn't know. Did we fall to our knees when we knew we had nothing left, nowhere else to go but down? Was I subconsciously asking God for mercy, for forgiveness, or for a savior?

My thoughts were scrambled, the fear at the forefront of my mind muddling everything else.

"Why?" I whispered to the floor. "Why…"

Confused, I was unable to finish my question, not knowing what my question was. Or maybe I did know, maybe I knew exactly what my question was. Maybe I wasn't asking why this particular and most recent tragedy had happened, but why it had *all* happened.

All of it. Why any of this had happened.

But there were no answers to be found. There never were.

Only emptiness. And consequences.

I wished with all my heart that I could have been stronger. Able to endure this new world, this new reality, with equanimity and grace.

As I stared off into nothing, I thought of Evelyn, my beautiful and courageous friend. Evelyn had endured as much as I had, been forced from her quiet, happy life as I had, had also lost the man she loved, and alongside me had been thrust into this cruel and cold world. Like me, she had been forced to marry a man she hadn't loved, forced to live a life she hadn't wanted. She had been forced to become a woman she wasn't. Had never known how to be.

But unlike me, she hadn't crumpled. She'd become an even stronger version of herself. Evelyn was capable of taking on whatever misery life decided to throw her way, embracing it even, utilizing it, molding it to her liking, and forever persevering.

I had done the opposite. Grief had consumed me, caused me to turn in on myself instead of facing my demons head-on. They'd piled up inside and eaten away at me, rendered me useless, unable to function properly, and created a whole new set of hardships.

My demons were always growing, welling up within me, until they were too many—too many to name or count, let alone deal with.

And so I'd snapped, unable to take another second of it. Of this life. Of his fist colliding with my face, of his body crudely taking what I wasn't offering, of his harsh words often followed by laughter and scorn. I'd snapped.

And there my consequences lay. Bloody. Mangled. Dead on our marriage bed. But even dead and finally silent, I could still hear his laughter. It echoed loudly throughout this old building, bouncing off the walls, coming at me from every direction.

You're worthless, Leisel. You're nothing. No one. Do you hear me? You're nothing, Leisel, nothing! You're a hole to fuck, a pretty face and an empty head. A stupid, good-for-nothing…

And his hand would crack across my face, causing me to stumble, to cry out in pain and fall at his feet. He would laugh again and again. Call me more names. Blame me for my inability to produce a child. And then more tears would fall.

From those tears of pain and humiliation came the worst consequence of all. My pain, my anguish, and my agony made him feel his most powerful, victorious, and like all men who succumbed to bloodlust, I was his prize to be taken.

Only tonight, there had been too many tears. Too much pain. And while he'd continued to ravage me, hurting me, suddenly I'd gone numb to it all. Numb and then…angry.

And as he slept, I'd paced. I'd mumbled, crying, cradling the sore places on my body. I'd paced until the anger had taken over, too many thoughts inside of me, too many voices shouting at me, too much pain radiating from my skin and from my broken heart, too many unanswered questions spiraling around and around, and then all of a sudden I could no longer bear it, bear another second of hearing him snore so peacefully, without a care in the world, after my world had been destroyed and he'd forced me into his world, his world of misery, of my misery, and suddenly the knife he kept in his boot was glaring at me from across the room, a shiny beacon in the fog that I'd become, and the beacon was beckoning me, screaming at me until it was all I could hear, all I could see, and so I took that knife from its sheath and I held it above my husband's body and as tears poured down my face, angry and full of determination, regardless of the consequences, I brought that knife down and drove it into his heart.

Again. And again. And again.

As I continued recalling the events that had concluded mere moments ago, a strange sort of calm began to spread across my goose-pebbled skin, soothing the burning nausea and relieving the crippling fear that held me hostage.

With a silent breath, I stood up and again surveyed the scene of my crime. Only this time, I wasn't looking at my consequence. Instead I was seeing something altogether different, something utterly surprising.

Surprising because…after all, I'd wanted out of this world, hadn't I?

I'd wanted to be free from this fear, from the pain, not just from that of my husband but from the world we now lived in. I wasn't built for it, wasn't built to survive in times of strife.

I was weak; I always had been. Only because of Evelyn had I made it this far. Only because of her had I not ended myself long ago.

And now I was free. I was finally blessedly free of this man.

"You were a terrible man," I whispered fiercely. "Not a man at all."

I'd known a good man, a true man. I'd loved him with all of me, and in return he'd loved me with all of him. Ours had been a partnership, a friendship, and a love affair all rolled into one. What I had lacked, he'd had in spades, and what he'd lacked, I'd made it my mission to make up for. And never once had he touched me out of anger or perversion.

That had been a marriage, and this…this had been a fallacy. A single-sided, self-serving game. This had been torture masqueraded as a duty to the continuation of the human race.

Killing him, that hadn't been a mistake. It hadn't been born of fear, but of anger. Killing him had been a necessity, a necessary evil. For the first time in my life, even if it meant the end of it, I'd finally done something brave. I'd finally saved myself.

With my bearings back, a steely resolve firmly in place, I turned away from what was left of the man I'd hated, from the life I'd detested. As I walked slowly toward my dresser with the intention of dressing, Evelyn's face once again invaded my thoughts. Knowing I would be leaving her alone, a sliver of guilt wormed its way into my newfound resolution. She was not without friends, but they were all the same, fair-weather and self-serving, survival their only concern. For so long all Evelyn and I had had was each other; we trusted each other, depended on each other, reminded each other of a life now long gone.

Shaking my head, I shoved those feelings away. It was too late to do anything about it now. The damage was done, and Evelyn…she would survive this too.

Fully clothed now in tattered jeans and a threadbare thermal top, I turned toward my mirror and let out a shaky breath. I didn't recognize this woman, the blood-spattered, bruised, and beaten-down woman. The same long dark hair fell past my shoulders, the same wide brown eyes stared back at me, the same pale, freckled skin shone white under the moonlight, yet I didn't know her. I didn't even want to know her.

Turning away from my reflection, I surveyed the room once again as my nails dug bloody half moons into my palms. Then I took another deep breath.

"Help!" I screamed at the top of my lungs. "Help me!"

A muffled shout sounded, followed by banging on the door and then a loud crash.

They'd come now. They'd see what I'd done and they'd take me away. Deliver me to my last stop on this long and twisted road.

CHAPTER TWO

Evelyn

JAMI PRESSED MY back against the wall, the cold bricks digging harshly into my heated skin. His kisses were persistent, never ending, and I willingly took them, devoured them, greedy for more. I was always greedy for more of him. The more of him I had, the more he'd wash away the bitter and hollow taste my so-called husband left behind. I needed Jami right now, needed him like a drug that could take me away to somewhere new, to somewhere else other than here with a man who repulsed me, in a life I hated.

Jami's mouth moved from my lips, traveling down my chin and neck, pushing my thin cotton blouse to one side and exposing more of my flesh to his voracious kisses. His hot breath danced across my skin, lighting my nerves to his every touch. My hands dragged through his hair, my leg wrapping around one of his, pulling him closer. He groaned deep in the back of his throat while his hands palmed my breasts in hunger. It was a sound that I loved to hear. A sound that ignited a fire in me, driving me onward to hear it again. Lowering his mouth to my chest, he pulled free my breast, sucking and biting on the hard nub of my nipple. I groaned again, wriggling beneath his weight, feeling as if I couldn't take another second of his teasing.

"Jami…" I said his name, loving the rough sound that followed from him, a satisfied rumble from deep inside his chest.

"Again," he murmured, his mouth resistant to leaving my nipple.

"Jami," I repeated breathlessly. He didn't need to ask, I would have said it anyway, would have screamed it over and over again. His name was an aphrodisiac to me, the lone word having so much incomprehensible power over me. It controlled me, controlled my body, and I felt myself melting more, succumbing entirely to his every touch, growing increasingly impatient for more of him.

Yet, even as hypnotized as I was by this man, my thoughts still turned often to Mason, my husband. His touch was still fresh on my body, his smell still potent in my nose. I could almost feel his fat fingers still pressing against me, intruding and eager, and it made my stomach heave. This was when I needed Jami the most, to replace Mason's taste and Mason's touches with his own.

Whereas Mason wasn't attractive, Jami was sinfully so. Whereas Mason was a good ten years older than me, Jami was thirty-three, only two years older than I was. No bath had ever done the trick quite like Jami's rough and zealous hands and his amazing mouth, always eager to please.

"Eve."

My eyes opened slowly and I found Jami watching me with hooded eyes, a grin dimpling his face. Reaching for me, he rubbed his thumb across my bottom lip, pulling my mouth open for him.

"Where'd you go?" he asked.

Calmer now, I smiled at him. "Nowhere. I'm right here."

His grin grew, and then he claimed my mouth once more, his hands deftly moving toward the hem of my skirt, pulling it up and dragging my panties down in a move both proficient and explicit. My own hands moved to his belt buckle, unfastening it quickly. With practiced fingers I undid his button, excited to free him from his clothing. Excited to feel him pressed up against me, pressing up inside of me.

My breath shuddered free from my lungs. I wanted him. God, I wanted him, needed him…

And then he was there, hard and ready for me. I whimpered as he gripped my thigh, lifted my leg, and eagerly pressed himself inside me. I sighed, my head lolling to one side, granting him access to the tender skin on my throat. He whispered sweet nothings into my ear as he moved inside me, his hips finding a perfect rhythm against mine.

Biting down on my lower lip, stifling my cry of pleasure, I allowed Jami to override Mason's touch, the ugly memories floating away with each pounding thrust that Jami gave me. He breathed heavily, a rumble stirring low in his chest, almost sending me over the edge.

"Eve!"

I opened my eyes, my body freezing in the midst of my breathless panting. Jami leaned in to kiss me again, but I shook my head and silently mouthed, *Wait*. Several moments ticked by.

"Eve!"

This time my name resonated through the walls and I paused, my breath catching in my throat as I waited to hear my name called out again. Straining my ears, my heart thudding wildly in my chest, I listened intently for any sort of noise. I heard it then, the distinctive sound of footsteps coming quickly up the path, the gravel crunching beneath boots.

Someone was coming!

"Shit!" I hissed, shoving Jami away hard enough to cause him to stumble backward. "Shit," I repeated, trying to compose myself, the loss of him inside me already too strong. "Someone's here."

A soft knocking sounded, echoing from the front door and through the dark and nearly empty house. Jami glanced around the room, his eyes suddenly wide and wild with worry. He grabbed his pants and began pulling them back up his legs, though I was glad to see that he looked just as flustered and red-faced as me.

Shit!" I cursed again, dragging my underwear back up my legs. Running toward the window, I looked to the ground beneath. Angela, one of the girls from the cookhouse, was standing at the door, her hands gripping her apron, violently twisting it. Glancing up, she found me in the window.

"Evelyn, quickly," she pleaded, gesturing for me to come down. Repeatedly, she glanced over her shoulder, back to me, and over her shoulder again, as if she was afraid that she'd been followed, or worried that someone was watching her. Looking her over, I realized that not only was she still wearing her apron, but she also had flour in her hair, all telling me that she must have departed the cookhouse in a hurry.

Fredericksville functioned like any other well-oiled machine. Everyone had a job to do, and everything worked fine as long as people did those jobs, and did them well. Just like before the infection, there were certain jobs that held more importance, more sway, than others.

Contrary to public opinion, it was my personal belief that every job held just as much importance as any other, simply because a leader could not exist without his citizens, and vice versa. Even the children responsible for recycling our garbage were important, and in my humble opinion, much more so than the cruel men in charge.

Not everyone shared my belief, though. My husband, the superior bastard that he was, was one of the many men around here always looking down on anyone he believed to be lower than him.

Turning away from Angela, I found Jami sliding his military jacket over his broad shoulders, his pants once again buttoned. Realizing another of our few-and-far-between moments had ended, a pang of regret passed through me. I watched him tucking his gun back inside its holster, until his gaze finally found mine.

Smirking and without another word, he turned away, already heading for the stairs. No kiss good-bye, not even a longing glance over his shoulder. I wanted to be pissed about his indifference; I should have been pissed. My adoring husband always gave me a kiss goodbye whether I wanted one or not, yet Jami gave me nothing. Nothing to cling to when he wasn't here, nothing to tide me over while Mason demanded I be his adoring wife. As was his usual MO, Jami just left, leaving me desperate for more of him.

I heard the soft click of the back door as it closed, signaling Jami's departure, yet I continued to stand there, waiting for one more minute—the longest of my life—before descending the stairs. Taking the steps two at a time, I shook my head, dismayed. That was too close; we were getting reckless. Or at least I was, although I wasn't exactly sure if I cared anymore.

No, scratch that. I did care. My thoughts veered to Leisel, my best friend. She was the only family I had left, and I couldn't deny that I still in fact cared. I had to care, for her sake, because if I didn't, she wouldn't have survived this place, this world. Her dependence on me and my strength could grate at times, but then, I couldn't fault her so completely. I had dark days of my own during which I longed to end it all, to eat a bullet, finally shutting the world out. Then I would think of her, and would be unable to go through with it. In a way, I guess you could say we were constantly saving each other.

We'd promised each other—back when this all had begun, when the world crumbled right before our eyes, taking with it everything we'd ever known, everyone we'd loved—that we'd never give up. That we'd survive no matter the cost, that we would always stay together. Always. Those promises had been hard ones to keep, and Leisel especially had suffered more than I. Daily, I hated myself for what she'd been forced to endure, for not being able to do more to protect her.

Reaching the dark foyer, I flipped the lock and pulled open the door, quickly backing away as Angela barged inside. She seemed frantic, a sheen of sweat glistening on her wrinkled forehead, and I began to fear that there'd been a breach in the walls. It had happened once before, during the first year when the walls had yet to be completed. A large group of the infected had managed to find their way inside, and were freely roaming the streets. But it had ended nearly as soon as it had begun. Our soldiers had controlled it, quickly and efficiently. Still, we'd lost people.

That had been three years ago. Three long years spent in this infection-free...prison.

"It's Leisel," Angela said, and my rambling thoughts came to a crashing halt. Grabbing the short, stocky woman by her shoulders, I lowered my face to hers.

"Where is she?" I demanded, the quiver in my voice laced with worry.

"She's—they took her!" She started to sob, hiccupping sobs that I didn't have patience or time for.

Still gripping her shoulders, I shook her hard. "Where is she?" I yelled. But Angela was still crying. I frowned down at her as annoyance and worry wormed their way into my panicked state. It wasn't as if Angela and Leisel were close, yet the woman was behaving as if they were.

"Stop crying and tell me where the hell she is!" I shoved her backward, slamming her back against the door.

My body, that only moments ago had been heated by lust, was now humming with anger. Leisel was a mouse, a quiet little mouse who had never done a damn thing to anyone. She'd never once caused trouble in Fredericksville, always keeping to herself, barely speaking to even me because of that bastard husband of hers. She was a broken and beautiful ghost, my sweet Leisel.

"I swear to God, if he's hurt her again..." I cursed under my breath, releasing Angela to begin pacing the length of the room.

Lawrence Whitney, Leisel's husband and our oh-so-enigmatic leader, was outwardly charming and charismatic, everything a leader should be. He was what the people of Fredericksville had needed in the beginning, someone to put their broken world to rights, and they'd followed him blindly. But privately, with Leisel, he was a monster. Beating and abusing her, using her in every horrific way possible, simply because he could. Because he knew that no one could or would stop him.

"I'll kill him this time," I mumbled. "I will." Tears began to form as a sense of helplessness washed coldly over me. Angela and I both knew I was full of shit; we both knew that I wouldn't do a damn thing. Because I couldn't touch that man without bringing hell down on both myself and Leisel.

Knowing how helpless I was made me hate him as much as I hated the infected that plagued the world beyond our walls. He was a monster, and no better than they were.

"He's dead, Eve. Lawrence is dead," Angela said, her eyes huge.

I scowled at her. "What?" I cried. "How?"

And then suddenly I smiled, because I didn't care how. What did it matter? He was dead and Leisel was free of him, free of his torture. Whoever she was passed on to next, they couldn't be any worse than Lawrence. So I continued smiling because this was a good thing, as good as life could get inside a walled community that had so easily disregarded a century's worth of women's rights in favor of a male-ruled totalitarian state.

"Where is she?" I asked, laughing despite myself. I suddenly wanted to find her, to be with her that very instant, wrapping my arms around her and sharing in what I could only imagine would be tears of sheer joy.

It was stupid of me to behave this way. Stupid and reckless. It was dangerous for anyone to know that I was this happy about Lawrence's death, but to hell with it, I didn't care. He was dead, and my best friend was free of him.

"It was Leisel," Angela mumbled.

"What was Leisel?" I asked.

"Leisel killed him." Angela's gaze dropped as more tears fell from beneath her lashes. "She killed him, Eve. And they're going to execute her tomorrow."

At her shocking words, I stumbled backward as if I'd been punched in the gut, as if Lawrence had just hit me with one of his vicious blows. Leisel, my innocent Leisel, had killed him? I shook my head, refusing to believe it, yet Angela was nodding like one of those obnoxious bobble-head figurines, smiling and forever bobbing its ridiculously large head.

Only Angela wasn't smiling.

"Take me to her," I said from between gritted teeth.

"I can't. They've locked her up. She's in the tower already. I have to go because if they notice that I'm gone…" Angela pressed her lips together and glanced away.

I didn't bother pressing her for more. What was left to say?

Several seconds of uncomfortable silence passed before Angela turned away and opened the door. Glancing back over her shoulder, she swallowed thickly. "I'm so sorry, Eve."

She really was sorry; I could see how genuinely sorry she was. She knew what Leisel meant to me, the lengths I would go to for her. And unlike the rest of the town, Angela had a vague idea of what Lawrence had put Leisel through.

Again, disbelief clouded my thoughts. Leisel had just killed a man in cold blood? It didn't make sense, though I supposed that everyone had their limits. Worry for her began burning through my veins. What had he done to get her into such a state that she couldn't take any more?

It all seemed so wrong, considering everything I thought I'd known about my best friend. How had such a sweet and caring woman, a total book nerd who'd taught half the kids in Fredericksville how to read and write, actually hurt someone? And she hadn't just hurt him, but had ended him.

I should have seen it coming, should have realized that she'd been near the end of her rope. There were only so many times a person could be beat down, again and again and again, before they broke entirely. Leisel had obviously broken, and why wouldn't she?

Hurting Leisel was like kicking a blind puppy—no one of sound mind would ever do such a thing. Lawrence, I finally decided, had gotten his just deserts, with no one to blame but himself.

How stupid we'd been, the both of us. Stupid for thinking that a small group of survivors that had happened on us in our darkest hour, promising safety and security, hadn't had ulterior motives. We'd simply traded one hell for another.

I found myself sneering at the wall, remembering how happy I'd been for Leisel when Lawrence had chosen her to marry. He'd seemed such a strong leader at the time. In his early forties, charismatic and handsome, and more importantly, seeming so willing to do whatever it took to help rebuild our crumbling world. I'd even been a bit jealous, wishing I had a man who seemed so dependable and caring.

Until the first bruise had appeared; then I'd felt only anger and regret.

"How did she do it?" I called out after Angela's quickly retreating form.

Turning, she anxiously looked in all directions. "She stabbed him," she said quietly, swallowing nervously, her eyes still darting back and forth. Another heartbeat passed, then Angela gave me a pitying glance before running off down the path and disappearing into the night.

Shocked and horrified, I clasped a hand over my mouth. Why stabbing was so much worse than anything else, I didn't know. Perhaps because it *was* so much more personal, so up close, and much more vicious than I would have ever expected of Leisel.

Surely this would help her. How clearly unravelled she must have become to resort to such extreme lengths, killing him in such a brutal and violent manner. In the old world it would have meant something, her defense would have been cut and dried, crystal clear to a jury as the evidence of her abuse was laid out for them. But in this new world, here in Fredericksville…

I stumbled forward, dropping to my knees, already knowing that Leisel had no defense. No matter what happened, her voice wouldn't be heard. Justice here wasn't justice at all, and no one had the time for sob stories. Surviving was all that mattered anymore, the protection of our community from outside threats, and ensuring that everyone continued to do their part to keep the cogs turning, to keep humanity afloat.

A sob began to build in my throat, making it hard to breathe. "No," I whispered to the darkness. "Please, no."

I'd promised to protect her, to keep her safe. But I'd broken that promise, told her to forget about her previous husband, her previous life, even though I hadn't—couldn't. I still thought about it every day, my first husband and our lives before the infection. I'd been a hypocrite and a liar, and part of me felt that if I'd been honest with her from the start, instead of always shielding her from my own pain, that maybe things wouldn't have ended like this.

Choking back my bitter tears, I slowly got back to my feet and looked around my sham of a home.

Three months after the infection had arrived in America, Leisel and I had both lost our husbands, our entire world. It took everything we had to carry on when all we wanted to do was curl up and die. I'd kept us strong, kept us fighting. I'd lied through my teeth, choking back my own sorrows in order to comfort and soothe hers, and now I was going to lose her anyway.

It had all been for nothing.

But then again, that was what I did. I stayed tough despite all odds, and even in the face of utter devastation, I'd always been the resilient one. I'd always refused to give up.

And, by God, I refused to give up now.

CHAPTER THREE

Leisel

SEATED ON A lone bench in the corner of one of two concrete rooms inside the Fredericksville police station, both my hands and ankles bound in handcuffs, I stared blankly through the candlelit cell at the guard stationed to watch over me.

Alex was younger than me by about five years, still in his early twenties, and I'd previously thought one of my late husband's most trusted friends. He'd been the one who'd always quietly spirited me away to the infirmary when I'd been too injured to walk, who'd made excuses for my absences, who'd ensured that my husband's sick secrets remained just that. Secrets.

Worse, he'd been Lawrence's personal escort, following wherever the man went, even standing watch outside our house at night. Because of this, it had been Alex who'd found me with my husband's dead body.

If anything, I'd expected to see anger or hatred in his features, or at the very least, shock and horror. Instead, he'd taken one look at my bloody, battered body, another at Lawrence's mutilated form, then lifted his eyes to mine filled with what looked like pity. And something else, something shocking and unrelated that I couldn't quite fathom.

Not a word was spoken as he'd slowly pulled his handcuffs from his belt and gently placed them on my wrists. Even more surprising was that he'd waited until I'd been securely locked inside a cell before alerting the others to my crime. It had dawned on me then that he'd been protecting me from the town's wrath, especially from those who had been a part of Lawrence's close-knit group.

I'd been here for an hour now, and yet hadn't had a single visitor other than Alex and a few other guardsmen passing through. No one had so much as looked at me, let alone spoken to me, leading me to wonder how many people had actually known about the four long years of abuse I'd endured.

Why hadn't anyone ever said a word about it? No one except Evelyn, that is. And even Evelyn had been loath to speak her mind in front of anyone who mattered. Speaking your mind in this new world was a crime in and of itself, and if the words you spoke were against Lawrence Whitney, you usually ended up minus a tongue.

I sighed, knowing I couldn't fault them for falling in line with the cruelty here, not when the outside world was as terrifying as it was. These men had saved us from the infection, protected us, given us a semblance of our old lives, no matter how warped that semblance might be. Something was always better than nothing.

Averting my eyes from Alex's, I looked out the lone window and into the inky black night, thinking of what was to come. I would be executed soon, there was no getting around that, and yet, much to my own surprise, I wasn't experiencing the crippling fear I'd thought I would when it came to facing my own death.

My calmness probably came from the knowledge that the world I was leaving was a barren one, devoid of everything I'd once loved. With the exception of Evelyn, there was nothing here for me. And maybe some small part of me was still hoping that there was a heaven somewhere out there in the great unknown. That maybe the human race hadn't been forsaken, and God would forgive me for my sins, allow me into heaven to be with my first husband again, to be the woman I once was without repercussions—simple, shy, and happy.

Without consequence.

Maybe someday I would see Evelyn again as well. Because if heaven was real, then she deserved to be there too.

The sound of a door rubbing against the concrete floor jolted me out of my musings. I jerked, then lifted my head to find Alex already on his feet and nodding to whoever was entering. I stiffened, preparing for the worst, thinking that my time had already come and I would be sentenced to die tonight.

A messy shock of dirty-blond hair came into view first that I instantly recognized as belonging to Jami, another Fredericksville guard and Evelyn's latest distraction from her husband. Following behind him, her face stained with tears, her strawberry-blonde curls unusually messy and her hands wringing together, was Evelyn.

My shocked gaze slid to Alex, who gave me a small, sad grimace in return. He was helping me? Yet again?

I jumped off my stool, entirely forgetting that my ankles were cuffed, and ended up falling forward. I twisted my body just in time so as not to land flat on my face, allowing my right arm to bear the brunt of the impact. Sharp pain radiated up the limb, exploding in my neck, causing me to inadvertently cry out.

While I lay there, breathing heavily, tears stinging my eyes, I could hear the jingling of keys, the sound of muffled cursing, and then she was there, kneeling on the floor beside me, her hands gentle as she turned my body.

"Oh God," Evelyn whimpered as she looked me over, her eyes widening at the sight of me. I couldn't imagine what I must have looked like; I hadn't looked in a mirror since the incident. But I knew from Alex's initial expression, and now Evelyn's, that I was a sight to behold.

"Eve," I said as I sobbed softly. "I'm so sorry. I'm so very sorry." Not for killing Lawrence but for leaving her here alone, because that was what she would be after I was gone—alone.

"Shh." She shushed me, smoothing her hand across my cheek and brushing errant strands of hair from my eyes.

"No," I whispered frantically, wishing I could hug her. "I'm sorry. I wasn't thinking, and I—"

"Lei," she interrupted, softly yet firmly. "You have nothing to be sorry for. He got what was coming to him! He got—"

"Eve!" The agitated mutter belonged to Alex. "Keep your voice down!"

"You can't be here," I said, grabbing her wrist. Using her arm, I pulled myself upright to a sitting position.

Evelyn wrapped both her arms around me, then bowed her head, pressing our foreheads together. As she held me, I let out a shuddering sigh of relief. I inhaled slowly, smelling the sweat on her skin, the faint smell of liquor and…Jami.

I looked up, over Evelyn's head at the guard she'd entered with. She wasn't alone here. She had Jami, and if he had been willing to risk bringing Evelyn into the station just to visit me, his feelings must run deeper for her than he'd ever let on.

"You need to leave," I said, pulling away from her as I forced back more tears that threatened. "You can't be seen here supporting me, not after what I did. They'll kill you for that, Eve."

"I'm going to talk to Mason," she said, refusing to let me go, squeezing me tighter. "There has to be something he can do, someone he can talk to."

"Don't get yourself in trouble for me!" I blurted out. Pushing away from her again, I attempted to scoot myself backward, a hard feat when handcuffed. "Why are you being so reckless?"

Realizing what I'd said, using the same words her late husband had always lovingly teased her with, guilt instantly flooded me.

Evelyn went still, her eyes filling with unshed tears. "You sound like Shawn," she said quietly. A long, pregnant pause followed. "And you know what I always said to him."

I nodded, feeling awful for her. "You always said, 'That's why you love me.'"

Evelyn gave me a sad smile. "And that's why you love me too, Lei."

My chest aching, I lowered my eyes. How I longed for our lives before the infection. For our silly, simple, and small lives in our quiet town where Evelyn had once been Miss Popularity and a doting housewife, and I had been the quiet and reserved preschool teacher. She had always been the complementary sun to my moon. I missed it all—our husbands, our weekly barbeques, our plans to vacation in Europe someday, our jokes about growing old together.

"I want to be with Thomas," I whispered, shaking my head. "I'm not strong like you are."

Evelyn threw her hands up in the air, her expression twisted with both hurt and exasperation. "Why are you so willing to leave, Lei?" she demanded. "To leave me! That isn't what Thomas would have wanted for you, to just give up!"

"He wouldn't have wanted any of this!" I shot back. "And he's dead, Evelyn, he doesn't want anything anymore!"

In a singular lithe movement, Evelyn jumped to her feet. Her hands planted on her hips, she glared down at me.

"I won't let you die, Lei." Her tone was forceful and stubborn, and so very Evelyn. "I won't let you die."

Then she turned on her boot heel, arms wrapped around her middle, and stormed out of my cell. Jami shot me a sympathetic look before quickly following her out.

When they were gone, Alex strode slowly into my cell. Bending at his knees, he offered me a hand. For a moment I simply stared up at him, taking in his features for what seemed like the first time, noting his closely shorn black hair and equally dark eyes. He looked tired yet alert, clean yet scruffy with several days' growth covering his jaw.

It was one of those moments where you realized that, although you'd lived side by side with someone, you'd never truly noticed him before. How odd to have known someone for so long only to realize you didn't know him at all, not even a little. I continued studying him, feeling as if I were missing something, wondering at all his recent kindnesses, when he'd never before seemed anything other than indifferent.

"I have a plan," he said in a low tone, barely a whisper. His eyes darted in the direction Jami and Evelyn had just disappeared, and then back to me. "I'm going to get you out of here. Out of Fredericksville."

Bewildered, I widened my eyes as my mouth fell open. "What?" I whispered.

He wiggled his fingers, beckoning me again to take his hand. Somewhat in shock, I took it, allowing him to pull me up and gently help me back to my bench.

Not another word was spoken as he turned away from me and crossed the cell, once again locking me inside. He did a full sweep of the hallway before turning around to face me. Through the bars, he stared deeply into my eyes, revealing so much emotion, more than I'd ever thought him capable of. But then again, I'd never really thought much of him before.

"Because, Leisel. I want out too."

CHAPTER FOUR

Evelyn

"MASON, PLEASE," I begged, clinging to my husband's leg as he attempted to walk away from me. "I'm begging you. Please, do something." I continued sobbing, my tears creating a damp spot on his pants. "Don't let her die."

"Evelyn, there's nothing I can do for her." He bent down, struggling to pry my fingers from his ankle, then huffed in frustration. "She killed Lawrence. He was my friend, you know. She couldn't have killed anyone more important if she tried!" Throwing his hands up in exasperation, his double chin wobbling, he looked down at me with pity in his eyes. "I'm sorry, Eve. I know how much you cared for her."

I looked down at the floor. My eyes were burning fiery holes into the wooden floorboards and I had to wait several seconds, breathing through my anger before I could manage standing.

"Cared?" I asked, seething. "I *care* for her, Mason. She's not dead yet." Turning my back on him, I stormed out of the room. Behind me, I heard him huff again in annoyance.

Now standing by the kitchen sink, I leaned forward, gripping the counter top with both hands as I stared out into the dwindling daylight. One day had already come and nearly gone; tomorrow I would lose her, and I couldn't lose her. I gripped the counter harder.

She didn't deserve any of this, and Lawrence had gotten exactly what he deserved. He'd been a bastard until the bitter end, and now he was going to take her down with him. My breath came in short, ragged pants, my anger and frustration threatening to swallow me whole.

Slow, deliberate footsteps shook me free from my thoughts as Mason attempted to stealthily enter the room. Only there was nothing stealthy about my husband, his slippers dragging noisily across the floorboards, his heavy breathing a telltale giveaway of his approach. A moment later his hands fell heavily on my shoulders, and as usual, I had to fight the urge to shrug him away.

"I'm sorry," he said, his hot breath on my neck.

In front of me the setting sun was a burning golden sphere in the sky, casting a fiery heat across the front of the house. The other houses didn't get as much sun as mine, and I had chosen it for that very reason. After our wedding, Mason had given me the option to choose whichever available home I wanted. I'd chosen this one for two reasons—it was close to Leisel, and the sun…my God, so much sun. It was always the last house to lose the daylight, and while the rest of my life consisted of so much darkness, I needed the sun, needed its warmth.

Mason pressed his lips to my neck, leaving sloppy, clumsy kisses. He was such a selfish man, only ever thinking of himself and his needs. Both disgusted and annoyed, I felt a shudder slither up my spine and across my arms, yet I did nothing. There was nothing I could do. He owned me in a way a husband should never be able to own his wife.

"Not tonight," I managed to say, somehow managing to not sound as repulsed as I felt. "I can't."

Slipping out from beneath his grip, I moved quickly to the other side of our small kitchen. When I chanced a glance in his direction, I found him red faced, embarrassed by my casual brush-off. No other woman in Fredericksville had ever gotten away with what I did. For the most part, I had Mason wrapped around my little finger. He knew it, and I knew it. Yet now, when I really needed the power, I had none.

There was only one way to save Leisel, something I had already begun to arrange but had hoped I wouldn't need to commit to. We needed to leave, to escape. We needed to go back out into the world we'd left behind—that everyone had left behind.

The thought was both horrifying and welcoming, especially knowing we could die out there. The infected still lurked; I'd gathered this much from Jami and the other guards who were often sent on scavenging runs. Although they weren't as quick as they used to be, the older infected and their rotting bodies were more shamblers now than when they'd first turned, they were still a blood-chilling sight to behold.

The remaining infected weren't my only concern. Everyone had heard the stories of people who had refused safety behind the walls, hell-bent on living in the open and among the infected. I had no idea what people like this were capable of, considering they'd survived both the infection and its endless rippling aftereffects.

But knowing that if I didn't at least try to get us out, that Leisel would die in here, it made the world beyond the wall seem much less frightening and much more welcoming.

"Will you help me, Mason?" I stepped forward, closing the distance between us, and placed my hands on his chest.

He swallowed nervously, licking his fat, greedy lips. He was hugely overweight, the only man left alive with so many extra pounds on him. It was ridiculous, really. Sometimes when he was on top of me, I could hardly breathe, let alone fathom enjoying myself.

"I told you I can't, Eve." His large hands roved across my back, pulling me closer to him. "You know I would if I could. I prefer your smiles to your frowns." His hands moved lower, cupping my backside.

"If you can't help me save her…" Looking up at him through my lashes, the way he liked me to, I continued in a whisper, "Then help us escape."

I stared at him, my eyes pleading for him to have mercy on my best friend, and on me. I knew he cared for me; some might even have called it love. But I knew the truth—what he felt for me wasn't love. I wasn't even sure the man knew what love really was. To him, his marriage to me, his ownership of me, that was what love was. And although he'd allow me a lot of things, Mason's warped idea of love wasn't going to allow me this. He wasn't going to let me go.

"You don't know what you're asking, Eve." He shook his head slowly, a look of sad resignation crossing his homely features, causing dread to pool in my gut.

"I do," I replied, unable to control the tremor in my voice. "I'm asking you to help me save my friend. My sister." Running my hands up his chest, I wrapped them around his barely distinguishable neck and brought us face-to-face. "Mason," I begged. "Please."

Gripping my hands tightly in his, he regarded me with pity. "You don't know what the world is like out there."

"So I'll learn," I pleaded.

"You'll be dead in a day."

"So will she." My voice finally broke, cracking on the last syllable. "Mason, tomorrow they'll execute her, and I'll die right along with her. Help get us out of here." Attempting to school my features, I looked up into his eyes. "If you love me, let me go."

The pitying look he'd had only seconds ago vanished, instantly replaced by one of sheer greed. The same greed he'd had in his eyes the day he forced this marriage on me.

I was his.

That was all there was to know.

Folding me against him, he forced my cheek against his chest as if to comfort me, and ran his hand lightly over the fall of my hair. This was typical of him, treating me as if I were a good and docile wife, helping him maintain his illusion that a woman like me would ever love a man like him. In reality, he was a disgusting slob who'd used the end of structured civilization to rise to heights he never would have in the old world, to have the sort of women who never would have given him a second glance. It was a harsh assessment, but when a man like Mason forced a woman like me into a life such as this, I couldn't help but be bitter and hateful.

Guiding me slowly from the kitchen, Mason began pulling me up the stairs. I tried to move away, insisting that I wasn't in the mood for sex, but as he continued pulling me, ignoring my protests, I gave up struggling. When we arrived at our bedroom, instead of following me inside, he shoved me into the dimly lit room and quickly pulled the door shut. The following sound of a click, signaling a key turning the lock, startled me.

"Mason?"

"It's better this way," he said through the door, his tone hopeful. "You can remember her happy."

My eyes rounded, wide with horror. "Mason, let me out!" I yelled, reaching for the handle. Desperately, I pulled on it, shaking it violently, but it didn't budge.

"Please, don't do this," I pleaded as I banged on the wood with my fists. "Please, Mason, you can't do this!"

"I'm sorry, Evelyn. I'm protecting you. I'll let you out in the morning…when it's done."

Over the sound of my pounding heart, I heard footsteps as he descended the stairs. Sheer panic gripped hold of me and I screamed for him to come back, to let me out. But he didn't return. Of course he didn't.

Running to the window, I attempted to push it open, but just like the damn door, it wouldn't budge. From my upstairs view, I could plainly see Mason bumbling down the walkway in front of our house. Looking up in my direction, his eyes found mine, his bulbous face, always covered in a thin sheen of sweat, was glinting from the reflection of the setting sun. His eyes were wide in apology, which was merely an act, because I knew he didn't truly care. The only thing Mason cared about was keeping me here—keeping me for himself. Looking away from me, he continued down the path.

I started pounding on the window, screaming at him, calling him all the names that I'd wanted to for the past three years, but never did. The hate-filled words that I'd kept buried inside me to keep both Leisel and myself safe, all came flying free from their cage. I continued pounding on the window, half expecting it to break, but it never did. Maybe I was too scared to hit it hard enough, though I wanted to. I wanted to smash it, to cause shards of glass to rain down on Mason's head, slicing him open, to hurt him the way he was hurting me.

"I hate you!" I screamed.

Screeching in frustration, I sank to the floor, my screams dissolving into self-pitying sobs. I couldn't help Leisel now. She was going to die, and I couldn't help her. I couldn't even be there for her at the end. As I pulled my knees up to my chest, my tears fell faster.

What would I do without her? Leisel had always told me that I was the strong one, but I knew now it wasn't true. Not when it was her I needed to keep me strong.

The moon was full, sitting heavy and pregnant in the sky when I heard Mason's return. I strained my ears, listening intently for his footsteps on the stairs, but he didn't immediately come for me. I could hear him stumbling around the house, no doubt having drunk too much, probably in an effort to wash away his guilt. Or perhaps he'd forgotten where he'd put me. Maybe he was so drunk that he'd even forgotten what had transpired earlier.

It had happened before, him locking me up for being what he'd considered insolent. There were times that he'd forgotten entirely and let me out without another word about it, looking at me curiously in the dark while he attempted to remember what I'd done to deserve such punishment. Although this—Leisel's execution—was hardly something I would consider forgettable. But this was Mason, a bumbling idiot, and anything was possible.

As hope blossomed inside me that today was one of those days, I got to my feet and tiptoed slowly toward the door. Pressing my ear against the wood, I listened to his slow and careful steps climbing the stairs, realizing that the footsteps I could hear were slow and cautious, and Mason was anything but. He was clumsy and heavy footed.

The handle on the door jiggled. Glancing around the room, I searched for something to arm myself with, because I would kill him if I had to. I refused to stay in this room and allow Leisel to die, not when there still might be a chance I could do something to stop it.

I decided on the table lamp; after all, it didn't work anymore. This house—every house—was full of many things that didn't work anymore, all set up to make us more comfortable, to help us forget the horror outside the walls.

As the handle twisted again, I readied myself to swing.

"Eve?"

Jami!

Bursting forward, I slammed myself against the door. "Get me out of here, Jami, please, get me out!" Again, I tried the handle, twisting it and pulling on it.

"It's locked," he said, his voice sounding deeper than usual through the thick door. "Is there another key?"

Though he couldn't see me, I shook my head in answer. "There's only one," I whispered loudly. "But Mason keeps it on him."

"Fuck me," he muttered. Several tense seconds passed and then he yelled, "Stand back!"

I dropped the lamp. It fell to the floor with a loud clatter and rolled against my feet. Quickly, I scrambled to the other side of the room just as something heavy banged against the door with a resounding thud.

Again and again, the loud noise echoed throughout the room, once, twice, and just after the third bang the door swung open, slamming hard against the wall. As it swung back, Jami caught it just before it could smack him in the face.

Our eyes met, and he was grinning at me, a grin that made me weak for him. I didn't love this man, but in that moment I felt something damn close to it. Running across the room, Jami met me halfway, and I threw myself up against his chest, pressing my lips against his, all while repeatedly mumbling my thanks.

"How did you know?" I asked when I finally pulled away.

He looked down at me, his eyes searching mine as if assuring himself that I was all right. "You'd never leave her alone like that." He kissed me again, still grinning against my mouth. "Let's go get your girl."

Pulling away from him, I took a moment to really look at him, his handsome face clearly expressing what he'd never said before. "Thank you," I whispered, feeling overcome.

Taking my hand in his, Jami pulled me through the house, not stopping until we'd reached the back door. There he pulled a ski cap from his back pocket, similar to the one he was wearing, then slipped it over my head and tucked my curls inside it. Grinning again, he pulled his gun from its holster, then led me from the house.

Adrenaline coursed through me, both from the fear of getting caught and the excitement that maybe, just fucking maybe, our plan would work. And Leisel and I would soon be free of this place.

CHAPTER FIVE

Leisel

"YOU SHOULDN'T BE helping me," I insisted, watching as Alex hurriedly unlocked my handcuffs. Ignoring me, he finished with my hands, then bent down to work on the shackles encircling my ankles.

"What if we get caught?" I continued, knowing that it was likely we were going to get caught. There were too many people living in such a small space, a place that was heavily guarded. "You'll be killed alongside me."

Alex remained as stoic as I'd always known him to be, notorious for saying as little as possible. Finished with my shackles, he shoved them away and got to his feet. I remained where I was for a moment, seated on the hard bench as I rubbed my sore wrists and stared up in wonder at him. For the life of me, I couldn't figure out why he was risking his own neck to help me escape.

"I have a truck outside the walls," he finally said. "Hidden in the woods about a mile and a half from here. Got food and water, a few gallons of gas stored inside. We just need to get there."

I gaped up at him. With the entire town on our heels, a mile and a half away might as well have been in China!

I shook my head. "We'll never make it."

Alex dropped to his knees, his dark eyes burning holes through my thoughts. There was a spark there, alit with a fever I'd never noticed in him before. But I had never noticed much, always consumed with my own problems, my own pain.

"I don't care," he gritted out through clenched teeth. "I've been outside the walls, Leisel. Many, many times. It's not pretty out there, but it's not pretty in here either, is it? I'd rather be free."

Free. The word sang through me like one too many cocktails, blinding me, drugging me with all its hazy, yet glorious possibilities.

His hand found my shoulder as he bent down to speak with me face-to-face, and it took everything I had not to flinch away from his touch. Being touched by a man, thanks to Lawrence, was not something I associated with tenderness or comfort. Not in a very long time.

"Don't you want to be free?" It was more a statement than a question. A proclamation. A declaration.

I shrugged his hand away. "We need to get Eve," I said. "I won't leave without her."

He frowned and his brow furrowed, causing delicate lines to appear on his otherwise smooth forehead, but he said nothing in response.

"I won't leave without her," I repeated, unable to imagine myself in life anywhere without Evelyn. I couldn't stomach the thought of leaving her behind in this awful place.

"You won't have to."

Both Alex and I jerked at the sound of another voice. As I shrank back in fear, Alex leaped to his feet and quickly whipped his gun free from the holster on his hip.

Jami stood outside my cell, a ski cap hiding his unruly hair, his normally impish expression now serious. Seeing Alex's gun, Jami's hands went up in the air, including the one holding his own weapon.

"I come in peace," he said, giving us a half smile. "And I'm glad I don't have to kill you too." He nodded at Alex.

"Too?" I whispered, fear slithering down my spine and chilling my blood.

"Michaels and Davidson?" Alex cocked an eyebrow in question, and Jami gave him a single nod in response.

"And Hamilton?" Alex asked, gesturing toward the door that led out into the hub of the station.

Jami shook his head. "There's too many out front," he said quietly. "I could only clear the back."

"Never thought I'd be so goddamn happy to not have electricity,"

Alex muttered, but he looked and sounded anything but happy. He turned back to me and unexpectedly held out his hand, the one currently holding his gun, and gestured for me to take it.

My lips opened and closed, and for a moment I could only stutter through several puffs of air. Finally finding my voice, I cleared my throat and tried again. "I don't know how," I whispered.

Panic was beginning to well inside of me. Both Alex and Jami were here, attempting to rescue me. And if Jami was here, that meant Evelyn was as well. Three people, three good people, all who could end up killed alongside me if we were caught. And two men were already dead?

True, there was no love lost between me and the majority of the men who policed Fredericksville. Most were self-centered, self-serving, violent men who were more than happy to adhere to the tyrannical rules of this place. But dead? I'd only ever wished one man dead before, and that wish had been granted by my own hand last night.

"This is the safety. Make sure it's off before you pull the trigger. Hold it like this. Leisel...Leisel, are you listening to me?"

I nodded dumbly at Alex, who was watching me impatiently and with more than a little annoyance. Clearing my throat again, I tentatively took the gun, clutching the thick handle in my seemingly too small and shaking hand. Then with a deep breath, I got to my feet. The weapon was heavy and awkward in my grip, making me feel like a child playing dress-up.

"Eve's watching the back," Jami said to Alex. "And we've got five...no..."—he paused, glancing down at his watch—"three minutes to get the fuck out of here before the patrol circles back around."

"Let's go," Alex said, his voice deep, laden with determination that I didn't share. I might have been standing, but it felt as if cement blocks had been strapped to my feet, my fear keeping me locked in place.

"Leisel!" Jami admonished me in a harsh whisper. "Eve is waiting for you! Risking her life for you! Move it!"

Evelyn. Her fate was my fate, and my fate would be hers. It was all I needed to propel me into motion. One step in front of the other, until I was sandwiched between my two unexpected saviors, and we were moving slowly but surely down the dark and narrow hall.

It was a mindless march on my part. Consumed by fear, the only thought that kept me going was that I would reach Evelyn, that there was finally a chance we could be free of this place and this life that wasn't a life at all. At least, not one that was worth living. Out there we might have a chance at some sort of happiness, and at the very least, freedom. Freedom was happiness, wasn't it?

My thoughts took a turn then, thinking of the infected, remembering how many there had been in the early days after the infection had hit, how quickly they'd ripped our lives to shreds. I quickly shook those thoughts away, knowing it would do me no good to overload my mind with more horrors than were already occupying it.

We hurried down a small flight of stairs and took a quick detour through a damp and dusty basement, the only light from a flashlight in Jami's hand. Then up another flight of stairs, through another corridor, fumbling in the dark until a faded exit sign finally came into view.

And then I was out the door and into the night, the cool fall air a welcome balm on my overheated skin. A slim pair of arms wrapped around my neck, a familiar scent enveloped me, and I let out an exhale filled with hope.

Until I saw the two dead bodies lying next to the Dumpster.

Evelyn squeezed me tightly, kissing my hair and cheeks. "It's going to be okay, Lei, I promise."

"One minute!" Jami hissed before pulling Evelyn off me. "We have to go now!"

With a final worried look from Evelyn, they took off running, and then Alex grabbed my hand, ripping me free once again of my dark thoughts and crippling fear.

We ran like the wind, like bats out of hell, toward the west end wall, toward our freedom, with only thirty seconds left before our escape would be discovered.

CHAPTER SIX

Evelyn

IF THIS HAD been a movie, an alarm would have been sounding right about now, blaring obnoxiously to let everyone know that something was wrong, that someone was trying to get out. Or worse, someone was trying to get in. Right then, I would have welcomed such a sound; at least then we'd know whether our impromptu escape had been noticed or not.

But in our world, such a noise was dangerous. A noise so loud would draw any and all infected from miles around straight to our walls. Insipid creatures with a one-track mind, hell-bent on tearing into anything and everything, but once they had a target, their one-track minds became even more deadly.

Jami glanced down at his watch, then looked at me. "Game time," he whispered, his words half lost to the wind as we continued to run.

The next guard shift was due to report. Any second now they would discover the bodies, discover that Leisel was missing, and soon we'd be apprehended and probably executed on the spot. That thought alone drove me faster, pushed me to run as fast and as hard as my body would allow.

At the far end of our community was a path that split both left and right, and when we reached it, we looped to the left and around the back of the houses. Weaving between gardens, hopping over skillfully trimmed bushes, we passed blooming rosebushes, bright hanging baskets, and lawns with neatly cut grass.

As if we were trapped in some crazy over-pruned oriental garden maze, we ran to the left one second and then to the right the next. Finally, we left the housing district behind us and headed directly into the farming and cooking quarter. Above us, tree branches hung heavy with ripe fruit, and at our feet were row after row of fresh vegetables.

It was all so picture perfect and proper, as if we were part of one big happy Brady Bunch family. But it was nothing more than a facade. Sure, the fruit was juicy and the vegetables ripe, but there was no soul. So pretty on the outside, yet inside everything had died long ago and since rotted to nothing.

A noise sounded off in the distance, something I belatedly realized was men yelling. I glanced to Jami with fear in my eyes, but he was already tugging harder on my hand, urging me to run faster.

The food warehouses were on the opposite side of the road we were on, and as we approached them, Jami pulled me to a stop. Panting heavily, I glanced back the way we'd come, watching as the dark silhouettes of Leisel and Alex closed in fast. Her hair was flying out behind her, her pale face a beacon to me, something to cling to in the midst of this insanity. Pulling her to a stop alongside Jami and me, Alex released her. She came crashing into me, and I crushed her body to mine.

Leisel's shoulders shuddered as she cried softly against my neck, her anguish painful to me as well. I held her against me for a moment, whispering reassuring things into her ear, promising her safety, promising her out of this nightmare, until eventually she calmed.

As she looked into my eyes, her own glistening with tears, I pressed a hard kiss to her lips. "We'll be fine," I said firmly, keeping our gazes locked. She tried to turn her head, to look away, to hide inside herself like she often did, but I refused to allow it, holding tight to both her body and her gaze. "Do you believe me?"

She said nothing, only nodded once, her chin trembling.

"Lei, I promise you." Pushing her dark hair away from her face, I pressed another kiss to her forehead. "I promise you," I whispered, pulling her in for another fierce hug.

Several more seconds passed while we caught our breath, trying to calm our nerves. I could no longer hear the shouts of the guards, and I had to believe that they'd moved away from us, instead of closer.

Finally relenting, I allowed Leisel to leave my arms. Pulling away, she lifted her hand, showing me her gun. Smiling, I showed her mine. It was almost exactly like hers, though I carried mine with more confidence. Before the infection, I'd loved going shooting at the local gun range. Even though it had been a while since I'd practiced, I hadn't forgotten the basics.

"Eve." Jami beckoned me toward him, gesturing at Alex to move toward Leisel, which he did immediately. Taking a moment, I watched as Alex sidled up beside her, his body language fiercely protective, and I marveled at how neither Leisel nor I had ever noticed the way he looked at her, the sheer intensity of it.

He was incredibly quiet, sometimes to the point of infuriating, yet the way he'd always stared at her, those deep brown eyes of his seeing all of her. She was blind to it—to him, hell, to anyone. She'd had enough of men to last her a lifetime, and she simply didn't care anymore.

But then there was Alex, and the number of times he'd had to escort her to the clinic for treatment, some humiliating and some just damn painful. Other than the staff at the clinic and me, only Alex had seen most of the horrors Lawrence had put her through; only he knew the full extent of her pain.

Leisel's pain, I surmised, and the threat of losing her for good, must have been his turning point. The reason why he was willing to risk his life to get us out of here. Knowing what I knew, having seen what I'd seen, Alex's behavior didn't really come as a surprise to me.

It was Jami who shocked me. Never in a million years would I have expected him to aid in an escape plan, let alone already have a plan of his own. He'd liked his job, this life, or I'd always assumed so, and I'd never thought that I was more than a passing distraction for him. But his willingness to help us, to leave with us, was evidence of much more caring than he'd ever admitted to me.

"I'm going across," Jami announced, his face hidden by shadows. "You wait here until you see my signal."

The three of us watched as Jami took off quickly across the street. Reaching the other side, he slipped between two closely erected buildings and disappeared from sight. Moments later, he reappeared and waved us across.

Shooting Leisel one last glance, I mouthed the words, *I promise*, right before bolting out into the street. It was dark in this part of town, the darkness our ally, but without the shadows of the buildings to hide us, I felt overly exposed and vulnerable to anything or anyone that might be lurking. Rattling in my own ears, my breath sounded overly noisy, a neon sign to our whereabouts. But I stayed the path, never faltering, not daring to look right or left. My footsteps were quick, surefooted, until I'd reached the other side of the street, slamming into Jami as he pulled me into the dark safety of another shadowed alley.

Not bothering to catch my breath, I peered around the corner, checking to be sure no one had spotted my mad dash for safety. Flashing lights snagged my attention, a flickering light from the lanterns that our guards carried, and though they were off in the distance, they were headed in our direction.

When Jami waved Leisel and Alex across, she hesitated. Thank God for Alex, because suddenly he pulled her across the street, nearly carrying her since she suddenly couldn't seem to run without slipping and nearly falling.

Checking back up the street, I noticed the lights were growing closer, the footfalls and quiet shouts sounding nearer. As Alex and Leisel finally reached us, I pulled her to me once again, noting that she was breathless and shaking with fear.

"This way," Jami said, already walking off. We followed him, Leisel and me in the center, while Alex covered us from behind.

We found the end of the alleyway heavily barricaded, secured by rusty corrugated metal and reinforced by wooden pallets and chicken wire. Seeing this, I started to panic, thinking that we were trapped, until Alex pushed past me and Jami bent down, slipping his backpack off his shoulders and pulling free a thick blanket. After handing the blanket to Alex, Jami bent down to give him a boost. Using Jami for support, Alex tossed the blanket over the top of the barricade and hoisted himself over.

It was too noisy, metal scraping on metal, and the sound echoed loudly in the dark. My heartbeat headed into overdrive, but my will to survive—for us to survive—was firm. Even as the voices grew louder, the heavy footsteps came closer, even with the hopelessness of this entire situation, I refused to give up. In fact, I damn well demanded that we would get through this night.

The soft fall of Alex's body thumping against the ground signaled to us that he was on the other side. We waited, the three of us, with bated breath, for what would come next. "Clear," he finally called out softly.

Jami gestured for me to go next. Shaking my head, I pulled Leisel forward. "I'll go once she's over."

Glancing up at the fence, her eyes as big and wide as a doe's, she swallowed hard and looked back at me. "I can't," she whispered, and shook her head.

"You can do this, Lei," I said to reassure her. "This is our chance, and you can do this, you have to." Gently, I pushed her toward the fence.

Nodding halfheartedly, she reluctantly climbed onto Jami's back. Immediately he lifted her, allowing her to reach higher so she could pull herself the rest of the way up. She fumbled clumsily for her footing, finally finding it, then heaved herself to the top. She soon straddled the wall and scrambled awkwardly over the top, and just before she was about to drop to the other side, she glanced down to give me a small, nervous smile, and then she was gone.

"Eve, you're next," Jami whispered.

The alleyway was darker now, more oppressive, the moon having hidden behind the clouds.

"Jami?"

"Yeah?" he asked, glancing back to the other end of the alley.

"Thank you for this. Words don't seem enough. I—"

Jami looked at me, his cocky smile back in place. "You can show me how grateful you are later, but for now, I need you to get your ass over there." Slapping my ass, he winked at me.

Suppressing a laugh, I grinned at him and shook my head.

After I climbed on top of Jami's shoulders, he lifted me with a grunt, and I found myself flailing for a moment before finally managing to grip the fence. As I pulled myself up and over, Jami's hands gave me the final push I needed to scale the remaining height. Just as I prepared to drop to the other side, I glanced down at Jami, finding him smiling up at me.

Freedom was so close, I could almost taste it, palpable on my tongue. Suddenly I found myself smiling back at Jami, grinning actually, my worry muted by the excitement I had for the future. Freedom and Jami had come at a price, but it was a price I was willing to pay, for both Leisel and myself.

"You can do it, Eve," he whispered, his eyes shining brightly, reflecting his own excitement. He kissed his palm, and then lifted it up to me.

It was the first time Jami had ever shown me that he cared, and it took me by surprise. He'd never kissed me good-bye, never before shown me that I was worth something to him. Fluttering in my chest, my heartbeat was erratic at this newfound knowledge. My charming, cocky Jami had just shown me that he gave a damn about me, something he'd sworn to never do again, not after he'd lost everything. But he'd finally let someone in—me—and I felt privileged and happy, trapped in a blissful bubble of hope for our future.

I was still smiling at him when my gaze caught on something moving behind him, and then my world slammed to a halt, everything suddenly moving in slow motion. The guards were nearly upon us, their lanterns lighting the area all around Jami. Men were yelling, running toward us with their guns drawn, shouting for us to drop our weapons and stay where we were.

And Jami, oh my God, my brave and cocky Jami, he turned and raised his gun.

"No!" I screamed. "Jami, no!"

"Go!" he shouted back. "Go, Eve!"

Jami didn't look back at me as he let loose the first bullet, and while I should have been dropping down to the other side and scrambling for my own safety, I couldn't move. I was frozen, caught in this horrifying, devastating moment.

Gunfire lit up the small space, small orange explosions of bullets being expelled at inhuman speed, and then suddenly, as if the wind had been knocked out of him, Jami dropped to his knees. My following cry was lost to the sound of gunshots and shouts, and still I could do little more than stare in horror as Jami continued to fire his gun, even as they fired back, riddling his body with bullets. He fired until his gun was empty, though his finger continued to click the trigger in hopes of more until his hand fell limply to his side, the gun falling from his fingers. The gunfire stopped then, the small space seeming smaller and darker than before.

I didn't even realize that I was still crying out until my throat began to burn. Just as Jami slumped forward, falling silent and still, something grabbed at my leg, promptly yanking me over the fence and into the darkness.

My fall was soft, Alex's arms catching me just before I crashed to the ground. As soon as I was standing, Leisel's hand found mine and squeezed it before pulling me from the wall, away from the shouting and yelling, away from Jami and into the forest.

We stumbled through the blackness, occasionally catching what sounded like the low moan of an infected. Keeping my grip firm on Leisel's hand, I refused to let her go, even for a second. When she stumbled, I stumbled; when she fell, I fell. We were in this together; she was all I had left.

It seemed as if hours had passed before the forest thinned and we reached a small clearing. In the moonlight, I could make out the outline of a truck, and as we grew closer, I noticed that it was old and rusted. What was once probably a beautiful blue now looked like a washed-out gray with patches of brown. Worse, it didn't appear as if it had been started in years, and I found myself holding out little hope of it being a worthy escape vehicle.

Regardless of its appearance, we piled inside. What choice did we have? The key was already in the ignition, and as Alex turned it, the truck sputtered several times before the engine finally turned over noisily.

As we drove away, leaving the forest behind us, Leisel's head came to rest on my shoulder. I could feel her body quaking, hear her soft sniffles as she cried silent tears while I stared blankly out of the window.

Maybe tomorrow I'd cry. But not tonight.

"He kissed me good-bye," I mumbled, still staring into the darkness surrounding us. Taking a deep breath, I slowly released it, refusing to be anything but grateful. Grateful because my friend, my very best friend, had evaded execution, grateful that both she and I were now free of Fredericksville and all its hidden horrors.

And that was all that really mattered.

CHAPTER SEVEN

Leisel

I AWOKE TO THE faint chirping of birds off in the distance, and the sound of trickling water. For just a moment I was at peace, happy in that gentle place between waking and sleep, ignorant of the crick in my neck from sleeping sitting up, and blissfully unaware of all that had transpired over the past two days.

And then it came back to me. Slowly at first—the pain, the violence, the crime—and I squeezed my eyes tightly shut, trying to block it out and enjoy the peace for just a moment longer.

But it wouldn't relent; all at once the rest of it poured in. My fear, my bloodstained hands, the bodies in the alleyway. And then later, while tucked neatly between Alex and Evelyn, when I'd cried and cried until the movement of the truck rocked me slowly into a blissful unconsciousness, all while Evelyn had run her fingers through my hair, pressed soft kisses on the top of my head, whispered soothing, calming words in my ear.

But it should have been the other way around. It should have been me comforting her. After all, it had been her who'd lost someone she'd cared for. Not me.

Weak.

The word pounded through my thoughts like a wayward drumbeat until I could no longer stomach another second of being alone with my thoughts, and my eyes flew open. I blinked through tear-encrusted eyes, trying to see past the sudden blinding sunlight streaming in through the truck's dirty windows.

"Morning." The sound of Alex's deep, booming voice startled me. Twisting in my seat, I found him standing just outside the driver's side door with his back to me. I blinked again, realizing that the sound I'd initially thought was trickling water was actually the sound of him urinating.

As my face heated with embarrassment, I quickly turned away and caught a glimpse of myself in the rearview mirror. The truck was an older model, the windshield short and squat, and the turned-down mirror gave me an up close and personal view of my face that I didn't much care to see. Dried smears of blood ran up and down both my cheeks, dark bruises ringed my eyes, my nose had a thin cut running across the bridge of it. My bottom lip was swollen, split in two places, and my neck…

I swallowed hard, glancing away from the mirror, vividly recalling what Lawrence's hand had felt like wrapped around my throat, his fingertips biting into my skin while I fought for my breath, while he took what he hadn't been given.

And then the blood. The memory of the blood covering me, covering the entire room, washed over me in one suffocating wave, so very real that I could taste the sharp metallic flavor all over again.

"Evelyn," I managed to croak out. Alex bent down, resting his forearms on top of the open window.

"You okay?" he asked.

Not trusting my voice, I simply nodded. He watched me for one long uncomfortable moment before pointing. Following his finger, I turned in my seat and took in our surroundings.

We appeared to be parked on the side of a deserted two-lane road, surrounded by mostly open land. I quickly spotted Evelyn, some several dozen yards away, as she emerged from behind a large oak tree. She was moving slowly, much slower than usual, looking disheveled and a bit dazed. I stared at her, squinting to see her better as she continued down the small incline of pasture. Her body language, her movements, her facial expression, it was all wrong and I hardly recognized her. This appeared to be Evelyn at her lowest, internalizing her pain, letting it press her down until something as simple as walking became strenuous.

I'd only ever seen this Evelyn once before. The day she'd lost

Shawn.

"Eve!" Alex shouted, bellowing from behind me, causing my entire body to flinch. "Three o'clock!"

My eyes darted right and found nothing, then left, *Evelyn's three o'clock*, and my breath caught in my throat. I'd seen the infected before, God knows I had, too many to count. But even so, they struck the sort of fear inside of me that no fist, no weapon, no living person ever could.

In the beginning, when Thomas and I were holed up in Evelyn and Shawn's home, the four of us had waited for weeks for someone to come and save us—the army, the national guard, the Red Cross, anyone to take us somewhere safe. During that time, the infected had been everywhere. Milling down the streets, in every nook and cranny, pounding on the house, trying to beat their way inside. Those who had once been our neighbors, friends, and family had all succumbed to the infection and become monsters.

I'd even had to endure the horror of watching my own husband turn, watch as the fever overtook him, as the bloody pustules formed all over his skin. I watched him cry tears mixed with blood, and gasp my name with his last few breaths. Then I'd watched as he awoke, his eyes clouded over, as a garbled cacophony of hoarse groans and animalistic gurgles erupted from his throat. And just as he'd lunged for me, his jaw snapping, his teeth bared, I'd watched as Shawn had speared my beloved husband through the skull with a butcher knife. The very same butcher knife he'd used to carve the turkey every Thanksgiving.

I'd seen the infected in Fredericksville too, the stragglers who had somehow managed to find themselves at our walls. But it was always from afar. Even during the one and only wall breach during the first year, the invasion had been short lived, resulting in very few fatalities.

But now here we were, in the great wide open, just the three of us, the birds, and the three infected shambling their way toward Evelyn. My only source of relief to draw from stemmed from the noticeable difference between these infected and the ones from the beginning. These were slower than I'd remembered them to be, less steady on their feet, and unable to move quickly.

Alex was already jogging around to the front of the truck, a rifle in his hands. He paused in front of the hood, drawing himself to his full height. Lifting the weapon to eye level, he squinted, peering through the scope. His index finger twitched on the trigger, and a bullet cracked in the air, the small explosion echoing around us.

I watched, clasping my hand over my mouth, as one of the infected fell. Its two companions paid it little mind as its body crumpled to the ground, their focus only on Evelyn. Who, to my complete and utter horror, wasn't running away from them, but toward them.

Something like a war cry flew from her lips as she rushed them head-on, her gun in her hand. My head buzzed with a pounding chorus of fear and anxiety as she flew across the lush grass, her arms and legs deftly pumping as she headed straight toward death itself.

What was she doing? Why would she be so reckless when here was Alex, complete with a rifle and an excellent shot, to boot?

"Help her!" I screamed, throwing myself at the windshield, pounding on the glass with clenched fists. "Alex! Do something!"

His rifle still raised, his body poised and ready to fire, Alex shook his head. "Can't!" he shouted. "She's blocking me! I might hit her!"

A full-body shudder racked through me, leaving my lips quivering and my hands trembling. I found myself frantically fumbling beside me, searching for the gun Alex had given me the night before. For what reason, I didn't know. I'd never fired one, had never even held one; Lawrence hadn't allowed me the liberty.

When I found it on the floor of the truck, I snatched it up and kicked my way out of the passenger side door, then rushed to the front of the truck. I reached Alex's side just as Evelyn had begun letting loose a barrage of bullets. Amid her screams, one crack after another rang through the air. My breath stuttered to a stop while my heart made up in beats what my lungs couldn't seem to produce.

One of her bullets finally found purchase in the knee of an infected, causing it to stumble and fall firmly on its backside. Another took a shot to the shoulder, the chest, and the side of its face, and yet it kept on coming for her, unfazed.

Then Evelyn, a mere kissable distance from the still-standing infected, finally hit her target. The bullet sliced through its forehead, blowing the back of its head wide open. Like a papier-mâché piñata, the prizes inside—bone and brains and various shades of indistinguishable sludge—all exploded into the air like confetti.

"Oh my God," I breathed, watching as the creature crumpled to the ground. But my relief was short lived as the remaining infected had somehow managed to get back on its feet. And Evelyn, looking victorious, was oblivious to the danger that was now nearly on top of her.

I screamed at the top of my lungs, frantically waving my arms in the air. "Eve! Eve! Behind you!"

Evelyn spun around just in time to catch the infected as it was reaching for her, its jaw open wide, ready to take a bite out of whatever piece of her it could manage. As she struggled to keep it at bay, shoving her hands into its chest, her gun fell from her grip. Screaming, Evelyn staggered backward under its dead weight, barely holding the monster off of her.

"Do something!" I cried, pleading with Alex. "She's going to die! Do something!"

"I can't get a shot," he muttered, still squinting into his scope.

Frustration and fear had me grabbing his arm, gripping tightly to the thick material of his canvas jacket and twisting. "This can't be for nothing!" I screamed, tears in my eyes. "And if I lose her, this will have all been for *nothing*!"

Evelyn continued to scream, barely managing to remain upright as she tried again to push the infected off her. But it wouldn't relent.

Lowering his gun, Alex turned to me, his calm gaze finding my hysterical one. It took only a split second, this strange look he gave me, and then he was shoving his rifle into my arms and running out into the field. Pulling a large hunting knife free from the sheath strapped to his thigh, Alex ran a circle around Evelyn and the infected, catching the infected's attention and allowing Evelyn the distraction and space she needed to give the thing a good shove. They both stumbled in opposite directions, Evelyn backward and the infected straight into the waiting arms of Alex.

With a swiftness that only came from experience, Alex laid the creature out flat on its back, and in the space of a heartbeat had sunk his blade into its skull.

Still cradling both the rifle and my gun, I sank to the ground, desperately trying to catch my breath. It was over now, everyone was safe, but…

This was life outside the walls, wasn't it? This was my supposed freedom. Tears burned behind my eyes, tears of both relief and regret.

Had we only traded one hell for another? And what would the cost of this new hell be?

"Lei!"

I lifted my eyes, watching as Evelyn came quickly down the incline, a small smile on her face. Incredulous, I stared at her, wondering how she could smile at a time like this. But I already knew the answer. Simply put, she'd been built this way, able to find a light when everyone else around her saw only darkness, able to hold herself together when everyone else was falling apart.

She'd lost Jami only hours ago and yet here she was, looking fresh faced, exhilarated, and...free.

"Are you okay?" she asked when she reached me.

Unable to answer her, so caught up in my own self-pity, I could do little more than bob my head once for yes.

"That was fucking amazing," she said breathlessly, shifting from one foot to the other. "Fucking amazing."

"You need to learn how to use that gun." Alex had strolled up casually beside Evelyn, his eyes on me.

Still on the ground and feeling awkward, I cleared my throat and attempted to get to my feet. Suddenly Alex was by my side, taking his rifle from my hands. With one arm around my waist, he pulled me upright.

"Thanks," I mumbled, moving quickly away from him and trying to subtly inch closer to Evelyn.

"She does," Evelyn agreed. "But first we need to figure out where we're going."

"Cold weather is coming," Alex said, still watching me. "We could head south, wouldn't have to worry about freezing to death."

"Sounds good to me." Evelyn turned toward me. "Lei?"

"The cold weather slows them down," I said softly, knowing I had nothing to offer and feeling silly because of it. "Doesn't it? Wouldn't that make it safer here?"

Alex continued to stare at me, his hard expression giving nothing away as to what he was thinking. "Don't know how safe we're going to be when we're freezing to death and can't find shit to eat."

"Hey!" Evelyn snapped. "She made a good point!"

"No," I said quickly, reaching out to grab her hand. "He's right, I wasn't thinking. We should head south."

Evelyn gave my hand a conciliatory squeeze but said nothing. However, it was hard to miss the fire in her eyes as she glared at Alex.

"South, it is," Alex muttered. "Let's go."

CHAPTER EIGHT

Evelyn

THE FIRE IN my belly burned long after the kill had ended. True, the kill had been messy and reckless, and I knew I needed more practice, but it had been glorious. To sink bullet after bullet into the infected, to watch them die…again. It had been a bitter ointment for my fractured heart.

The ache in my chest was a constant reminder that at some point I would have to stop and think about Jami. I'd have to think about the loss I had taken, the life he had given up, both for me and for the chance at freedom. His death was another reason I wouldn't let this all be in vain, another reason why we had to survive.

But not now. I couldn't think about it now.

Gritting my teeth, I jutted out my chin as we all climbed back inside the truck, willing myself to stay strong. We continued down the vacant road, and Alex turned onto the first highway we came across. It was a dusty graveyard, a never-ending obstacle course of cars, skeletons, fallen trees, and debris. There was no sign of any infected for miles, but even after several hours had passed, I found myself still longing to kill more of them. That last encounter had lit a fire in me, and I found myself itching to sink a bullet or a blade into another, and end it.

He'd kissed me good-bye.

My breath snagged in my throat, Jami's face coming to the forefront of my mind. Leisel squeezed my hand, and startled, I glanced at her, giving her a reassuring smile.

"Are you hungry?" I asked her. "You need to eat. No point starving yourself, you'll get weak."

"There's some food in the bag, but it's not much," Alex said, not bothering to take his eyes off the road.

Climbing over Leisel's knees, I found Alex's backpack wedged behind the bench seat. There was some bread and fruit, apples and berries mostly, and some meat. I scowled at the meager supplies, knowing we needed to ration our food and water; this wasn't going to last us more than a day, two at most.

"How did you get the meat?" I asked Alex.

Meat was a rarity. In Fredericksville, only once a month would there be a culling of our livestock. The majority of it was cured so that it lasted longer. But this meat was fresh, and still unsalted.

"I stole it," Alex said, his voice as blank as his expression.

I nodded once, my mouth flattening into a thin, determined line as I began to divide the food between us, giving us equal amounts of meat, bread, and fruit. Alex ate while he drove, one hand never leaving the wheel, while Leisel picked at hers for a long while before falling back to sleep.

"How you doing?" Alex asked quietly, glancing at me.

"Fine, you?" I retorted cockily.

I could tell he thought I was just a feeble woman, that I'd break down anytime and soon he'd have to care for two broken women. But I wouldn't break down. I had to be strong for Leisel, and that thought gave me enough strength to keep my tears at bay.

A small smile curved his lips. "Pass me the water," was his only reply.

We slipped back into silence, the low hum of the engine lulling me, making me drowsy. I was just on the edge of sleep, about to slip over into oblivion, when Alex called my name. I was instantly alert, sitting up straight in my seat and searching for threats, only to find Alex pointing to an upturned car in the middle of the road up ahead, blocking our path. Heavy steel guardrails boxed us in on either side, leaving us little choice but to somehow move the vehicle.

Leisel was still sound asleep, and I decided to leave her be. She needed her rest, a chance to calm and gather her thoughts, find a way to accept everything that had happened over the past several days, and hopefully wake up ready for this new world.

After Alex pulled the truck to a stop, I followed him out to the road, tightly gripping my gun as I scanned the area for any infected. When we didn't find any signs of others, living or dead, we proceeded toward the car. It was little more than a rusted-out shell, with bits and pieces of mangled metal strewn across the road.

As we drew closer, we noticed something odd, some sort of movement coming from within. We got closer to the vehicle, squatting down on our heels to look inside, only to find the driver of the vehicle, or what was left of him, was still seated behind the wheel, pinned in place by the broken steering column. Hearing us, it turned toward us, its jaw snapping, a raspy hungry noise erupting from its decaying throat.

I raised my gun, ready to shoot it and put it out of its misery, but Alex placed a hand on my arm, stopping me.

"We need to save our bullets," he said, and handed me a knife. "Straight through the head. He's an old one, should be soft."

I knew why he wanted me to do it, instead of him. He was testing me, determining whether I would be of any use to him out here. Taking the knife from him, I purposefully stalked closer to the car. As I reached the driver's side and bent down to look inside again, the infected became frantic. It reached out an arm weakly for me, flailing against the door to get to me as its neck strained, its jaw still snapping wildly.

I raised my knife, my gaze flitting to the backseat of the car to find the skeletal remains of the rest of the family. Oddly, I found myself giving each skeleton a name—Mary, Jack, and sweet little Katie—and suddenly wished I could give them a proper burial, not leave what was once probably a happy loving family out here in the middle of the road like a circus sideshow.

The infected groaned, drawing my attention back to its snapping jaw. Without hesitation, I raised my blade and brought it down swiftly, burying it deep within its head, and the infected stilled instantly. With an easy tug, the knife pulled free, dripping black sludge that splattered against the pavement. Wrinkling my nose at the gory mess, I stood up and turned to Alex, offering the knife back to him, but he shook his head at me.

"That's yours now," he said, handing me the sheath that had been strapped to his thigh. "Now help me move this thing."

It only took us a few minutes to realize we couldn't move the car; it was too heavy and too mangled. Deciding to use our vehicle to push it out of the way, we made our way back to the truck.

Leisel was still sound asleep, softly snoring, yet I decided to wake her so we wouldn't scare her senseless with the sound of metal rubbing against metal. When I shook her gently, she bolted upright, her hand immediately reaching for the gun resting between her thighs.

Standing just outside the truck, Alex glanced from me to Leisel with his ever-present scowl firmly in place. His gaze finally landed on me, and he pointed to the driver's seat. "You drive, I'll push."

Putting the truck into gear, I began slowly driving the truck forward. With Alex as my guide, I brought the truck head-to-head with the car and began to nudge. The noise was truly awful; the screeching metal on the blacktop was louder than I'd anticipated, the pop of glass resonating as one headlight exploded. I winced, hoping we weren't going to break our own in the process.

Mercifully, after fifteen minutes we were able to move the car enough to give us the space to pass through.

"You okay?" I asked Leisel as I slid across the bench seat, giving Alex back the driver's side.

"Yeah," she said quietly, and let her head fall to my shoulder.

"Promise?" I asked her.

Lifting her face, she offered me a small smile. "Promise."

I studied her for a moment before planting a kiss on the top of her head, and fell silent.

"Town up ahead," Alex announced loudly, the sound of his voice making me jump.

He was an odd one, going for hours without uttering a single word, then out of nowhere he would speak, scaring the shit out of everyone. I turned to frown at him, but his eyes stayed on the highway as he slowed down in front of an exit sign.

"Keep going?" he asked, rubbing one hand over his short black hair. "Or check it out," he added, answering his own question. He spared a glance in our direction, his eyebrows raised expectantly.

I shrugged. "Check it out?" I said, unsure, my gaze skimming over the town's welcome sign.

> WELCOME TO COVEY
> POPULATION 1,600
> HAVE A NICE STAY!

"Why wouldn't we check it out?" Leisel asked, her voice timid and laced with worry. "We need supplies, right?"

"Women like you are currency," Alex answered, his expression still infuriatingly blank.

Leisel's sharp intake of breath resonated through the cab of the truck. "Then keep going!" she cried out softly. "Keep going!" Leaning forward in her seat, she looked at me, staring at me, willing me to agree with her.

Biting down on my bottom lip, I didn't answer right away, instead thinking of our options.

"Eve," she whispered, sounding desperate.

Pressing my lips together, I shrugged my shoulders again. "We don't even know if anyone is there, Lei. And we need supplies. We're not going to make it much farther with what we have."

"We're going to need gas," Alex said, glancing toward the fuel gauge. "Soon."

"Eve!" Leisel whispered harshly, grabbing for my hand and squeezing it hard.

I knew what she was afraid of; I was afraid of the same thing. Running into people much like the ones in Fredericksville, who thought themselves entitled to whatever the infection had left behind.

Or worse. And when it came to worse, the possibilities were endless.

"It could be abandoned," I continued. "Maybe some infected roaming around, but nothing we won't be able to take care of."

At least, I was hoping that was all we would run into. A few infected would be easy enough to get rid of. Unless the town was overrun.

"There's too many possibilities," she said, homing in on my thoughts.

"We need to make a decision." Alex pointed toward the sky.

"We're running out of daylight."

Scowling at him, I turned back to Leisel. For someone who'd been so uncommonly helpful, he was largely insensitive to Leisel's fears.

"Let's check it out," I said, not entirely sure of my decision, but needing to make one regardless. And Alex was right, night was coming and we needed somewhere to spend it. Somewhere safe, and a car with no gas was not a safe place to be.

"Please, no! Eve, please."

Leisel was crying again, and I felt like shit that I was the one who had caused her tears. But I was doing this to protect her, to get us somewhere safe. Pulling her into a hug, I planted a kiss on the top of her head.

"We'll be fine. I promise," I said, with far more reassurance than I should have been allowed to dole out.

Nodding against me, she attempted to stop her tears, but I was still left feeling awful. Leisel had known nothing but fear for the past four years, and I would do anything to ensure she'd never have to feel unsafe again.

Alex drove on. As we drew closer and the small town came into view, the niggle of worry already fluttering inside my stomach only worsened. There was no movement, nothing alive or dead that I could see, but looks were always deceiving.

Take Lawrence Whitney, for example. The threat that lay behind closed doors, lurking in the shadows, was always far more deadly than the danger in plain sight.

CHAPTER NINE

Leisel

THE TOWN OF Covey was small, even smaller than Fredericksville, and it appeared to be utterly abandoned. As Alex turned slowly down what was probably once the main drag, I stared out the window in shock at what I was sure was once a quaint little village. Mom-and-Pop-type shops lined the street, a wooden sign boasting an apothecary hung haphazardly from a broken post, and there was an honest-to-God barber shop, complete with a candy-cane-striped pole.

I continued staring, trying to imagine what this place had looked like back before the infection, picturing happy people strolling the sidewalks. It was a place I would have gladly visited. I would have forced Evelyn to come along with me, dragging her into shop after shop, smiling as she laughed at my purchases and good-naturedly teased me for being so easily amused by simple things.

But that was then and this was now. And the now was a cracked and overgrown street, the earth beneath the pavement reclaiming the land and everything man had built on it. The stores were mere shells of their former selves with broken windows, missing doors, faded and cracked paint, and the ever-present aura of death.

It was a ghost town, a graveyard without headstones, a forgotten and decaying museum of what life used to be. And if life went on this way, if the infection continued to rage, eventually there would be no one left, the human race would soon be gone. In time, so would all of our towns and with them, any last shred of proof that we ever existed at all.

"Looks clear," Evelyn mused, though her body stayed tense and alert.

Alex let out a small snort. "Looks can be deceiving."

Her expression pinched with irritation, Evelyn slanted her eyes in my direction, rolling them ever so slightly.

I attempted to give her a smile in return, but didn't quite manage one. My stomach churned with fear, my head pounded from anxiety, and with every mile we traveled, my fear of the unknown only continued to grow, increasing my discomfort.

"Lei?" she whispered, cocking her head in question. "You okay?"

"F-fine," I stuttered hoarsely, but I was anything but fine. I tried to envision myself searching out these buildings for food or clothing, things that had once belonged to others—others who hadn't been as fortunate as me—and my apprehension only grew. I felt like an interloper in this new and foreign world, and worse than that, like a burden on Evelyn and Alex.

What good would I be if we were attacked by an infected, or even by another person? What good was I even if we weren't?

Closing my eyes, I inhaled slowly and deeply, the stale air of the truck smelling strongly of unwashed bodies. I let out my breath, wishing I could have a private moment alone, somewhere behind closed doors so I could block out the world. Just a minute was all I needed to regain my composure.

I took another breath and let it out, another fruitless attempt at calming my nerves. It was hot in the truck, the three of us pressed up against one another, Alex on my left, his right leg situated firmly up alongside my left, and on my right was Evelyn, her entire left side pressed uncomfortably against me. We were touching from our shoulders to our knees, unable to move even a fraction of an inch without the other being entirely aware.

When I cracked open an eyelid, the truck's dashboard loomed in front of me, and beyond that abandoned cars blurred in and out of focus as we passed them, Alex swerving every so often to avoid garbage strewn in the road. His elbow would press into my bicep and every time, I cringed and closed my eyes, my breath lodging in my throat.

I needed out of this truck; it was too small and stifling. I needed fresh air and a moment alone. I needed a bath to wash away the blood, the sweat, and the stench of fear. I needed—

"Don't worry, Lei," Evelyn said gently, interrupting my panicked thoughts. "It's going to be fine. I'm going to protect you."

My eyes flew open just in time to see her reaching for me, more than likely to give me a reassuring pat or a comforting squeeze. The thought of it, of being treated or thought of like a useless child again, sent my emotions into overdrive, and I did something I'd never done before, never thought of doing before.

I slapped Evelyn's arm away.

"Stop it!" I cried. "I'm not a child. It's not my fault I don't know how to use a gun. It's not my fault I don't know the first thing about surviving out here. It's not my fault that I'm not as strong as you, or as brave. And it's not my fault that I'm weak!"

Evelyn's mouth fell open, then closed, and then opened again as her eyes widened in shock at my sudden outburst. For the first time, my friend was at a loss for words. There were a lot of firsts happening lately, most of them at the most inopportune times. And all of them were my fault.

"You're not weak."

I was so busy glaring at Evelyn, and her gaping at me, that neither of us noticed for several moments that the truck had come to a stop. Blinking with confusion, I turned to find Alex staring straight ahead, his hands gripping the steering wheel so tightly that his tanned knuckles had turned white.

"You're not weak," he repeated, this time more forcefully.

Without another word, Alex roughly pulled the key from the ignition and exited the truck, slamming the door loud enough to make me wince. I watched him walk a few feet into the empty street before I looked back at Evelyn, an apology forming on my lips.

"No," she said, flashing me a wicked smile. "Don't you dare say you're sorry. Not for that."

Flabbergasted, I searched her face, confused by her smile, trying to discern the reason for it.

"Why the hell not?" was all I could say.

"Because," she said pointedly. "It's so fucking good to finally see you stand up for yourself again."

The first three stores we ventured inside had been picked clean of anything useful quite some time ago. All that remained were fragments of what these buildings had once held, an abundance of cobwebs and dust, and a few scattered human bones.

For the most part I stayed on lookout, remaining at the entrance. My sole job was to alert Alex and Evelyn of any threats, be they infected, animal, or another human, while the two of them searched for provisions.

By our fourth stop, at what looked to have once been a bank, I was more sure of myself than I had been in quite some time. The gun felt good in my grip, solid and heavy, and despite not having yet fired it, I was oddly reassured to have it there.

That wasn't to say I was no longer scared, because I was. Actually, I was downright terrified. The sun was setting on the horizon, giving the entire town an overall gray and spooky appearance. Without electricity, the interiors of the buildings were already too dim to see clearly, even with the aid of Alex's flashlight. Added to it was the unnatural silence and stillness in a place that I knew had once been full of footsteps, voices, even the buzz of the streetlamps. It was the perfect setting for a horror movie. And as the sun sank deeper on the horizon, my recently won smidgen of courage began to form into a hard lump of fear in my gut.

"We should get going," I called out over my shoulder, my voice quivering with my growing anxiety.

"One minute!" Evelyn replied. "There's something under this... goddamn it, this is heavy!"

"Leisel."

Alex was suddenly beside me, so close I could feel the heat of his breath against my cheek. Squeaking in surprise, I jumped backward, out of the doorway and onto the sidewalk.

"You scared me," I breathed out. Placing my hand over my pounding heart, I took in a much-needed gulp of fresh air.

"Sorry," he said, not looking the least bit sorry. Much like Evelyn had earlier in response to Alex, I found myself wanting to roll my eyes.

He was a strange man. Handsome and unreadable, and if the events of the last two days were anything to go on, entirely unpredictable.

"Why did you help me?" I blurted out, suddenly needing to know. "And don't tell me you wanted out of there. Life was good for you and Jami in Fredericksville. Why would anyone trade that for…" I trailed off and gestured toward the empty, ruined street. "This," I finished. What I really wanted to ask was, why would anyone trade a comfy and predictable life for what could end up being a very short life, one filled with unfathomable dangers.

As I already presumed, he didn't answer me readily but instead just stared down at me, his dark eyes appearing black in the waning light.

"You think you're weak," he finally said, his voice unusually ragged and thick. "But you're not. Weak people don't live through the kind of shit you lived through. Weak people don't drive a knife into someone's heart, and weak people don't just willingly accept the fact that they've been sentenced to death."

Alex took a rather menacing step toward me, and I again found myself fighting to remain where I stood. I didn't want to be the woman who was afraid of all men just because one man had hurt her. I didn't want to be weak anymore. So I stood my ground and lifted my chin, though my knees began to tremble.

"I was weak," he continued, twisting his lips into a snarl filled with self-hatred. "I stood outside your home, day after day, year after year, listening to what he did to you, and I never lifted a hand to stop it." He swallowed hard and shook his head as his nostrils flared, his gaze unfocused. "Weak people do nothing. Weak people let life happen to them, and I was weak. I knew what it was like out here, knew the kind of shit people were doing just to live another day, and I didn't want to come back to it, to this. So I let him hurt you, didn't say a word, didn't try to stop it, because I was goddamn weak."

My lower lip began to quiver as my eyes filled with tears. One blink and they spilled over, running down my cheeks faster than I could catch the breath I needed to stop them. Who was this man? This wasn't the Alex I knew, the silent, stone-faced, emotionless Alex who'd been by my side this entire time, and yet the same I'd thought had never really seen me before.

I shouldn't have been so surprised. Whereas Lawrence had appeared easygoing, always had a smile on his face, was well spoken, and moved in a way that wasn't at all threatening, he'd actually been the very opposite.

People, I'd come to learn, were rarely congruent to the face they put on. Lawrence certainly hadn't been, and Alex wasn't either. Evelyn, however, Evelyn was always herself. The one person I could always count on for honesty, the one person I could always trust. She was my constant, my rock, my heart, and I loved her for that.

"You have nothing to apologize for," I whispered tearfully. "I don't blame you for taking care of yourself. You didn't owe me anything."

"But I did—I do," he said, his jaw clenched tight, his eyes flashing fire.

I watched him internally battle his anger, and yet I was strangely not afraid of him. It was the smiles that now worried me, the gentle touches and the softly spoken words that turned into something much more horrifying. Thanks to Lawrence—who had been at his most calm and his happiest when hurting me—Alex's sharper, much harsher demeanor was almost comforting.

"I owe you my humanity, Leisel. Or what the hell is the point? What are we trying to survive for?"

I opened my mouth, an instinctual response when someone asks you a question, only to realize I didn't have a ready answer, and more tears fell. Through blurry eyes I saw Alex's hand rise, and for the first time in three years, I didn't flinch at the sight of it. But before it could reach me, his hand suddenly stilled a hairbreadth away from my cheek, and hovered for a moment before falling away.

"I'm sorry," he said quietly, all the anger now drained from his expression.

I didn't want to repeat myself, to tell him again that he had nothing to be sorry for, not after he'd confessed what appeared to be something that had been weighing so heavily on his mind for some time now. To do so would be to dismiss his pain, and I knew better than anyone what that felt like. Never would I wish the same on another person, to ignore the wounds they carried within them.

"Nothing," Evelyn announced, and we turned to her, finding her expression crestfallen. Kicking at some debris in her path, she made her way toward us. "Not a single thing."

The three of us stood there for a moment, not looking at one another, not looking at anything in particular. We were all hungry, dirty, and the weather was quickly turning. Soon the days would no longer be warm, and the nights even colder.

"Without gas, we'll be traveling on foot soon," Alex said, both sounding and looking grim. "And dead if we don't find anything to eat."

"What about other people?" Evelyn asked. "There must be other survivors."

Alex turned his hard stare on Evelyn. "Trust me, we don't want to find other survivors. You think Whitney was a ba—"

"Evenin', friends."

My head spun left toward the new voice just as Alex grabbed my arm. I barely had time to see who it was that had spoken, only getting a glimpse of a dark figure that looked decidedly male, before Alex yanked me backward and nearly threw me into Evelyn. Quickly, he moved to stand in front of us, shielding us both with his body. Evelyn's hand immediately sought out mine and we both squeezed each other tightly.

"You look hungry," the voice continued. "And tired."

"We're fine," Alex snapped. "Just passing through."

"We've got food, friends, and—"

"I'm not your friend," Alex fired back, sounding more agitated than I'd ever heard him before. I watched, barely breathing, as his shoulders tensed, the muscles in his back bunching under his clothing.

"Are you sure about that?" the voice replied, sounding casual, easygoing, and far too jovial for my liking. "We could all use a friend these days."

A crash sounded from behind us, just as a bright light temporarily blinded me. Gripping Evelyn's hand tighter, as well as my gun, I blinked rapidly, aiming my weapon uselessly, trying to see against the blaze of light. All around me I could hear shuffling, muffled curses that sounded like Alex, unfamiliar murmurs, and then all at once Evelyn was ripped away from me.

Momentarily alone, I flailed, fear holding my scream hostage in my throat, until hands suddenly grabbed at me, and pain erupted in my skull. Like from a blow to the gut, breath whooshed from my lungs as my knees gave out. I began to fall, dropping down a seemingly endless hole of nothingness, surrounded by silence and a shade blacker than night.

CHAPTER TEN

Evelyn

I AWOKE TO THE sound of singing.

Groaning, I grabbed my aching head and found something sticky coating my hair, the scalp beneath tender and raw. The trilling sound of several voices singing in harmony only made the ache worse.

I was suddenly reminded of attending church as a child. Every Sunday we'd wear our prettiest dresses, my sister and I, my mother as well, and my father would wear his perfectly pressed suit. The minister had been a grumpy old bastard. Never a smile for anyone, not even for the well-behaved children who'd sat patiently and quietly for fear he'd scold them. In fact, as I'd grown older, it had become a longstanding joke between my father and me as we debated the reason behind that old man's misery.

When I was finally able to pry my heavy eyes open, it wasn't only the sound of singing that reminded me of my childhood. I was seated in a church—the front pew, to be precise—and there was a choir standing off to my right singing the last hymn, a benediction I knew by heart.

Similarities aside, the minister standing behind the podium was the exact opposite of my minister. This man was anything but miserable, and instead appeared to be hopped up on happiness. His smile was warm, his eyes shining as they scanned his congregation. A full head of thick brown curls framed his youthful and friendly face, and when he turned that face in my direction, he winked at me, his smile growing even wider.

Blinking, I shook my head as if it would somehow help clear the fuzz from my brain. When that didn't seem to work, I closed my eyes and counted to ten, because this must be a hallucination or a dream.

That was it! I was dreaming.

Giving myself a good pinch on the arm, I opened my eyes, yet nothing had changed. Confused, I blinked several times, and then a few more for good measure. But nothing had changed. The merry minister was still there, bouncing about happily, clapping while he sang. Out of nowhere, the song suddenly reached a new volume, and my body responded by sending a sharp shooting pain screaming through my head from temple to temple.

When I glanced to my left, I found an older woman with gray hair, her eyes kind as she beamed at me. Scowling, I looked away, only to find the space to my right occupied as well. Another friendly face smiled at me, this one belonging to a middle-aged man who was lovingly cradling a shotgun in his lap.

Startled by the gun, I flinched and inched closer to the woman instead. She placed a gentle hand on my shoulder, and I flinched again. My behavior didn't seem to faze either of them, they continued to smile as they sang, looking expectantly at me as if awaiting me to open my mouth and jump right in.

Shrugging the woman's hand from my shoulder, I attempted to stand, but was immediately forced back down by both the woman and the man. Once I was seated again, they each took one of my arms, gripping the limb in their grasp. It was then that my mind fully cleared and I realized that Leisel and Alex weren't here with me, wherever the hell *here* was.

Twisting around in my seat, I searched through the sparsely filled pews for any sign of my friends, coming up empty. Feeling suddenly sick, panicked, and more than a little afraid, I started to yell.

"Lei!" I screamed, interrupting the third verse of the hymn. "Leisel!"

Despite my cries, the choir sang on with wide, contented smiles on their faces. Not even a glance was spared in my direction, as if this insane scenario was utterly normal for them.

"Get off me!" I screamed, still twisting in my seat, trying to shake free of my captors. "Get the fuck off me!"

The minister chose that moment to finally stop singing, and once he did, the entire church fell silent. His happy expression remained firmly in place, though something had changed. His eyes seemed different now, as if a darkness had crept in.

"You're awake!" Clapping his hands together, he gave me a toothy grin. "Wonderful. Let me introduce myself, friend!" he continued cheerfully. "I'm Mr. Peter, and the good people seated next to you are Mr. Michael and Mrs. Mary!"

"Friend," Mr. Michael greeted me, bowing his head.

I gawked at all three of these crazy people, my eyes bugging out of my head, my brain having trouble grasping what was really happening here.

"Friend," Mrs. Mary said, releasing me in order to offer her hand.

Instead of taking it, I jumped up, catching Mr. Michael by surprise, and wrenched free from his grip on my arm. As I scrambled backward, both Mrs. Mary and Mr. Michael were already on their feet, reaching for me. Suddenly Mr. Peter was there, his white robes swishing around him as he stepped in front of them, blocking them from reaching me.

"That won't be necessary, Mr. Michael," he said, his eyes on me. "We're all friends here, no need to panic."

I scowled at him. "Where's Leisel!" I demanded.

The minister cocked his head to one side, looking thoughtful. "I'm afraid I don't know of a Leisel, friend."

"The woman I was with!" I screamed, my hands twitching with the urge to wrap them around his neck. "Where are the people I was with?"

"Ah, your companions," he replied calmly. "Why, they're here. With us." He gestured behind him, toward the congregation.

Desperate, I swung my head around, my eyes now wild as I searched for any sign of Alex or Leisel.

The church was small and dark, its windows boarded up. The walls were white, the carpet red, and candles have been placed throughout the entire space. There were more people here then I'd previously thought, twenty or so, although there might have been more considering I couldn't see straight through to the very back. Still, I saw no sign of Leisel or Alex.

"Leisel!" I shouted again. "Leisel!"

Mr. Peter placed his hand on my arm. His grip was not harsh, in fact, his touch was gentle, probably meant to be a calming gesture, yet it had the opposite effect on me.

"They are here," he said, his tone lower than before, with a hint of a threat. "They are within us all." He pointed to himself and then spread his arms open wide, emphatically gesturing to everyone.

Sharply, I turned to look out at the congregation, finding them little more than happy statues. When I glanced back at Mr. Peter, my panic and fear reached their pinnacle and I lashed out. My fist connected with his jaw with a sickening crunch, and we both cried out in pain. But pain was the least of my concern. As he stumbled backward, I leaped, jumping on top of him, and sent him sprawling flat onto the floor. Screaming obscenities, I sent my fist again into his face, clawing at his skin, slapping at him, until hands gripped the back of my clothing and promptly yanked me to my feet.

I was still flailing, screaming and kicking, when Mr. Peter was helped to his feet. His nostrils flaring, he glared at me through swollen eyelids. Licking the blood from his bottom lip, his once happy expression was gone, replaced with a deadly snarl.

"That wasn't very nice of you," he practically growled. "I thought we were friends."

"Where is she?" I yelled, my throat burning with grief.

Without warning his hand lashed out, connecting painfully with my cheek. My head snapped back and stars danced in front of my eyes as I blinked repeatedly, desperately trying to focus. But the slap was like a mallet to my already dazed skull. Suddenly my legs were like jelly, and I slumped against the men holding me up.

"Take her to the altar," Mr. Peter said to the men holding me, his now cold and disappointed gaze landing on me. "We're forever grateful for your sacrifice, friend," he said softly, a wicked smile curving his lips.

No longer with the strength to yell, I mumbled something incoherent in response before I was dragged away from the candlelit room and through a door. It was dark in the bowels of the church, my already strained eyes unable to make out much more than shadows.

"Don't worry, friend!" Mr. Peter called out, his voice sounding muffled and far away. "You'll be with them soon. Both the Lord and I want you to know that we are indebted to you. Forever grateful."

I didn't have the energy to fight them, whoever was dragging me along. And what would have been the point? Not only did they outnumber me, but Mr. Peter's parting words had stripped away any fight I had left. It no longer mattered anymore what happened to me.

Nothing mattered if Leisel was gone.

I felt myself being pulled down a set of stairs, hearing the *thump-thump-thump* of my feet as they dully hit against each concrete step. It was even darker down here, and foul smelling. As the rank smell of death and decay washed over me, I gagged and almost sobbed. That smell reminded me of the early days, of the disease on every corner, in every home. It reminded me of the families lost, the children massacred. Worse, it reminded me of Shawn, of his final moments.

A low buzzing sound surrounded us, a strange humming, not unlike the sound of an electrical transformer. But my throat was thick with unshed sobs, and burning with a grief so all consuming, I couldn't even find the strength to lift my chin from my chest to locate the source of the noise.

Several moments passed, then a flicker of light caught my attention. When I lifted my head, my gaze fell on someone's legs. I tilted my head up, letting my gaze travel up the legs and body until I found the blurry face of a man.

"Please," I begged. "Just tell me where she is, just let me see her." My chin trembled as I spoke, but I refused to cry, refused to give in to my grief until I'd seen her, until I knew for sure what had happened to Leisel.

But the man didn't respond, didn't even look at me. Instead he moved away, allowing the men dragging me along to pass by him.

There was a draft down here, a chill that worked its way through the damp corridors, similar to the one making its way down my spine. My heart hammered heavily, and a drop of sweat slid slowly down my back. Off in the distance I could hear the sound of footsteps, each one echoing all around me.

Letting my eyelids drop, I swallowed another threatening sob, not quite able to believe that it had come to this. That after everything I'd lived through, this was how I was going to die—at the hands of a bunch of whack jobs in serious need of therapy.

Really, God? Really?

We continued for what seemed like an eternity, until one of the men holding me up began to grunt with the effort it took him to keep me from falling.

I lifted my head, just enough to catch a glimpse of him in the dim light. He was younger than me, yet he had an aura of darkness surrounding him that aged him beyond his years. There was a familiar look in his empty eyes, one I'd seen a hundred times before. It wasn't sadness or anger, but the look of someone who'd seen too much, done too much, someone who knew they were going to burn in hell for it all when push came to shove.

"You're going to burn," I whispered hoarsely, wanting to remind him of what he already knew, and his eyes flitted to mine, staring blankly down at me. Disgusted, I turned away from him. There wasn't hope for someone like him, lost to their madness.

We finally came to a stop just outside a large wood-slatted door. One of the men holding me unexpectedly released me, shoving me entirely into the arms of the other. He was older, and surprisingly heavy-set considering we were in the midst of a damn apocalypse. I was reminded of Mason then, his greed when it came to everything, but most of all when it came to me. I hoped that having lost me, he was drowning in self-pity.

Casting a quick glance over my head, the man pulled a set of keys from his pocket and thumbed through them. After several tense moments as I waited for the horrors behind the door to be revealed, he unlocked it.

The door creaked open ominously, revealing a dark room, and the smell of decay wafted from within, even more potent than before. It wasn't just the smell of decay, but the smell of death itself that hung in the air, and my stomach lurched at the thought of what new horror I'd just stumbled into. Squinting my eyes, I could make out what looked to be a concrete stand in the center of the room, a velvet blanket thrown over the top of it. There were no windows, and no doors aside from the entrance. Of course there weren't.

The man still holding me pushed me forward, shoving me into the foul-smelling darkness. At first, I tried to resist but it was futile, and I was shoved hard onto the cold concrete floor. Quickly, I scanned the room, but saw nothing but the concrete stand and velvet blanket. But as my eyes began to adjust to the darkness, I found that it wasn't a blanket at all. It was blood, thick and red, covering the stand.

"Why are you doing this?" I whispered, turning back to the men, my eyes wide with horror as my brain struggled to process what was happening.

"It's not our choice," the heavyset man replied. "It's the Lord's." And then he gazed up to the ceiling, making the sign of the cross in front of him.

"You're telling me that the Lord asked you to kidnap three people off the street and kill them? The Lord wants you to murder three innocent people who have done nothing to you?"

"You're not going to die," the younger man said.

"I'm not?" I asked, dumbfounded.

"No, silly, you're going home." He smiled then, though it wasn't a friendly smile, leading me to think he didn't quite believe what he was saying.

"You're speaking in riddles!" I yelled, fixing them both with as menacing a glare as I could muster, but it was wasted on them as they were both now smiling.

"Where are my friends?" I asked, feeling the slightest bit hopeful, though my voice had cracked on the last syllable. "Have you killed them? Please, just tell me."

"We're sending them home too," the older man replied, his voice distant, his gaze suddenly far away. "They shall protect our flock from the wolves."

Tears began to build behind my eyes. These people were insane; they were completely fucking nuts. I had no idea what they had done to Leisel and Alex, no idea what they were going to do to me. My heart began to beat so incredibly fast that it felt as if my chest might explode from all the pressure. But I'd held it together for this long, managing to keep everything always bottled up and buried deep down inside me, that I refused to release it here, especially in front of these lunatics.

And then, just when I'd thought all was lost, a scream, piercing in its intensity and utterly familiar, cut sharply through the otherwise silent hall.

Leisel!

Jumping to my feet, I lunged through the doorway, blindly reaching for either man standing there. Punching, kicking, clawing, biting,

I attacked them with everything I had left, drawing my strength from the sound of Leisel's fear.

CHAPTER ELEVEN

Leisel

I COULDN'T STOP SCREAMING. The smell was foul, vile, enough to make my eyes water and my stomach heave. Only I didn't have time to lose my stomach contents. Not locked in this tiny room, lit by a lone candle on the floor, chained to a stone altar, my only companion a hungry infected.

I'd never been this close to an infected before, only Thomas and Shawn when they'd been newly turned. Shawn had quickly ended Thomas's life, and when Shawn had awoken as an infected, it had been Evelyn who'd taken his.

Although I'd seen other infected through the years, it had always been from afar. Even our encounters most recently, I hadn't been up close and personal with them, not like Evelyn or Alex had. I'd always been shielded by something, by someone.

Not anymore.

My head was still pounding from the blow I'd suffered, and the shackles around my wrists were cutting into my skin, chafing and tearing it. But I continued pulling on them, my adrenaline overshadowing my pain as I ran in circles around this bloodied stone altar. I had only myself to protect me now. No one was coming to save me, and there was no time to break down, to freak out and give up. Not unless I wanted a very painful and awful death.

The infected was desperate to take a chunk out of me. It shambled mindlessly after me, its arms outstretched, its maw strained wide open, exposing rotten, jagged teeth. Even worse, this was not a newly turned. From what I could tell in the flickering shadows, this looked to be a first- or second-wave infected. What had once been skin, smooth and plump and flush with life, was now sunken and shriveled by age and decay, giving the thing an overall brown and leathery appearance. It was utterly hairless, its cloudy eyes were sunken in, and what little muscle mass remained wasn't enough to shield the infected's bones from protruding from its skin. Since it was utterly devoid of any body hair, I couldn't even begin to determine what sex it was.

First-wave infected were rarely seen anymore, most of them having been killed or no longer able to get around as easily as in the early days after years of decomposition had taken its toll on their bodies.

However, this particular one had been well cared for. No exposure to the elements to quicken the decaying process, no human attacks had left it missing limbs or with gaping bullet holes. Sure, it smelled something awful, like meat that had been left in a freezer long after the electricity had gone out, but at the same time it had been routinely cleaned, clothed…and fed.

This infected, as hard to believe as this was for my fear-addled brain, had been loved. Was loved. And I'd been so lovingly given to it for dinner. But I wasn't going to be an easy meal. Whereas fear might have paralyzed me in the past, in this tiny room it had become my motivation.

With the stone altar the only thing keeping the creature from easily getting to me, I ran left, then right, then left again, or sometimes in a complete circle, as it slowly but surely continued to come at me. It was a tireless creature, uncaring about the energy it expended, whereas I was the opposite. I was cold, exhausted, my body not yet recovered from Lawrence's final beating. I didn't have Alex's physical strength or Evelyn's seemingly tireless stamina, and although I wasn't out of shape, I certainly wasn't in the best condition. Eventually I would tire or make a mistake, and then become fodder for the dead.

Then the worst thing possible happened—I slipped. I didn't know how or why it happened, not that it mattered once I was flat on my backside, my arms hanging above my head, my wrists still chained to the altar. As the garbled groans grew closer, I grabbed hold of my chains, kicking at the floor, attempting to pull myself back up to my feet, but I wasn't fast enough. The infected reached me, and with its bony arms outstretched, descended on me.

I knew I was screaming, I could feel the vibration in my lungs and in my throat, yet I couldn't hear a thing. My heart was pounding, my cold, sweaty hands sliding down the chain as I continued to try to pull myself upright, my fingers slipping with every attempt. Instinctively, I swung my right leg up and forward, hitting the infected square in its open mouth and sending it staggering backward. It hit the wall, the force of which pushed it forward, giving me only a split second to pull myself up.

I managed to regain my footing, but the chains had become twisted and tightened when I'd fallen, and now running in circles around the altar was no longer an option.

The infected came at me again, steady and sure, and again I swung out with my leg, this time catching it in the knee. With an audible crack, the limb bent and the infected stumbled. But still, it kept coming, entirely unbothered.

Frantic, I tried to untangle the chains, screaming as I yanked and pulled, uncaring that I was openly bleeding, uncaring that I was now probably missing most of the skin on my wrists. I hadn't lived this long—surviving the loss, the pain, and the brutality of this new world—only to end up locked in a room, chained to an altar like a sacrificial lamb, and given to an infected as a gift.

I took too long trying to untangle myself, not giving myself enough time or space to get another good kick in, before the infected came barreling back toward me. I screamed as it reached for me, thrusting out my elbow into its chest, but without enough strength. The shove didn't do much, only alerted the infected to the ready meal I'd just shoved into its face. As its rotten teeth clamped down on my arm, I screamed again, this time with tears in my eyes.

"No!" I cried out, struggling harder. "No!"

My jacket ripped beneath the onslaught of teeth, and I squeezed my eyes shut, knowing my shirt and skin would be next. I was too tangled now, no room for any evasive maneuvers. The sickly sweet smell of rot and decay was all around me, the breathless monster on top of me, clutching at me with frozen hands. It was over. This would be my bitter, ugly end.

At the first scrape of teeth against my skin, my heart skipped a beat. A visceral reaction burst forth and I swung my arm upward, and even with as little room as I had, my elbow dislodged from its mouth, finding purchase against its jaw. The force of the blow wasn't enough to send it backward, nor distract it, but it gave me enough room to back away just enough to lift my leg and send my foot straight into the same knee I'd already broken.

This time its fragile bones shattered and the infected fell to the floor, its head slamming against the concrete. I didn't waste another second. I lifted my foot and sent it down and onto the creature's face. With the force of my stomp and the amount of decay the infected had already endured, my foot sank easily through its skin, its face giving way beneath my weight. Skin split and bones cracked beneath my shoe, but I pressed on, grinding my heel, screaming and crying until I both felt and heard a resounding pop. Like a broken water balloon, the head of the infected deflated, sludge pouring from it.

The infected was now still, unmoving, and what was left of its face entirely engulfed my tennis shoe. Still screaming, I began kicking, attempting but unable to dislodge it. With my refusal to touch the thing, I eventually had little choice but to sink to the ground beside it. Not that it mattered much. The infection would soon take root inside me and the fever would spread quickly, giving me a day, maybe two before I succumbed and then awoke as one of them.

As my bottom hit the cold concrete floor, the rest of my fleeting energy leaving me entirely, my screams turned to whimpers, my cries to a quiet choking that resulted in bile erupting from my throat and down my chin. I sat there, coughing through my emotion, fear snaking through my body so wildly that I could hardly think straight, and then my bladder unwittingly released, warm and wet, coating my jeans.

And that was how Alex found me. Covered in my own vomit, in a pool of my own urine, with my foot still lodged in the skull of an infected.

So consumed with my own circumstances, I hadn't even heard the door open, didn't see Alex until he was standing in front of me. I stared up, feeling momentary disbelief until I noticed the arm in his hand. Connected to the arm was the entire body of a man I didn't recognize. A man who, considering he had what looked like a human bone jutting from his eye socket, was obviously dead.

Alex took one look at me, at my expression, then dropped the body and rushed to my side. Belatedly, I noticed the large key ring in his hand, courtesy of the dead man, I supposed.

"Ev-Ev-Evelyn," I managed to sputter out between sobs.

Yanking on my chains, Alex shook his head. "Haven't found her yet. Only found you because you were screaming."

"Bi-bitten." I sobbed, trying to move my right arm to show him.

There was a momentary pause as Alex's eyes grew wide with alarm, and then he ripped off the remaining shreds of my sleeve and frantically inspected my skin.

Dropping to his knees, not caring what he was kneeling in, he rocked back on his heels and smiled at me. "Not bitten," he whispered.

Not bitten. Those two words were like fuel to my dwindling fire. My waning energy erupted, my worries for myself instantly gone, replaced with nothing but concern for Evelyn.

After dislodging my foot from the skull of the infected and helping me to my feet, Alex kept one arm looped around my waist, holding me up as he unchained me from the altar. It took several attempts, but he finally found the right key and removed my shackles. I winced at the sight of my bloodied and mangled wrists, but then quickly forgot about them.

"Evelyn," I whispered frantically. "We need to find her."

Alex, his back to me now, was bent down next to the body he'd dragged into the room. Roughly rifling through the man's clothing, he was pocketing whatever he could find.

Getting to his feet, he thrust a small blade at me and I readily took it, grateful for it. The smooth handle was hot in my cold hand, steady and sure against my shaky resolve. I could do this if I had to. It wasn't as if I was any stranger to using a knife on someone, even if that person had been sleeping. My apprehension stemmed from the fear of retaliation. I wasn't a fighter, with very little physical strength. If a full-grown man came at me…

Gritting my teeth, I shut down that line of thinking. I would do what I had to do. I would be strong and fight, if need be. I'd be like Evelyn.

"Stay behind me," Alex said, his voice a hushed whisper. "If anything happens to me, you run. Understand? Just run."

I managed to bob my head up and down, my relief at finding out I hadn't been bitten short lived. We still had to get out of here…wherever we were. The last thing I remembered was being torn away from

Evelyn, and then I'd woken up here, shackled and alone, only to have an infected shoved into the room with me.

"What is this place?" I asked as we crept quietly toward the door. "Where are we?"

With one hand on the knob, the other clutching a handgun, Alex turned his head just enough to look at me. In the bouncing light that gave his already shadowed features a menacing glower, he swallowed audibly.

"Hell," he replied darkly. "Just another version of hell." His expression and his words were a window to his soul, and for the first time since I'd known Alex, he seemed honestly afraid.

Instinctively, I reached out, placing my palm on the small of his back and fisting the material of his shirt. It was a reassuring gesture, both for him and for myself. His eyes shut, just for a second, but in that moment I saw his features relax. The worry seeped from him, and when they reopened, he was the Alex I knew once again.

Hard. Determined. And ready to fight his way out of hell.

Again.

CHAPTER TWELVE

Evelyn

"YOU'RE GOING TO regret that, friend."

Somehow I'd backed myself into a corner, the heavyset man blocking any chance of escape I might have had. At least he was no longer smiling. In fact, he looked furious, so much so that his saggy jowls were quivering with rage.

Glancing behind him, toward where his companion lay unmoving, and hopefully, not breathing, he turned to back to me, his upper lip rising in a crude snarl. "The Lord will not be pleased."

Crouching lower, I backed even farther away, my back now pressed against the cool, damp wall. I'd been lucky with the younger one. Leisel's screaming had spurred me on and I'd struck out wildly, gripping hold and ripping out his hair, my nails digging into his eyes, but it had been his own weapon that had been my saving grace—a long-handled police baton that had been tucked into his belt. Taking hold of it, I'd swung as hard as I could, feeling the crack against the man's skull, the force of the impact radiating down the baton and into my arm. Then I'd taken off running down the hall, in the wrong direction, no less, only to find myself boxed in.

Now the other man was advancing on me, a shotgun in his hands, and I knew there was no way out of this. You didn't bring a metal club to a gunfight and expect to make it out alive.

Tears, unexpected and unwelcome, formed behind my eyes, startling me as one by one they slid down my cheeks. Trying to staunch my emotions, I took a deep breath, and ended up whimpering instead. I was suddenly furious, hating myself for allowing this man, this lunatic, to see my weakness. Hating that it was this stranger who was the first to see my tears after so many years of containing them. Not Shawn, not Jami, not Leisel, but this vile, hateful, murderous man who used God as an excuse to hurt others.

And that was where I found it, my strength. In the knowledge that I was better than this man, than these people. That even if I were to die here today, I would die with the knowledge that I was a survivor, a true fighter, who didn't resort to violence, who hadn't lost my mind just because the world as we'd known it had ended.

Gritting my teeth, I unfolded from my crouch and stood to my full height, ready to meet my fate head-on. So focused was I on my quickly approaching death, I nearly screamed when Alex was suddenly there, running up behind the man with his own gun drawn. Alex jumped up into the air, and as he came crashing down, slammed the butt of his pistol into the back of the man's head.

The shotgun fell first, falling free from the man's hands as his eyes went wide. The man himself fell next, slumping into a heap on the floor. But Alex didn't stop there. He leaped on top of the man's lifeless form, using his gun to hit him again and again, over and over until blood sprayed from several gaping wounds in the man's head.

"Stop!" Leisel screamed, running up from behind. "Alex! Stop!"

She was alive. She was alive and Alex was alive, and even more amazing, so was I. My gaze flickered between Leisel and Alex and the bloodied body on the floor, and then back to Leisel.

She was alive.

Grunting, Alex climbed off the body, using his coat sleeve to wipe away the blood that had spattered across his face. He then tucked his pistol into his waistband and reached down to retrieve the man's shotgun.

"We need to go," Leisel whispered.

I knew we needed to go, but I couldn't seem to stop staring at her and move my feet. I'd been convinced she was dead, that fear driven home when I could no longer hear her screaming. Yet she wasn't, she was here, and I still couldn't quite believe that she was real, that she was still alive.

"Lei," I choked out, reaching for her, my chin trembling. "You're alive."

Her face crumpled at the sound of my broken words and then she rushed forward, nearly tripping over the mangled body at our feet as she fell into my waiting arms. Wrapping my arms around her, feeling her warmth and her trembling, feeling the dampness of her tears on my face, only served to reinforce the fact that she was truly alive, and I wasn't dreaming or imagining that she was here. I breathed out a sigh of relief and slumped against her.

"We need to go," Alex muttered. "Now."

He was already moving, heading down the hall, and Leisel and I hurried to catch up. We followed closely behind him, me still clutching my baton in one hand and Leisel's hand in the other.

"This place is huge," I whispered when we breached a third set of stairs. "And creepy as hell."

Wherever we were now, I could hear singing, the same hymn being belted out by the same joyful voices, the sound of it all the more chilling now that I knew what was happening here. In the Lord's name, no less.

"You ready for this?" Alex asked when we reached a large wooden door, the singing coming from just beyond it.

Nodding, I showed him my weapon, and he rewarded me with what might have been a smile. With Alex, whose smiles and grimaces looked nearly identical, the possibilities were endless.

Tightening my grip on Leisel's hand, I gave her a hard yet gentle glance, trying to will my strength and reassurance into her. She looked petrified, yet determined, and it was then that I noticed a small blade clenched in her fist. Knowing that she had some way to defend herself if we got separated was a comforting thought.

Raising my baton, I looked at Alex and nodded. "Ready," I whispered.

As he took hold of the handle, I had a moment of panic at the thought that it might be locked, that we might have to bust our way back into the bowels of the church. If that were the case, we'd lose the element of surprise, no longer have the upper hand.

But my fears were baseless. As the door clicked open and the room we were standing in flooded with light, the three of us moved forward and into the nave of the church.

The room was exactly the same as when I'd been forcefully

dragged through it. There were still people lining the pews, the choirs was still situated on the chancel, and the minister, Mr. Peter—apart from his swollen lip—was still smiling, still singing his heart out with his arms raised toward the sky in worship.

"SHUT THE FUCK UP!" Alex bellowed, startling everyone in the room, including Leisel and me.

The singing abruptly ended. A heartbeat of silence followed before a chorus of gasps and murmuring finally rippled through the pews as the parishioners watched us creep slowly into view. Only Mr. Michael was brave enough to stand, though his hands were trembling, giving away his fear and causing his gun to quiver in his grasp.

Alex smiled at the armed man, a menacing show of teeth. "Put it down, or your man over there"—he gestured with his gun toward Mr. Peter—"is going to eat a bullet."

With a quick nod, Mr. Peter signaled for Mr. Michael to do as Alex asked. Mr. Michael did, gently setting his weapon down by his feet before sitting down again.

Mr. Peter, no longer smiling, his eyes wide as he looked the three of us over, opened his mouth to speak.

"Don't say anything, asshole," Alex gritted out, cutting off whatever the man was about to say. "Get your people and go stand over there." He pointed to the far aisle of the nave, the one directly opposite of where we stood.

The church went silent, the choir and the parishioners all looking at Mr. Peter in question. Sheep, that was what they reminded me of. Unable to think for themselves, to eat, sleep, or breathe without some sort of direction.

"Stay here," Alex muttered before he stalked forward. With his shotgun raised, the barrel fixed on the center of Mr. Peter's chest, Alex approached him slowly.

"You would kill a man of God?" Mr. Peter asked in shocked disbelief as he eyed the gun in Alex's hand. "You would murder innocent church folk for simply spreading the word of the Lord?"

Reaching him, Alex pressed the barrel of the gun against his chest. "Tell them to move," he growled. "Or I will kill you."

The two men stared at each other, Alex's eyes full of hard determination, and Mr. Peter's full of hatred. Pure, unadulterated hatred glowered beneath the facade of kindness.

"Do what he says," Mr. Peter said, lifting his chin obstinately. "Get up and move to the east side, and let these sinners pass. The devil has a different path for them."

Another murmur rippled through the pews as people glanced back and forth at one another, some looking fearful, others looking angry, until eventually everyone was on their feet and shuffling slowly across the room.

"Arms up!" Alex shouted, glaring toward the gathered crowd. "All of you."

Again, Mr. Peter nodded, signaling for them to do as Alex asked. Once their arms were raised and Alex noted that their hands were devoid of weapons, he reached for Mr. Peter. Taking hold of his neck, Alex shoved him forward. Pressing his gun into the man's back, he kept his grip on his neck and urged him to begin walking.

Gripping Leisel's hand, I pulled her forward into the center aisle and followed closely behind Alex, only stopping to reach down and scoop up Mr. Michael's fallen shotgun. We continued down the aisle quickly as I kept a close watch on the crowd to my right, looking for any sign of movement, ready to run if someone pulled a weapon.

"You're leaving us unarmed, you know," Mr. Peter said, his tone suddenly oddly friendly. "We'll have no way to protect ourselves against the risen."

Alex laughed, a cold and cruel sound. "You tried to kill us, and you think I care what happens to you?" He barked out another angry semblance of a laugh, and pressed his gun harder into Mr. Peter's back.

When we reached the set of double doors at the entrance, Alex looked at me and I hurried forward, trying the handles and finding them locked.

"Where's the key?" Alex growled, shaking Mr. Peter.

"It's here!" a voice called out, and an elderly man stepped forward from the crowd. Graying and wrinkled, he wore a pair of tattered suspenders and a golfing cap. He reminded me of a grandfatherly type, a great uncle, or an elderly neighbor, someone who looked harmless, kind and caring even. Holding up a set of keys for us to see, he shook them. "I've got them."

Alex gestured for the man to join us and when he did, still keeping his grip on Mr. Peter's neck, Alex used his shotgun to shove the old man toward the doors. "Open them," he demanded.

The old man complied, his hands shaking with age and fear as he attempted to locate the correct key. It took several tries, each failed attempt causing the man to glance back at Alex with wide, fear-filled eyes, until finally the doors were unlocked. Pulling them open, the man tentatively peeked his head out, looking both left and right before stepping back.

"The way is clear," he said, swallowing hard. "Though your conscience will not be if you harm Mr. Peter."

Alex snorted. "I should kill him," he gritted out through clenched teeth. "I should kill you all."

The old man swallowed again and shook his head. "No, friend, you should be grateful for what we had planned—for what the Lord had planned for you."

"What is wrong with all of you?" I cried out, looking from the old man to Mr. Peter to the crowd of people still gathered together. When no one bothered to answer me, I shook my head, feeling both sickened and saddened. "Alex," I said. "Let's go. Right now."

"Yes, go," Mr. Peter snarled. "Get out of my church, and take with you the evil you've brought into my home. Go back to the vile cesspool the world has become, full of sinners and whores," he said pointedly, looking at Leisel and me as his face contorted with disgust, his eyes burning with madness.

I was shaking, not with fear but with a burst of uncontrollable anger, and as Alex shoved Mr. Peter forward, just barely missing the elderly man, I found myself releasing Leisel's hand, raising my gun, and pulling the trigger. My aim was wild and the first bullet sliced through Mr. Peter's shoulder, causing him to lurch backward and cry out in pain. Again, I pulled the trigger, this time hitting him squarely in the chest, piercing his most vital organ. He stumbled backward, his eyes wide, and hit the wall behind him before his knees gave out and he dropped to the floor in a heap.

Gasps and screams erupted from the gathered crowd as the old man fell to his knees, his hands covering the growing red stains on Mr. Peter's shirt.

"What have you done?" he screamed, his voice shrill and thick. "You've doomed us all. You've doomed us all!"

Alex, aiming his gun at the old man, let loose a mouthful of spit, sending it directly onto the toe of his shiny black shoe. "You've doomed yourselves."

I was shaking, my gun still aimed at the man I'd just killed, wanting to kill him all over again, wanting to kill every last person inside this church. Though they deserved worse than a quick death, they deserved the very same death they nearly inflicted on us, and who knew how many other innocent people.

"The blood attracts the risen," the old man wailed, his words barely distinguishable amid his groans of grief. "We'll need an offering!" he cried, looking toward his people.

Much to my horror, several of the parishioners stepped forward. Their heads were bowed as they silently offered themselves up at the old man's request.

"We need to go," Leisel cried out as she grabbed my arm and tried to pull me through the doorway. "Now, Eve, now!"

The three of us ran through the doorway and out into a dark and empty street. Though I didn't stop running long enough to get a good look at the place, I garnered from what glimpses I did see that it was a quiet sort of neighborhood. It had once probably been full of families, with children laughing and playing, neighbors borrowing sugar, the sort of town where Christmas caroling was a yearly event looked forward to by all.

We passed house after house, the windows dark, no signs of people or of infected, but we kept running, not wanting to stop until we were as far away from this place as possible.

Eventually the houses were spaced farther apart. The road was wider here, the trees larger and thicker, their heavy branches blocking the moonlight. I slowed first, my steps staggering, my chest burning from breathlessness. Leisel's body was pressed heavily against my side, and she smiled at me, seeming glad for the reprieve.

"Alex," I called out, my voice strangled, my throat dry and sore from exertion.

Still jogging ahead of us, he turned, slowing down when he saw we were unable to keep up with him. Nodding, he circled back around to us, taking the place on Leisel's right.

"We can't stop yet," he whispered hoarsely. Sweat glistened on his forehead as he looked at Leisel. "Are you okay?"

Leisel raised her head, her glistening eyes meeting Alex's. "I'm okay," she answered, sniffling.

She didn't sound okay, not even a little okay, yet the fact that she was attempting to be strong given our current situation made me almost smile. Almost.

We traveled without speaking for what seemed like miles, the sound of our footsteps accompanied by the trilling of crickets and the breeze rustling through the top of the trees. My feet were sore, aching with a tiredness that they hadn't felt in a long time. It was the sort of pain that reminded me of the world before the infection took hold.

Strangely, it felt good.

Good, only because it reminded me that I was finally free.

CHAPTER THIRTEEN

Leisel

WE WALKED ALL through the night and straight into morning, not stopping for anything other than bathroom breaks. We walked until my feet were numb, and my legs and arms were aching with fatigue and strain. And then finally, when I wasn't sure I could go any farther, when I had begun to sway from exhaustion, growing dizzy with hunger, Alex finally stopped walking. He stopped so abruptly, I almost slammed into the back of him.

"What?" I asked, looking around. I saw nothing, only the heart of the forest we'd been traveling through for miles now. Nothing but trees, a veritable color wheel of leaves, and the dirt beneath my feet.

"We can sleep here," he said, gesturing with his gun. My eyes followed the barrel of the weapon to a nearby tree.

"Oh," I said, sighing happily.

The small hunting platform looked quite rickety, obviously unused in some time, and weathered by the elements. The rope ladder hanging from it was tattered and heavily frayed, but I couldn't have cared less. I was dead on my feet and would have passed out right there on the ground if it would have been safe to do so.

The past couple of days were finally catching up with me. The exertion, the trauma, the heartache, and everything that went along with it all. My body was thoroughly exhausted, hardly a drop of energy left inside me, as was my mind. But it wasn't safe down here, and we didn't have the luxury to sleep in shifts. Neither Evelyn nor Alex had slept since leaving Fredericksville, and what little sleep I'd gotten on the road hadn't been nearly enough. This was the perfect place to catch a few hours of shut-eye without having to worry about any stray infected happening on us.

"I'll go up first," Evelyn offered quietly.

I looked over at my friend, searching her dirty, bloodstained face for a reason behind her recent silence. It wasn't like her to be so quiet, and yet for the past several hours she'd hardly said more than a few words.

"Hey," I said, reaching for her. Threading my fingers through hers, I pulled her several feet away from Alex, attempting a semblance of privacy. "Did something happen?" I whispered, purposefully brushing a lock of her hair out of her eyes in an attempt to gain her full attention.

Her head raised and she finally looked directly at me, her beautiful and poignant features twisted with pain, her big blue eyes so full of sorrow. Seeing this, seeing her so openly hurting and vulnerable was so unexpected, so unlike Evelyn, that I had to catch myself from taking a startled step backward. She seemed so broken, even worse than before.

"Eve," I said, my voice cracking. "What did they do to you?"

It hadn't occurred to me until now that something else, other than being sacrificed to an infected, could have happened to Evelyn.

"Other than having to endure mass at gunpoint and terrible singing?" she joked, attempting a smile. But like her words, her forced happy expression fell flat.

Her false smile fell away and she sighed, giving my hand a squeeze. "I thought you were dead, Lei," she admitted in a small voice. "And there was nothing I could do. And all of this..." She shrugged and looked away, her eyes scanning the forest. "This would all be for nothing then."

I felt a prickly sharp sensation in my chest, not unlike pain, but at the same time the feeling went deeper than any sort of physical pain could.

"I'm not your responsibility," I told her gently, rising emotion causing my eyes to fill. "And you're not mine. We're in this together, Eve, because without you, all this would still be for nothing."

"Seems sturdy enough," Alex called out, drawing our attention up into the tree. Standing on the platform, Alex peered down at the two of us and kicked at the rope ladder. "Welcome to Hotel de la Zombie."

My eyes widened with surprise. Had Alex just made a joke? Emotionally spent, half delirious from exhaustion and physical exertion, I couldn't stifle the giggle that slipped past my lips.

"Ooh," Evelyn cooed, nudging me with her shoulder. "Mr. Strong, Silent, and Sexy has jokes."

My eyes widened in her direction, my giggle falling away as my mouth fell open. "Sexy?" I whispered, frowning. "You think Alex is sexy?"

She lifted one shoulder, letting it fall, a halfhearted shrug. "Sure, if you like pretty boys who are constantly brooding and moody."

I stared after her, wondering how she could go from nearly crying to making jokes so quickly. She grabbed the frayed end of the rope ladder, and I watched as she deftly swung herself up, taking her only moments to climb to the top.

"Mints on the pillows, Lei," she said in a singsong voice. "Very ritzy!"

Blinking and feeling strangely like crying, I shook my head and took a step forward. Pain shot up through my feet and into my calves, causing me to wince, and I found myself moving faster, despite my pain. After all, the sooner I got myself up there, the sooner I could sleep; and the sooner I slept, the faster I would heal.

As for the rest of it—what I'd done back in Fredericksville, my close encounter with becoming an infected's dinner, Evelyn's strange shift in moods, and the human deaths that were quickly piling up at our feet, either by my own hand or because of me. Well, I'd deal with it all later. Or never. Whichever seemed easiest.

A cold breeze swept over me, waking me and causing a wave of goose bumps to pebble my skin. Along with it came the delicious aroma of cooking meat. Turning on my back, I stretched languidly, wincing as pain in both my wrists and ribs flared to life. My head hurt as well, a dull pounding that only grew, drawing me further out of sleep and into full consciousness.

Opening my eyes, expecting to see a brightly lit forest, I blinked in surprise. The sun was nearly gone, only slivers of the fading light peeking through the heavy canopy of branches and foliage. Alex was seated across from where Evelyn and I lay beside each other, his legs crisscrossed in the small space allotted him. In front of him was what looked to be a large coffee can, and inside it a rather impressive fire was raging.

"Squirrel," he said, lifting a small dark shape out of the flames. On a stick, the ends whittled to a sharp point, was speared the small body of a skinned and thoroughly cooked squirrel. My stomach growled again, this time louder, catching Alex's attention and drawing out a smile.

Groaning, I pushed myself upright, trying to ignore my body's protests. I was sore everywhere, more so than before. Everything that had happened over the last day or so—the beating I'd taken from Lawrence, the stress, the blow to the back of my head, the fight with the infected, our long trek on foot into the middle of nowhere—it had all caught up to me.

To make matters worse, I smelled awful, the most predominant odor being the urine coating my pants. Despite having dried, the urine had developed a bitter stench, as well as left the material stiff. Shifting uncomfortably, I folded my legs beneath me and hoped Alex couldn't smell me.

"How?" I whispered, so I wouldn't wake Evelyn.

He shrugged. "Found this can and some snare wire on another platform. Set a few traps and got lucky."

"Wow," I breathed out, significantly impressed. Give me a coffee can and some wire and I could have possibly potted a plant. Catching squirrels never would have occurred to me.

"Eat up," he said, holding out the squirrel kabob in offering. "Plenty more where that came from." He gestured to a small pile of squirrels beside him. I counted three more little bodies, already skinned, and all appearing to have had their necks broken.

"Thank you," I said, taking the food, my chest near bursting with gratitude toward this man and all of his unexpected kindness. "Thank you for everything."

Alex's eyes shifted upward, and he loudly cleared his throat. "There's a creek nearby," he said, sounding suddenly uncomfortable. "Decent place to wash up in the morning."

He was purposely changing the subject, obviously uncomfortable with my gratitude. I didn't understand it, but neither did I push it. Instead, I blew on my hot meal, simply grateful to have one, grateful that my very best friend was alive and safe and sleeping beside me, and forever grateful to the man seated across from me who'd made all this possible.

We ate in silence, the only sounds from our continuous chewing, the bird calls from the hidden life within the depths of the forest, and Evelyn's soft and peaceful snoring. Then, when my belly was full and exhaustion once again crept up on me, I lay back down beside Evelyn on the hard and uneven wood planks and closed my eyes. Only this time, before sleep could overtake me, I felt a light touch against my fingertips. Jerking, I opened my eyes to find Alex had moved closer to me, his hand barely touching me.

His eyes on me, he threaded his fingers through my own, his dirt-caked and calloused hand curling around mine. I was uncomfortable for a moment, then a soft, contented sigh escaped my lips and I squeezed back. I wasn't sure why, maybe to convey the gratitude he didn't seem to want to hear, maybe to share with him some sense of comfort. Either way, it felt oddly right, and I soon drifted off to sleep.

The creek was only a short distance from our shelter. Although my body ached fiercely and I felt as though I could have slept for weeks, I was able to manage the quick walk.

The sight of fresh water, clear and clean, was enough to rejuvenate me despite my injuries. Evelyn was the first to undress and I hastily followed her, though unlike her, I remained in my undergarments.

As it was, the moment I was free of my shirt, both Evelyn and Alex averted their eyes and the woods grew suddenly silent. I knew their reactions were because of the sad story my body told. Old scars and fresh bruises riddled the skin on my stomach and back, reminders of the beatings I'd endured at the hands of that bastard. My body was no longer a pretty package, something to be proud of or coveted, but instead a living reminder of the hell I'd lived through. I didn't hate it, wasn't ashamed of it, but neither did I like to look at myself for any length of time.

But seeing their faces, the cringes they both tried but failed to hide, caused a wave of humiliation to barrel through me. I didn't want their pity; I didn't want anyone's pity. We'd all lived through our own horrors, and whether they showed on our skin or not, we all bore scars, didn't we?

Evelyn's scars were internal, buried down deep. She never spoke of her pain, of the past, of the people she'd loved and lost, but instead concealed them, hiding from them using whatever distraction she could, drawing strength from our nightmare.

And Alex, his scars were there, though shrouded by his silence and his perseverance. I didn't know his story, the life he'd lived or what he'd endured before he came to live behind the walls of Fredericksville. But whatever it was, it had left a mark.

Wordlessly, I followed Evelyn into the creek, the stark contrast between the warm day and the cool water was glorious against my chafed and broken skin. I sank down quickly, feeling the silt and stones beneath me, and closed my eyes with a happy sigh.

"You know what would be amazing right now?" Evelyn asked.

I cracked an eyelid, squinting through the sunlight to find her perched on a small rock, bringing handfuls of water up to her face.

"Soap?" I suggested. "Clean clothes? Starbucks?"

From a few yards away I heard Alex snort, causing my own smile to form. Evelyn too, having raised her head from her hands, was grinning at me.

"Yes," she agreed, laughing. "Soap, clean clothes, and Starbucks would all be amazing. But I was thinking more along the lines of a frosty cold one, straight out of the cooler. Getting a nice buzz going and lying naked out in the sun."

She threw her head back, her face pointed toward the sky, and closed her eyes. Sitting there on that rock unabashedly, the sun beaming down on her, her luxurious hair hanging down her back, her naked and nicely toned body half in the water, half out, she arched her back in such a way that she looked like a mermaid, an ethereal beauty not from this world.

For reasons unknown to me, I found myself glancing over my back to where Alex was, kneeling in the shallow water, expecting I'd find him looking at her as well. The shock of his nudity momentarily startled me, and I found myself looking over every finely honed inch of his suntanned skin. He was a beautiful young man, his dark hair and scruff shining wet and black against his golden body, his dark eyes...

Our eyes met, mine wide with shock and his dark with guilt. He wasn't looking at Evelyn at all; he was looking at me. And the intensity of that gaze wasn't just surprising, but somewhat stifling. He looked away quickly and I did as well, only to find Evelyn watching me. She glanced between the two of us, her brow arched knowingly, a smirk on her lips. I stared at her, pleading with her with my eyes to keep her devilish mouth shut and not worsen what had just become an awkward situation.

Her impish grin turned gentle, and with a wink she turned away. Relieved, I set to washing myself as best I could, trying hard to ignore the sudden elephant that had just bumbled its way into my already complicated world.

Why had he been looking at me like that?

Although, I'd be lying if I were to say I wasn't somewhat pleased to find that he hadn't been looking at Evelyn.

CHAPTER FOURTEEN

Evelyn

SEVERAL DAYS PASSED while we recuperated. We slept, ate, and healed, though some scars would never go away. I felt fractured, as if deep gouges had been ripped through my heart, hurting far more than my physical injuries. It was as if my soul was sad, almost crushed with the gravity of our situation. Was this it? Was this all we had to look forward to now? Meeting crazy people as we struggled to live—to survive each day?

I didn't for one minute regret my decision to break Leisel out of Fredericksville, but I had hoped that there would be more to offer her out in the world. That perhaps man had been surviving, and we'd been merely locked away from the efforts that were being made to bring us back from near extinction. But I'd been wrong.

There was nothing good left in the world, and I didn't know how to deal with that. I didn't know how to make things better. That was my job, after all, who I was at heart. A people pleaser, someone who fixed things, made them work again. But I couldn't make this better, didn't know how to make this right. And the more I worried over it, the more I ached because of it, the harder it became to keep everything locked up tight inside me.

Things began to bubble to the surface, emotions and feelings that I'd kept locked up tight for so long now, cracks beginning to appear in my facade. Without Jami here, I didn't have an outlet to rid myself of all this nervous energy simmering just below my surface. Without

Jami, I didn't know how to rid myself of my own demons, to quash them, rebury them before they started to show. The truth was, I could actually feel myself breaking apart and once I broke, who was going to put me back together?

I looked at Leisel, who was sitting on the forest floor, her back against a thick tree trunk, staring off into the distance again. It was something she'd always done, but she'd been doing it a lot lately, her mind going elsewhere for hours at a time. Once she came back to us, it was usually with a start, as if she'd forgotten for a moment where she was. She'd been like this for a while now, ever since Alex had left to check his traps for food, and I couldn't help but think that if I couldn't hold it together, it wouldn't be Leisel who would save me. Not with her being so emotionally wrecked. My gaze dropped to her wrists, noting that they were healing well after her skin had nearly been scraped completely off. Thankfully, scabs were beginning to form, easing my worries that she might develop an infection from the wounds.

As my stomach began to growl, I placed my hand over it and turned away from Leisel, searching out the woods for any sign of Alex. We'd been lucky so far, with plenty of squirrels and snakes as our food source, and even a bush with some edible berries to give us more variety in our diet. In fact, we'd been very lucky, probably luckier than most. Luckier than Jami had been, anyway. That thought made my stomach twist painfully, and I purposely forced all thoughts of him away.

Focusing back on Leisel, I found her looking at me, her eyes wide.

"Did I do it again?" she said, her cheeks flushed.

Nodding, I smiled at her. This was the first time that she'd acknowledged she did that—disappeared into herself. Maybe it was because Alex wasn't around, and she felt somewhat comfortable to speak of it.

"How are you holding up?" I asked.

Cocking her head to one side, she raised an eyebrow in question.

I shrugged. "I hate to say this, Lei, but you killed a man this week, and that's a new record for you." I purposely kept my voice light to show her that I wasn't judging her. Being a murderer myself, I had no room to judge her or anyone, but more so because I thought what she did—killing Lawrence—was pretty amazing, and she was coping with the aftermath better than I would have expected her to.

"He wasn't a man," she said, sucking in a sharp breath. "He was a monster."

I nodded fervently in agreement. "Can't argue with that."

"Real men were people like Thomas and Shawn," she continued. "And I haven't seen a man like that..." Her words drifted off, her eyes glossing over, her expression growing sad at the memory of our first husbands, our husbands before everything was destroyed.

"Where do you go?" I asked in an attempt to change the subject. "When you zone out?" Picking up a twig, I began breaking it into small pieces, tossing each one aside.

"To the past," she said without hesitation. "I go back to the past."

I shook my head, unsure of what to say to that. I never thought of it—the past. Once a day, I would close my eyes and try to envision Shawn's face, only so that I didn't forget him, but I refused to think back to the happy times, to birthdays and barbeques, to Christmases and vacations. Thinking about better days just made reality that much harder to live through.

"What?" she asked, looking surprised. "You don't? Not ever?"

"Why torture yourself?" I retorted, hearing the annoyance in my tone, and then wincing in regret.

"Because." Averting her eyes from me, she looked at the ground. "I don't know..."

"It's okay," I said hurriedly. "We don't have to talk about it."

Mostly because I didn't want to talk about it, couldn't actually bring myself to talk about it. And I couldn't fathom any reason why she would want to talk about it either. It was far too much pain for any one person to have to think on. How much pain could one person live through? But to purposely dredge up the past, knowing full well you were never going to have that life back? No, I couldn't. It would break me completely, drive me insane with sadness. I couldn't think of those days, those lost lives, because I wouldn't want to come back from those beautiful memories. Not ever.

"No, no, it's okay," she said. "I want to. Actually, I think I need to." Her eyes flitted to mine and I found her smiling, the smile distorted among the many bruises still visible on her pretty face. "If that's okay?"

I shrugged noncommittally, silently hoping she wouldn't force me back there. "Sure, if you think you're up to it."

Leisel's smile grew wider, her eyes lighting up from within. "I think about it all the time. Things like the first Christmas we all shared together. You and Shawn came over, you brought me that awful chocolate cake—your first attempt at baking, remember?"

She started to laugh and it was such a foreign sound, an infectious one. Despite myself, despite now vividly recalling the memory of that very Christmas that had just forced itself out of the dark recesses of my mind, I found myself chuckling with her.

"It was disgusting," I said, still laughing. "Why would you think about that?"

"Because it makes me smile, and because it was that day that I knew we'd be friends forever." Her words were spoken with so much conviction that tears suddenly sprang to my eyes.

Biting down on my bottom lip as a dull pain sprang to life inside my chest, I shook my head. "A shitty chocolate cake makes you think the weirdest of things, Lei. Maybe you're just being overly emotional—you're probably about to get your period or something."

I tried to laugh then, only to remember that Leisel hadn't gotten her period in nearly two years, not since recovering from the beating that had nearly killed her. "Shit," I mumbled as my own tears slipped free of my lashes. "Shit, I'm a fucking idiot. I'm sorry."

Unfazed by my tactless comment, Leisel edged closer to me, taking my hand in hers. "Remember when I told you how much I hated fruitcake, that all I'd ever wanted as a kid was a damn chocolate cake at Christmas, but my mom continued making fruitcake? Remember, Eve? We were drinking tequila in your backyard, and for some reason I told you my Christmas cake sob story, and then six months later you made me that chocolate cake—albeit a shitty one—and gave it to me for Christmas."

My chin trembled, my heart stuttering in my chest. "Don't," I pleaded, more tears building in my eyes and threatening to break free. Tears that I'd long refused. Tears that I'd always been able to resist in the past. "Please don't do this, Lei."

Raising our joined hands, Leisel pressed a kiss to my knuckles. "When you gave me that awful cake, I knew what I meant to you, how much you cared for me. I knew from that day on that I would always be able to depend on you." Leisel stared into my face, her eyes glistening with love. "And in return, I swore to myself that you would always be able to depend on me."

I swallowed and looked away, choking back my tears. Her hand found the bottom of my chin, and she tilted my face back to hers.

"You made me so happy that day, Eve, and every day since. I love you, and I am grateful every single day that you married my husband's best friend, that you became my best friend. You make the days worthwhile. You make everything worthwhile."

My first sob broke free. It was loud and tragic, and made my gut twist painfully. Fat, salty tears trailed down my cheeks as I continued to shake my head, wishing she would stop. But I couldn't find my voice, couldn't tell her to hush because my throat felt too tight, and I was too busy sucking down air, trying desperately to breathe.

As I sobbed again, louder this time, Leisel tried to pull me into her arms. I resisted at first, pushing back against her, but she refused to let me go, refused to loosen her grip on me. Eventually my dam broke, my barriers came crashing down, and I found myself clinging to her as I sobbed, my pain finally finding purchase in the world. Memories flooded in; there was no hiding from them any longer.

The tears were never ending, a tsunami of emotion that threatened to swallow me whole, over and over again dragging me into the abyss of pain that I'd been hiding from for years. And all the while, Leisel held me tightly, humming softly and sweetly, keeping me tethered to her and refusing to allow my pain to consume me.

I must have dozed off, because when I woke my face was dry of tears, but I was still in Leisel's arms.

"I still remember how you looked when Thomas introduced us," I said, my voice hoarse and my throat sore from crying. "You were scared shitless."

"You were intimidating, Eve!" she said with a laugh.

Sitting up, I wiped the remaining tears still clinging to my lashes. "I overheard you talking to Tom that day, you know?"

Leisel's brow furrowed with confusion.

"At the table," I explained. "I think a waiter had just brought you a fresh drink. You were never much of a drinker, so in your defense you were probably a little drunk when you said it..."

Leisel shook her head. "Said what?"

"That you hoped you weren't going to have to spend too much time with me. That I'd been a whore in high school, and you hoped I was just another one of Shawn's flings, and that we wouldn't last. That he could do a lot better than me."

Her eyes wide, Leisel reached for me. "I'm so sorry, Eve, I didn't mean it!"

"Yes, you did," I said, and grinned. "And you were right. Shawn did deserve better than me, so I set out to be better for him and to prove you wrong. To show you I wasn't a total loser."

"I don't even remember that," she said, sounding guilty.

"I told you, you can't drink for shit. But it doesn't matter. All I wanted you to know was that you'd been right. Hearing you say that, it made me want to be better for him, and what started out as me trying to prove you wrong, turned into me falling in love with Shawn. You didn't know it, but you saved me. I was heading down a path that eventually there was going to be no coming back from. You saved me from that, you and Shawn."

"But you only had two years together." Leisel's face crumpled. "You both deserved more."

"Two years with a man I loved," I said, nudging her. "And you gave me that. No one could have known what was going to happen, Lei. And having two years with a man like Shawn was worth it. It's better to have loved and lost than to have never loved at all, right?" Turning toward her, I tossed my arms around her neck and squeezed her to me. "Thank you for giving me those two years with him."

We were both crying now, crying and hugging each other, but beneath the tears I was smiling. "Do you remember when you crashed Tom's car into the back of Mr. Reilly's truck?"

"And you flashed your boobs at him so he didn't report the accident!" Leisel added, laughing.

"And we told Tom that he didn't call the police because he was just being a good neighbor!"

We were both hysterical now, laughing so hard that we were crying again. I couldn't say that it had been better to remember, to let it all out. The pent-up emotions were still there, and there were a million more memories that were yet to be freed, a million more tears yet to be shed, but it had been good to let some of it go, to not have to be the resilient one for just a little while. The air smelled cleaner than it did before, my head seemed a little less crowded, and my body a bit more rejuvenated.

A noise in the forest drew our attention to where Alex was standing beside a large oak tree, holding two dead rabbits in his hand. "Is it safe?" he asked, raising his brow.

Nodding at him, I rolled my eyes as Leisel beckoned him forward.

"I found a small cabin about a mile north," he said, stepping forward. "I staked the place out, waited for about an hour to see if anyone showed up, but no one did. We need to scout out the area first, but I think we should check it out."

He paused, his gaze landing on Leisel. He looked concerned for her, but more than that there was a possessiveness in his expression that I'd never noticed before. He'd always stared at her, but never with such intensity. I supposed that now we were all finally free of Fredericksville, none of us felt compelled to hide our true feelings any longer. We were all finally free.

"Let's eat first," I said, "and then go check it out."

CHAPTER FIFTEEN

Leisel

THE CABIN WAS just as Alex had said, not too far off and yes, very small. But it didn't look abandoned, not in the way everything else seemed to look. It was run-down, the burnished red paint in need of a touch-up, and the windows were boarded up. Yet, from our vantage point hidden amongst the trees—and everything else considered—the tiny cabin looked pretty good.

"I don't know about this," I whispered. The town of Covey had looked even worse than this lone cabin, and after what had happened there... Well, I didn't want to put anything to chance.

"We need clean clothes, Lei," Evelyn whispered back. "At the very least, something to bandage your wrists."

"I'll go first," Alex said. "If it's safe, I'll whistle once. If not, twice, and you two...run."

"We're not leaving you," I blurted out, instantly feeling ridiculous. Who was I kidding? It had been Alex who'd saved me, twice now. If anyone was going to be doing any saving, it certainly wouldn't be me. Still, I meant what I'd said. I wouldn't leave him, not for anything. I owed him; Evelyn and I both did.

"We're not leaving you," Evelyn agreed, then smirked. "Who will catch our dinner?"

Alex grunted. "Good to know what I'm worth."

Despite myself, I smiled. The past few days of peace and quiet had been a soothing balm to my aching heart. The time that Evelyn and I had spent talking about life before the infection had been the most freeing moment I'd experienced in quite some time. Of course, it had helped that that we were now actually free.

Be careful, I mouthed to Alex.

Out of the corner of my eye I saw his arm move, his hand lift, and even though I was still staring up at his face, in my peripheral vision I watched as his hand continued to rise toward its destination. My cheek.

Unlike last time, back in Covey when he'd nearly touched me yet didn't, this time his large, warm hand made contact, gently cupping my cheek. The unexpected intimate touch sent a shiver of something foreign slithering through me. Not good, not bad...just odd.

And there was something else, something in his eyes not unlike the way he'd been looking at me back at the creek. It was every bit as intense, but even more so. Stronger, and infinitely more private.

Suddenly nothing made sense, the shared looks and the hand holding, all seemingly simple gestures and usually meaningless, but they no longer seemed simple or meaningless anymore. I didn't know what this new revelation meant, or if it meant anything at all. All I did know was that it frightened me, curdled my insides like old milk, and sent my heart aflutter in a fitful cadence of beats that pounded their way up to my throat.

"Listen for my whistle," Alex said as he dropped his hand, breaking our connection and scattering my thoughts. Slightly dazed, I watched as he crossed the small distance of forest and stepped out into the clearing.

His body taut with aggression, one hand gripping his handgun, the other a blade, he walked slowly yet with purpose toward the cabin. I studied him intently, something I'd never bothered doing until this very moment. I took in the pride in his stance, the predatory way he walked, and his overall masculinity, and I felt a swell of appreciation burst to life deep down within my belly. Even though he was five years younger than my twenty-nine years, he both looked and acted much older. Maybe that was due to his life before the infection, or maybe it stemmed from whatever horrors he'd endured after. Or maybe he'd just always been an old soul.

I continued to watch him, thinking that maybe his dark, fierce features weren't quite so intimidating anymore; that maybe, just maybe, they were part of his charm. For several seconds my thoughts continued to wage a war with one another in relation to Alex, agreeing and then disagreeing, finding plausible reasons for my strange line of thinking, and then more excuses for why I should put a stop to it. It wasn't until he turned the corner, out of sight, that my mind finally freed me from its babbling.

"I don't like this," I whispered nervously, sensing my anxiety rising. Several more seconds had passed silently, and yet no whistle had sounded. What-ifs began racing through my thoughts, the endless possibilities of what awful things could be happening behind that cabin, and me unable to help.

The sound of crunching leaves echoed in the stillness as Evelyn inched her way closer to me. Her hand slipped into mine and together, like we always had, we gripped each other tightly.

"You know how he saved you, don't you?" she whispered. "Back in Covey, from those freaks?"

Turning to look at her, I shook my head slowly. "No," I said. "I didn't really think about it." I paused as a memory struck me. Alex and the dead man he'd been dragging into the room, the one with the human bone jutting from his eye socket.

"I asked him," Evelyn said. "He was locked in a room just like you were, chained up and given to an infected. He used his chains to strangle the thing, and ripped its head clear off. Then he tore open the body, dug out a leg bone, snapped it off, and waited until someone came looking."

I gasped at the image that intruded on my thoughts, the ugly memory of that moment pushing forward.

"Are you listening to me, Lei?" she continued. "That man took the head off an infected and used its bones to kill an armed guard. And he did this all while still chained up."

I stared at her, not blinking, a little light-headed at the thought of it all.

"My point is, Lei, you don't need to worry about him," she said matter-of-factly.

Feeling both bewildered and proud, I turned away from her and back to the cabin. No, I really didn't have to worry about him, did I? At least, not when it came to protecting himself.

In the distance, a low piercing whistle sounded and my breath caught. I waited to hear another, two whistles to signify that danger was afoot and it was time to flee or fight. But it never came. Instead, I watched as Alex appeared from around the side of the cabin, looking entirely well.

With a sigh of relief, I dropped Evelyn's hand, got to my feet, and together we started for the clearing.

According to Alex, all the windows were still intact, yet had been boarded over on the outside as well as the inside, something that would require making a mess and a whole lot of noise if we tried to enter that way. In the end, it was the front door that seemed to be the safest and most logical way inside, but first we'd have to get past the two large padlocks sealing us out.

"This is a good thing," Alex murmured, using his knife to fiddle with the top lock. "Means ten to one there's something useful inside, and most likely no nasty surprises."

I still wasn't convinced that we were safe here. Something about this place felt off to me. Unlike everywhere else we'd seen, it didn't seem dead; in fact, it was teeming with life. Of course, that could have been all the burgeoning forest surrounding me, the animals and insects within, all who'd been untouched by the infection. Still, my worry didn't lessen, and I found myself constantly scanning the tree line for any sign of movement.

"Got it," Alex said, releasing the first lock from its loop and pocketing it. As he started on the second, Evelyn grinned at me, excitedly shifting from foot to foot as she eagerly waited to see what was inside. She reminded me of the old Evelyn, before the infection, always eager to do and try new things, clapping excitedly when she was happy, bouncing around like a ten-year-old girl who'd just gotten the thing she'd always wanted for her birthday.

With a happy smile on my face, I turned away, again scanning the tree line for any sign of threats. There was nothing, just the various shades of greens and browns of a forest, the low hum of insects, and turned leaves dropping from their branches and fluttering slowly to the ground. I followed one leaf in particular as it snagged on the breeze, turning in a circle to watch as it floated and spun through the clearing. I followed it on its happy journey, until I had nearly turned in a complete circle when something caught my eye and I froze in place.

"Eve!" I whispered, reaching out blindly for her. "Alex!"

A man stood at the edge of the clearing, not yet breaching the tree line but still discernible to the naked eye. He was dirty and bloody, his long hair disheveled and his clothes torn. His eyes were wild, and in his arms…

"Oh God," Evelyn breathed. "Oh no."

My gaze traveled down his body, my heart skipping a beat in my chest.

In his arms, hanging limply and covered in blood, was the tiny body of a little girl.

CHAPTER SIXTEEN

Evelyn

"HANDS UP!" ALEX yelled, dropping his knife in favor of his rifle. Quickly, he slung the weapon around himself and raised it, showing the man that we were armed.

The man's eyes narrowed, his mouth pressing into a tight line as he lifted the little girl in his arms higher, closer to his chest. It was a protective maneuver, and seeing this, I placed a hand on Alex's arm.

"He can't," I said simply, my eyes trained on the little girl in his arms, her hair bloody and draped across her face.

The man still hadn't moved. His face, partly hidden behind a long, scruffy beard, was frozen in some emotion that I couldn't place. Not anger, though he did seem angry, and not sadness, though considering the condition of the child in his arms, he should have been sad. Shifting from foot to foot, in obvious indecision as to how to proceed, he wrinkled his brow in consternation, as if trying to decide if we were yet another threat to him and the girl, who was probably his daughter.

"Is this your home?" Leisel called out, her soft voice carrying across the clearing.

The man grunted loudly in response, but didn't vocalize an actual yes or no.

"I'm guessing that's a yes," I said quietly.

"We'll leave," Alex said loudly, lowering his gun and taking a step away from the door.

I responded immediately, moving to Alex's side and readying

myself to leave, but Leisel, ever the compassionate one, didn't budge. She looked at me, frowning ever so slightly, and I knew exactly what she was thinking—that my lack of compassion for this man and this child made me a bitch. Yes, I couldn't deny it; I was more than willing to turn tail and leave these people to fend for themselves. They weren't my problem, and I didn't want them to become my problem. The blood dripping from the girl's tiny body would undoubtedly attract the infected, it always did, and I wasn't emotionally ready to fight.

Not only that, but I'd seen enough death to last me a lifetime. I didn't need to bear witness to more if I didn't have to. This child was clearly going to die, if she wasn't already dead, and I didn't have the stomach to stand by and watch how this was going to unfold.

"Leisel," Alex said. "Let's go." He reached for her arm, meaning to pull her away from the door just as the man, as if finally breaking free from his indecision, began walking forward. His gait was strong and determined as he moved across the small clearing toward us.

No one said a word as he came to a stop beside us, and now that he was near us, I could smell him, and the stench was awful. Whether it was coming from the little girl's wounds or their unwashed bodies, I wasn't sure, only that it was a struggle not to gag from the awful stink.

His clothes were filthy, his skin and hair greasy to the point of appearing wet, yet he didn't seem like a vagrant just barely getting by. If anything he seemed well fed, his shoulders large, his biceps strong.

We looked on while the man balanced the little girl in his arms as he fumbled with the second lock, opening it with ease and then kicking the door open. He kept his back to us the entire time, obviously having decided that were weren't a threat. That, or he simply didn't care.

"We should go," I said quietly. "If she's bitten, she's going to turn, and I don't want to see that."

Because no one in their right mind wanted to see that, to watch a child die, let alone turn. And if that poor little girl died and one of us had to put her out of her misery, then what? What would happen when this man—her father—flipped out and attacked us? Because he would; I'd seen it happen too many times to count.

"Woman!" the man yelled from inside, his voice gruff and impatient.

Leisel jumped, looking from the doorway to me and back to the doorway before quickly slipping into the cabin. I cursed her loudly, and Alex did the same. We shared a knowing glance, me rolling my eyes and Alex looking grim, before both of us followed her inside.

It was dark, and it took my eyes several moments to adjust, but when they finally did, I found myself shocked. The place was surprisingly clean, almost homelike, with shelf after shelf of jars and boxes in different sizes and shapes. The entire place was no larger than a ten-by-twelve room, with a twin-sized bed on one side near a wood-burning stove, and at the other end was a small wooden table and three lawn chairs. The man was kneeling beside the bed, the little girl lying on top of it. Her breaths were dry, crackling, as her little chest rose and fell at a rapid rate.

The man was attempting to bathe her neck, only succeeding in cleaning the blood away for a moment before the wound would gush again. I swallowed hard. I was right; she'd been bitten, and she would turn.

To my horror, Leisel was kneeling beside the man, tenderly brushing hair away from the child's face. "What can I do?" she asked, her voice full of urgency.

"Leisel!" Alex said, his tone sharp. He was clearly not happy about her proximity to either the man or the bitten child, and I couldn't say I blamed him. I felt the same, concerned by the entire situation.

"She's just a little girl, Alex," Leisel snapped, shooting us both a look of disgust. "She needs our help. They *both* need our help!"

I dropped my gaze, knowing she was right. This poor girl, she was only a child, a beautiful girl of maybe seven or so, with long blond hair and the lips of a cherub. She was sweet and innocent looking, apart from the bite on her neck. But it was that very bite that made her a monster to me, one I didn't want to go anywhere near.

"She's not going to be a little girl much longer," Alex said darkly.

The man turned then, fixing his narrowed gray eyes on Alex, and if looks could have killed, Alex would have been dead where he stood.

"Say that again, boy," the man growled, and slowly pushed himself upright.

Alex, unfazed, cocked his head to one side and looked the man directly in the eye. "I said, she's just a child...*for now*. She's been bitten, she'll turn into one of *them* soon. Who knows how long she's got," he said, gesturing angrily toward the bed where Leisel was still kneeling. "And I don't want her turning anywhere near my…"

His words trailed off as his gaze moved away from Leisel, but I knew what he'd been about to say, what he'd wanted to say and why he'd stopped himself. He and Leisel weren't anything, no matter how much he wished they were.

Placing a hand on Alex's forearm, I stepped in front of him, not to shield him from this man, but in an attempt to keep the peace. My heart was telling me one thing, but my head was telling me another. My head wanted me to run, get the hell away from this time bomb of a child, but the other part of me, a small voice buried deep down, told me that she was just a little girl and this poor man, her father, deserved our help.

"How can I help?" Leisel asked again.

Several more tense seconds ticked by while the man continued to stare over my head, his angry gaze on Alex, until finally he gave his head a small shake and turned away. He headed toward the small stove, his worn boots scraping noisily on the wood floor, then bent down and poked at the small fire glowing within.

"A bowl," he mumbled. "Get me a bowl. I need to sterilize the water."

Still sitting with the child, Leisel stared up at me, her eyes burning with an unrelenting pleading until I couldn't take it anymore, the guilt she forced me to feel. I turned abruptly, going off in search of a bowl, bumbling along the shelves filled with odd bottles of liquid, rusty cans, and mangled boxes.

Eventually I found a bowl, a heavy metal pot with a thick handle. Pulling it down from the shelf, I crossed the cabin and handed it to the man. He promptly filled it with water from a canister hanging at his hip, and after setting it on top of the stove to boil, he busied himself with a pestle and mortar that he used to grind some herbs. The entire time he was grinding, his gaze flicked between the child and Alex, as if he expected Alex to make a move when he wasn't looking.

When the water began to hiss, bubbling over the top of the pot, the man carefully removed it and sprinkled in some of the crushed herbs, then mixed them together. When he seemed satisfied with his concoction, he headed back to the bed, grunting at Leisel to move out of his way.

Looking from the pot in his hand to the gaping wound on the little girl's neck, Leisel shook her head, but reluctantly stood. Making her way back to me, her eyes were glassy with unshed tears. While I was sad for the little girl, and for her father as well, I was more concerned with our personal well-being. The pustules had started to form all over her body, big white blisters filled with pus and blood. Once that little girl turned, rigor mortis having not yet set in, she would be a quick and efficient weapon of death. And only sometime after, when her muscles had become stiff, would she slow down, until eventually she'd begin to decompose, making her movements still slow, but fluid once again.

"We need to go," Alex said through gritted teeth.

"She'll be fine," the man said, not bothering to turn around. "Once I clean it, she'll be fine."

His voice was strained, shaking ever so slightly, and his shoulders were hunched, but his hands worked quickly at applying his homemade herbal paste. From what I could tell from where I stood, it seemed to have stopped the bleeding, but it would do nothing for the infection. If the CDC hadn't been able to figure out a cure or even a preventative treatment, then I doubted this man's herbal paste had succeeded where they had failed.

Though that didn't mean I wasn't hoping. That I wasn't standing there waiting for the blisters to retreat, for her breathing to return to normal, for her eyes to open, to look up at her father with a smile on her innocent face.

But that wasn't what happened. She took a sudden gasping breath, her chest heaving one last time, and then she fell still, her lips forever parted in a silent *O*.

"She's dead," Alex said, bluntly enough that I rewarded him with an elbow to his ribs.

Standing, his shoulders slumping even more so than before, the man turned to look at us. I waited with bated breath, imagining him turning feral, attacking Alex for his cruel words. Instead he faced us, a sad and defeated man, his long hair hanging around his face like a dark curtain of despair, his nostrils tightly flaring as he struggled to contain his crumbling emotions.

"She was my little girl," he whispered brokenly, his eyes finally meeting mine. "She was all I had left." His voice cracked over the last few words, and then he began to cry. Not the subtle, unassuming tears of someone we didn't know, but the exhausted, heartbroken tears of a man with nothing left. His sobs were loud and pitiful, and the more he tried to control himself, the harder he cried.

The three of us stood frozen, unsure of what to do, what to say, and what was there to say? We couldn't fix this—no one could fix this. This was what the infection did. It attacked, it killed, it destroyed all things, beautiful and not. It held no regard for the young or the old, for the color of their skin or religious beliefs, for social standing or perceived importance.

It just killed and killed and killed.

It killed everything.

Leisel began to cry with him and then, before I could stop her, she crossed the room and wrapped her arms around the man, this stranger. Pulling him against her, she cradled his large shaking frame while whispering soothing noises in his ear, much like she had done with me. One hand rubbed his back in slow, sure circles. The familiarity of her actions was almost choking in its awkwardness. We didn't know him, not who he had been, nor who he was now. Yet she was treating him as if she'd known him her entire life. This was who she was—the caretaker, the peacemaker, the woman people went to when they needed comfort.

An odd thought struck me then, a painful realization. Leisel wasn't weak, not in the true sense of the word. She might be fragile physically, she might be easily upset, always wearing her emotions on her sleeve, but out of the three of us—Alex, Leisel, and myself—she was the one who'd held on to her humanity the most, not an easy task in a world gone to hell. And all this time, I'd assumed I was stronger than her because I would easily—and gladly—walk away from situations like this, because I was prepared to kill and maim and to damn others to misery if it meant keeping the two of us safe.

Somewhere in the midst of my strength and courage, I must have lost a part of myself. The part that cared about others, even strangers. Somewhere, somehow, I had lost my humanity.

The thought was shocking, choking even, and I suddenly needed air and space from them all. I turned and stumbled outside, my eyes burning from the sudden brightness. I began to sob and retch, gasping for air, feeling as if I were every bit as bad as one of the infected, because I'd never felt or shown an ounce of remorse for anything or anyone that I'd killed or hurt. Just like the infected.

A noise up ahead startled me out of my pity party and I looked up sharply, seeing an infected on the outskirts of the clearing. It had come because of the smell of blood, just like we had expected. It was a man once, but Christ, this wasn't a man anymore. It was barely dressed, with rags clinging to its bony, graying body.

Drawing myself upright, I gripped my knife and took a step forward, watching as he—*it*—looked up and toward me. Noticing me, it growled loudly and stumbled out of the trees and into the clearing, but I suddenly couldn't move, as if my feet were glued to the earth. My knife was still firmly in my grip, but may as well have been a spatula for all the good it would do if I couldn't find the will to act. I saw so much of myself in that monster right then, knowing I was no better than it was.

The infected continued its broken shamble toward me, growing closer with every limping step, yet I still couldn't move. As it stumbled over a large tree branch in its way, I found myself snorting, then laughing. Laughing! Coughing, I attempted to clear my throat, but I was still unable to stop laughing. The infected seemed somewhat incensed by the sound, or maybe that was only me projecting my emotions on a creature that didn't feel anything but hunger and the urge to kill.

Just like me. Hungry to live, and willing to kill to continue to do so.

It was within arm's reach now, and I was at least able to raise my blade a little higher. But my damn arm was shaking and I knew—I just fucking knew it was going to bite me if I didn't do something. But I couldn't; I just couldn't.

"Jesus, Eve!" Alex charged past me, barging into the infected just as it reached for me, and threw it to the ground. Dropping to his knees, Alex smashed the grip of his rifle into its head, the sickening sound of bones cracking and brain splattering under the impact causing me to feel even sicker.

Scowling up at me, Alex got to his feet. "What the hell is wrong with you?" he demanded angrily.

I opened my mouth but no sound came out, not even air. I was literally at a loss for words to explain myself or my behavior.

Giving me a hard look, Alex shook his head and turned away.

"Get your shit together," he called out over his shoulder as he stormed back inside.

Dizzy and disoriented, I slumped to the ground. This wasn't me. I didn't do this. I always had my shit together; I'd had my shit together for the past four years. I didn't lose it like this, yet my vision was tunneling right in front of me and still, I could barely breathe.

From within the cabin, I could hear the faint sound of arguing, and then what sounded like a physical scuffle. I knew I needed to pick myself up and get in there, to see what was going on, but I couldn't make my legs work. Just the thought of standing felt strenuous, in fact everything felt strenuous. It was just too much, it was all way too much for me to cope with.

A short, sharp scream rang through the air but was cut off as quickly as it had begun, and then a mere moment later, the man stormed out of the cabin and took off running into the woods. Another moment passed before Leisel exited the cabin. Her eyes found me and she headed in my direction, taking a seat beside me on the ground. Draping an arm over my shoulders, she rested her head against mine.

"Alex killed her," she whispered. "She woke up and lunged for her dad. He wasn't quick enough, but Alex was."

Taking a deep breath as my vision cleared, I felt my lungs finally expanding fully, enabling me to take a much-needed breath of air. I glanced at Leisel, debating whether to respond to what she'd told me, but found her looking off into the distance as tears glistened on her cheeks, and decided for the moment to just let it be.

Eventually Alex joined us, his teeth clenched and his jaw locked. "Sort your shit out, Eve," he said shortly. "You can't screw up like that again."

Sniffing, I nodded. He was right; I was being weak when I needed to be strong. But I also knew that this—his anger—was his way of dealing with what had just happened. That like me, he had his own coping mechanism, and right now he wasn't coping well. He was mentally and physically strong, but everyone had their breaking point.

"I'm sorry," I whispered, blinking rapidly in an attempt to stop my threatening tears from falling. Because I was sorry. Sorry for losing it, for nearly getting myself bitten as well as putting everyone else in danger, and sorry because of the terrible thing he'd just had to do.

"Don't apologize for being human," Leisel said softly, squeezing me closer as she glared accusingly at Alex. "Don't ever apologize for that, Eve."

Hours passed before the man returned, and when he did he didn't as much as look at us, let alone say anything about us still being there. Honestly, I didn't know why we were. We didn't owe him anything, yet we stayed.

Noises erupted from within the cabin, as if objects were being tossed around. The loud banging and clanging only lasted for a minute before the man reappeared with a small shovel in hand. With a defeated-sounding sigh, Alex joined him and together they took turns digging a small hole in the ground.

The three of us stood by silently while the man brought out his daughter, wrapped tightly in a blood-soaked sheet, and laid her gently in the ground. Alongside her he laid a ragged-looking teddy bear and a folded piece of paper that looked to be a wrinkled photograph. After she was buried, the upturned dirt packed around and above her, the man walked back inside the cabin without a word to any of us, and closed the door behind him.

No one spoke; there were no words. This shouldn't have happened, this wasn't fair, she's gone to a better place, and she's at peace now, *blah-blah-fucking-blah*. It all seemed pointless to voice.

"Should we see if he has any weapons we can use?" I asked, rubbing my temples. "Or maybe ask him if he knows where we can get a vehicle?"

"Let's come back tomorrow," Leisel suggested. "Give him time to grieve."

All of us agreeing on that being the best course of action, we headed back to our tree stand. It wasn't yet dark out, the sun still hanging heavy in the sky, mirroring how heavy I felt.

Children offered hope, and when a child was taken from this world, it made it seem a lot darker of a place to try to live within.

I lay awake for hours that night, staring up into the treetops, exhausted but unable to sleep. I listened to Alex's snoring, the branches blowing in the light breeze, until eventually I turned, finding Leisel wide awake and watching me.

I offered her a small smile and she returned it, cuddling closer to me. I knew exactly what she was thinking—that days like today made it all seem so damn hopeless.

The sun woke us early the next morning. Quickly, we washed up in the creek and then headed back for the cabin, but when we arrived, we found it empty. Even the blood-soaked sheets on the small bed were gone.

A small note was pinned to the open door, and on it two simple words had been penned:

THANK YOU.

CHAPTER SEVENTEEN

Leisel

"NOW WHAT?" EVELYN asked, sounding irritated. "Now what the fuck are we supposed to do?"

Neither of us had gotten much sleep the night before, but Evelyn looked worse than I did. Large dark circles ringed her bloodshot eyes, her shoulders slumped, and her hands trembled slightly.

"He didn't owe us anything," I told her gently. "We just met him at a bad time."

"I know that!" she shouted, growing even more agitated. "But... but now what?" She gestured around the empty cabin, her eyes wide, her nostrils flaring. "We have nothing, Lei! Nothing!"

"Not nothing." Alex interrupted us, and we both glanced to where he was standing. There was a small chest at the end of the bed, and Alex was rifling through it, pulling out articles of clothing and tossing them onto the bed. Evelyn and I both stared at the varied shades of pinks and yellows, clothing that so obviously had belonged to the little girl we'd helped bury yesterday.

I couldn't help it, couldn't stop the tears that formed. Memories of her dying breaths, her sweet little face contorted in pain, and her father's grief-stricken wails filled my thoughts. Just yesterday they'd both been here, alive and surviving, and now the child was dead and her father was gone. Gritting my teeth, I pushed back my emotions. Now wasn't the time for it, not when there were three of us right here, fighting through another day.

"We can't use those, Alex," Evelyn said tersely. "They're too small."

Alex didn't pause in his digging. "We can use them as rags, as bandages, and a million other things, Eve. There's more," he continued, holding up a woman's dress. "I'm guessing he had a wife at some point."

Alex tossed another pile of clothing onto the bed, and as I walked forward to inspect it, I noticed Evelyn had hesitated. I glanced back at her with a questioning look that seemed to jolt her into motion, and together we headed for the bed.

Not many of the items Alex found were functional clothing, at least not in this new world. There were dresses, many of them sleeveless, and lightweight dressy tops that would have been perfect had I needed to go to a job interview, not dodge the living dead and half-crazed humans.

More importantly, I didn't want to wear someone else's clothing. Clothing that belonged to a family now destroyed. But what choice did we have? The stench of decay and death, blood, sweat, and other foul smells wouldn't leave our current clothing, no matter how many times we tried rinsing them clean.

Eventually we managed to find a few things we could use. For a bra, I used one of the little girl's tank tops. It was chest-compressing tight, only reaching to above my belly button, but was already doing a better job of supporting my breasts than the bra I'd been wearing since we'd escaped Fredericksville. Over that I slipped on a black loose-fitting, long-sleeved cotton shirt that had ridiculous lace insets in the back and belled sleeves. Thankfully there had been a pair of jeans inside that trunk as well. They were too big for Evelyn's slim figure, and far too long for my short legs, but after rolling them a few times, they fit me comfortably.

Evelyn was less fortunate, having to settle for a pair of gray dress pants, and a pale pink child's long-sleeved nightgown to use as a shirt. Both of us looked utterly ridiculous in our ill-fitting, mismatched outfits, but anything was better than nothing. Or so I kept telling myself.

Alex fared far worse than we did. The only men's clothing to be found was a white button-down shirt, a long black tie, and a wrinkled pair of dress pants. He opted to keep his filthy BDUs on, but decided to exchange his ruined and blood-stained T-shirt for the button-down.

I found myself watching him as he pulled the shirt over his head, mesmerized by the way the muscles in his back and arms would flex with even the simplest movement. Thomas had always been in great shape, but Alex—the breadth of him, his stature, and the size of his muscles—put Thomas to shame.

I felt a chill then, not from the weather, but brought on by the direction of my thoughts. What was I doing staring at this man like this? And comparing him to my husband, my first husband, who I'd loved more than anything? What was wrong with me?

I started to turn away, ashamed of myself, when Alex turned back around, fully dressed, and slipped quickly back into his military-issued jacket. Seeing the button-down beneath the dark and dirty canvas, I started to laugh.

"You look handsome," I blurted out.

"Yeah?" He smiled at me. "Should I put the tie on too?"

Before I could answer, Evelyn stepped between us. She looked from me to Alex and then back to me again. "What's the plan?" she asked, her tone serious, instantly breaking the lighthearted moment.

Not knowing, I looked again at Alex, whose smile was now gone. Sighing, he closed his eyes.

"South," he said, and when he opened his eyes, his usual grimace was back in place. "We head south like we'd planned."

We spent the night in the cabin, searching every nook and cranny for anything the man might have left behind. In the end, when we gathered our finds, it didn't amount to much. Other than a few articles of clothing, a tin mug, a rusty old hammer, and a plastic jug, there was nothing of worth left.

While Alex went out in search of dinner, Evelyn and I busied ourselves tying together some of the little girl's clothing to make a sling purse of sorts, and used that to store what we'd collected.

By the time Alex returned it was dark out, and Evelyn had started a small fire in the pot-bellied stove for both light and warmth. Huddled together around the small stove, we ate our dinner, consisting of two chipmunks and some berries, mostly in silence.

Evelyn, I noticed, was more withdrawn then I'd ever seen her before. She was moody, her highs and lows becoming more and more noticeable. She outright snapped at Alex, and avoided any sort of conversation at all with me. Although she stayed by my side, still seeking me as a source of comfort, I could tell something was definitely wrong. There was an inner turmoil I could see, anguish and anger written all over her face. I felt helpless, not knowing the right thing to do or say to ease any of it for her, so in the end I didn't say anything at all.

During the night, while Evelyn and I were occupying the small bed together, and Alex had lain on the floor in front of the door, the wind began to pick up, causing the temperature to drop drastically inside the cabin. Without blankets or the added body heat of Evelyn, who'd curled in on herself and was facing the wall, I woke to the sound of my own teeth chattering.

Freezing, I sat up in bed, finding Alex wide awake and propped up against the wall beside the stove, a small fire still blazing within.

"It-it's c-c-cold," I whispered, rubbing my hands up and down my arms.

"Come over here," he whispered. "The fire is warm."

Not wanting to wake Evelyn, I hesitated only a moment before I tiptoed toward him, crossing the creaking floorboards as quietly as possible. Holding up his arms in welcome, Alex spread his knees apart, indicating that I should take the space between them. Part of me balked at such an intimate embrace, but the other part of me, the part that was cold and feeling dejected about our current circumstances, wanted to readily accept the warmth he was offering.

Still, I couldn't bring myself to do it, to be that close to him, and took the empty space of floor beside him instead.

"Lei…"

I glanced up, meeting his gaze, finding his features twisted with some sort of internal pain.

"I would never hurt you," he said softly.

Feeling my cheeks heat, I looked away and out across the cabin. I knew he wouldn't hurt me, of course I knew that. But some part of me, even the part of me that knew I could trust him, still couldn't fathom being that close to him, or being that close to anyone other than Evelyn.

"I should have killed him," he continued, his tone having drastically changed. Instead of soft, meant to be comforting, he sounded darker, angrier.

Surprised, I glanced back up at him, finding him staring off much like I had been doing. Only he was rigid now, his body having gone taut, his jaw hard and starkly outlined, ticking ominously in the firelight.

"It wasn't your responsibility," I said gently. "I wasn't your responsibility, Alex."

His eyes slanted toward me, his expression impassioned and enraged. "You don't get it," he said through clenched teeth. "You don't know how I—" He cut himself off abruptly, his eyes flashing angrily, and looked away again.

I stared up at him, feeling both helpless and confused, not wanting him to lay blame of the outcome of my forced and abusive marriage at his feet, yet not knowing what to do or say to change how he felt. He was such a quiet man, usually only speaking when spoken to or when he believed it absolutely necessary, but I had to imagine that there was so much more going on inside him, far more than he ever let on.

"You have no idea how grateful we are," I said. "If it wasn't for you, we would have never gotten out of there, Alex."

He didn't respond, didn't turn to look at me, or acknowledge in any way that he'd even heard me. He continued staring ahead, the hard lines of his body still unyielding, his expression still so furious. So I did the first thing that came to my mind, the first thing that I could think of doing to ease the sudden tension.

Grabbing his arm, I moved to my knees in front of him, forcing him to look at me. "I'm still cold," I said, sounding surprisingly forceful to my own ears. "I can't get warm."

I don't know why it mattered to me that he didn't carry so much guilt, that he didn't bear the weight of my world on his shoulders, but it did. For some reason, easing this man's conscience suddenly mattered.

His hard expression instantly softened, his legs falling open as he gestured for me to come closer. I did so, half crawling into the space he'd allotted me. His arms wrapped around me, pulling me closer to him, hugging my body tightly to his. Although, already feeling blessedly warmer, it was still an uncomfortable position for me. To be so intimately close to someone, to a man, no less. Yet I didn't fear him; I could feel that truth ring loud and true within me that this man wasn't a man to be feared, that he deserved as much comfort as I could provide him.

I turned my head, tentatively pressing my cheek against his chest, hearing the sound of his strong heart beating a steady rhythm. How long had it been since I'd been held by a man without the heavy hand of fear pressing down on me, turning much-needed comfort into something else entirely, something dark and cruel?

Too long. So long, in fact, that I hadn't realized how much I missed it, not until this very moment, enfolded neatly within Alex's arms.

"Better?" he whispered. His chin tickled against the top of my head, his thick scruff catching like Velcro on my hair.

I tilted my head up, meaning to answer him, not expecting his face to be so close to mine. Our noses nearly touching and our breathing momentarily intermingled, I stared up at him in the flickering firelight as shadows danced all around us.

"I wanted to do this so many times," he said, his warm breath fanning across my face. "Every time I heard you crying, it ate away at me. I wanted to hold you...or do something, anything to make it better."

Feeling exposed, I sucked in a sharp breath. Alex knew things about me—had seen and heard things—that not even Evelyn had known. In fact, Alex knew me almost as well as Evelyn did. While he might not have known of my life before the infection, he'd known of my life after, known all of my secret pain.

"Not your fault," I managed to whisper. Still staring at him, I was somewhat awestruck by how oddly right this felt, being in his arms, both our secret shames openly revealed. I was so used to hiding, hiding everything, every part of me from nearly everyone else that I couldn't help but feel so...so...taken by this moment. This very freeing moment.

Alex breathed harder, his chest rising and falling rapidly beneath me. His arms tightened around me, and yet I still felt no fear, no stifling sensation threatening to overwhelm my emotions. There was most definitely anxiety, an ugly burn in the pit of my stomach, but there was none of the familiar sense of fear and dread I'd felt when Lawrence had touched me.

I continued watching him, staring up into his half-lidded eyes, desperately wondering what he was thinking. Was this pity he was feeling? Pity for the woman he'd had to watch be beaten down both emotionally and physically, day after day, year after year? Or was it his guilt for simply standing by while Lawrence did to me whatever he wanted?

Or was it more than that? Did it go beyond Lawrence entirely? The thought that maybe whatever it was that was happening here had nothing to do with Lawrence Whitney was a joyous one. Yet at the same time, it was terrifying.

I wasn't like Evelyn, I wasn't able to just lose myself in a moment, forgetting everything else but the here and now, nor had I ever allowed myself to become distracted by the opposite sex. That was Evelyn's thing, her way of dealing with her emotions, how she made the days a little less long and our situation a little more bearable. Instead, I resigned myself to a lifetime of frigidity, the thought of being touched by any man leaving me queasy and uncomfortable.

But out here, thrust into the middle of nowhere, our fate unknown, when any moment could be our last, I suddenly found myself feeling quite different in that regard.

I wanted more and yet…I didn't. Or I couldn't; I wasn't sure which.

Looking up into Alex's dark eyes, I found myself shivering again, only this time it wasn't from the cold; I was anything but cold. An unexpected warmth invaded that forever chilled place inside of me, creeping in much like the morning sun. Tiny tendrils of light gently hit here and there, making it not quite so cold anymore. In fact, it was downright intoxicating.

His hand moved slowly up my back, leaving ripples of gooseflesh and anxiety in its wake. Brushing my hair away from my face, his fingertips gently smoothed along my jawline until he'd taken my chin in his hand, tilting my face toward his.

Was he going to kiss me? God, it had been so long since I'd been truly kissed, just for the sake of kissing. Even longer since I could remember wanting to return the gesture.

Was it wrong to want to kiss him? It seemed wrong, and yet…I wanted this. I wanted this comfort and warmth, this intimacy. I wanted something to relieve the fear, the cold, the crippling guilt and regret.

Just for a moment, for a single moment, I wanted to remember what it felt like to be alive.

Of my own accord, I tilted my head even farther. My eyelids dropped, a single tear slipping down my cheek as I waited for him to kiss me. Instead, I felt his thumb wipe away my tears, and a moment later his lips pressed down softly against my damp cheek. A tremble rippled through me and my lips parted, sucking in a much-needed breath of air just as his mouth brushed lightly over my own.

My eyes still closed, I both gasped and whimpered against his lips, feeling his warm breath mingling with mine.

"Leisel…" So tightly pressed against each other, I could feel the rumble of my name vibrate within his chest. "Leisel, look at me."

I didn't respond; I couldn't open my eyes. I was frozen in place by the duality of my emotions, unable to make a decision one way or the other.

"Please," I whispered, not quite sure what I was begging for, not sure of anything at the moment. What did I want? What was I doing?

He kissed me then, just another brush of his lips. Once, twice, and then he molded his mouth softly against mine. Of their own accord, my hands began to move, one finding its way up to his neck and then farther, into his hair. The other found his bicep, my fingers digging gently into the hard muscle there. His mouth grew hungrier, more demanding, and then, as his tongue touched mine, I was thrown for another loop, my growing fervor going into overdrive. I gripped him harder while turning in his arms to have better access to his mouth.

Something was happening to me, something that made me feel both strong and weak. Weak for succumbing, for letting my body override what my brain and heart couldn't rationalize, and yet strong for letting go, even if it was just for a moment, of the guilt and the regret that never seemed to leave me.

"Lei," Alex muttered against my mouth. His hands cupping my cheeks, he pulled away from me.

My eyes fluttered open, seeing him for the first time since before we'd kissed. I stared up at him, staring into the deep depths of his dark eyes, watching the firelight bounce within. And he stared down at me, searching my features. Searching for what, I didn't know; I was only aware of my racing heart and my ragged breathing.

"Alex," I whispered tearfully as the stirrings of warmth began to recede. Releasing my grip on him, my hands fell to his chest, fisting in his shirt. I couldn't lose this moment, I wasn't ready to go back to the cold, to the fear and the guilt. To my memories. More than anything I wanted right now, just for this one moment, to have a worthwhile *right now*.

He must have found whatever it was he'd been looking for. Still holding my face, he then lowered his head to mine and covered my mouth with his once more.

CHAPTER EIGHTEEN

Evelyn

IT WAS LIGHT out when I awoke, the sun squeezing into the cabin through the small cracks in the boarded-up windows, casting crazy illuminated shapes on the wall by my head. Blinking away any residual sleep, I rolled onto my back, watching as the dust motes floated about in the chilly air.

My chest felt heavy, full of burden and dislike for myself. I didn't want to be anything less than human, like the infected were, or the lunatics in Covey, but neither did I know any other way. Other than Leisel, and maybe Alex, everyone else was expendable. That was how I'd survived, the only way I knew how to survive.

Reaching out beside me, I felt around for Leisel, needing her to ground me, to make me feel less wretched. Confused when my hand didn't find her, I turned over on my side and found the bed empty. Sitting up abruptly, my hand curling around the handle of my blade, I hurriedly glanced around the cabin.

And then I smiled.

Seated up against the wall near the stove, Leisel was wrapped in Alex's arms. Pressed against his chest, her features were slack in a peaceful sleep, while Alex was curled around her, his posture relaxed, his scowl gone, making him appear younger, like a man his age should look. I stared at them both, looking so at ease, that for a moment I forgot. Forgot where we were, forgot what happened to the world around us, forgot the pain and the torture and the ever-mounting guilt.

It was a beautiful thing to see, two people released of their burdens, if only temporarily. And for a moment, seeing them released me of mine.

Leaning back against the wall, letting my blade fall away, I continued watching them sleep, imagining a life for them. A softer life, with chocolate Christmas cakes and backyard barbeques.

Time passed slowly, the soft, soothing sound of their heavy breathing comforting me to the point that I began to drift off again. Still thinking of better days, I closed my eyes, envisioning the four of us—Leisel and Alex, me and Jami—at the beach, laying out in the sun, cold beers in our hands. There's a live band playing off in the distance, the sound of music floating on the summer breeze. Maybe there are even children playing beside us. Their tiny voices, and innocent, tinkling laughter. I'd always wanted children. Shawn and I had planned to have at least two.

But then I saw Shawn as I'd last seen him, infected and dying, begging me to kill him before he ended up hurting me.

Gritting my teeth, I quickly shook away the image of Shawn's face, replacing it with Jami's. Picturing our children with my strawberry-blonde coloring and his impish smile.

He'd kissed me good-bye.

A sob lodged in my throat, choking me out of my daydream and back into reality, into this harsh, ugly reality where Leisel, Alex, and I were inside a boarded-up ramshackle cabin where only a day ago a little girl had died.

Rubbing my eyes, I moved to sit up straighter when a growling sort of groan sounded from just outside the cabin. Immediately I jumped out of bed, once again clutching my blade.

The sound of my feet hitting the floor woke Alex, his eyes instantly alert and his body rigid. Leisel's eyes were now open as well, wide and unblinking, and focused on the door.

Another growl sounded, this time followed by a *thump-thump* on the wall, causing the door and windows to rattle.

"Think we've been spotted?" I whispered dryly, already moving toward the boarded-up window.

"It's the blood," Alex whispered back. He and Leisel had gotten to their feet and were quietly creeping toward me.

I cursed quietly, silently berating myself for not remembering the trail of blood that little girl had left in her wake. It was probably all through the forest, leading the infected straight to us. I should have covered it, attempted to mask it somehow.

"Shit," I muttered, peeking through the boards. "This is bad."

I counted six infected, and that was only what I could readily see through the small gaps between the boards. There could be many more, and probably were. Worse, they clearly knew we were inside, and once they had their sights set on something or someone, nothing could divert their attention.

As Alex joined me at the window, I moved aside, allowing him room to bend down and take a look for himself. He said nothing as he stared through the small space, though his hands curled into fists, his knuckles turning white.

Running his hands through his hair, worry etched on his features, Alex moved away from the window and back to Leisel's side, his body language fiercely protective. "We're going to have to run for it."

"Run for it?" Leisel exclaimed softly, stepping around Alex. "But how many are there?"

Rising up on her tiptoes, she peered through one of the cracks, her breath hitching. Backing slowly away, her shoulders trembling, she looked from me to Alex. "Are you kidding me?" she said shrilly, her eyes as round as saucers. "We can't make it through that many. They'll charge the door the second we open it!"

At the sound of her voice, another *thump-thump* sounded on the wall of the cabin, followed by another and another.

"Leisel!" Alex growled, glaring at her. "Keep your voice down."

Pulling my hands through my hair, I began to pace the room. They became noisier, more agitated, and the louder they became, the more attention they were going to attract. Soon we'd be blocked in by any and all nearby infected, and who knew how many that was. Fifty? A hundred?

"Shit, what are we going to do?" I whispered frantically.

"I told you," Alex said. "We're going to run for it."

Heading past me, Alex looked at the ceiling, probably for any sign of an alternative escape route. Shaking his head and muttering to himself, he moved toward the back wall, where he gently rapped his knuckles against the slatted wood. The answering sound was a hollow one, especially against the backdrop of all the noise the infected were making.

"Alex?" Leisel whispered. "What are you doing?"

"We make as much noise as we can on this wall," he said, pointing. "We attract as many of them as possible to the back of the cabin, and then we make a run for it through the door." Turning, he looked at us both, his expression determined. "It's the only way out of here."

Leisel looked terrified, and though I refused to show it, I felt much the same. It was a shitty plan, yet it was the only plan we had.

"Let's do it," I said, then lifted the makeshift bag of items we'd packed the night before and strapped it tightly to my back. Gripping my blade in one hand, I handed Leisel the hammer we'd found.

"Leisel," Alex said. "Be ready to open the door when I say to."

Holding the hammer like one would a baseball bat, she swallowed hard and nodded. Creeping slowly toward the door, she placed one hand on the lock, ready to flip it open when Alex told her to do so.

Jerking his chin toward the wall, Alex began to bang on the wood, signaling for me to do the same. As his large fists repeatedly bashed against the wall, I both slapped and kicked at it, making as much noise as I could.

"It's working," Leisel whispered loudly. "They're moving, not all of them, but some are moving away."

We doubled our efforts, banging against the wall even harder and more enthusiastically than before, until eventually a thin sheen of sweat lined my forehead. I found myself envious of Alex's strength; he wasn't even remotely winded by the physical exertion, whereas I was quickly tiring. More determined than ever, I gritted my teeth and pounded harder. I would survive this world; Leisel and I would both survive this world.

Soon, we weren't the only ones pounding on the back wall. The infected were on the other side, their fists pounding in answer to ours, the growls and groans even louder than before.

Looking over his shoulder, Alex glanced at Leisel. "How's it look?"

"There's three that I can see," she whispered back.

Still banging on the wall, he glanced back to me. "On three, we run." He waited for us both to nod in agreement before beginning to count, "One, two...three. Open the door!"

We grabbed our weapons, Alex pausing to pick up a nearby chair as Leisel popped the lock open on the door.

The door swung open, revealing three infected. They were older ones, their skin sunken in and blackened from exposure, their limbs little more than skin covering bone. They were missing their eyes, the reason they hadn't followed the others, yet their ears seemed just fine as they growled ferociously in our direction, already bumbling toward the noise we'd made by simply opening the door.

Using the chair, Alex shoved them backward and onto their backs, and then he grabbed Leisel's hand and yanked her out of the cabin. We ran blindly through the clearing, not bothering to see if the other infected had spotted us.

The trees were a blur as we ran, our footsteps loud and clumsy in the underbrush. Branches snagged my hair as I sped by but I never slowed, not even when my lungs burned and my muscles ached. Not even when sweat was slipping down my face and burning my eyes.

Outside the clearing, the trees were denser, making it difficult to see where we were or where we were going. Yet we didn't stop, not until we came to a steep bank that dropped to a wide river, another bank just as steep on the opposite side.

Dizzy, I dropped to my knees and bent forward, my hands digging in the dirt as I tried to catch my breath. Leisel slumped to the ground beside me, her pale skin reddened from exertion, her dark hair slick with sweat. Together, we sucked in air at a rapid pace.

"We…need…" Alex gasped, taking a moment to steady his breathing. "We need to…get across this."

Wiping her sleeve across her forehead, Leisel glanced up at him. "Why can't we go around?" she asked, still breathless.

"You don't normally go around rivers," he told her. "They could go on for miles."

"So, over?" she asked. "Or through it?"

"Too dangerous to go through it," Alex said, frowning as he surveyed the water below us. "If the current is strong enough, we'll be pulled away." Looking frustrated, he shook his head. "There are too many variables to consider."

Getting to my feet, my entire body protesting any sort of movement, I placed my hands on my hips and sighed noisily. "Then we go around," I said pointedly, annoyed at our indecision. "There's no point in just standing here talking about it."

About to offer my hand to Leisel, I found that Alex was already doing so. Taking her hand in his, he pulled her easily to her feet. For a moment the two of them just stood there, him looking down at her, her looking up at him, leaving me feeling incredibly awkward.

Clearing my throat, I turned away, purposely letting my steps fall heavier than usual. Soon, I heard the two of them walking behind me and I slowed, allowing them to catch up.

As we walked on in silence, constantly on guard, I couldn't help but think how fortunate it was that we'd woken up as early as we had. We were going to need as much daylight as possible in order to find a safe place to spend the night.

CHAPTER NINETEEN

Leisel

"WHAT DO YOU miss the most, Eve?" I asked, slowing my pace until we walked side by side. We hadn't seen an infected for hours, something that wasn't surprising considering how deep in the woods we were. The trees were unbelievably thick here, proving to be formidable obstacles in some places, and the ground wholly uneven, all of it making for a tiresome journey. Still, it was beautiful to look at. The normally green leaves, having begun to succumb to the changing seasons, were turning vibrant shades of amber, crimson, and violet. It had been so long since I'd had the peace of mind to simply enjoy nature in its true glory.

Peace of mind aside, by mid-afternoon, the sun high in the sky, I was growing weary and in desperate need of a distraction, something to keep my mind from dwelling on my mounting aches and pains.

"That's a silly question," Evelyn said, wrinkling her nose at me. "You know what I miss the most. *Who* I miss the most."

"No." I hurried to fix my mistake. "I didn't mean it like that. I meant what stupid and insignificant things do you miss? Not from Fredericksville, but from...before?"

I was taking a risk by bringing up the past yet again; Evelyn never talked about it. But after our heart-to-heart she seemed more open to it, finally willing to remember what life had been like before the virus had taken a foothold in our lives. At least, until the incident back at the cabin.

"Oh." She pursed her lips. "Hmm, you mean other than Starbucks and cold beer and bikinis?" She smirked at me. "I miss ice." Sighing happily, she said, "I miss ice and ice cream and popsicles and frozen margaritas. I miss anything that isn't room temperature." She shrugged her shoulders and sighed again. "What do you miss the most, Lei?"

"Hot showers that don't require boiling water," I offered. "And shaving. God, I really miss shaving. Oh, and Butterfingers, water that doesn't taste tinny… Oh! And I really miss my slipper boots, you remember the ones, right? Pink with—"

"How could I forget them?" Evelyn interrupted, making a face. "They looked like giant fuzzy pink marshmallows."

"They were really comfortable."

"No, Lei, they were really ugly."

I stuck my tongue out at her before sparing a quick glance down at my baggy outfit. Letting out a little huff, I said, "I miss my clothes too."

"You have never cared about your clothes!" Evelyn protested. "I had to practically drag you to the mall with me."

"I didn't care *much* about my clothes," I said, correcting her. "But the difference is they were my clothes, and I happened to like them very much." I gestured down at my ridiculous ensemble. "This," I said pointedly, "I dislike very much."

Evelyn slowed her pace, leveling me with a look of disbelief. "Are you the one wearing a skintight pink nightie, Lei? With hearts and stars on it?"

Ahead of us, Alex barked out a harsh-sounding laugh, startling me. Evelyn and I looked at each other, our eyes wide with surprise. Had Alex just…*laughed*?

Readjusting her makeshift sack, Evelyn brought a hand to her face, cupping her mouth. "I think that's the first time Alex has ever laughed," she whispered. "*Ever*."

"I agree," I whispered back. "It did sound a little rusty."

"I can hear you," Alex muttered, not bothering to spare us a glance. "And I think you both sound like spoiled little girls. Your clothes are clean and dry—it shouldn't matter what the hell they look like."

Evelyn turned to me, her eyes wide with amusement. *You both sound like spoiled little girls*, she mouthed mockingly.

Looking away, I clapped my hand over my mouth, swallowing

back my threatening laughter. Yet Evelyn continued to mimic Alex, even going as far as to imitate the way he was walking, his shoulders squared, his back ramrod straight. All in all, he had a sort of marching quality about him.

"By the way," Evelyn whispered again, and I felt a soft pinch on my arm. "Did you kiss him last night?"

My eyes widened, and I dropped my gaze to the forest floor. Feeling my face grow warm, I bit my bottom lip and continued walking, studiously ignoring her. I felt another pinch, and another, and then Evelyn began poking me, over and over again. It didn't matter how fast I walked, her legs were longer and quicker than mine. Each time I tried speeding up, she was still right there, still poking me in the arm. Only once did Alex glance over his shoulder, seeing what we were doing, acting like ridiculous children. He'd rolled his eyes and quickly looked away.

"Yes!" I suddenly hissed, unable to take another second of her incessant poking. "I kissed him!" Coming to an abrupt stop, I spun on her, pointing an accusatory finger. But when I found her smiling, grinning actually, I couldn't stay mad. I just couldn't. Not with her.

The news seem to thrill Evelyn, who proceeded to let out a small squeak of excitement. Looping her arm through mine, she pulled me close, and together we started walking again.

"Hurry up," Alex called out. "You're falling behind."

"I hope he's more fun to kiss than he is to travel with," Evelyn whispered.

"Shh!" I admonished softly. "Shut your mouth!"

"I can still hear you," Alex called out, his tone dry, yet with a hint of amusement. "Loud and clear."

Feeling a startling amount of contentment, I pressed my lips together and cast my gaze downward, smiling to myself. I couldn't recall the last time I'd felt so...okay.

I couldn't lie and say that I was happy, not with the infected as well as the living an ever-present threat. Not when there was no way of knowing how or when we were going to get our next meal, let alone find a safe place to spend the night.

But at the very least, in that singular moment, I felt better than I could remember feeling in a long time. Freer, and more like myself than I had been in years.

Hours later, when the sun was beginning its downward descent, the trees starting to thin out some, we happened on a narrow dirt path. Alex bent down on one knee, inspecting the man-made trail. "It's not overgrown," he mused aloud. Standing up, he looked left and then right, his expression quizzical.

"Do you smell that?" Evelyn asked, lifting her chin and sniffing the air. I gave her a questioning glance, and sniffed as well.

"Like...something's burning?" Alex suggested. "Or was burning."

At first I couldn't smell anything out of place; the forest smelled like you'd expect—damp, cool and crisp, hints of moss and pine and the bitter woodsy scent of leaves beginning to decay. I inhaled harder, sucking in air through my nostrils and down my throat until I began to sort out the intermingling smells, finding the one scent that was out of place. It was something like the aroma of a doused campfire, when the fire had been put out but the embers were still steaming.

"I can't be sure," Alex said, peering down the path. "But I think it's traveling with the breeze. We could head west and check it out, or east and see if this path leads us to a road."

He turned to face Evelyn and me, waiting for our response. How did he know which way was west, I wondered, without a compass?

"The sun rises in the east," he said, answering my unspoken question with a wink. "And sets in the west. And moss," he continued, pointing to a large oak. "Supposedly it only grows on the north side, but I'm not exactly sure how accurate that is."

"What did you do before?" I asked, intrigued and suddenly wanting to know more about him. "Before the infection?"

He lifted one broad shoulder, then let it drop nonchalantly. "Nothing really. I was only nineteen when the infection hit the States. I was in community college, played football every weekend with my friends, hunted with my dad, still didn't know what I wanted to do with myself." He shrugged again, more so with his face than his body. "Still don't."

"What do you miss the most, Alex?" Evelyn asked abruptly. "From before?"

He didn't answer right away, his eyes taking on a sort of far-off, glazed-over quality. I watched him, wondering if that was how I looked when I thought about the past.

"Music," he finally said, refocusing on me.

Still watching him, I felt my heart thump painfully inside my chest, my good mood quickly deflating. It wasn't what he said, but the way he'd said it. Quiet and full of longing, but at the same time, sounding resigned. As if he truly believed that music, along with cold beers and pink fuzzy slipper boots, had all become extinct, and only in our memories would we ever have those things again.

Evelyn cleared her throat. "How about we head west?" she asked. "And see what's causing that smell? Who knows? Maybe we'll find a pair of pink slippers."

Ever the protector, Alex was insistent that Evelyn and I stay behind him as we made our way down the dirt path. We stayed to the side of the trail, mostly, Alex wanting quick access into the forest if we happened to need a quick getaway. I kept my hammer tightly in my grip, though I had no idea that if it came down to actually using it on an infected, if I would be able to muster up enough courage.

For at least a half an hour, it didn't seem to me that the path was leading us anywhere. I began feeling like Dorothy in *The Wizard of Oz*, on a long road to nowhere good, with the possible threat of monsters waiting to jump out at me at every twist and turn. But for Dorothy, it had all just been a dream.

If only it were really that simple, I thought, feeling suddenly sullen. To click our heels together and chant, "There's no place like home, there's no place like home." And then, poof, we would wake from this nightmare, safe and sound in our own warm beds, the monsters gone.

"Dorothy was a lucky bitch," I muttered under my breath.

"What did you say? Did you just curse?" Evelyn asked, watching me curiously. "Who's a bitch?"

"No one," I mumbled, feeling silly.

"The smell is getting stronger," Alex announced, slowing his pace to a mere crawl. "Look." He pointed up ahead and around a small bend. "A driveway."

I squinted, trying to see better, and found a gravel-covered path hidden among the trees and up a small incline.

We continued walking, the three of us on constant alert for any hint of movement or sound that seemed out of place, Alex with his rifle held in front of him, and Evelyn clutching her blade while I kept a firm grip on my hammer. Slowly and silently, we approached the driveway, and Alex held out an arm, signaling that Evelyn and I were to stay put while he checked it out.

I reached out, tugging on his sleeve to get his attention. As our eyes met, I didn't know exactly what I wanted to say, just that I felt I should say something. Every other second, it seemed, we were walking into some form of danger or another, and just in case we weren't able to walk away from what we were about to walk into this time, I just wanted Alex to know…

Actually, I wasn't exactly sure what I wanted Alex to know, maybe only that I did care about what happened to him. Yes, I wanted him to know that I cared, so I tried to convey that emotion by standing up on my tiptoes, lifting my face to his, and pressing a soft and quick kiss on his lips. Alex's hand found my waist, pulling me tightly against him as he deepened what had only been meant as a small gesture, turning it quickly into something so much more.

"Be careful," I murmured, then pulled away. Déjà vu washed over me, dizzying and powerful, and suddenly it wasn't Alex standing in front of me, but Thomas. Together with Shawn, ready to scour the neighborhood for food and water, standing in front of me, kissing me good-bye, and me whispering to him, "Be careful."

Four hours later he'd returned covered in bite marks, Shawn half carrying him into the house. The very next day he'd succumbed to the fever.

I stepped away from Alex, feeling nauseated and a little breathless, and searched out Evelyn's comforting hand. She was there, she was always there, slipping her hand into mine and gently squeezing.

"I'll whistle," Alex said, looking between the two of us. "Once to come up, and two to run."

Hand in hand, Evelyn and I stood at the bottom of the small hill, watching as Alex made his way up it and out of sight. We waited there for what seemed like an eternity, not speaking, barely breathing, until we finally heard it—a single whistle.

Together, Evelyn and I jogged up the driveway. Alex came into view, first his dark hair, then his broad back. There were more trees, then a large clearing, and was that a truck? Yes, it was a truck! And then, as the rest of the scene revealed itself, we stopped dead in our tracks.

Off to the far left of the clearing sat the shell of what was once a home. Thick splintered beams reached toward the sky, blackened and charred, towering eerily over a foundation of ruins—piles of broken glass, black dust, and burned, twisted wood.

"Oh my God," Evelyn breathed. "There are so many bones..."

My eyes widened, my mouth falling open. What I had thought were twisted pieces of burned wood were actually bones. And now that I knew exactly what I was looking at, I could make out what appeared to be a rib cage, and beside it, a skull.

"We have company," Alex said, his voice low as he gestured toward the truck.

What had once been a man, but was now a monster, was pressed up against the blood-splattered driver's side window. His face was twisted into an unholy snarl, his teeth bared and chomping on air while his hands pawed at the glass, drawing dark smears up and down as he struggled.

"He's newly turned," Evelyn said, swallowing hard. "He'll be faster than the others. Stronger too."

"That truck looks like it might still work," Alex said quietly. "This fire was recent. And look." He pointed to the bed of the truck where three gas cans were neatly stacked inside, and a dark outline of liquid could be seen in all three. "Fuel."

The entire scene was devastating. Something obviously horrible had happened here, and to people just like us, hidden away and simply trying to survive. There was no way to know what had actually occurred, but I envisioned a family, maybe some friends, who'd secreted themselves in a house in the woods only for one of them to somehow become infected. That one had probably infected everyone else, even the sole survivor who'd tried unsuccessfully to escape in his vehicle.

Tearing my eyes away from the ruins, I looked at Alex. "What should we do?" I asked, my voice thick with emotion.

It was Evelyn who answered, her sentiment starkly different from how I was feeling. "We kill it," she said, her tone matter-of-fact. "And we take the truck."

CHAPTER TWENTY

Evelyn

WE KILL IT, and we take the truck.
Of course we do, that was the humane thing to do, right? And we needed a truck. So why did I feel so guilty? I'd said it so candidly that I'd even shocked myself. Yes, this new Evelyn was a much more manic version of me than any other version I could remember. My violent ups and downs, my unraveling emotions with oddly thrown-in periods of indifference, it was the part of me that I'd always been able to keep hidden in the past. But here, in the great wide open, it seemed as if everything was spilling out of me, all my secret pain. It made me feel useless, and in turn, vulnerable. My typical escape from my emotions was gone, impossible without Jami here to distract me, and now I found myself questioning every thought I had, and every single action.

Scrubbing his hand across his chin, Alex scratched thoughtfully at the scruff that covered his once clean-shaven jaw. "Eve, you go to the passenger side and distract it. I'll take the other side and open the door, and when it comes out, I'll kill it."

"What about me?" Leisel asked as she clutched her hammer a little tighter.

"Stay here," Alex and I answered together.

Leisel's lips flattened, and her gaze fell to the gravel beneath her feet. I felt a pang of guilt for brushing her off so carelessly, but the truth was she had no real experience killing these things, aside from the one at the church. She'd always been protected from them, and I wouldn't risk losing her at the hands of one lone infected. And Alex apparently shared my feelings.

Watching as she'd looked on in horror at the smoldering pile of bones had only solidified my fears for her. She hadn't cried, but she had been clearly horrified, telling me she wasn't ready to take on the world outside the walls on her own, not just yet.

Nodding at Alex, I stalked toward the passenger side, my knife raised just in case. You could never trust these things to do what you wanted or expected; they lived by their own set of rules, hunger the only thing on their mind.

"You ready?"

Alex stood across from me with the truck between us. Squaring my shoulders, I brought my blade forward and nodded.

"Of course," I said, ensuring that my tone reflected confidence and strength.

The infected thrashed, throwing its body against the window in its eagerness to get to Alex, so much so that I couldn't imagine him paying me any mind no matter how much noise I made. Only when I tapped my blade against the passenger window did its cloudy eyes jerk toward the sound, and it launched across the bench seat, its obsession with Alex officially over.

When it plastered itself against the window, the glass audibly bent with its weight, and a slight crack began to fissure downward. Again, it slammed its face into the window, its teeth gnashing, its tongue—a dried-up and putrid slab of meat—glided across the glass, causing my stomach to turn over.

While I had its undivided attention, Alex produced another blade and opened the door, then took a step back and lifted the knife. As the scent of fresh human meat wafted into the cab of the truck, the infected seemed to pause in its thrashing, its head whipping in the other direction. All at once it growled and groaned, launching itself in Alex's direction.

Unaware of the drop between the cab and the ground, it tumbled headfirst out of the door and promptly fell out of my sight. His knife still raised, Alex dropped to his knees and a sickly crunch echoed through the air, followed by a wet slapping sound.

As I rounded the truck, still holding my knife in front of me, ready to use it if needed, I found Alex getting to his feet, his blade in one hand, dripping with red and black sludge, and in the other a set of keys. The infected lay facedown in the dirt at his feet, utterly still.

Glancing inside the cab, I looked over the seat, the entirety of the bench covered in dried blood and unidentifiable gore. And the smell, the smell was wretched, like a combination of sewage that had sat out in the sweltering sun, along with the sickly bitter stench of death all the infected carried with them. Similar to rotting flesh, but indescribably worse.

"That's disgusting," Leisel said, coming to stand by my side. "I call dibs on the backseat."

With a snort, I started to laugh. "Be my guest," I said, gesturing to the small backseat where what was left of a human carcass lay in an abnormally contorted heap. It was only a skeleton, having been picked clean of most of its organs and entrails, though the slimy gunk that remained was smeared and dried all over the seat and floor.

"Oh!" she exclaimed, taking a step backward. "Never mind."

Grunting in irritation, Alex stepped between us and shook his head. He pulled open the half door to the backseat, then grabbed the feet of the skeleton and dragged it out. There was a loud sucking sound and then an audible crack, and suddenly Alex went staggering backward, tripping over the body still lying on the ground, and promptly landed flat on his backside.

Leisel clapped a hand over her mouth, while I burst out laughing at the sight of him flat on his ass, holding a skeletal foot in each hand. Raising his eyes toward us, he scowled, which only made me laugh harder.

"Oh my God!" Leisel exclaimed, wiping away tears from underneath her eyes. "Do you need a hand up?" she asked, offering him her hand.

"Are you being funny, Leisel?" Alex retorted, one eyebrow raised. Before she could answer, Alex had tossed away the feet and grabbed hold of her hand, yanking her down. Pulling her over top of him, he rolled them, reversing their positions and covering Leisel's body with his. And then he kissed her.

Left standing there, entirely forgotten, I stared openmouthed at them as my face grew warm. This was so unlike Leisel, the way she kissed him with such wild abandon, full of passion, and right beside the body of a recently deceased infected, no less. Even with Thomas, a man she'd been so very much in love with, she'd never been one for public displays of affection, and this…

Feeling awkward, I coughed and backed away just as they pulled apart. Alex jumped to his feet, pulling Leisel up with him. Although her cheeks were red and flushed with embarrassment, she smiled at him, a genuinely happy smile, the kind I hadn't seen grace her pretty face in far too long. Alex wasn't smiling—not that he ever did—though he was staring down at her, his usually hard features relaxed with a sort of contentment I found myself jealous of.

I'd known how Alex felt about her, but Leisel, despite her proximity to him all these years, barely knew him. And yet, here she was, allowing herself to live in the moment for the first time in her life. Which left me feeling confused, my thoughts and emotions running amok, but worst of all, feeling alone and entirely without the luxury to live in the moment with anyone.

I should have been happy for her, and for the most part I was glad for her. Glad that she was finally experiencing the sort of freedom she'd been long deprived of, but at the same time I was left wondering where I fit in. Who I had become in this equation, and was I even needed any longer?

"If you two are done playing footsie," I said, attempting to keep my tone light, "we need to see if this thing still runs."

They both looked up and over at me. Alex looked surprised and Leisel somewhat embarrassed, as if they only now remembered that I was still there. Jerking my thumb toward the truck, I quirked a brow.

With his hard exterior back in place, Alex rubbed a hand across the back of his neck while sighing heavily, then headed for the truck. Ignoring the gore covering the seat, he slid inside. His first attempt at starting it produced nothing, only a desperate-sounding whirring noise on the truck's part as it attempted to turn over. He tried again, pumping the gas pedal several times until eventually the truck roared to life, an expulsion of black smoke pouring from the exhaust.

Cutting his eyes toward us, he jerked his chin. "Get in."

Leisel and I exchanged a look, neither of us wanting to make a move toward the truck. Pointing to the body still in the backseat, I shook my head. "No way, not until that's gone."

"What?" he asked. "You expect me to clean it? Take it to a car wash? Maybe get it detailed while I'm at it?"

"Maybe just take the body out of the back?" Leisel suggested softly, her nose wrinkled with disgust.

Sighing angrily, Alex jumped out of the cab and flipped forward the front seat. Leaning into the back, showcasing the fact that the bottom and back of his pants were smeared with gore, he forcefully pried the remaining skeleton off the seat and swung it out of the truck. It broke apart in midair, bones scattering about as it came crashing to the ground.

"All good now?" he asked, rolling his eyes.

The roads were bumpy and uncomfortable, and obviously hadn't been driven on for some time. Debris covered them—everything from trees to broken-down cars. As we passed through the outskirts of another town, a trail of dust flew up in our wake, the only movement we'd seen for hours.

The day was scorching. Sweat trickled down between my breasts, making me even more uncomfortable in my pink nightshirt, leaving me hot and sticky, hungry and thirsty, and with the urge to pee all at the same time.

Seated behind me, Leisel had taken to staring out of her open window in a daze. She'd wound up her long brown hair into somewhat of a ponytail, reminding me of the time she'd cut it all off into a sharp chin-length bob and had cried for weeks. It had grown out since then, taking the four long years since the start of this nightmare to get back to the length she'd always loved.

Four long years…

I sighed noisily, drawing Alex's attention. Ignoring him, I closed my eyes, my thoughts drifting away with me. By talking about the past, Leisel had opened a wound inside of me that had yet to truly heal, forcing me to remember things I couldn't afford to remember, happier times that were of no use to me now.

Yet I couldn't stop the flood of memories, the image of Shawn lying in bed beside me, snoring softly, a silly smile on his lax features after a full night of lovemaking. And of Leisel, the way her nose had always wrinkled in disgust when I'd attempted cooking, and of how she'd eaten it regardless of the taste. Every last bit of it.

I thought of my mother, my father, my juvenile delinquent of a little brother, the smell of pine and cookies at Christmastime, the warm sand beneath my fingers during summers spent lounging at the beach, of Leisel's horrible fashion sense, and the way Thomas had never once looked at her with anything but utter adoration.

How much simpler things had been, and how naive we'd all been because of it, complaining about mundane things like bills and dentist appointments.

What I wouldn't give to have all that back, where my only real concern was making sure I paid my mortgage on time.

CHAPTER TWENTY-ONE

Leisel

WE DROVE ENDLESSLY, only stopping to eat, sleep, or when Alex would hunt for food and fresh water. We drove down sad and desolate highways and back roads, too many to count, always careful to avoid towns, no matter how empty or debilitated they seemed from afar. No, we'd learned our lesson and would not be making the same mistake twice.

We continued to drive, stopping at night to sleep, and only sleeping in shifts. Either Alex or Evelyn would remain awake, keeping guard outside the truck, while I was always allowed a good night's sleep. When morning came, either Alex or Evelyn would drive while the other slept. And there I would be, feeling more and more useless with each passing day.

For the most part, the states we passed through seemed to be in a stasis of sorts, not a sign of life to be seen or heard. Occasionally, we'd pass small, sleepy groups of infected who, as soon as we drove on, became quickly disinterested in us. We searched abandoned vehicles, taking anything that could be of use to us—clothing, tools, anything that could be used as weapon, and then we'd move on, avoiding neighborhoods or once-populated areas at all costs.

Through a long stretch of land, where the patches of forest were few and far between and small game was scarce, we'd been forced to stop twice in search of food. Once at a rest area just off the interstate, and again at a gas station on the outskirts of a large city.

Both places had been overrun with infected, something we hadn't realized beforehand. And both times Alex and Evelyn had come running out of the buildings, shouting and screaming for me to "DRIVE!"

With barely enough time as groups of infected chased behind them, I'd hopped into the driver's seat. Just as Alex yanked closed the passenger door behind Evelyn and him, and the infected were throwing their mangled bodies into the side of the truck, I'd slammed down on the gas pedal and peeled away in a cloud of smoke. All of that, and only for a meager bag of sugar-coated candy that hadn't spoiled, and a lone bag of beef jerky so rock hard I could hardly manage to sink my teeth into it.

After that I demanded to be allowed to drive, allowing either Alex or Evelyn to sleep while I took my turn. I even went as far as to offer to take guard during the night, but was quickly shot down by both my best friend and my…my boyfriend? Was that what Alex was, or was becoming?

To date, there hadn't been much time for conversation, at least nothing of the personal variety, so I'd kept my questions and my musings to myself. The nights Alex wasn't on guard, I'd slept in his arms, and the nights he was, I missed his warmth. We snuck kisses here and there, gentle touches and sweet embraces, but only when Evelyn was asleep or off relieving herself in private.

As we made our way farther south, the leaves on the trees grew greener, the foliage fuller, the cold nights and dropping temperatures receded into warm nights and even hotter days. In addition to feeling disgusting and dirty, I was restless, both physically and mentally. I wanted to have the privacy with Alex to take our blossoming relationship to the next level of intimacy. I was tired of just kissing, sick of being handled so carefully by him.

In fact, I was sick of the both of them, Alex and Evelyn, never allowing me to do much of anything. One or both of them always seemed to be glued to my side, never allowing me a moment to myself.

Only three days after breaching a warmer climate, we ended up running out of gas, and some small part of me, agitated and only worsening with each passing day, raw from overthinking and needing more of…anything, was glad for it. We were all hungry, we were warm and uncomfortable, and strung out from having spent far too long living basically on top of one another. None of us were in a particularly pleasant mood, but Alex and Evelyn seemed hell-bent on taking their frustrations out on each other, leaving me stuck in the middle.

"We should have stopped at that barn," Evelyn grumbled as she wiped the gathering sweat from her brow. I climbed out of the truck after her, taking in our new surroundings.

It was warm here, much warmer than up north, the temperature rising with every mile we traveled. Three days ago I'd rid myself of my long-sleeved shirt, trading it for one of the summer dresses we'd found back at the cabin. It was a thin, gauzy sort of linen, an olive-green color with spaghetti straps, and a hemline that ended just above my knee. I'd completed the look with Alex's duty belt, the same one he'd been given in Fredericksville. On it, Alex had replaced his gun holster with a knife sheath from his boot, and now my small blade rested securely at my hip.

My hair was filthy and greasy, because washing it without shampoo just wasn't cutting it, so I piled it on top of my head in a messy partially braided bun. But even so, I still felt awful, itchy from dried sweat and the healthy coating of dirt that covered us all. I was in desperate need of a good, long soak with at least a sliver of soap. We all were.

"There were infected all over the place!" Alex shouted, slamming the driver's side door shut. "Who knows how many more were inside."

"That's just great," Evelyn snapped, her hands on her hips. "And now we're who knows how many miles away from anywhere else! With nothing but...but..." She spun around, gesturing to the endless stretch of golden wheat surrounding us on both sides. "But grass!"

"Wheat," I corrected her tersely, annoyed with both her and Alex, and their nonstop bickering.

"What?" she demanded. "Who cares what it is. Jesus, Lei!"

I shrugged. "You should care."

"Why?" she demanded, practically shouting the word at me.

"Because," I shouted back, feeling my temper rising. "We can eat it, *Eve!*"

This seemed to give her pause, and slowly the anger drained from her features. "We can?"

I rolled my eyes. "Yes. We can eat the berries. We need to soak them first, but after that they'll be edible."

"How do you know that?" Evelyn asked. She narrowed her eyes suspiciously at me, as if I'd purposely kept this wheat-berry secret from her for our entire friendship for some nefarious purpose, and my just now revealing this wicked knowledge meant I must have more secrets, maybe bigger, badder ones, secrets that could possibly change the course of the entire world.

I snarled my answer. "I used to read, remember? Books? You remember them?"

"FUCK!" Alex suddenly bellowed, startling me. Silent now, Evelyn and I watched as his fist took a nosedive onto the hood of the truck. "Fuck!" he shouted again, and again went his fist.

"Fucking great," Evelyn spat. Spinning around, she gave us her back.

I glanced between them both. At Evelyn, who was basically pouting in a metaphorical corner, and Alex who was throwing an adult-sized temper tantrum, taking it out on our only means of transportation. Out of gas or not, the thing still ran.

I took a deep, not-so-calming breath, full of hot air and truck fumes, which only served to further agitate me. Turning, I squinted down the highway, looking for anything at all, some form of shelter where we could rest and regain our bearings, maybe have some blessed privacy from one another. Yet, there was nothing. An endless stretch of nothing.

Sighing, I took a step toward the wheat, the golden stalks at least four feet high, nearly reaching my chest, and ran my hand over the top of their soft and silky stems. It would take ten, maybe twelve hours to soak them, but then they'd be edible. And something was always better than nothing.

I gritted my teeth, my hand suddenly clenching around one of the stalks. Crumpling the grains in my fist, I wondered how many times I would have to tell myself that, to try to convince myself of it before I actually began to believe it.

How much more surviving for the moment would we be forced to endure? Would it ever let up? Was there anywhere safe to go? Was there anything left at all?

As I was standing there, angry at the world and feeling sorry for myself, something touched the toe of my sneaker, and a low growl erupted from within the thick of the wheat stalks.

Seeing the bony, blackened fingers reaching for me, the dirty, nearly skinless arm parting through the wheat, I jumped backward, a scream forming on my lips. But the scream never came.

The infected was little more than a skeleton, really. Most of the skin on its face was missing, along with one eye, and it was using the earth to pull itself toward me. As its fingertips found purchase in the ground and it came slithering into view, I realized that it no longer had any legs, or even much of a torso left. Where its rib cage ended there was little that remained, only leathery ribbons of hanging flesh and dried-up entrails.

As it came for me, I continued backing away. Every inch it gained, I afforded myself a foot of distance, all the while staring down it, feeling scared, but something more than just fear. The raw sensation returned to me, the impression that my insides, my emotions, had all been sandpapered, rubbed clean of their protective coating and left open, exposed and bleeding.

Anger, pure and unadulterated rage began to well within me, making me feel too small for my body, my skin suddenly too tight, and feeling close to bursting. I just knew I couldn't take another setback, stomach another letdown before I was going to explode. Because this couldn't be all that was left, just this rot and decay, this abomination of what once was, all this…all this…godforsaken—because yes, if there was a God, he had surely forsaken us all— *nothing*.

Nothing. There was nothing left. Just me and Evelyn and Alex, searching for something we would never find, and *this thing*, this nightmarish monster creeping out of a beautiful wheat field, intent only on one thing. To destroy, destroy, destroy.

What did it matter anymore? What did any of it matter? How much longer before there was no more food to be found, before any and all shelters crumbled to dust? How much longer did we have before we too succumbed to the death of this world?

My scream, the one waiting on the tip of my tongue, finally bubbled free. A garbled and meaty-sounding explosion of anguish and suffering—and most of all rage—ripped its way up through my lungs, singeing and searing whatever it touched, and was sent soaring into the world.

Then I yanked my blade free from my belt, dropped to my knees, and sent it straight into the exposed skull of the infected. Not once, not twice, not three times. The pain, the fury, the fear, it all burst forth, all consuming and all controlling, and my hand, gripping tightly to that tiny knife, sent the blade into that monster's skull an uncountable number of times. Over and over again until I could literally feel something inside me snap, break, split wide open, and then…I no longer felt so constrained, so uncomfortable inside my own skin.

Breathing hard, partially blinded from the sweat dripping into my eyes, I got to my feet and sheathed my blade. Both Evelyn and Alex were instantly at my side. Alex kicked the dead infected, ensuring it was truly dead, and Evelyn wrapped her arms around me. They expected tears, I supposed, or me to collapse weakly into their arms, needing comfort and soothing. And then they would oh-so-sweetly tuck me into the backseat of the truck, cooing at me about getting some sleep and feeling better when I woke.

But I didn't cry; I wasn't sad. And when they reached for me, I pushed them away, pushed right past them and headed for the truck. Hastily, I grabbed what little belongings we'd appropriated along our journey, shouldering a tattered backpack, wrapping my hand around a plastic milk carton a third of the way full with dirty water, tucking a hammer into my belt, and then I turned to face them.

They still stood where I'd left them, standing in the middle of the road, the dead infected at their feet. And I swore to myself that if either one of them were to say a word, be it soothing or comforting or full of false positivity, I was going to send my little blade directly into one of their feet.

"Let's go," I said, my voice unwavering, my tone uncommonly hard, even to my ears. "The sun will be setting soon, and we'll need light to kill those infected."

"The barn?" Alex asked as he assessed me curiously, and much to my amusement, cautiously.

I nodded firmly. "The barn."

CHAPTER TWENTY-TWO

Evelyn

WE MARCHED ALONG, one behind the other, each of us keeping to our respective places since we couldn't stand to be near one another. The only good thing about being stuck in the middle of nowhere was that we were in the middle of nowhere, and it was unlikely that anything was going to sneak up on us. I couldn't say that I was completely at ease, but as I walked, or rather, stomped, I found the tension in my shoulders beginning to fade.

The fresh air, the warm sun beating down on me, it was all somewhat soothing after being stuck inside the cramped and filthy truck, breathing in the sweaty foul air for long hours at a time. The stench of the dead body and the infected that had been trapped inside had yet to leave the truck, and despite the open windows, the smell clung to our skin. To be outside in the fresh air was invigorating, and I took breath after deep breath, feeling calmer and better as the smell finally left my nose.

I watched Leisel's confident steps as she followed behind Alex, and found myself smiling slightly. He'd silently refused to let her take the lead, walking purposely faster every time she'd attempted to walk ahead, his stubbornness nearly outweighing hers. Eventually she'd relented, but her scowl remained.

I knew her well enough to know she was reading too much into the situation, taking his behavior as a personal insult against her, when in reality, he cared about her so much more than she realized. To a man like Alex, protecting what he cared about was how he expressed his feelings, but it made me nervous as well. So I couldn't blame her for wanting to stand strong and fight her own battles.

Accepting that she didn't need me as much as she once had wasn't an easy feat for me. Her budding relationship with Alex and her own desire to finally exert some independence had come as such a surprise, that at first I hadn't known how to handle the mixed emotions her new behavior had stirred within me. And I was still struggling with where I fit in here, within our little group as well as in this world. To be honest, I wasn't sure if I'd ever figure it out, or if there was anything left to figure out anymore.

Kicking a rock, I watched listlessly as it bounced down the road, passing both Alex and Leisel, but neither took any notice, too consumed with their frustrated stomping. Rolling my eyes and wanting to throw rocks at both of their heads, I let myself fall even farther behind them.

It was another hour or so before the barn finally came back into view. Still surrounded by infected, too many to count, there seemed to be even more than when we'd passed by earlier. It reminded me of the cabin, and the infected that had gathered there. There had to be some reason why they were crowding this barn, desperate to get inside. Something had to have drawn them here, the same reason that was keeping them here.

Coming to an abrupt stop about fifty yards from the barn, Alex turned to look at Leisel and me, waiting until we'd both caught up to him before speaking.

"Something is attracting them here," he said, giving voice to my thoughts. "But the sun will be setting soon, and I don't have a damn clue where we are. Either we clear it, or we walk back and spend the night in the truck…again." He grimaced.

The thought of spending another night in the truck, with barely any room to move, with no choice but to have the doors locked and the windows closed, trapping us inside with that god-awful smell, made me cringe. Alex and Leisel both seemed to share my sentiment, all of us looking positively nauseated at the very idea of it.

"No truck," Leisel snapped. "We need to clear the barn."

Alex's narrowed gaze landed on her. "You killed one infected, and now you're ready to take on an entire group of them?"

Leisel's delicate nostrils flared in response. "I'm so pissed off right now," she shouted, "that I'm ready to take you on!" She shoved him hard in the chest, but he barely flinched at the contact.

With his arms folded across his chest, Alex didn't respond, only glowered down at her. Gritting her teeth, Leisel gave him the same hard stare, neither of them willing to back down. I glanced back and forth between them, realizing that neither of them were going to willingly give up their ridiculous battle of wills, then I stomped forward, stepped directly into their line of sight, and threw my hands up in the air.

"Can we save your lover's quarrel for after we've cleared the barn?" I said witheringly. "As in, after it's safe here and I can be as far away from you both as possible?"

Leisel lifted her lip in an ugly snarl that looked so out of place on her innocent-looking features that I nearly laughed out loud.

Alex, unlike Leisel, seemed grateful for my distraction. Sighing, he glanced toward the barn. "I'm not sure we should risk it."

I realized then that he was anxious, if not downright nervous at the idea of us taking on so many infected. I'd become accustomed to his gruff and usually no-nonsense demeanor, that hearing him sound so apprehensive made me suddenly feel unsure about attempting to clear this place.

"Maybe we could draw them away somehow?" Leisel suggested with a sigh, though she still looked annoyed and more than a little put out.

"There's too many now," Alex said, shaking his head. "Way more than there were earlier."

I raised an eyebrow but didn't voice my annoyance. After all, I had suggested we stop earlier when we'd first passed by. "They aren't fresh," I offered instead. "They won't be quick. I think we can clear them."

Dragging a hand through his short beard, Alex pressed his lips into a thin line. His eyes were darker than normal, his uncertainty spilling over into his features.

"Anything goes wrong, you run," he said, his gaze landing on Leisel. "Got it? You goddamn run." He looked at me than, and I found myself grateful that I hadn't been overlooked, that he'd wanted me safe as well, even if it was merely because he knew Leisel wouldn't survive on her own. It gave me back some sense of purpose.

Leisel's eyes narrowed in response, but instead of coming back at him with another smartass remark, she simply nodded her head in acceptance. Glancing at me, she gave a slight shake of her head, and I knew there was no chance in hell she'd run, not without me, at least. I was her best friend, her only family left, and she'd never leave me anywhere, just as I wouldn't leave her.

Alex had somehow gotten absorbed into our family as well, though his place in it was still somewhat uncertain to me. I trusted him, I respected him even, as well as Leisel's feelings toward him, but if it came down to it, I would choose Leisel over him. And I hoped she would do the same for me.

"Then let's do this," Alex said, pulling a tire iron from his belt loop. Though he still carried his rifle, there were no bullets, the weapon more for show than anything else.

As I gripped my blade and Leisel her hammer, the three of us started forward. The closer we drew to the barn, the more aware the infected became of us, and slowly they began to stumble in our direction. A rush of adrenaline burned low in my belly, making my entire body quiver with nerves. I glanced at Leisel, wondering at her well-being, but found her looking far more determined than I felt.

"Split up!" Alex shouted, and jogged off to the side as the first infected closed in. It was an ugly-looking thing, its gender no longer distinguishable in the mass of rotting skin and jutting bones. Alex, having circled it, sent the sharp end of his iron into the back of its skull, killing it before it had the chance to turn fully around and face him. Yanking the weapon out quickly, Alex sent the infected crumpling to the ground, and then he swung left, sending the iron straight into the face of another approaching infected, tearing off its cheek and causing it to stumble to the side.

That was the last I saw of him, as I was suddenly faced with my own battle. Two infected rapidly approached me, and as I shouted a warning to Leisel, I found that she was no longer beside me but running in a wide arc around the two coming at me, headed straight for a third that was gaining on us. My heartbeat spiked with worry for her, but there was nothing I could do, not with the two still coming at me.

Avoiding its gnashing teeth, I shoved the first of them, pushing it backward. It staggered, bumping into the second, though it didn't fall like I'd hoped. I was forced to run a circle around it, slamming my blade into the skull of the second, leaving me very little time to pull my weapon free before the first managed to bring itself fully around.

Shouting, I ripped my blade free from its head, shoving the prone body of the second infected into the first, thankfully with enough force that I managed to topple it over. About to bend down and put it out of its misery, I paused as something sharp grazed my arm, and I whipped around to come face-to-face with yet another one. I slashed out wildly, the tip of my blade shredding the remaining skin on its throat into ribbons of leathery flesh, causing thick black gunk to well out from within. The wounds I created did nothing to divert its attention from me.

As it continued to come at me, I hurried backward, not watching where I was going, and ended up snagging the back of my foot on something. I glanced down, only for a second, though long enough to realize I'd stumbled on the two previous infected, one dead and the other still alive beneath it.

It was only a matter of seconds, the time I spent looking down, righting my balance in order to avoid the teeth of the pinned infected, but it was enough time for the approaching one to reach me, to wrap its decaying hand around my wrist and lurch forward. Screaming, I shoved at its chest, desperate to avoid its teeth. It nearly bit me, its chin grazing my forearm as I struggled to free myself from its grasp. I felt a tug on my pant leg and then another, and when I spared a glance downward, I found the pinned infected had managed to somewhat free itself, and with chomping teeth was about to take a bite out of my leg.

Still screaming, I gripped the throat of the infected, its skin dry and yet rubbery beneath my fingers. I pulled and sent us both sprawling to the right, where we fell in a heap of tangled limbs. The thing writhed on top of me, and just when I thought it was hopeless, its mangled face mere inches from my own, there was a flurry of movement, a crack and a thump, and though its body remained on top of me, its head was suddenly gone.

Above me stood Leisel, holding her hammer in a two-handed grip. She was covered in sweat, but her brown eyes were gleaming. "You okay?" she asked, breathless.

Shoving the headless body off of me, I rolled over and jumped to my feet. I gave Leisel a winded whisper of thanks, then scoured the area for Alex, finding him surrounded by six infected, with several more on their way toward him.

"Let's go!" I shouted, taking off across the field.

What used to be a woman shambled into our path, its tattered dress swaying over its bony body. It growled loudly, sounding pained, and the sound sent shivers down my spine. Running behind it, I slammed my blade into the base of its neck, and though it fell to the ground, it continued to twitch and groan. From behind me, Leisel came forward swinging and sent her hammer into the infected's temple, crushing it like a watermelon. Black sludge poured out amid the shattered bits of its skull, and a toxic foul smell was released.

More growls erupted to our left from a small group making their way toward us. Waving frantically at Leisel, I motioned for her to help Alex while I took off running into the oncoming fray.

As I was running, I ducked and wrapped my arm around the waist of the first infected in the group. With a grunt, I shoved it into the ones behind it and they all fell like bowling pins, one by one, leaving them all piled on top of one another.

After wiping the sweat from my eyes, I bent down and took out the first of the pile, sending my blade into its eye and twisting. After that, it was easy pickings. Over and over again, I slammed my blade into each of their heads and finished them off quickly.

Turning, I found Alex and Leisel down to two remaining infected, a walker and a crawler. Leisel was bent down in the tall grass, her hammer lifted high above her head, waiting as it crawled closer toward her before sending the blunt end down onto the top of its head, shattering what remained of its skull.

Alex was wrestling with the walker that used to be a man, tall and large, and not nearly as decayed as the others. There wasn't enough room between them to manage a good swing with the iron. Grunting, Alex sent his fist into the base of its jaw, knocking it back a few steps, and giving him the space he needed to lift the tire iron over his head and send the lug end of it directly onto the top of the infected's head. Skin split and rotten blood, both black and red, sprayed out from the wound, a sign that this infected had been recently turned. With a shout, Alex lifted his arm, shielding his face from the splatter.

Unfazed, and despite the blood running down its face, the infected kept coming for him. Just as I was beginning to worry, my stomach sinking as it quickly gained on Alex, Leisel appeared behind it, sending her hammer into its side.

It turned to face her, reaching for her just as Alex righted himself and again brought the tire iron down on its head. This time, its skull split wide open, and after swaying for a moment, its large body folded and crumpled to the ground.

Without the growling and moaning from the infected, it was suddenly eerily quiet as the three of us made our way toward one another. Sweating, all of us breathing hard, we came together in an awkward hug, Leisel sandwiched between Alex and me.

Leisel was grinning, her eyes lit with an excitement I was positive I'd never seen on her before, while Alex was staring down at her in a stupor. I mirrored his feelings, completely taken aback by how well she'd fought, how determined she'd been, and how it had been her alone who'd saved us both.

"We did it!" she exclaimed, and I could tell she was more proud of herself than either of us.

"We did," I said, smiling at her.

"And you were right, Eve," she said, still smiling. "That was fucking awesome!"

I choked on a laugh. Leisel almost never cursed, and to hear her do so was yet more evidence of how far she had come and how much she had changed. The timid Leisel I knew was slowly disappearing as a stronger, more independent woman appeared before my eyes, and I was proud to witness it.

Alex pulled away from us, his gaze lifting over my head and beyond. "There's still the barn, and whatever is inside it."

Across the way, the barn loomed ominously over us, the setting sun in the distance causing the dilapidated structure to cast a large shadow over the field. An answering shiver rippled up my spine.

"Do you think there are people inside?" Leisel asked.

"If there are," Alex said, his gaze fixed on the barn, "then they're assholes for not helping us."

"They could have been bitten. Maybe they turned?" Leisel suggested innocently.

"Only one way to find out," I said. Threading my fingers through hers, I clutched her hand tightly. "Ready?"

Placing an ear against the barn's large double doors, Alex listened intently for any sound coming from within while Leisel and I waited in silence behind him. Seeming satisfied, he attempted pulling at the doors, only to find them locked from the inside. Glancing over his shoulder, he grimaced. "Someone is in there," he said, his voice low. "Or some...thing is in there."

Curling his hand into a fist, he brought it up to the door and hammered at the wood. "You can come out!" he shouted. "It's safe now!"

Alex backed quickly away, his tire iron ready to swing, then gestured for us to follow him. Seconds ticked by as we waited for any sort of sound, yet nothing came.

Grinding his teeth together, Alex stormed forward and again banged on the doors. Glancing up at the waning sunlight, his scowl only deepened.

I knew how he felt. We were tired, hungry, beyond thirsty, needing more than anything a safe place to set our aching bodies down for just a moment.

"I'm going to count to three!" Alex shouted. "And then I'm breaking in! One! T—"

The doors rattled, the sound cutting him off. Immediately he took a step back, his body shielding us from whatever might be inside. Another sound rang out, much like that of chains clanking together, and then one of the doors slowly opened, revealing the pale, dirty face of a teenage boy. A man appeared behind him, older, in his midforties, with long dark hair streaked with gray and an equally long beard.

They were both frowning, looking less than pleased to see us. Worry coursed through my body, and I clutched tighter to Leisel's hand. If they had guns...

As if only now noticing Leisel and me, the older man's frown lifted into a smile. "Well, well, well," he said, stepping out from behind the boy as his eyes raked us over from head to toe. "Mighty fine of you pretty ladies to come and save our sorry asses."

His eyes flickered back to Alex, and his smile disappeared. "I'm Bryce," he continued, holding out his hand. "This here is Mike."

Warily, Alex took his hand, giving it a firm shake before quickly releasing it. "Alex," he grunted.

"Are they yours?" Mike asked, looking around Bryce to Leisel and me. "Or are they up for grabs?"

Beside me, Leisel sucked in a breath, her fingernails digging into the skin on my hand. Remembering what Alex had told us—that women were currency—my chest suddenly tightened as my heart began to hammer painfully inside it.

"They're both mine," Alex growled. The hand gripping his tire iron began to twitch, his knuckles turning white as his entire body tensed.

"Forgive the boy," Bryce said, giving Mike a shove backward. "He ain't got no damn manners. Damn shame, though." Sucking in his bottom lip behind yellowing teeth, Bryce grinned at me. "This one looks right up my alley."

Despite myself, I scowled at him, only succeeding in earning myself a small chuckle from both Bryce and Mike.

"How did you get stuck in there?" Alex gritted out.

Bryce shrugged. "We were scavenging for supplies when Mike here tripped and cut his damn leg open. Before we knew it, we had goddamn rotters coming at us from every direction. Couldn't find anywhere to stop and bandage the wound, not until we got here, but by then we had a whole mess of 'em following us."

"So you locked yourself inside," I said dryly. "How smart of you."

Bryce looked back at me with an appraising grin. "That we did, sweetheart. Wasn't too sure how we were gonna get outta here, neither. Speaking of, we should all get inside."

Shoving Mike backward, Bryce headed back inside the barn, gesturing for us to follow him. The three of us shared a wary glance, but having few other options, we eventually followed.

It was murky inside, dark, and just plain filthy, dust and grime clinging to everything. A small tractor sat on the left, moldy bales of hay stacked on the right, and above us was a second-story loft, the ladder leading up to it hanging splintered and broken.

"There's a barrel of rainwater over there, ladies," Bryce said, pointing off into the dark depths of the barn. "Something to clean up with, at least, while us men have ourselves a little chat."

Even in the fading light, I could see him grinning, and I had to bite my tongue so as not to respond with something biting in return. Tugging on Leisel's arm, I pulled her off into the darkness, leaving Alex behind.

The barrel was old, the water inside it smelled awful, but it was water and we were filthy. Glancing behind me, ensuring that no one could see us, I lifted my top over my head and dunked it inside the barrel, using it to clean my face and torso. Although hot and sticky, the water was surprisingly cool and refreshing. Following my lead, Leisel pulled the top of her dress down to her waist then proceeded to bring up handfuls of water to pour over her bare chest.

"Do you think this is safe?" she whispered as she slipped back into her dress.

"I don't know," I answered honestly. "But it's safer than being outside."

"And when we sleep?" she bit out, making it clear that she didn't approve of us staying, didn't trust these men, and that if the shit hit the fan, Alex and I would be to blame.

"Sleep with one eye open," I quipped back, purposely avoiding her glare.

Eventually Alex joined us, taking the space between Leisel and me, and quickly removed his T-shirt. He dunked it into the water and brought the soaking material up to his chest, squeezing it and sending water cascading down his body. Leisel, her worry suddenly forgotten, openly gawked at him, watching with wide eyes as his biceps flexed with his every movement. Water poured down over his rippled abdomen, and I worried she might start drooling at any moment.

Though I wanted to laugh at her expression, I didn't blame her. Alex was an attractive man, young and muscular with sharp, distinctive features. Back in Fredericksville I'd never given him a second glance; he'd always seemed too clean-cut for my taste. But now, having gotten to know him, I'd since begun to appreciate him.

The beard had definitely helped.

"I think they're okay," he whispered, turning his gaze back on us. "They said they have a large camp not far from here, where we can load up with supplies."

My eyes widened at the revelation. "A camp? Do you trust them?"

"I don't trust anyone," he said with a shrug. "But they seem harmless."

"Harmless?" Leisel whispered angrily. "Did you see the way they were looking at us? We need to keep going. *I don't trust them.*"

"I tried to tell you," Alex hissed, sounding equally as angry as Leisel. "The world is broken. I've seen places worse than Fredericksville, women being traded like food. But it doesn't change the fact that we need gas and food and weapons and clothes…" His hands gripping the edge of the barrel, he glanced between us, his features twisted in frustration, his nostrils flaring as he tried and failed to compose himself. "Shit!" he whispered. "We need everything!"

I felt sympathy for him, because as a man in this world he held a great advantage over women, and though I truly hated that concept, I had no choice but to accept that this was the way things were now. But that advantage also weighed heavily on him. Every option we had could potentially be a dangerous one, a burden he had to carry all on his own.

Reaching across the barrel, I placed my hand on Leisel's arm. "Let's just see how we feel in the morning. Alex is right—we need so much, and right now we won't make it much longer without supplies." Glancing up at Alex, then back to Leisel, I gave her a pointed look. "I trust Alex's opinion," I said, "so let's just see how this plays out."

Leisel outright glared at me, as if I'd just gone and broken the number-one girl code of honor by siding with a man over her. Undeterred, I held my gaze with hers, staring back at her until she sighed and rolled her eyes.

"Fine," she snapped, yanking her arm free. "But I'm not sleeping anywhere near them." Turning abruptly, she marched off and disappeared into a dark corner, as far as possible from where we'd left Bryce and Mike.

Giving me an exasperated but somewhat grateful look, Alex wrestled quickly back into his drenched shirt before stalking off after her.

Sighing, I dipped my hands back into the barrel and brought a handful of water up to my face. Leaning forward, I watched the droplets drip slowly back into the black pool, making circular ripples in the water while I prayed that Alex and I weren't wrong to trust these men.

CHAPTER TWENTY-THREE

Leisel

I DIDN'T TRUST THEM, I didn't like them, and I didn't want to be anywhere near them or their shifty eyes. Both Mike and Bryce were too friendly, seeming jumpy and on edge. They were always assessing both Evelyn and me, and not in a good way. I didn't want to spend the night in the barn with them, and I definitely didn't want to journey out on foot with them to their supposed so-called camp in the middle of nowhere. But that was exactly what I did, what we all did, taking a necessary risk in order to obtain the supplies we so desperately needed.

Once morning came, the sun high and hot in the sky, we headed out, passing our truck along the way. We walked for hours, the sun burning down on our already sweltering backs, and just when I was about to accuse them of lying, wondering what kind of trap we'd just blindly walked ourselves into yet again, their "camp" came into view.

Camp was a one hell of an understatement. This wasn't a camp, this was an industrial city. Many acres were filled with old factory buildings, some up to ten stories high while others sat squatty and wide beneath them. A tall and heavy formidable-looking gate, topped with razor wire, seemed to encircle the entire complex. Every so often a spark on the gate would catch my eye, followed by a zip, crackle, pop.

Electric fences, I mused, feeling both awed and wary at the same time.

"Fries 'em up good and crispy," Bryce said, waggling his eyebrows at me. "Keeps 'em cooking 'til someone comes and blows a fucking hole through 'em."

Evelyn and I shared a glance, and I could tell she was apprehensive too. Gates like these didn't just keep the infected out, they kept the living in. Gates like these were a little too similar to the walls of Fredericksville for my liking.

"Who's in charge?" Alex asked.

"Man named Jeffers," Bryce answered. "Him and his old lady run everything. You'll be meeting them soon. They like to greet all the new arrivals in person."

There was a note of pride in Bryce's voice, and I couldn't help but think that maybe this could be a decent place, especially with a woman at the helm. Because with a woman in charge, things couldn't be all bad for the women inside, right? God, I hoped so.

As we approached the camp I began counting, estimating there were ten, fifteen, no, nearly thirty buildings in all, probably more that I couldn't yet see. Vehicles were everywhere, taking up the numerous parking lots and scattered across the lawns. And interspersed through it all were people. Hundreds and hundreds of people. Milling around, running, walking, talking, laughing, and shouting.

An array of tents was lined up between the buildings, some big, some small, in a large variety of colors. From this distance I couldn't exactly be sure what they were for, but from the shouts carrying across the way, it seemed like a street fair, with vendors selling their wares. And far off, on the opposite side of the property, I could see several dozen rows of wind turbines, the blades turning slowly in the breeze.

"This place is huge," Alex muttered. He appeared somewhat at ease, but his gaze was everywhere, darting left and right at a rapid pace, taking in everything. And his body language was taut and rigid, his posture ramrod straight, all things that belied his calm and cool exterior.

"Entrance is this way," Mike said, glancing over his shoulder. His gaze found mine and he gave me a toothy smile. I attempted to smile, but more than likely only accomplished a somewhat strained grimace. Mike might be young, but he was of the age where sexuality was the first and foremost thought above everything else. His roaming eyes moving up and down my body made me want to slap him silly and send him home to his mother. But he probably didn't have one, at least not anymore, and had been forced to grow up around the likes of men like Bryce.

Averting my eyes, I suppressed a shudder.

"Bryce! Man, we sent you out for supplies and you brought us pussy back instead!"

Three men had appeared on the opposite side of the fence, close but careful not to touch the electrical death trap. They were all older, heavily bearded, and in their late forties or fifties. From our vantage point on the road, they appeared to be triplets, all of them hairy, overweight, and carrying two or three large rifles each.

"They ain't mine!" Bryce grinned at his friends. "Paul Bunyan over here has claim."

Immediately all three sets of hungry eyes sought out Alex. "How much, man?" one asked.

"I got a stash of some pretty sweet steel," another called out. "You give me a two-for-one and I'll set you up real nice."

I quickly inched toward Evelyn, who was also closing the small distance between us. Our hands found each other, our fingers interlocking as we squeezed each other tightly, silently conveying our apprehension and fear. Suddenly, my rather modest dress seemed skimpy, as if this were my fault for exposing too much skin. Skin that was starting to crawl with dread.

"Alex!" I hissed under my breath. "Alex!"

But Alex wasn't looking at me. Still walking, he fixed his stony glare on the three men at the fence as they walked in tandem with our small group, then shrugged his shoulders.

"Not for sale," he called out. "Got a truck, though. Broke down a couple miles that way. Good condition, just needs some gas."

"Got enough trucks to last me a lifetime," the man answered. "But I ain't seen a real redhead in years." His beady gaze shifted to Evelyn and his lips twisted into a greasy smile. "The carpet match the drapes, honey?"

Alex froze mid-step, his hand on his gun, and turned to face the men at the fence. "They aren't for sale," he said slowly, forcefully, spitting each individual word out between his teeth with enough venom that the tiny hairs on my arms and neck rose to attention.

I'd known Alex was formidable, dangerous even, and could hold his own more often than not. But this show of dominance over these men, his claiming us in order to protect us from the dangers of this new world, caused a different sort of appreciation to blossom within me. He wasn't just our savior and our protector, he was more than that. He was the kind of man who stood up for what he believed, a real man who did everything he could to prevent evil from spilling over into the remnants of good. He was a man like Thomas had been, despite his young age, a man of honor through and through. And I couldn't help but think that Thomas would have liked him.

"Told ya so," Bryce said cheerfully. "Can't say I blame 'im myself."

The men grumbled under their breath, shaking their heads, their expressions conveying disappointment and irritation. One by one, they walked away, no longer interested in haggling with Alex.

"Just a little ways up." Bryce gestured at a small bend in the fence, where just around the corner several dozen heavily armed men wearing fatigues were gathered. "Don't mind the artillery, gotta keep this place safe somehow."

"You know the rule, Bryce," one of the soldiers called out, coming to greet us. "Strip down or stay out."

"What?" Evelyn asked, her eyes wide.

Bryce, already unbuttoning his jeans, gave her an apologetic glance. "Them's the breaks, kiddo. Gotta show some skin, all your skin, if you wanna get in."

Horrified, I looked at him with wide eyes as my mouth fell open. "Why?"

"Looking for bites," the soldier said, his steely gaze on me. "Or any signs of infection."

"Isn't th-there somewhere p-p-private?" I stammered, my voice trembling. "Less out in the open?"

"Boss man's rules," another soldier said, coming to stand beside the first. "Nobody's allowed in until they've proven themselves clean." He gave me a shark-like smile while deliberately running his gaze up and down my body.

I pressed my lips together, turning away from the quickly gathering crowd of men, and sought out Alex. He didn't look happy, in fact, he looked downright pissed off and ready to bite the heads off anyone who dared to come near me. Yet, he was already pulling up his T-shirt.

"Let's just get this over with, Lei," Evelyn whispered, squeezing my hand. "They can look all they want, but no one's going to be touching, okay?"

No, it wasn't okay. None of this was okay. I understood the need for this, for keeping any sign of infection out of such a heavily populated area, considering how quickly it spread. But this was overkill. At the very least, they could have set up some sort of makeshift shelter outside the perimeter, giving people a semblance of privacy.

With a sigh, Evelyn dropped my hand and began unbuttoning her pants. Whistling and catcalls immediately commenced, and vulgar, sexually explicit innuendos erupted from the growing crowd of men. Women too, I noticed. I continued to stand there, fully dressed, even after both Alex and Evelyn had rid themselves of every last stitch of their clothing, and alongside an equally nude Bryce and Mike, drew closer to the fence for their inspection.

"Arms up," a soldier demanded, licking his lips as he appraised Evelyn. "Spread 'em and bend over." He grinned, his eyes still firmly fastened on her.

"Lift up your hair, princess," another soldier said, drawing closer to Evelyn.

She did as she was told, her blue eyes burning with a fire that promised retribution if anyone laid a hand on her. Not that they could, the gate prevented any contact. But once those gates were open…

Queasy and light-headed, I turned away and pressed a hand against my stomach. I couldn't do this; I couldn't strip for an entire crowd of people, leering and jeering at me as if I were some sort of sideshow animal. I was a person, a woman; I had feelings and emotions and pride. Oh God, why didn't anyone seem understand that anymore? Or care at all? Where was the humanity?

Dead, I thought bitterly. Dead, like everything else.

"If that one doesn't strip, or leave, within the next two minutes, I'm putting a bullet through her head."

I squeezed my eyes shut, clenching my fists into tight little balls. I couldn't do this; I just couldn't. I'd already been subjected to enough torment and torture to last me several lifetimes, and I'd be damned before I willingly subjected myself to it.

"You hear me, sweetheart?" the same voice called out. "I'm counting down, starting now!"

"Lei…"

I opened my eyes to see Alex standing in front of me. Already dressed again, he gazed down at me with dark eyes full of compassion.

"Lei," he repeated, his tone gentle. "I'll be right there next to you. You don't have to look at them, you just look at me, okay?"

Staggered breaths caused my mouth to quiver. "We don't need this place," I whispered. "We don't need them. We were fine on our own."

But even I knew I was lying. We were far from fine. Daily we had to scavenge, usually finding nothing of use. We had no safe place, no guarantees, nothing but the clothes on our backs and one another.

Alex shook his head. "We do. I wish we didn't, but we do." His voice was desperate, his eyes pleading with me.

He didn't like it either, and I could tell it was killing him to admit defeat, especially after making it this far with just the three of us. But even a king knew he couldn't survive without his subjects, and whereas Alex was much like a king in this new world, powerful yet just, he too knew when he needed help.

I closed my eyes again, trying to find someplace inside myself where I could go, where I could hide inside my own skin in order to get through the next several minutes. I already had enough shame to last me several lifetimes, and the thought of adding more to it was sickening.

"One minute!" the voice called out.

"Lei, please." Alex sounded somewhat frightened now, whether it was his fear of never finding another place like this one, or his fear of me being gunned down like an infected, or maybe both, I didn't know.

"I can't lose you," he whispered fiercely.

"You barely know me," I snapped, trying to pull free of his grasp.

Tightening his hold on me, he bent his head close to mine, forcing me to look at him. "I do know you," he hissed. "I know you hum songs from the sixties and seventies when you're bored or sad. I know that most nights you cry yourself to sleep. I know that you're usually thinking about Thomas when you smile. Lei, I know where every bruise and cut on your body is and what caused them, and I also know Eve is the only person on this planet who makes you feel safe. *I know you, Leisel.*"

Shocked, I stared up at him as my entire body trembled. "You make me feel safe too," I whispered as tears pricked my eyes.

He swallowed. "Don't take that away from me," he whispered back.

"Thirty seconds!" the guard bellowed.

Yanking free of Alex's hold, I spun away and marched with purpose over to the gates. Purposely, I avoided meeting Evelyn's eyes, part of me hating that she seemed to always be able to do what I couldn't.

Keeping my gaze firmly planted on the ground, I let my belt drop first. Then, reaching around, I began to struggle with the buttons on the back of my dress. As I continued to fumble, silently cursing both myself and this awful situation, Alex appeared at my left and Evelyn to my right. Brushing my hand away, Evelyn began to work the buttons while Alex kept his eyes steadily focused on mine. When my dress fell away, leaving me standing in nothing but a pillaged pair of underwear, I couldn't hold back a full-bodied shiver. Keeping my gaze on Alex, trembling from head to toe, I tucked my thumbs inside my underwear and pushed them down.

"Turn around and lift your arms," the soldier demanded.

Swallowing hard, fighting the urge to cover my breasts, I turned slowly, giving my back to the gathered crowd. They weren't nearly as zealous with me as they'd been with Evelyn, something I attributed to my scars and numerous bruises. Although most of them had turned an ugly shade of yellow and purple, they were still visible. For that, I was grateful. If the crowd had been nearly as crude to me as they'd been to Evelyn, I might have taken off running.

"Spread your legs," the soldier said, "then bend down and touch your toes."

I did as he demanded, feeling my cheeks burn hot from the humiliating position. I stayed that way for several seconds, my legs spread wide apart, my backside thrust high into the air while I attempted to reach for my toes.

"Clear!" he called out, and I sprang up, closing my legs and slapping my hands over my breasts. Alex, still standing beside me, had already begun helping me back into my dress.

"What happened to her?" I heard someone ask. Still busy with my underwear, I didn't turn to answer.

"A man," I heard Evelyn snap.

"What man?" the voice asked. "That man?"

I spun around then, facing the several soldiers and the crowd of onlookers behind them. "No," I said bitingly. "Another man did this. And I killed him for it."

Not one person who heard me seemed surprised by my answer, most of them disinterested in us now that we were clothed again. Only one soldier, the voice behind the question, stared back at me. He was young, maybe around my age, with light brown hair spiked up in all directions, and rather hollow-looking blue eyes.

"Welcome to Purgatory," he said flatly. "Weapons are allowed, but if you kill someone inside these gates, you'll answer for it. You got that?"

"Got it," Alex replied tersely.

"I'm talking to her," the soldier said, his eyes still on me. "The self-proclaimed murderess."

"I got it," I said evenly.

Lifting up two fingers, the soldier spun an invisible circle in the air. "Let 'em in!" he shouted, and the gate began to open, its hinges squealing in protest.

When the gate was fully open and there was no danger of being electrocuted, we stepped inside as a group. Bryce and Mike took off together, disappearing into a crowded market area, while Alex, Evelyn, and I stood in a tight circle, unsure of what to do or where to go.

"This way." The soldier who'd welcomed us inclined his head. "Time to meet the boss man."

As we followed him down the crowded path, the throng of people growing thicker and noisier, I couldn't help but wonder why they would name a safe haven something as awful as Purgatory? Because it was the last stop before heaven or hell? A place of judgment that would test our resolve and strength?

Or was it just as it implied. Purgatory, a place or state of suffering. For all eternity.

From behind us, the gates closed with a thump and click, electrical sparks shooting out in all directions.

I turned away, still following our armed guide. I supposed I'd find out soon enough, one way or the other.

CHAPTER TWENTY-FOUR

Evelyn

MY HEART WAS beating furiously in my chest, anger and frustration still burning through me as I gripped Leisel's hand, trapping her fingers within my own. Being naked was nothing to me. Being gawked at, stared at, ogled, and scrutinized, it all meant nothing...*to me*. Yes, I hated them all staring, of course I did, but I'd found it more infuriating than embarrassing. Yet to Leisel, to someone whose own body had been repeatedly used as a tool to both shame and embarrass her, it was everything. And after everything that bastard Lawrence had put her through, her body was finally her own, and I hated that these men had made her feel anything differently.

Alex walked ahead of us, with Leisel and me following closely behind, and like a small triangle we trailed after the guard. I hadn't even met this supposed boss man, yet I hated him already, hated him for the uncomfortable welcome his men had given us. But as I looked around, taking in our new surroundings, I couldn't deny that I respected him as well. He'd accomplished a lot with this place, especially safety, and that was worth my admiration.

Life literally teemed from every corner of this place, as if Purgatory were a busy New York City sidewalk, not an old factory complex stuck in the middle of nowhere. It was both fascinating and frightening, so much life all in one place, filled with people who didn't seem afraid like the citizens in Fredericksville. In fact, these people seemed the opposite, laughing and joking as if this were just any other day, not four years into the crumble of civilization.

Eyes followed us as we passed, dirty faces assessing us from head to toe. Some people offered us friendly smiles, others were more apprehensive. But the men all had the same look in their eyes—greed—evident by their lascivious grins, their hands rubbing together, knuckles cracking, their appraising eyes running up and down the length of us.

Jutting my chin out, I ignored the catcalls, ignored the quivers that ran up Leisel's arm and into my own. Picking up our pace, I ensured that we stayed directly behind Alex, no more than a distance of two steps at all times. Even so, Alex's presence didn't calm me as I'd hoped it would, not when I could still see all those greedy eyes.

Eventually, at the far end of the open area, we turned down a quiet corner and entered a tall building. On either side of us, the walls were crudely painted with names and dates, images of both the past and the present. The hallways were lined with large metal drums, men filling them with some sort of yellowish liquid, as if preparing for something.

The entire place was surprisingly cleaner than I'd thought it would be, the floors swept free of debris, items piled up and organized on shelves or neatly stacked in containers. Amazed, I continued to stare, wondering how many different supplies they must have in a place this size, and how they'd obtained it all.

Finally we approached a set of concrete steps that led to a heavy steel door, two armed guards stationed at the bottom.

"He up there?" our escort asked the guards, jerking his chin in the direction of the door.

One of the guards answered, a short, stocky man with shockingly red hair. "Yeah, you know the drill, knock and wait before you go in."

We started up the stairs, only to be stopped by one of the guards placing a firm hand on Alex's chest. "What do you need?" This guard was taller than the other and lankier, but his gaze was hard and forbidding.

Cocking his head to one side, Alex eyed the man disdainfully. "Everything," he bit out.

The soldier's gaze slid away from Alex, landing on me. Seeing him, the look in his eyes, I knew what was about to happen, and a shiver of anxiety slid up my spine.

"I can get you anything you want for a night with that one." Biting down on his bottom lip, the guard switched his appreciation toward Leisel. "Or that one," he continued. "We haven't had fresh pussy here in months, and I'd like a workout with 'em before they end up in the Cave." He looked back at Alex, his brow arched in question.

"They're not for sale," Alex answered, the muscles in his back tensing.

"You're tapping both?" The soldier laughed once before looking back at me. "He satisfying you?" His gaze shifted between Leisel and me. "Both of you?"

It was Alex who answered. "I am," he practically growled.

The guard let out an unsatisfied breath of air, yet his smile remained. Stepping aside, he gestured to the door, allowing us access.

One by one, we climbed the stairs, and for reasons unknown to me, I chanced a glance back down. Both guards were still watching us, smiling widely, and I couldn't help but think that maybe we'd made a huge mistake, that maybe we shouldn't want to find out what was behind that door.

When we were through the door, we were faced with yet another set of stairs that led to a corridor, then two more sets of stairs. Finally we came to a long dark hall lined with broken windows. A lone door was at the end, painted a bright red. As we trudged down the hallway, we couldn't help but peek out the windows. From our vantage point here, high above the camp, we were able see a great deal of the entire spread, and even I had to admit that I was slightly awed by it all. This place was huge, much bigger than Fredericksville, and a lot less *Truman Show*, with more of a *Mad Max* vibe.

We came to a stop in front of the opulent red door where our escort raised his fist and knocked twice. Several heartbeats passed, during which my apprehension mounted, and then a gruff, inaudible reply sounded from within.

I gave Leisel's hand another squeeze; she looked like she needed it. In fact, she looked downright petrified, and knowing that was all the incentive I needed to swallow my own fears and reservations.

"We'll be okay," I told her quietly, and breathed a sigh of relief when she nodded in response. "Together, okay?" I smiled at her. "Always together, I promise."

The room we entered was a huge open expanse, large concrete pillars standing from floor to ceiling and spaced evenly throughout.

Sections of the space had been cordoned off to create the ambience of an actual home, and it was just that—homelike, yet in a fucked-up sort of way.

There was a living area consisting of three sofas, none of them matching, all of them with an insane array of colorful throws and mismatched cushions. The bedroom area was covered in mirrors—the walls, the ceiling, even the headboard. Near a row of partially boarded-up windows, I saw a bathroom area with a large claw-foot tub, which caused me to cringe in sympathy for whoever had been responsible for lugging it up all those stairs.

Like the rest of the building, the place was clean yet eclectic, with colors splashed over walls, and a variety of throw rugs of different sizes and shades scattered over the floor. It was visually jarring and oddly welcoming at the same time.

Through the center of it all, a man and woman approached us, unsurprising in my expectation of their appearances. The man was huge, not just muscular, but downright huge, covered with muscles. And as he continued toward us, a fierce scowl on his face and his bare chest on display, I was slightly more impressed by the sheer strength he radiated than by the place he presided over.

A thick stripe of gray ran through his hair, making me wonder if he'd placed it there intentionally. But the closer he came, the more obvious it was that it was natural. With a toothpick jammed between his two front teeth, his scowl deepened as he closed in on us, and I briefly wondered if we should just say *screw it* and run.

The woman beside him was less imposing, yet her very presence seemed to suck all the air out of the room, making her seem even more frightening than him. She was slight with a slim waist, heavily tattooed arms, and chin-length hair that had been dyed a bright pink. Someone of her size and stature shouldn't have seemed so daunting, yet there was something off about her, something that suggested a raw edginess, as if a sleeping violence lurked just beneath her surface.

We were watching them and they were watching us, while this woman hung off her man like a leech, her nose ring twinkling each time she made the slightest of movements.

Several tense moments ticked slowly by, and just when I thought I couldn't take another second of the silence, when I was feeling as if I was suffocating under this tiny woman's hard gaze—not the man's, because his eyes hadn't left Alex—Leisel spoke up, shocking the hell out of everyone in the room.

"I don't know about you, but I would really like to sit down," she said with a shrug. She let out a nervous laugh, trying to be brave, attempting to break the ice on this awkward situation we'd found ourselves in.

"We've been walking all day, avoiding the infected," she continued. "I swear, it's like there's a damn apocalypse going on out there." She offered another soft laugh, her gaze darting over to mine.

Trying not to gape at her audacity and her bad attempt at a joke, I wondered about how strangely calm she seemed, when here I was, feeling as if I might vomit from anxiety.

Even stranger was the man, who'd since begun to smile at Leisel's nervous twittering. His smile widened until he plucked the toothpick from between his teeth and grinned from ear to ear. Suddenly, his grin became a full-bellied barking sort of laugh that left all three of us shifting uncomfortably.

Looking perplexed and more than a little annoyed, the pink-haired woman glared up at her man. When he noticed her eyes on him, the man turned to face her, and after seeing the look of confused disdain twisting her features, his smile quickly fell away.

"Come. Sit the fuck down," he said, his voice full of gravel, his original snarl once again firmly in place. Together, although the woman was clearly leading the show, the couple started for the sofas.

Alex looked first at me, then at Leisel, his eyes burning with questions that he didn't dare voice. Not here, not yet. Shrugging ever so slightly, he headed for the sofas as well, leaving Leisel and me little choice but to follow him.

Like lambs sent to the slaughter, one by one we took a seat, Leisel on Alex's left, and me on his right. I didn't like the seating arrangement, sure that Leisel should be in the middle, protected by both of us. But this place, this world, it wasn't our reality. It was their reality, this new world where men lorded over women as if we were property. I could only assume we were seated like this because Alex sensed this, and was acting accordingly.

Seconds ticked by, one by one, and still no one spoke until Alex finally broke the silence. "We, uh, helped two of your men escape a horde of infected. In return—"

"Jeffers," the man said, interrupting Alex, then tucked his toothpick back in place.

"What?" Alex asked.

"His name is Jeffers," the woman explained, her voice thick with an accent I didn't recognize. "And I'm Liv."

Suddenly she grinned at me and inched her way closer to Jeffers. Draping a long skinny leg over his thick muscular one, a little too much thigh and the noticeable curve of her backside revealed in the process, she arched into him and darted her tongue out, stroking a long, leisurely lick up the length of Jeffers's neck. It was all very vulgar, the act reminding me of a dog pissing on a tree, marking its territory. Instantly, I concluded that I didn't like her.

"You been living in the wild this whole time?" Jeffers asked, his brow puckered.

"Yeah," Alex muttered. "Anyway...Jeffers...we helped two of your men—"

"The three of you?" Jeffers looked at Leisel and me, his eyes narrowing.

Alex nodded, clearly annoyed at the interruption. "Yeah, the three of us helped two of your men. They were trapped inside a barn, the whole place was crawling with infected, and we—"

"Rescued them?" Liv offered, lifting one thin eyebrow. Her sly gaze landed on Jeffers. "You hear that, baby? These three wild rats rescued two of your boys."

Turning toward me, she grinned again. "Who was it? The men you rescued? What were their names?"

Liv's tone had become challenging. She ran her tongue across her lower lip, every so often biting down on it. I couldn't tell if she just disliked me as much as I did her, and she was toying with me because of it, or if this was all some odd attempt at flirting with me. All I knew was that I didn't trust her. Not at all.

"Bryce," I answered with hesitation, my gaze on her steely and hard. "And Mike."

Her body still draped across Jeffers, Liv started to laugh, a sharp, short, mocking laugh that sent gooseflesh pebbling up and down my arms. "Jeffers, baby," she cooed, a little too sweetly. "These ladies rescued two of your boys. Meaning we have a couple of badass bitches ripe for the taking, don't we?"

Jeffers appeared less than impressed, his face still hard and unreadable. Every so often the muscles in his chest and arms twitched, a jumpy, unsteady tempo that did nothing but add to the already uncomfortable situation. Eventually he leaned forward, his elbows resting on his knees. Tonguing his toothpick from left to right, his cold stare fell on Alex.

"I'll want to settle that score," he said darkly.

"Settle the score?" I exclaimed loudly.

Jeffers's eyes shifted languidly toward me. "Keep your mouth shut unless you're spoken to, and maybe I'll let you stay." He turned back to Alex. "You fight? Or you just big and useless?"

Leisel's hand suddenly found my arm, her nails digging painfully into my skin, and I was right there with her, both spitting mad at this audacious man, and fearful of what he had in store for us.

"I can fight," Alex said, his tone flat. Leisel's nails were now digging vicious little holes into my flesh, and I had to squelch back a yelp of pain.

"You fight, you stay," Jeffers said. Spreading his arms out over the top of the cushions, he leaned back against the sofa. Liv followed him, curling herself around his large body like an attention-starved cat.

Ignoring Liv, Jeffers glanced between Leisel and me. "Goes for you two as well. You either bring something to the table or you're useless to me."

Leisel's *I told you so* echoed inside my head, eclipsing the ringing in my ears caused by rage. I glared at this man and his ridiculous pink-haired toy, my humiliation burning hotly inside me. He knew we had nothing, nothing but our bodies, and I would die before I let another man hurt Leisel that way.

"I'll fight in exchange for all of us," Alex said, his words coming fast and hard as he struggled to control his anger.

Uncurling herself from Jeffers, Liv turned to Alex. "Sorry, sexy," she purred seductively, running her eyes up and down his body, much like she had with her tongue on Jeffers's neck. "That's not how it works around here. No one is accountable for anyone else. You either hold your own or you're out."

That imperious bitch. I wanted to punch her, rake my nails up and down her face, gouge her eyes out with my fingertips, rip her silly pink hair from her scalp and make her choke on it. But I did nothing, just sat there beside Alex, playing the part of the good little woman who knew her place, while praying that Alex would speak up in our defense.

"They're not for sale," Alex said, and got to his feet. He glared down at Jeffers and Liv. "And if that's their only option, then we're done here."

Jeffers rose as well, matching Alex's glare. "You might be done here, but I said there was a score to settle, and I'll have my fight."

The men stared each other down, both pumped full of testosterone and ego, neither willing to bend for the other. It was a dangerous situation, Alex with only two small women in his corner, and Jeffers with an entire army.

"So this pussy doesn't put out," Liv said, leaning forward with an amused smirk on her face. "Is that the problem? They only have eyes for you?" Without waiting for Alex to answer, she shrugged. "Then we'll just find something else for them to do." Her eyes landed on Leisel. "Do you like to dance, little mouse?"

Beside me, Leisel flinched, and I could tell she was mere seconds away from completely losing it. Her breathing was frantic, her grip on me bruising.

"I can fight," I said suddenly, drawing all attention to me.

Liv's mouth curved into a cruel smile, making my stomach sink. What had I just gotten myself into?

"I was kinda hoping you'd say that," she sneered. Turning to Leisel, her grin only grew in its awful intensity. "And you, little mouse? Can you fight like this pretty little kitty can?"

"No," Alex growled, moving to stand directly in front of Leisel, blocking her from Liv's line of sight.

"Ah..." Jeffers drawled knowingly. Glancing down at Liv, the couple shared a shrewd look. Suddenly I felt worse, my anxiety spiking yet again. They now knew how Alex felt about Leisel, and I couldn't imagine them respecting those feelings. If anything, these were the sort of people who took advantage of them.

"There has to be something else she can do," Alex said. "Cleaning or cooking..."

Liv raised her index finger in the air and ticked it back and forth like a metronome. "Ah, ah, ah," she said, smirking. "We don't cook for the masses here. Some people have the resources and have set up restaurants of sorts, while the others either rely solely on their wages or end up fending for themselves. As for cleaning, we reserve those jobs for the elderly. The men and women who no longer have the strength to fight, or the sex appeal to sell themselves."

Releasing me with a resigned sigh, Leisel got to her feet, slipping out from behind Alex's towering frame.

"I can dance," she said.

CHAPTER TWENTY-FIVE

Leisel

"NO, LEI, ABSOLUTELY not! Four years of intermediate ballet when you were a teenager isn't what these people have in mind for you!"

Evelyn had been yelling at me for close to an hour now, only pausing in her rather shrill screeching to studiously ignore me, after which she began yelling again. And I was getting a splitting headache from it all.

"Four years of ballet," I said tersely. "Two years of modern dance, six years of hip-hop, and three years of Zumba, Eve. Remember? You took the classes with me. I *can* dance."

"Classes, Leisel, classes! This isn't a class full of girls and women, this is you wearing next to nothing and dancing in a cage for an audience of men! You couldn't even take your clothing off at the gates without having a panic attack!"

I sighed noisily. Yes, this was much different from anything I was used to, or comfortable with, for that matter. But Liv had assured me that I wouldn't be naked, not that I trusted that seedy woman in any way, and that the cage dancers were just that, dancers. As long as Evelyn and I made sure to have our property brands completed before we began working, a tattoo that would be identical to the one Alex was currently getting, no man could touch either of us without Alex's permission. Considering the way Alex was acting—refusing to look at me, and his expression murderous—I didn't foresee it being a problem. Him selling me to another man, that is.

"We don't have a fucking choice," I spat out, increasingly agitated with her incessant mothering. "This place isn't exactly a pillar of women's rights!"

"Who are you?" she shouted, her face suddenly far too close to mine. "What is with this split personality disorder? One minute you're cowering, the next you're killing infected, the next you're crying, and then you're willing to dance for men? I don't know you, Leisel. I don't know this person and I don't understand it!"

"I'm doing what I *have* to!" I screamed. Without thinking, I slapped my hands against her chest and shoved her backward. "I'm trying to adjust! I'm trying, Eve, I'm *trying*!"

"I don't want you to adjust!" she cried, and shoved me back. I caught myself before I could fall, and when I raised my head to glare at Evelyn, I found tears forming in her big blue eyes. "You were fine the way you were!" she continued shrilly. "You were caring and sweet, the only truly good person left in this world!"

"I wasn't fine!" I yelled, the sight of her tears causing my own to fall. "I was *weak*, I was weak and stupid, and because of that I ended up married to a man like Lawrence! He knew it, he could see it in me, see that I was a doormat he could walk all over. I don't want to be a doormat anymore, Eve, I want to be strong! I want to be strong like you are."

People were beginning to stop and stare, openly gawking at Evelyn and me as they passed us in the hallway. The building we were in was a smaller one, full of what looked to have once been managerial offices. Now they were separate places of business. Evelyn and I were currently standing outside a door laughably marked BRANDING.

"I used to wish you were stronger," Evelyn whispered raggedly, drawing closer to me. "And then…now…it's like I don't know who I am if I don't have to worry about you. What is my purpose here, Lei, if I have no one to take care of?"

Despite her tears and her now quiet tone, her eyes were wild, frenzied even. I'd thought her mood swings had calmed some, but it seemed as if the past week might have been the calm before the storm, a storm that was only just beginning to brew.

"Oh, Eve," I whispered, reaching for her. As I took her into my arms, hugging her fiercely, two men passed by, slowing down at the sight of us. Both of them wore sickly smiles; one of them winked and the other waggled his eyebrows. Disgusted, I buried my face into Evelyn's shoulder.

How easily the world had reverted to what it once was, where men lorded over women and treated them as if they were little more than cattle. In a way, the new world was much like the old West, full of gun-toting cowboys, danger at every turn, and where a woman was only safe if she was spoken for. If not, she was fair game.

I should be grateful Evelyn and I had Alex, and I was, yet I couldn't help the anger that followed in its wake. Anger, because I shouldn't have to feel this way, and because of how far we'd come as a nation, only to lose it all in only four short years.

"We're safe now," I said soothingly. "We have electric fences and an entire army keeping the infected out. We have Alex protecting us. You don't have to be strong at the moment, Eve, you can take a breath. You can take a hundred breaths."

My words were kind, and as genuinely spoken as I could muster given our current circumstances. I hoped that Evelyn was too upset to hear the doubt I felt, that she wouldn't pick up on the little white lies laced between the truths. Because we weren't safe, not really. Safety was now a thing of the past, a wish on a star, the kind of dream you never wanted to wake from. In this waking nightmare of ours, anything could happen. Alex could die, leaving us alone, two women ripe for the plucking once more. Or the infected could come, too many for these gates to hold at bay, and then this somewhat safe haven would fall, leaving us as food for the infected, or again lost to the big, wide open.

"You're right." Evelyn pulled out of our hug, sniffing and wiping the tears from her cheeks. "I'm being ridiculous. It's probably that time of the month." She attempted a smile and I attempted one back, but our facades quickly evaporated once the door beside us opened, revealing a very pissed off Alex.

He held up his wrist, revealing his branding. Two identical *A*s in bold lettering had been inked into his skin with two circles surrounding them.

"A-A?" I asked.

"Alexander Adams," he answered through his teeth, his gaze hard as he stared at me. "My name."

"One more *A* and you could start a travel club," Evelyn joked without humor, but neither Alex nor I even attempted a smile. There was nothing funny about any of this.

"Who's next?" Alex asked.

I looked at Evelyn, who shrugged in return. "I'll go," she said. "You guys need to talk."

As she disappeared inside the room, pulling the door shut behind her, I suddenly couldn't bring myself to look at Alex. He was glaring at me, no, his eyes were wishing a thousand daggers to pierce my heart. And even though I knew I didn't owe him an explanation for my decision, his behavior was making me feel as if I did.

"It could be worse," I quietly told the floor. "I could be stripping, or…" I finally looked up at him and raised my arms in a helpless gesture. "I can't fight, Alex! What did you want me to do?"

He didn't respond, just continued to stare, those dark eyes of his burning angry holes straight through me.

"Alex," I whispered, my tone taking on a hint of desperation. "Say something!"

He didn't, of course he didn't, but my words seemed to trigger something in him. His shoulders sagged, and his scowl faded. Shaking his head, he leaned against the wall behind him and folded his arms over his chest.

I sighed and reached for him, attempting to pry his arms away from his body. It took several pulls, me getting nowhere against his strength until he finally chose to relent. Dropping his arms, he allowed me to wrap mine around his waist and press myself against him.

Several moments passed, his stubbornness knowing no bounds, me gripping him tightly and him refusing to reciprocate. But I wasn't going to give up, wasn't going to allow something so meaningless to drive our small group apart. I kissed his chest, dug my fingertips into his lower back, and kissed him again and again through his dirty T-shirt until finally he sighed. Reluctantly, he lifted his arms and brought them around me.

Another moment passed, and then he lifted me up off my feet and into his arms, holding me so tightly I could barely catch a breath.

As I followed behind our newest guide, a prostitute named Bethany who couldn't have been more than twenty and was noticeably naked under her nearly sheer robe, I took in what was one of the many living quarters in Purgatory. This particular building was five stories high, resembling a college dorm with door after door after door, and very few windows. But this was far from a dorm, the walls decorated with an odd mix of spray-paint art and framed art, the paintings all easily recognizable as past works from historically famed painters.

And there were padlocks on nearly every single door.

"Doorknob locks didn't cut it," Bethany offered when she caught me staring. "Too many break-ins."

I gaped, wondering what anyone still had these days that would be worth stealing, and why people would be willing to take such a high risk. Maybe I was just being naive about it all, but Purgatory's rules were laid out to us by Liv, and they were strict and harsh. The first time you stole, you lost a hand. The second time you stole, you were put in a cage, infected, and left to turn. You took another man's woman, you lost another vital body part and got strung up in a cage, infected, and left to turn.

Each incident had the same outcome. You became an infected and were left in a cage to rot. I hadn't yet seen any cages or infected, but it was a horrific and painful death to contemplate, and a terrible reminder to everyone not to steal or cause trouble, yet apparently not a complete deterrent.

"When you're home," she continued, "you keep your door locked from the inside, and when you leave, make sure you lock it from the outside."

We followed her in silence, the three of us simply taking in our surroundings. We passed a pair of young children playing alone in the hallway with a set of colorful blocks. I offered them a smile that they both returned with apprehensive looks, which only made my mood darker.

"Since you've got two claims, Liv wanted you all in the family building." Bethany shrugged, dramatically flipping her long black hair over her shoulder. Slowing her pace, she turned to look over her shoulder, giving Alex a long, appraising look. "If you're looking for another girl, I'd be more than happy to give you a freebie, give you a taste of heaven, honey."

She stopped walking altogether, forcing the rest of us to stop as well. Placing her palm against Alex's chest, she ran her red-tipped fingers across his T-shirt. Her tongue darted out, sliding slowly over her full bottom lip. "That's what they call my pussy 'round here," she whispered as she slid her hand down his stomach.

Shocked, I watched with more than a little anger-fueled jealousy as she boldly took a handful of Alex's crotch. "Heaven," she purred throatily, her fingers flexing.

My breathing grew shallow, seconds seeming like hours as my heart pounded an unsteady rhythm inside my chest. Why didn't he slap her away, or better yet, take her by her slutty throat and squeeze the life from her? Resentment flared inside me, and I struggled to contain my annoyance at both her and him.

Alex's hand covered hers and peeled her hand off him before he pushed her away and took a step back. "Maybe another time," he said stonily, thankfully looking as disgusted as I was feeling.

Bethany's instant disappointment was palpable. Miffed, she gave both Evelyn and me a scathing glance, speaking volumes as to how she felt. Who were we? What was so special about us that a man like Alex would claim us and not her?

I found myself feeling sorry for her, my anger doused nearly as soon as it had flamed. Instead, I was saddened by her circumstances, and though this woman wouldn't want my pity, I felt it for her regardless. Take Alex out of this equation, and Evelyn and I could both be in her shoes, desperate for any sense of security and ready to do anything it took to obtain it.

"Whatever," she muttered, then turned away, leaving us all with an up close and personal view of her backside. "We're here anyway." She flipped her hand carelessly toward a door on the right. Like the others, it was also fitted with a large and formidable-looking padlock. A key appeared in her hand—*Where had she been hiding that?*—and then, without turning to look at him, offered it to Alex.

"I'll be back for you tonight," she said flippantly in my direction. "Make sure you shower before work. The bathhouse is on the first floor."

With another flip of her hair over her shoulder, Bethany pushed between Evelyn and me, her shoulder purposefully colliding with Evelyn's. And then she was off, down the hallway and eventually out of sight.

While Alex fumbled with the padlock, Evelyn and I exchanged uneasy glances.

I'm worried about you, her eyes told me.

I was worried about me too, but instead of conveying that, I glanced away, my gaze landing on the two children still playing in the hallway. There wasn't much I was grateful for in this new world, only Evelyn and now Alex, yet I found myself suddenly grateful that I'd never been able to conceive a child. Not with Thomas and not with Lawrence.

This world wasn't for children, it wasn't conducive to growing and learning, and it definitely didn't perpetuate morals. These two children would know nothing but violence and death, and I counted myself grateful that I would never be laden with the guilt of bringing life into an already dead world.

"Home sweet home," Alex muttered as he pushed open the door. A moldy smell wafted out into the hall, intermixed with cleaning solution. One by one we entered, taking in our new residence. It was a small room, no bigger than a bedroom. Off to the right, a stained mattress had been dropped haphazardly onto the floor, and to the left was a battered old armchair, threadbare and missing half an arm. A shoddy countertop lined the wall beneath a row of windows, all of them cracked and covered in duct tape.

But the walls were another story. Hanging over the poor paint job, a sickly green color, were several familiar art prints. The *Mona Lisa*, *Starry Night*, and *The Scream* all hung side by side, an odd sort of mix.

I stared at *The Scream*, thinking how fitting it was. The thought also occurred to me that, much like children, art seemed to have little place in this world.

CHAPTER TWENTY-SIX

Evelyn

"WHAT NOW?" LEISEL was perched on the edge of the broken armchair, looking from Alex to me and back again. Her eyes pleaded with me to give her something of substance to latch onto inside this strange place, but all I could do was shrug.

We'd only been in this place for a couple of hours, and already I was edgy and ill at ease with everything. It would be nightfall soon, and the thought of being somewhere behind walls, fences, barriers… whatever you wanted to call them, made me uncomfortable. I was supposed to feel safe now, yet I felt anything but.

Alex had been silent for hours now, ever since Leisel had insisted that she was going to dance. Clearly, he hated the idea, loathed it, and I could almost taste his anger at the idea of other men looking at her. Refusing to even take a seat, he'd been standing in front of a window, looking out through the broken glass at the world below since we entered our room.

Jerking my head in Alex's direction, I gave Leisel a pointed look, silently conveying to her to get her ass up and go to him. Mouthing the word *no*, she shook her head, and in return I glared at her, again jerking my head. Reluctantly, she finally stood and walked slowly across the room before reaching him. Tentatively, she reached out, gently placing her hand on his back, only to have him flinch away from her. Closing her eyes, Leisel took a deep, shuddering breath, before opening them and trying again. This time, Alex remained still, allowing her to touch him, and eventually she began gently rubbing his back and he began to visibly relax.

Biting down on her lower lip, she looked at me with an expression on her face that clearly said, *What do I do now?* Smiling softly, I simply shook my head and turned to leave. There was only one thing I knew to do to win a man over. Use your body.

"Where are you going?" Alex said sharply, making me jump from the sudden sound.

I froze in place, my hand barely touching the doorknob. Glancing over my shoulder, I found him glaring at me, his deep-rooted scowl still in place.

"It's dangerous out there," he growled, his frown and fury all melding into one menacing expression.

"You don't actually have a claim on me," I told him, my tone matter-of-fact. "So if it's all right with you, I'm going to check this place out. Besides, I need to find us some food." Glancing down at myself, I wrinkled my nose. "Maybe even some clothes that fit. And I definitely need a bath, and I don't need a chaperone, not with your initials forever branded into my skin." My last words were said with the intonation of bitterness I was feeling. Lifting my arm, I flashed Alex his initials that were now forever marked on my wrist.

Alex's eyes darkened with something close to guilt, and I could tell he felt bad about the branding. I wasn't upset with him because it wasn't his fault, but I remained silent, letting him steep in his guilt.

"Fine," he eventually spat, snarling. Then he looked at Leisel, and his scowl deepened.

"You should go too," he told her, his tone harsher than I'd ever heard it before. "You need to wash up for tonight, right?" He laughed once, a sharp, humorless bark, then turned away from her, his eyes once again trained on the ground below.

Rolling my eyes, I sighed loudly. Alex's moods were giving me whiplash. Which was probably fitting, considering how annoying it must have been for him to have dealt with Leisel and me, and our constant ups and down during the last few weeks.

Still, Leisel looked as if she might cry; her chin was trembling, and her hands beginning to shake. I was about to say something snarky in return, something to lighten the mood, until I noticed the fire in her eyes. It was a small one, but it was there, hidden amongst all her tears and fears. That fire created a warm sensation deep down in my belly, causing me to smile with pride.

"What about your claim on us—on me?" she said, her tone surprisingly snarky. "Are you sure you want me wandering around without you and your leash?"

She was trying for angry, but she'd never pulled off angry very well, coming across instead as a stubborn, headstrong child. Alex turned, staring down at her, his eyes softening the longer he watched her attempt to keep up this silly angry charade. Eventually her features gentled, and then she gazed up at him in that beseeching way I remembered from before. When she'd want something new for the house, something expensive that Thomas believed was frivolous or too extravagant. He'd always caved. Always. And Alex was no different. Only a moment passed before Alex's shoulders slumped in defeat.

She reached for him again, and this time he didn't flinch away from her. This time he wrapped one arm around her waist and pulled her against his chest. Her face lifted and his lowered, and they gazed into each other's eyes in a way that suddenly made me feel as if I was a Peeping Tom, intruding on a private, intimate moment.

Smirking to myself, I started to leave the room when Alex's sudden shout of protest sounded behind me.

"Eve! Stop! If you're dead set on going, then let's all go take a look around."

I turned back to look at him, a little stunned that he was relenting so easily. Though, I knew firsthand the effect Leisel had on those who loved her.

"Until we all know what type of people they are," he continued. "I think we need to stick together." He frowned at me, and I frowned right back.

"You mean you want me to stick with you," I said pointedly.

Folding his arms across his chest, he glared at me. "If it means that you're safer, then yeah, that's exactly what I mean."

I had opened my mouth to protest when Leisel stepped forward, interrupting our argument before it could even begin. "I think he has a point, Eve. I'd feel safer if we were all together."

Huffing in annoyance, I rolled my eyes to the ceiling, pissed off that she had chosen to play that card on me. She knew I would never turn her down, that I would never dismiss how she felt. I always wanted her to feel safe; in fact, I needed her to.

"Fine," I snapped. "Fine."

The air was cooler outside, daytime giving way to early evening, abandoning the stifling heat of the sun in favor of the moon. It was quieter now, lights shining from inside several of the buildings.

This place was creepier now that nightfall was approaching, now that it was quieter and almost deserted, apart from the odd person scampering from one building to another. Shadows, big and black, cast on us as we traveled through what suddenly seemed eerily like a deserted town, tall structures towering over us from either side.

It somewhat freaked me out, feeling all too similar to when the outbreak had first begun. Our hometown had been busy, always bustling with life, until the infection had hit. Then all too soon it had grown quiet, each street seeming darker than the last.

This place—Purgatory—had not so long ago been teeming with life, yet with the setting of the sun had gone nearly silent. The only sound I could easily discern was a low beat, a mixture of bass and loud whispered words, coming from somewhere within one of the structures. I looked up at Alex to find his features creased with irritation, as if the music provoked him somehow, and with each step toward it, he seemed to grow even more standoffish.

Yet we continued to follow the beat, making our way through the winding paths between the buildings, hunting out the source of the noise until we found ourselves in front of a smaller building nestled between two of the larger ones.

I stared up at it in wonderment. I hadn't heard music in such a long time, even in Fredericksville, for fear it would attract the infected. But these people were almost brazen with their noise levels. It scared me, yet at the same time, I couldn't deny the excitement that welled inside me.

I turned to Alex and Leisel, finding the same wonder-filled, excited expression on her face, though Alex looked more pissed off than anything else, irritation still rolling off him in waves.

His hand was latched onto Leisel's, their fingers interlocked. He surveyed the building warily, swallowing slowly, his Adam's apple bobbing in his throat.

"We should get back to the room," he said, already turning to leave and pulling Leisel along with him.

"Alex," she protested, digging her heels into the ground.

"Really?" I snapped. "You're going to leave? Just like that?"

He turned back, his shoulders already sagging in defeat as he glanced at Leisel and saw the disappointment creasing her features.

"It's noisy in there," he said, to which I rolled my eyes. "It could be dangerous. We don't know these people."

Snorting, I gestured toward the sky as I held my arms wide open. "Alex, look at where we are. This whole place is dangerous, this whole fucking world is dangerous!"

His mouth pressed into a thin, hard line. "This is different," he said flatly. He was a man of so very little words, always using simple straightforward sentences, very rarely showing any sort of emotion, though right now I could tell I was pissing him off.

He looked down at Leisel, at her pleading expression, the one that had always gotten her exactly what she'd wanted when she'd been with Thomas. I held back a smile, waiting and watching as Alex's willpower began to crumble.

"Please, Alex?" she whispered sweetly, too sweetly, even for Leisel. "We can just take a look around. We'll leave if you don't like it. I promise."

Alex glanced between Leisel and me, and a frustrated noise erupted from the back of his throat. Frustrated, yet defeated.

"Fine," he conceded unhappily, "but you stay next to me at all times."

"Deal," I answered. Even as much as I hated having to answer to anyone, I would do it if it meant I got to listen to music, for the first time in what seemed like forever.

Frowning at me, Alex shook his head and started for the door. Inside, it wasn't dark like I had expected it to be. In fact, it was lit all along the hallway, as if the lighting was meant to lead us to an underground den. We followed the path down a flight of stairs, passing by other people, couples who barely gave us a second glance. Their eyes were glazed over, and their hands far too busy with each other to notice, or care, about our little trio.

At the end of a second hallway, the narrow space abruptly opened into a large, yet infinitely darker room, my eyes struggling to adjust to the dimmer, drearier lighting. Despite the size of the room, it was cramped, chokingly so in places, filled with bodies pressed against one another in a strange macabre dance, moving together in a perfect yet chaotic mayhem. Heat poured off the dancing crowd in waves, thick and stifling, yet the beat chilled me, the sounds of an earlier lifetime dancing eerily over my skin like a ghost, raising the hairs on my arms and the back of my neck.

When we reached the edge of the throbbing crowd, Alex grabbed hold of my hand as he edged closer to Leisel, pulling her tightly against him. I understood his fear. This place, it was strangely intoxicating. I could already sense it—the ambience—making us forget, pulling us apart. Suddenly, I was lonelier than ever in a room full of people.

"Can we dance?" Leisel shouted. Her eyes were round; she was obviously electrified by the sight. She'd always loved to dance, yet never in public. This would be a first for her…if Alex allowed it.

Before Alex could answer, the crowd surged against us, knocking us backward and separating my hand from Alex's. Grabbing a nearby arm, I was easily able to regain my footing, yet I had lost sight of Alex and Leisel entirely.

I continued searching, pushing and shoving my way through the mass of people, sweaty bodies pressing up against me as sweat trailed down my back.

A warm breath danced against my ear. "You shouldn't be here."

Startled, I turned, shocked at the sight of pitch-black eyes meeting my own, eyes that seemed to suck the air straight from my lungs. He was a large man, twice my size, even taller than Alex. His arms were heavily tattooed with dark images that ran up and down the length of them. His neck was thicker than my thigh, his dark hair shaved into a short Mohawk that began at his widow's peak, ending at his neck. A beard as dark as his hair framed a squared and hard jawline. All in all, he was an intimidating man, but it was his eyes that terrified me. They were an angry, dark, coal-burning black, with a deep-rooted intensity that made my stomach start to ache.

I glanced around, searching for Alex and Leisel but finding neither. Glancing back at the man, his features almost lost in the darkness, I swallowed hard.

"I can handle myself."

A slow grin arose on his mouth. "Didn't doubt it."

Something like pride sparked to life inside me. Maybe it was what he'd said—believing that I could actually handle myself—or maybe it was the way he'd said it. Either way, I found myself smiling at the compliment, and my cheeks flushed.

Tilting his head, he gestured for me to follow him, and for some reason I did. Though I knew it was ridiculous to follow this man—a complete stranger, and an intimidating one at that—I couldn't seem to stop myself.

Trailing after him, I watched his large frame move through the crowd as people everywhere hurriedly moved from his path. Who was he that they regarded him in such a way? Was it fear? Or was it respect?

We came to stop at a table, one of many set up in the far end of the room. He sat first, watching me as I emerged from the thick throng of people. Hot and sweaty, I wiped a hand across my forehead, feeling somewhat nervous, but infinitely more reckless. This place was a drug, an aphrodisiac tempting me on to a path that I knew was wrong.

Taking the seat opposite him, I watched as he laid his forearms on the table, enabling me to clearly see his many tattoos. Numerous skulls trailed up both his arms, disappearing under the sleeves of his T-shirt.

He seemed even bigger now that he was seated, his imposing stature engulfing both his chair and the small table between us. My eyes darted up to meet his, and I found him watching me intently with a strange expression on his face, a mixture of longing and anger.

"Lots of skulls," I said lamely, my gaze dropping to his arms.

"One for every kill," he said matter-of-factly, as if this was something every person did when they killed an infected.

My thoughts trailed off as my eyebrows rose. "Infected?" I asked. "Or people?"

His lips curved into a grin, yet he didn't bother to respond. A scantily dressed woman appeared at our table, diverting his attention as she set down a drink in front of him. He picked up the glass and took a long swallow, then offered it to me.

I could smell it from where I sat, the bitter tang that emanated from all liquor, knowing that this was not the sort of man you simply took a drink from. He was dangerous; I knew that much just from looking at him. But as I continued to study him, I realized he wasn't just dangerous, he literally radiated danger. Violence. From every pore on his skin, every taut, bulky muscle in his body.

And yet, I found myself reaching across the table, taking what he offered, then brought it to my lips and swallowed the burning, foul-smelling liquid. Feeling oddly like Alice in Wonderland, I licked a spilled drop from my bottom lip as the rest of the swallow burned a hot path down my throat.

"This one is mine."

I glanced up, surprised to find Alex and Leisel standing beside me. Grabbing my arm, Alex pulled up my shirtsleeve, showing this man the brand on my wrist. My gaze flitted to Leisel, her big brown eyes watching me, radiating something like pity. I swallowed back a wave of shame. She knew me, knew how I worked, how I'd always worked, the things I did to fill the emptiness inside. Though my guilt and shame were obvious, my anger probably wasn't. And I was suddenly so very angry.

Looking away, I found the man across from me glaring up at Alex before looking back at me. I shrugged apologetically, suddenly feeling like a moron for forgetting my place. It was imperative that the people here believed I did actually belong to Alex. For my own protection, and for Leisel's.

Nostrils flaring wildly, the man pushed away from the table and cast hard glances at both Alex and me before walking off, his retreating form instantly swallowed by the pulsating crowd. Watching him, my chest began to ache—for the freedom he had, able to just get up and walk away. To get lost in a crowd, in the dark.

"We're leaving," Alex said, his expression one that brooked no argument. Neither Leisel nor I protested.

CHAPTER TWENTY-SEVEN

Leisel

"EVE?" I WHISPERED, nudging Evelyn's shoulder lightly. An incomprehensible murmur slipped past her lips in response, signaling to me that she was sound asleep. Sighing, unable to sleep myself, I pushed up on the musty mattress and surveyed the dark room. Finding Alex seated upright in the armchair, his head lolling off to one side and his eyes closed, I rolled off the mattress and tiptoed carefully across the floor.

"Hey," I whispered, bending down and placing my hand gently on his knee. Alex's eyes flew open and he shot up and out of his chair, startling me and sending me falling backward.

"What?" he said loudly, his eyes darting wildly back and forth. "What's wrong?"

"Nothing!" I whispered. Getting to my feet, I glared at him. "Shh! You're going to wake Eve."

As understanding dawned on his face, his shoulders relaxed and his panicked expression morphed to confusion. "Why are you awake?" he asked. "Are you okay?"

Reaching for him, I nodded slowly. "I couldn't sleep," I said, and fitted my body against his. His arms encircled me and he moved us backward as one, dropping back down onto the chair and bringing me with him.

Curling into his lap, I wound my arms around his neck and pressed a kiss to his jaw. "You're starting to look like a mountain man," I said softly, smiling against his beard.

"I don't like it here," he said in response as he stared off across the room. "I want to try and get as much as we can as quickly as we can, and then keep moving. I don't trust this place."

"It's better than nothing." I pulled away from him somewhat, disappointment coursing through me at his lack of response to my kiss.

I didn't trust this place either, but as far as I could tell there were no forced marriages happening here, no religious zealots feeding the living to the dead. And the brand still stinging on my wrist gave me a sense of comfort I'd never thought possible from a tattoo. We each had to work to stay, to contribute, but we were able to carry weapons to protect ourselves, we had a bed to sleep on and the promise of food and water come tomorrow. It was almost too good to be true, yet I found myself not wanting to wait for the other shoe to drop, just for once to not be consumed by fear of the unknown.

Alex didn't respond. His gaze remained fixed on the shadows cast by the moonlight on the opposite wall, but he lifted his hand and slipped it beneath the back of my shirt, settling it heavily on the small of my back. His warm, comforting touch caused a small sigh of pleasure to escape me. Arching my neck, I moved in to kiss him again as Evelyn emitted a small noise in her sleep, the springs in the mattress creaking loudly as she rolled over restlessly, then nestled herself against the wall.

"I'm worried about her," I whispered, watching her legs twitch.

Alex's gaze moved to her fidgety form. Frowning deeply, he shook his head. "She was stupid tonight."

"You don't understand her," I whispered. "She needs..." I bit my bottom lip, unable to find the words to convey why Evelyn did the things she did without making her sound like a slut.

Though I knew Alex was right, she had been stupid tonight, I also recognized how lonely she was, still suffering from the loss of Jami. It was how she dealt with it, using men—using her body to fill the loss. It was how she kept going.

"No," he said flatly. "I understand her. Jami wasn't the first guard she hooked up with. And he wouldn't have been the last. They all talked about her—"

"Don't," I snapped, sitting up straight and shrugging his hand off my back. "You don't get to talk about her like that. You don't understand her."

Alex's hard gaze focused on me. "Lei," he said gently, "I get it. We all deal with shit differently. But she can't do this here. She could get hurt. She could put us all in danger. That guy she was with, he was pissed. She should have been up front with him."

Feeling calmer, I relaxed in his lap, nestling my head in the crook of his neck. "She doesn't know who she is without a man," I whispered. "It's not her fault."

Again, his hand found my back, traveling upward, higher than before, his fingertips lingering on each bump of my spine. I shivered slightly at his touch, wrapping my arm around his firm waist.

I still felt the same sort of restlessness as when we'd been on the road, itching for something more with Alex. But as he simply cuddled me closer, continuing his gentle exploration of my back, I knew I wasn't going to get it, not without expressing exactly what it was I wanted. It would mean being bold, more so than I'd ever been before, and taking matters into my own hands, something I wasn't used to doing when it came to the opposite sex.

"Get some sleep, Lei," Alex murmured, then dropped his face into my hair. "We all need it."

"Alex..." I pulled away, glancing up at him through my lashes, suddenly feeling foolish. When he glanced down at me, his gaze questioning, I swallowed hard and cleared my throat. "I don't want to sleep," I said, and pressed my fingertips into his skin, willing him to understand. "We're safe right now." Glad for the darkness, glad that he couldn't see the blush I could feel creeping up my neck, undoubtedly coloring my cheeks, I said, "Eve is asleep..."

Alex's eyes met mine as a small, knowing smile curved his lips. His hand pulled free of my shirt and lifted to the back of my head, cupping it. I leaned forward, eager for his mouth, my own hand digging more deeply into the skin on his side.

Our mouths met softly, too softly for what I was feeling, and I instantly deepened the kiss while maneuvering my body until I was straddling him. The broken chair beneath us tilted precariously but I couldn't have cared less; I was already lost to him, to what he made me feel when he was kissing me, touching me.

He grew hard beneath me, and the knowledge of that only furthered my want. Of their own accord my lips moved faster, my tongue delving deeper as I pulled his shirt up over his abdomen, then greedily ran my hands over the rippled muscles covering his stomach.

Alex had such a beautiful body, soft but hard, powerful and strong, and I needed more of it, needed more of him than he'd given me yet. Reaching between us, I fumbled with his belt, the desires of my body now overriding any embarrassment I'd felt. Continuing to kiss him, I pulled his belt open, softly rocking my hips over his.

"Lei." Breaking our kiss, he circled his fingers around my wrists and pulled my hands from his pants.

Breathing hard, I blinked, focusing on his face. "Don't," I whispered. "Don't make me stop again."

Tears formed in my eyes, born of frustration without an outlet. I was instantly embarrassed, but more angry than anything. Twisting my arms in his hold, I tried to free myself, but his grip only tightened.

"Not with Eve in the room," he said.

"She's asleep!" I hissed. "She won't care!"

"She will care," he said. "You know she will."

My body went lax, disappointment causing me to sink listlessly against him. He was right; she would care. And after tonight, with her being so careless with a strange man, if she happened to wake up…

"Dammit," I whispered as a tear slipped free. My body ached while my thoughts spun wildly. I wanted to let go for a moment, to feel instead of think, to get lost in the tornado Alex created inside me whenever we kissed.

"Lei, don't." Releasing my wrists, Alex hugged me tightly, bringing me flush against him. I tried to fight him, to pull away, the closeness of him only increasing the maelstrom of need still flurrying within me, but he didn't relent, pressing my body hard against his.

"Shh," he whispered, his voice raspy, more affected by our circumstances than I'd thought. His hips raised slightly, pressing forward between my thighs, causing me to whimper as the throbbing ache there grew stronger.

If possible, his hold on me grew even tighter, making my already shortened breaths come faster and harder. His hips retreated and returned as he dragged the length of himself purposefully against me.

Biting down on my lip, I buried my face in his shoulder, allowing my body to relax as best I could. He repeated those same movements, stoking the already raging fire inside me to a roaring intensity, bringing me to that edge I was craving, time and time again until I finally reached it and fell weightlessly over the cliff. I floated on air, my body throbbing, humming, as I fell into oblivion.

As I sagged against him, he loosened his grip on me, and for a moment neither of us spoke, both of us breathing heavily as the sound of my own heartbeat echoed loudly in my ears.

"What about you?" I eventually managed to whisper. He was still hard beneath me, his body still pulsing, trembling ever so slightly.

Choking out a quiet laugh, he pressed a kiss to the top of my head. "It's been three years," he said, his tone full of humor. "I can wait another day."

I pulled back from him and sat up straight, meeting his dark gaze. His eyes dropped down, taking in all of me, my heaving chest and my quivering legs, before returning to my face.

"Three years?" I whispered, shocked. "You haven't been with anyone... No one in Fredericksville?"

Alex said nothing, easily falling back into his typical silence. But words weren't needed in that moment; his eyes spoke volumes. His feelings for me, I could only guess, went far deeper than I'd ever realized, or could have ever imagined they would.

Not knowing how to respond, I dropped my head, pressing my cheek against his chest as I closed my eyes.

CHAPTER TWENTY-EIGHT

Evelyn

I WAS HUNGRY.
    I was always hungry, but this was a need of a different type, an angry hunger that I could feel straight through to my bones. Part of me was afraid of having to fight, yet a sick part of me was eager to beat on someone—to hit, kick, scratch, do whatever the fuck I needed to rid myself of my anger.

The pain I wrestled with on a daily basis made me more than angry, pissed off with myself and everyone else. My rollercoaster emotions, and my frustration with this whole damn crazy-assed world were spilling forth, trying to breach the surface. It was all too much, like a pan of boiling water precariously bubbling over, that any moment was going to spatter, making a mess too hot to clean up.

I had heard Leisel and Alex last night, heard their heated whispers, listened to their heavy, lust-filled panting. I hadn't meant to, but once I woke up I was unable to fall back to sleep. And so I had lain there, my lashes damp from silent tears, my thoughts dark and angry, feeling cold and alone until morning had finally come.

Quietly, I crept from the mattress, and after slipping my feet into my boots, I turned to look back at them. They were curled up together in the chair, Leisel looking small in Alex's arms. They were perfect for each other, complementary, the yin to the other's yang, and I was happy for them. Happy that they had found each other in such a shit-filled, horrible world. He would be good to her in the way that she deserved, in the way that Thomas would have been.

My chin trembling, I quickly left the room, clicking the door silently closed behind me. I leaned back against it, the realization that I no longer needed to stand tall for Leisel was a foreign thing for me. Knowing that now I only needed to be strong for myself, that I could finally take a breath, take a hundred breaths if I needed to, was an incredibly hard adjustment. I imagined that it was something like what a parent experienced the moment they realized their child was growing up, wasn't as dependent on them as they once had been. It was an empty sort of feeling, and inexplicably lonely as well.

I rushed down the hallway to the stairs, suddenly desperate for fresh air. But when I pushed outside the heavy doors, I was greeted with the smoky scent of fire pits and the bitter tang of body sweat, the oaky smell of alcohol brewing, and the unmistakable scent of sex, all hanging thickly in the air.

I continued on, feeling the stares of eyes everywhere, watching me, appraising me from head to toe as if I were prime beef at a cattle market. Unnerved, I kept walking, refusing to look down, to look anywhere but directly in front of me. They could look all they wanted, look down at me as if I were little more than an object or something to trade, but I knew differently. I was a woman, a survivor, just like everyone else here. Even if they refused to treat me with the respect I deserved, I was determined not to fall victim to it.

As I explored the area, weaving around buildings, going farther than we'd ventured last night, I was surprised to discover that Purgatory was even larger than we'd first thought. There were pathways everywhere, leading between buildings, and something was happening at every turn, on every corner.

It was overwhelming at first, especially after being on our own with only endless miles of nothingness surrounding us. Even back in Fredericksville, it hadn't been like this. Things were quiet and organized there, everything and everyone in their rightful place. This was far different, an organized sort of chaos. It was noisy and smelly and crazy, filled with so many people from different walks of life, all simply trying to survive.

Suddenly, I found myself no longer angry with them, not even at the men staring at me as I passed them. Instead, I shared a sense of common ground. None of us had anything left, and we were all doing what we could to make this life somewhat worth it—worth living through the horror, even if that meant using the only thing we had left to barter with. Men had their fists; women had their bodies. We used, we abused, just like in the old world, but at least here, this seemed to be accomplished with some element of control. At least here it was an honest and up-front way of life. They didn't hide what they were or what they wanted, not like in Fredericksville where everything was done behind closed doors. Here there was no upper class, no middle class, and no lower class, we were all on equal footing, and there was a surprisingly strange comfort in that fact.

Stopping, I stared at the small bodies of animals roasting on top of a metal barrel that had been fitted with a grill, flames burning low from inside its depths. Their fur had been stripped, revealing the soft, meaty flesh beneath, and the scent coming off their quickly crisping bodies was utterly delectable.

Behind the barrel, both a man and woman were working the grill, flipping the animals, replacing the fully cooked with new pink meat. I watched them work for a moment, noticing that the woman had a similar brand on her wrist, as well as a wedding ring on her finger. She was pretty in a basic sort of way, clean and pale, with long brown hair tied back in a low ponytail.

"You from the wild?" she asked, her voice surprisingly rough, like that of a pack-a-day chain-smoker.

"The wild?" I asked, hungrily staring down at the meat. Jeffers had said something similar, but I had no idea what he'd meant.

"Out there," the man answered and glanced behind me, past the electrified fences, beyond the gates. "The wild."

He was clean shaven, and I could see the small scars that covered both his chin and neck. He watched me a moment, looking thoughtful while running his tongue along the edge of crooked yellow teeth.

"Oh," I replied. "Yeah, I am."

"How is it?" the woman asked, her hands still busy working the grill. She was in the process of skinning a rat, deftly freeing its wrinkled skin from its little body, revealing the muscle underneath, and placed the fur in a neat pile with the rest. "Is it still—"

"You know it is," the man interrupted her gruffly, giving her a hard glare. "Don't ask stupid questions." He turned to me, his irritation evident. "You buying?"

"I, um, how do I buy something?" Rat or not, I was famished. "I don't have anything."

"Then you ain't buying," he replied harshly, turning his attention to the small crowd that had formed behind me. As my stomach continued to growl, the woman threw me an apologetic glance before resuming her work.

Wishing I had pockets to sulkily shove my hands into, I stepped away, resuming my walk.

I passed by clothing stalls, homemade jewelry for sale, accoutrements of all kinds, even little corner cafés that boasted homebrewed beer. At the mere thought of a cold beer, of the frothy liquid running down my throat, my mouth began to water.

"Hey!" a deep gravelly voice called out from behind me. "Hey, woman!"

A heavy hand landed on my shoulder and I flinched. Snatching the hand that was holding me, I twisted it, pushing backward. Jumping away and spinning around, I found the bearded man from last night stumbling backward. As he caught his balance, all the while glaring at me, I noticed the food in his hand—two grilled rats on skewers.

"Oh shit," I mumbled. "I'm so sorry, I didn't know. I'm a little jumpy."

Snickers erupted all around us, making the man's already deadly expression darken. Angrily, he thrust a cooked rat in my direction, grunting at me to take it. And I wanted to, I really did, but how could I? How could I trust him? Nothing was free, not anymore. Not even what appeared to be a simple act of kindness.

But I was hungry, God, I was so hungry. Yet this man didn't seem like the type of person I'd want to owe anything to.

"I'm not hungry," I lied, holding his stare, though my eyes were burning with the need to look away.

"Eat it," he grumbled. "You're too skinny." He dropped his eyes, purposefully raking his heavy gaze up and down my body, and again thrusting out the rat in offering. I stared at it, at the fat dripping from its body over this man's thick, dirty fingers, making them glisten in the sunlight. Then I looked up into his face, wondering what hands like his could do, the sort of painful damage they could inflict.

"I said I'm not hungry," I repeated, holding my chin high, yet my voice was a mere whisper.

His beard twitched as he fought the urge to smile. "You the fighter, right?" he asked. "New girl from the wild?"

Still staring up at him, I could only nod in response.

"Then I need you to eat, because I'll be betting on you." Grinning, he fixed his eyes on mine as he took a bite of one rat, sinking his teeth into the flesh, easily tearing the meat away from the small bones. I decided then that his grin made him handsome, though not a typical sort of handsome like Alex. No, this man looked far too menacing to be considered simply handsome.

"I'm someone else's," I said and flashed him my brand as Alex had last night, suddenly glad to have it there. "As you know."

"I'm aware," he said flatly, and again thrust the meat toward me.

My stomach decided to take that very moment to growl loudly, something this man found extremely amusing. His mouth still full of rat, he began to chuckle. "Just take the damn food, woman. I won't ask you again."

My stomach burning with hunger, I relented and accepted the rat. But just as I brought it to my mouth, ready to tear into it, he spoke again.

"You better win for me, Wildcat." Tossing me another grin, he turned and walked off.

"It's Evelyn," I yelled after him obstinately. "Not fucking Wildcat."

I stared after him for a moment before realizing I still had food in my hand, and instantly the man was forgotten. Biting into the rat, the taste of well-cooked meat exploding in my mouth, I groaned loudly. Ravenous, I took another bite, then another, smiling as I wiped an errant drop of grease that found its way to my chin, then sucked on my finger. Soon, I had nothing left but a pair of greasy hands and a small pile of bones.

Pleasantly full, I walked on, searching out a garbage can or some other means of disposing of the bones.

"A moment on the lips, a lifetime on the hips," a breathy voice announced from behind me.

I jumped and turned around, coming face-to-face with a woman in a darkened doorway, her body looking somewhat distorted by the shadows.

"I'm Dori," she said as a wide smile grew across her full pink lips. A dainty hand slipped free of the darkness in offering, and I took it. Her gaze dropped to my brand, and still holding tightly to my hand, she nodded. "Seems fresh."

"It is," I told her. "I just got here." Trying to pull my hand free, I found her grip oddly strong and unrelenting.

"That's a shame," she said, finally releasing me. Her own hand still lingered in the air between us, her gaze dropping to the bones in my other hand. Smiling broadly, she gestured for me to hand them over. With a frown, I did, watching as she greedily sucked the marrow from the small bones, reminding me of myself only moments ago.

Uncomfortable, I moved to leave, and it was only then that I was able to finally see her, all of her as the remaining sunlight pierced the shadows. She was nearly naked, her top so sheer I could see her two rosebud nipples peeking through. My eyes traveled lower, then widened considerably.

"Don't judge," she said, then wheeled herself forward and into view.

"I wasn't, I…I…" I was desperately trying not to stare at the empty space where her legs should have been, but the more I tried to look away, the longer I found myself staring.

"Sure you were," she said with a laugh. "It's okay. I'm just lucky that I still have a hole for these assholes to fill." She laughed again, a dainty chuckle that matched her dainty hands and pretty face.

Realization slapped me in the face. A hole for them to fill…and my stomach began to churn.

"Ain't much a girl like me is good for in a place like this, but you'd be surprised what men like these days." She grinned again, and I suddenly felt downright sick. My newly digested rat was quickly turning to stone in the pit of my belly.

I struggled to think of a reply, the silence between us uncomfortably awkward. "What did you do before?" I blurted out, instantly wishing I could take the words back.

"I was a professional cheerleader," she answered, unbothered by my question. She laughed again, louder this time, as if her answer was the funniest thing she'd ever said, and I couldn't help but laugh with her. If I hadn't laughed, I probably would have cried.

In the midst of our laugher, a shadow fell over me, and I turned to find a man sidling up beside me. He was slim, not just the half-starved look of some of the men around here, but really thin, his skin pockmarked and greasy. As he looked me up and down, a leery smile arose on his face.

"Uh-uh." Dori chastised him immediately. "Not this one, Steven, this one's claimed." In a flash, his smile vanished, replaced quickly with a frown.

"Baby, don't pout," she crooned. "You know I always take good care of you. What did you bring me today?"

He held up a small filthy bottle of water, though I couldn't tell if it was actually water inside or if the bottle was just that dirty.

"And?" Dori asked with a soft smile.

Outstretching his other hand, he revealed a small packet of white powder. A greedy, eager smile lit up his features.

"Perfect," Dori purred, pulling open her blouse.

Steven's eyes were now solely on her, glazing over as his tongue darted out to slide slowly across his bottom lip. When I glanced back to Dori, I found her hand had disappeared somewhere beneath the layers of fabric pooling at her waist. As he pushed past me, Steven slyly rubbed a hand across my backside, and then together, the two of them disappeared inside the building.

I stared after them a moment, still sick to my stomach.

"What the fuck have we gotten ourselves into?" I muttered to myself.

CHAPTER TWENTY-NINE

Leisel

"YOU'LL DO," BETHANY said as she lifted her chin and sniffed the air around me. "At least you don't smell like week-old garbage anymore."

Narrowing my eyes, I turned away from the girl before she could see the snarl twisting my lips. It was bad enough that in only a few short minutes I would be dancing for a crowd of drunken perverts. I didn't need to add complications with my coworkers into the mix. While Bethany wasn't a dancer, she would still be working the crowd, giving it up to whoever could afford her.

Surveying the crowded dressing room, which was more or less a broom closet, I found my reflection in one of three full-length mirrors lined up against the back wall. Swallowing back a wave of nervousness, I ran my hands down the sheer material covering my body. It was supposed to be a dress, but in reality it was more like half a dress. Although the sleeves were long and the neck was high, the flimsy, nearly see-through black mesh barely covered my backside. Underneath it I was wearing a matching bra and thong made of finely scalloped lace I'd been given, both a deep shade of red. All in all, combined with my freshly washed hair that was brushed to shiny perfection, and my smoky eyes and matching red lipstick, it was a very sexual look. Sexy even, without being overly slutty...if it were something I'd be sharing with only one man, not an entire room full.

However, I had a plan, a little trick I'd learned thanks to Lawrence's cruelty. It had happened by accident at first, during one of his many beatings. I'd just suddenly slipped away, finding myself emotionally and mentally detached from my body, as if I were watching the abuse instead of experiencing it firsthand. I planned to apply that same method, escaping my here and now, to my dancing tonight. I would close my eyes, find a happy memory somewhere deep inside me, and use that as my rock, as my anchor that would see me through.

"Dancers! Get ready to take your places!"

An older woman called Mattie, with long black hair heavily intermixed with sparkling strands of silver, clapped her hands together in earnest. She was, for lack of a better word, my boss, and more importantly, the madam of Purgatory. She handled all of the women, more or less, responsible for designating them to certain areas of the complex to sell themselves. She also distributed the girls' payment, as well as clothing and accessories, pretty much all the things an old-world madam had done, Mattie did as well.

She was surprisingly kind, a once-handsome woman with a sharp edge about her that I instantly appreciated. In a way, she reminded me of Evelyn, beautiful yet gruff, rough around the edges but with a heart of gold.

"New girl!" she called out, beckoning me with two fingers. "You first."

When no one else made a move toward her, I glanced around me, looking at the other girls for an idea of why I was being made to go first. Was this some sort of cruel new-girl initiation?

"Go, little mouse," Bethany said, obviously taking her cues from Liv as she gave me a not-so-gentle shove on my shoulder. "Nobody's here yet, the doors open in five. And you're going to need a minute to adjust."

My stomach did a funny sort of dip straight down into my intestines as my already sky-high anxiety skyrocketed. Adjust to what, I wondered. The possibilities were endless, and as my imagination ran away with itself, all of them seemed more horrific than the last.

Despite my fears, I dutifully placed one foot in front of the other, grateful that I hadn't been forced to wear heels. I could dance, yes, but in heels? No. Although I wasn't too sure how sanitary it was to be walking around Purgatory barefooted, at least I didn't have to worry about falling flat on my face.

Together, Mattie and I left the dressing room and entered the bar, aptly named the Drunk Tank, which was still silent and empty, with the exception of several men who were busying themselves behind the bar. The space was huge, the size of a high school gymnasium, and had been fitted with mismatched low-hanging chandeliers. It was filled with tables of all shapes and sizes, painted much like the rest of Purgatory, in a rainbow of colors without rhyme or reason.

"Lower the cages!" Mattie called out, snapping her fingers.

One of the bartenders, a burly-looking man with a shaved head and his arms covered in tattoos, jumped up and over the bar. With a salute in Mattie's direction, he headed toward what looked to be a set of gears affixed to the wall. His muscles bulging, he raised a heavy-duty lever and the gears began to turn, slowly at first, gradually speeding up. A grinding, clicking sound erupted from above me, and I watched as large wrought-iron cages came cascading down from the high vaulted ceiling.

My hand clasped over my mouth and I stumbled backward, again grateful for the absence of heels. Half of the cages were empty, but the other half…were not.

"Don't be afraid," Mattie said kindly. "They can't hurt you."

Gaping up at the occupied cages, I made a choking sound behind my hand. No, they definitely couldn't hurt me. They were missing half their faces, their lower jaws appeared to have been sawed off entirely and their eyes plucked from their heads, but none of those facts made such a gruesome sight any less horrible.

I surveyed the caged infected, noting that all of them had once been women. Some were naked, their sagging breasts and rotting genitals exposed to all who cared to look, while others were dressed in skimpy, sexy clothing, much like the ensemble I was wearing.

All in all, it was a heartbreaking sight. Yes, they were no longer human. Yes, they were monsters who, if given the chance, would destroy every last one of us. But once upon a time, back when the world had been something worth remembering, they had been people—women. Mothers, sisters, daughters, and friends. Why couldn't these people see that? Didn't they remember? Didn't they care?

"But why?" I stammered out between choking breaths.

"Because nothing goes unpunished around here, and men like to be victorious over their conquests."

I frowned harder as my head began to pound. What was wrong with these people that they would think there was anything okay with any of this? Did they find it sexually satisfying? Seeing women caged and rotting away? Sick to my stomach, I clasped my belly as it twisted in on itself, matching the fear that climbed up my spine.

"Listen to me," Mattie said forcefully as she took my shoulders in her firm grip. "If you cry, you're going to ruin your makeup. Makeup is hard to come by these days, only reserved for my prettiest girls. I'd hate to have to punish such a beautiful face for something as trivial as makeup."

When I heard her words, the tears welling behind my eyes froze. I blinked repeatedly, trying to squelch any errant drop that dared to leak free.

"I was told you were from the wild," Mattie said, frowning at me. "Forgive me, honey, but you don't strike me as near tough enough to survive out there among the rotters."

My lips flattened, my nostrils flared, and I swallowed back any last shred of pain I was feeling for the caged infected. "I am from the wild," I said thickly. "I'm just not an animal."

Mattie clucked her tongue at me. "Now that's where you're wrong," she said, her tone as smooth as melted butter. "We're all animals. Always were. The only difference is we're no longer caged."

A vision of Lawrence, snoring peacefully in our bed, danced behind my eyes. And then of me, holding that blade over his body, my eyes wide, my hands shaking, my heart bursting…

Folding my arms across my chest, I cleared my throat and glanced around. "Which cage is mine?"

Mattie smiled. "Atta girl."

It was an eerie thing, an odd conglomeration of past and present—residents of this new world, dancing and drinking, laughing and shouting to the rhythms of the old world. It was a head-on collision of what was and what would never be again, much like the famous paintings lining the walls marred by graffiti.

It felt wrong, it looked wrong, like a dream you couldn't seem to shake. You woke up again and again, only to fall asleep and pick back up right where you'd left off. The moment the doors had opened and the crowd noisily poured inside, an odd sort of haze quickly enveloped me, leaving me feeling surreal, as if I were floating along a breeze, an incorporeal essence, and everything around me...only a mirage.

Still, I danced. I danced and I danced and I danced to the beats of yesteryear. To rap music, to hip-hop, to show tunes, and to the oddly thrown-in recordings of car commercials and the closing credits of television sitcoms. Every so often a wild-looking man would jump on top of the bar, yelling obscene things into a microphone, further winding the crowd up to the point where, even as barbaric as it was, I was glad to be locked in a cage and hanging high out of reach.

All around me, both men and women were crowded together, some half-naked, others entirely nude, their hair plastered against their faces, their sweaty bodies straining. They danced and they sang as they guzzled drink after drink, groping one another. Some even decided to have sex right then and there—on the floor, up against the wall, bent over a table or the bar—their shame left at the door.

Even stone-cold sober, I felt drugged by it all...the atmosphere, the barely restrained violence, the fervent sexuality oozing from every pore of every person.

Somewhere in this room full of bodies were Alex and Evelyn, since both of them insisted that they'd be present despite my protests. I'd thought, at first, that their presence would make the whole awful situation that much worse for me, like having an audience to your shame. Only now, unable to pinpoint anyone's face or even distinguish between the sexes, I no longer cared. In fact, I was glad for it. Glad that somewhere among all this insanity was a tether to what remained of my sanity.

And so I danced. I danced slowly, I danced wildly, I danced sexually. I raised my arms above my head and danced to the beat of my own drum. I sent my hands skimming down my body, feeling my way through the music and the wants of the screaming crowd.

I danced and danced, and I ignored them all. They shouted requests for me to take off my clothes, to pull my underwear to the side, to flash them my breasts. I ignored the glasses and lit cigarettes thrown at my cage, much as I ignored my dance partner, the infected hanging no more than three feet from me, bumbling around to a hungry beat only it could hear.

I ignored and ignored and I just danced, losing myself to it all, and yet strangely felt as if I'd found some long-lost piece of myself in the midst of it all.

When the sun finally rose, the bar emptied except for a few straggling employees. My cage was lowered, and Alex was there waiting for me.

"Hi," I whispered as I stumbled forward.

Alex's dark eyes burned. He seemed so incredibly alive in that moment, as if he were actually lit from within, his fire radiating from the inside out.

"Say something," I said softly, placing my hand on his chest. Beneath my palm, I could feel his heart racing.

"I wanted to hate it," he said slowly through gritted teeth. "You up there locked inside a cage looking…like that." His feverish gaze dropped down, taking in every exposed inch of me. My stomach flip-flopped, and I nearly found myself preening in the face of his admiration, even as lust-fueled as it was.

"And these sick shits watching you," he continued as his eyes glazed over. "Wanting to touch you, and…" He swallowed hard, his eyes never leaving me.

"But you didn't hate it," I finished gently for him.

His teeth clenched, and he shook his head slowly. "I didn't hate it."

"And?" I prompted him, wanting—no, needing—to hear what he couldn't seem to bring himself to say.

"I'm not like them, Leisel," he ground out, his eyes flashing angrily as they refocused on me. "I know I'm not like them."

My hand fisted in his shirt, and I tugged him down until our faces were nearly touching. "I know," I whispered. "But you can tell me. You can tell me you liked it, and it won't change anything." I needed to hear it from him, felt it desperately in the pit of my stomach.

He stared into my eyes, his heart pounding a furious beat beneath my fist. Then his hand slid from my back to my backside where he grabbed hold of me, bringing me flush against his body, his hand squeezing possessively. I could feel him, all of him, hard and eager, his body tense, yet trembling just beneath the surface. I knew we were being watched, could hear the whispered giggles from some of the other girls, but I didn't care. Nothing else mattered in this one moment.

"I liked it," he admitted, his voice hoarse.

I let out a sigh of relief and fatigue. I was exhausted, tired, and sore to the point where I knew I wouldn't be able to stand upright for much longer. But this moment, it was an important one, a turning point in both my life and Alex's, in our blossoming relationship, in finding our places within a world we hated, and I didn't want to dismiss it or him.

"Alex," I said, arching my neck and brushing my lips against his. "I liked that you liked it."

What I didn't say, what I couldn't even admit to myself, was that some small part of me had liked it as well. Though, for the life of me, I couldn't figure out why.

CHAPTER THIRTY

Evelyn

IT WAS MIDDAY before Leisel finally began to stir, and Alex still had yet to sleep. After carrying her back to our room, her cradled against his chest, he'd held her for hours, watching her sleep, staring at her so intently, so full of sexual energy, that I barely recognized him. Gone was the silent, brooding, usually moody man who'd saved our lives. This was an infinitely more sexual version of Alex, reminiscent of a man possessed.

As for me, I hadn't been able to stomach an entire night of watching Leisel dance in that ludicrous cage, watching the men and women below her using her body as a sexual stimulant, pleasuring themselves as they stared up at her. But Alex, he'd been the opposite, seemingly obvious to everyone else in the room, to anyone but her. With his hands shoved deep into his pockets, his eyes glazed over with raw fascination as he simply stared.

He was still staring. Leisel hadn't had the energy to even change her clothes when we'd gotten back to our room. Sprawled across the dirty mattress, she was still wearing the same provocative ensemble, and Alex still couldn't seem to take his eyes off her.

I, however, was staring at the delivery that had arrived a few hours ago for Leisel. Leisel's old clothes, and her payment for services rendered—a pitiful bag of canned food, bottled water, and a single T-shirt emblazoned with a trucking company's logo. That was her wages for an entire night of dancing nearly naked, for giving those greedy bastards a part of her she never should have had to. And how had she been repaid? With virtually nothing. Her soul and her pride were only worth a couple of meals and a lousy T-shirt.

Even worse was the stream of visitors we'd had. Mattie had dropped by first, informing us that Leisel would be working again tonight. After that, two men had knocked, wanting to speak with Alex. I hadn't told him what they had wanted, how they had tried to barter for Leisel's body. Then Liv had graced us with her horrible presence, simply to inform us that Alex and I would both be participating in the fights today.

Through it all, Leisel had slept.

"Do you think we should wake her?" I asked Alex softly.

"No," he replied without bothering to look my way, his gaze fixed firmly on her sleeping form.

My shoulders slumping, I turned back to Leisel's insulting payment and fell silent again, wondering what it would be like to be a man in this new world instead of a woman. Wishing, not for the first time, that Leisel and I didn't have to rely on Alex for safety, unable to trust anyone or anything.

"Will you be okay?" Alex asked suddenly, and I turned to face him, surprised.

"What?"

"The fight," he said, finally looking away from Leisel. "Will you be okay?"

My brows raised; I was shocked that he was even asking. "I think so," I said slowly. "I guess it depends on my opponent."

What I didn't say was that I wondered if it was going to be worth it. After seeing Leisel's meager earnings, I couldn't help but doubt it would be. It just made it clearer to me that we needed to bargain, beg, or earn what we could as quickly as we could, and then get the hell out of here. Sooner rather than later.

Alex suddenly stood, towering over me as he rolled his shoulders. His usual scowl missing, he looked younger somehow, more like the young man he would have been if the world hadn't gone to hell.

"Do you even know how to fight, Eve?" He quirked one thick, dark eyebrow in question.

Rolling my eyes, I snorted out a laugh. "Yes, Alex. I know how to fight."

"Show me," he said as he slowly approached me, his hands raised, his palms facing front.

I shrugged, figuring a bit of practice might actually be good for me. Who knew what kind of training my opponent would have? Plus, I hadn't fought in years.

Getting to my feet, I shifted my body into position, raising my arms and curling my hands into fists. Smirking, Alex circled me, assessing and judging my stance until he was once again standing in front of me.

"You've fought before," he said with a small smile, appreciation warming his eyes.

"Three years of kick boxing."

Leisel's quiet voice shocked us both, and immediately I dropped my arms and rushed to her side. As I knelt on the floor beside the mattress, Alex took a seat beside her on the bed.

"So, did I earn my millions last night?" She laughed softly, looking at me. "Am I famous now?"

"You did great," Alex answered. Glancing over top of her head, he gave me a stony look, silently telling me to keep my mouth shut regarding her pathetic earnings.

"More than great," I said, my smile suddenly strained. "How are you feeling?"

"Hungry," she replied. "Please tell me we got some food."

"Sure did." I turned away, reaching into the bag to rifle through it. I chose one can in particular, mostly because it looked to be in better shape than the rest, and pulled it free.

"Creamed corn?" I asked, doing my best to sound cheerful. Leisel's eyes flickered to the can in my hand, a sad-looking little thing that had probably been traded back and forth a hundred times before coming to us.

Meeting my eyes, a small frown furrowed her forehead as Leisel slowly shook her head. "Tell me there's more than that." Her eyes stay glued to mine, watching me intently.

"Of course there's more!" I laughed gently. "There's split pea soup, pickled asparagus, and canned pasta."

Her eyes wide, Leisel looked from me to Alex. "That's it?"

Swallowing hard, I pulled the bag out from behind me and set it down on the mattress. "That's it."

For a moment, Leisel only stared at the bag. Then all at once her nostrils flared and she angrily pawed through the bag, tossing its contents aside one by one until it was empty.

"It doesn't matter—" Alex started to say, but was abruptly cut off by Leisel, who crumpled the bag and sending it flying across the room.

Shrugging off Alex, she jumped to her feet and shouted, "It was all for nothing!"

"No, Lei." Getting to my feet, I placed my hand over her trembling arm. "It wasn't for nothing, and this is fine, this is great."

Because it was great. If you were starving—and we were—any sort of edible food was a great and wonderful thing.

"It is not fucking great, Eve!" she screamed. "This is bullshit!"

Snatching the can of creamed corn from my hand, she sent it flying across the room. It smashed into the opposite wall, nearly hitting one of the paintings hanging there before crashing to the floor and rolling behind the armchair.

Idly, I found myself wondering if this was exactly how the can had come to be in such poor condition, dented and dirty, its label peeling and stained. I inexplicably found myself feeling oddly protective over this poor can of corn, unloved and unwanted by all. Dropping to my hands and knees, I started hunting for its whereabouts.

"What are you doing?" Leisel yelled.

"Finding the stupid can," I yelled back.

"Leave it!" she screamed. "It's shit, this is all shit!"

Finally, I could see the can. As I flattened my body, stretching out my arm in an attempt to reach it, I ignored the cockroach that scuttled by my fingertips, as well as the sudden frantic beating of my heart *that* caused, until I finally found it, all alone beneath this equally sad chair. Wrapping my hand around the poor can, I dragged it free.

When I got to my feet, I found Leisel glaring at me, incensed by my actions. Suddenly, she lunged at me, reaching for the can, and I quickly darted out of her way, flinching when she tripped and stumbled into the armchair.

"This is bullshit!" she yelled as tears ran down her face, smearing what little makeup remained. "This is *all bullshit*!" Curled into fists, she brought her hands down hard against her thighs.

"You did this, Eve!" she screamed at me. "You made me go there, you made me leave, and now this is our life! This is all your fault!"

Biting down on the inside of my cheek, shame and guilt flooding me, I realized she was right. This was all my fault. I'd made her go to Fredericksville, then I'd made her leave it. And despite her protests and her willingness to die, I'd agreed to follow Bryce and Mike to their camp, to Purgatory.

This was all my fault. Her misery, her pain, it was my burden to bear.

Alex was staring at me, glaring actually, silently willing me to set the damned can down, but I couldn't, I wouldn't, and instead clutched it closer to me. I was holding this stupid can as if it were a lifeline, this poor can that nobody wanted, that nobody loved, that was only good for one thing. This sad little can that people only deemed good enough to pass along to someone else.

"Calm down, Lei," Alex said, his tone surprisingly conciliatory. Dropping beside her, he attempted to gain her attention. "Food is food. It doesn't matter. Eve and I are both fighting today, we'll earn more. Between the three of us, we'll make do."

He reached for her only to end up smacked away as Leisel began to sob again.

Making a strangled sound deep within his throat, Alex's features hardened. Grabbing hold of Leisel's wrists, he forcefully yanked her from the chair and into his lap. She struggled at first, trying to wiggle her way free from him, but he only gripped her tighter, forcing her to remain where she was. She began to cry angry tears, her sobs sounding more frustrated than sad, and eventually she gave up fighting and instead sank against him, burying her face into his chest.

"It wasn't for nothing," he said, cupping the back of her head. Leisel looked up, and directly into his eyes while Alex attempted to wipe her tears away. "You did an amazing thing, Leisel, you earned us this food." He paused briefly before continuing. "And you looked goddamn amazing doing it."

No longer crying, Leisel looked up at Alex as a blush rose in her cheeks. A moment passed by in silence, and then another and another. Then suddenly they were kissing fervently, Alex's hands buried in her hair, Leisel gripping the back of his shirt. It was noisy and messy and extraordinarily passionate, and I was left standing there feeling awkward and incredibly jealous.

It wasn't that I wasn't happy for her, for them, because I was. But I hated that I was happy for them, and I was jealous that I didn't have what they did. My thoughts quickly strayed to Jami and the ways he'd always eased my pain with his experienced hands and sinful mouth. And right then, I needed him—needed that. I needed something, someone to fill this hole inside me, to fill this hole that watching them just made worse.

Still clutching tightly to my can of corn, I padded toward the door and slipped quietly out into the hallway, forcing back my angry, bitter tears.

Once I was outside, I headed toward the marketplace, the delectable smell of grilled rat calling my name. But when I arrived, I found myself feeling guilty at the idea of trading this can for something better, something more fulfilling. It wasn't the can's fault that no one wanted it. The can was simply doing its best, making do with what it had to offer, hoping that one day someone would...

I glanced down at the can, suddenly realizing that I was being ridiculous.

"You hungry, Wildcat?"

I didn't bother to turn. I'd sensed his eyes on me the second I reached the marketplace, as if he'd been waiting here for me, waiting for me to leave my room and find him. As if he had already somehow known that I would need him.

Eventually, he came to stand in front of me, leaving me no choice but to look up at him. He looked the same as he did the day before—big, tattooed, and scary as shit. Without breaking eye contact with me, he gestured toward the man and woman manning the grill. Out of the corner of my eye, I watched them, their eyes flitting between him and me, until the man silently handed him two skewered rats without him having to ask. Or pay.

He offered one to me and as I stared down at it, still clutching tightly to my can, trickles of traitorous guilt welled inside me at the thought of giving it away. But eventually I held it out in offering, this poor can of corn, simply because I was weak. Weak and hungry.

Breaking eye contact, he glanced down at my can, his mouth twitching, his dark eyes dancing with laughter. Seconds passed, during which he still didn't take my can, and I didn't take his rat. It was him who ended our standoff, laughing and turning away. As he walked off, he glanced over his shoulder and jerked his chin, signaling that I should follow him.

As he walked off, his obscenely large frame casting dark shadows down the walkway, everywhere people hurried to move out of his way, their reactions telling me this man was exactly what I'd figured him to be. Dangerous.

Several more tense moments passed before I found myself trailing after him, part of me curious as to where he was going and wanting to know why he wanted me to follow. The other part of me already knew exactly what he wanted from me, and knew that I was going to give it to him.

Right before he was about to round a corner, he stopped, waiting for me to catch up. I didn't hurry, simply took my time reaching him, already knowing how this game worked. I'd played it before I married Shawn, and then again after I lost him. In a way, with the exception of my first marriage, my only real marriage, I'd been playing this game my whole damn life.

But for the moment, I didn't care. I needed this. Needed someone to take away the ache and fill the emptiness. Someone to quiet the insane buzzing inside my head.

Because this was what I did, this was my thing, the only way I knew how to survive. It was what I did, who I was. I needed that connection to make me believe I was complete and whole and sane again, something to still the constant churning of useless emotions that coursed through me. We all had our ways. Alex was quiet, forever internalizing his demons, always a silent soldier. Leisel was the victim, constantly relying on everyone else to save her from herself. And I was…

I was the whore.

CHAPTER THIRTY-ONE

Leisel

"YOU'RE HOLDING BACK," I accused Alex, narrowing my eyes at him. Here I was straddling his lap, wearing nothing but my lacy red bra and matching thong, and he was being so infuriatingly gentle. While his kisses had initially been demanding and full of hunger, they had slowed and softened, his touches nearly nonexistent as his hands barely skimmed over the surface of my skin. I wanted the Alex I'd seen last night, the one with the fire in his eyes, his body strung tight with wanting.

"And don't say it's because of the bruises. They're all nearly healed and you know it."

As was typical of Alex, he didn't respond, just continued to sit there, his face an unreadable mask as his hands gently held my hips.

Throwing my hands up in the air, I let out a huff. "Fine," I snapped, readying to move off him.

"Stop it," he said quietly.

I paused, glancing back at his face. "Stop what?"

"Stop acting like Evelyn."

My eyes flew open, widening. Hurriedly, I scrambled off his lap and stood. "What is that supposed to mean?"

He looked up at me, his expression still giving nothing away as to what he was truly feeling, and rolled his eyes. "You're pissed off, Lei. You're pissed and you only want to fuck because you're pissed."

"That's not true!"

Only it was true, maybe a little bit. I was pissed off, pissed that I'd been shortchanged after eight hours of continuous dancing, pissed off that I'd had to swallow my pride and my standards yet again, and pissed off at myself for blowing up at Evelyn like I had when she hadn't done anything to deserve it. And now I was pissed off at Alex for being such a big fat know-it-all.

"You wanted to last night!" I yelled, pointing at him. "So, what's the problem now? No infected around to turn you on? Or was it the other dancers that got you going? Or maybe it was—hey!"

Taking hold of my waist, Alex lifted me clear off my feet and stormed across the room with me half hanging over his shoulder. When he released me, I landed on my back on top of the mattress, and a loud whoosh of air burst past my lips. But before I could do much of anything, even blink, Alex was on top of me.

"This what you want?" He practically growled the words as he jerked down my bra strap.

With no ready response, I simply lay there, glaring up at him as he continued to somewhat violently undress me, even going as far as to rip my new underwear as he yanked it down my legs.

When I was naked beneath him, thinking he would soon kiss me, he surprised me by gripping my arm instead and flipping me over onto my stomach. I tried to push myself upright, but he was already behind me, pushing me back down.

"You want me to treat you like you're one of the whores here?"

The thought wasn't an altogether unwelcome one. I wanted to be with him. After weeks of heavy make-out sessions and every night spent lying in his arms wishing we could do more, now that we could, I very much wanted it. I wanted to be powerful, the way Evelyn was, the way she could wrap men around her finger and get what she wanted. I was sick of being the timid mouse...I was sick of being me.

"Or do you want it the way Whitney used to give it to you?"

I went utterly still, unable to even blink as I tried to process what he'd just said to me. What *Alex* had just said to me. And suddenly I couldn't see straight, or anything at all, I didn't know. All I knew is that I was screaming at the top of my lungs, and fighting desperately to twist my body free from under him. Somehow I managed, though I had no idea how. Then I was face-to-face with him, still unable to see clearly, still screaming.

My hand cracked across his handsome face, sending it flying to his right. Unfazed, he turned back to me and I slapped him again, this time across his other cheek. The second slap was hard enough that not only did his head jerk to the side, but his shoulders twisted and heaved as he tried to right himself.

"Feel better?" he asked, rubbing his left cheek as he faced me again.

"No!" I screamed.

I was exactly the opposite of better. How could he have said that to me? What was he thinking, bringing up something—some*one*—so awful at a time when it was supposed to be just me and him being together for the first time. Could he really not be the sort of man I thought he was? It was a possibility; I'd only recently gotten to know him. And considering it was me and Evelyn who did most of the talking while Alex either grunted or rolled his eyes or spoke in two- to three-word sentences, it was a very good possibility that I didn't know this man at all.

But I refused to believe that. I did know him, probably better than anyone else still alive today, better even than those who were dead, simply because I knew the Alex of this world, a man who hadn't existed before four years ago. This man might be quiet and ridiculously gruff at times, but he wasn't stupid. There was method to his madness; whether it be for survival or showing someone he cared about them, there was a well-thought-out reason behind every one of his actions.

Dropping back down onto the mattress, I tucked my legs beneath me, overly aware of my nakedness, but not ashamed enough to do anything about it. "Why did you do that?" I asked quietly, my voice hoarse.

"You needed it," he said, and shrugged. "You were pissed off, hurting too, and about to use me to make you feel better."

"Would that have really been so awful?" I asked, feeling bewildered. "Having sex with me? Because I thought that's where we've been heading..."

God, listen to me. Two weeks ago, I would have never had the courage to ask such a question. In fact, just a few days ago I was shying away from stripping down at the entry gate. Now, look at me. Either Purgatory and all its sins were starting to corrupt me, or I was just that damn angry, hungry, and exhausted from...everything.

I decided on the latter, figuring it would take more than two days to corrupt someone. Or at least hoping that was the truth.

Sighing, Alex scrubbed a hand across his scruffy jaw. His stubble was more of a beard now, something I'd never liked on men before, but on Alex, I liked it very much.

"I've wanted to be with you for years," he said, meeting my eyes. "And now I have you, you're all mine, Leisel." Lifting his brow, he looked at my wrist, where his brand shone dark against my pale skin. His lips twitched as a small, satisfied smile appeared. "And your first time with me isn't going be some bullshit screw." He lifted his eyes to meet mine.

Three things were going through my mind in that very moment. First, had Alex just told me he'd wanted to be with me for years? And if that was the case, was that why he'd helped me escape?

Second, what was with his "You're all mine" caveman-type nonsense?

And third, if I'd known how to swoon properly, I would have been swooning. It may have been crudely said and more than a little chauvinistic, but it had been said all the same.

He wanted our first time to mean something.

I'd been right about him. There was always a reason, always a carefully constructed plan of action forming behind his dark eyes.

"I like you," I told him, and reached for him. Cupping his cheek, I pulled him forward and kissed him gently on the mouth. It was Alex who deepened the kiss, slowly pushing me back until I was lying flat on the bed with him propped up over me.

"I love you," he said, and then, before I could respond or do much of anything other than gasp at his words, he kissed me. It was a deep kiss, a very thorough kiss, a kiss that made my body go soft and weak beneath him. It was a kiss that made me forget about my anger, my hunger…my everything.

He broke our kiss and I relaxed into him, suddenly content with simply holding him. Content with simply being near him. I didn't love him, not in the way I'd loved Thomas, but then again, the world had been different then, and I had been different too. This was the new world, full of fast-paced living because there were no more guarantees, no rainbow to reach the end of. There would be no one to jump out and exclaim, "Surprise! You're on *Candid Camera*! Sorry for scaring the shit out of you and making you suffer for the past four years!"

This was all we had, this right here and right now. So I decided in that moment that it didn't matter how much or in what way that I loved Alex, only that some part of me did.

"Where are you taking me?" I asked Alex. Jogging through the throng of people gathered outside as he pulled me along with him, I was struggling to keep up. My legs were much shorter than his, so I had to work twice as hard just to keep from being dragged on the ground behind him.

"You'll see," he said, glancing at me over his shoulder and grinning.

Another grin. How many was that now? Two, three?

His smiles, the genuine ones, and his full-fledged grins, were a sight to behold. They were so few and far between, causing his hard features to soften, giving him this overall youthful and playful look. They made me feel giddy and excited, especially when they were directed at me, or because of me.

Was this what happiness was like? It had been so long since I'd experienced any form of it, so long since I'd known what it was like to simply clutch the hand of a man, to see him smile at me and find myself returning that smile. Was this how it had been with Thomas?

I tried to remember, to wade through the last four years of muddied horrors back to when I'd been married. I remembered our first kiss, the day he'd proposed, the day we were married, the day we found out I couldn't have children and he'd held me so tightly while I cried. Thomas had rocked me, soothed me, told me that it didn't matter, that I was all he'd ever need.

Had his smiles made my belly flutter? Yes, they had. Did the warmth of his hand on mine spread throughout my entire body? Yes, it had.

It was an odd sort of sensation, this sliver of happiness that had been thrust so unexpectedly into my lap, and along with it had come twinges of guilt as well, as if I were somehow betraying Thomas by falling for another man.

But I shook those feelings away because if Thomas had known

all I'd endured, if he'd known what Lawrence had done to me, or even had a glimpse of what the world was today, he would never begrudge me something that made me smile, that melted the ever-present cold inside me. He'd been a great man, a kind man, a man who'd put others' needs and wants before his own. He'd been a man…like Alex.

Many times I'd already compared the two men, Thomas and Alex, more or less hoping that Thomas would approve of Alex, maybe even like him. But the more I thought about Thomas, remembering exactly the kind of man he'd been, the more I knew I was no longer just hoping.

Thomas would have liked him, simply because Alex made me happy.

I was still smiling, oblivious to the people shoving past me, to the incessant shouting that seemed to come from every corner of this place, reminiscent of a twenty-four-hour carnival. There was so much noise, too much noise, but today it didn't bother me or leave me feeling like a lowly sheep among prized cattle. Today I was smiling.

He finally came to a stop at the far end of the complex, outside a small but colorful awning with heavy flaps hanging down on all sides, hiding whatever was within. Alex gripped a tent flap, about to pull it open when a man appeared beside us. I recognized him instantly, remembered he was one of several bartenders from the club last night.

"What's up, man?" He offered Alex his hand, and Alex dropped mine in order to shake it.

They were roughly the same size, Alex being just a tad taller with a good half inch more muscle mass. They even appeared to be around the same age, both in their early twenties, but whereas Alex was tanned, his hair and features dark, this man was dirty blond, his skin as pale as mine.

"She's yours, yeah?" the man asked, jerking his chin in my direction.

Alex dropped the man's hand. "Yeah," he said gruffly, his carefree demeanor dissipating.

"Heard you got two of 'em," the man continued. "And if the other one can dance half as good as this one, I was thinking you might be interested in having 'em do a private show for some of the guys. Figured you wouldn't be opposed to some girl-on-girl action. Ain't no one going to be touching either of them, not with your mark on 'em."

My smile fell away, disgust causing the warmth inside me to quickly cool. The bitter realization hit me that no matter how much happiness I could eke out for myself, nothing could ever truly block out the sad state of the world around me.

"Fuck off," Alex said, his tone low, yet deadly. "Fuck off right now, asshole."

Neither Alex's anger nor his warning seemed to faze this man. In fact, he smiled and shook his head.

"You're a greedy son of a bitch, aren't you?" He shrugged. "No offense meant, man. I'm just a guy looking to fill some time. Ain't got nothing but time to fill these days."

"Fill it with somebody else," I snapped, drawing the attention of both men to me. I glared at the blond man, hoping the disgust I felt was being properly conveyed. "I'm not a *plaything*," I continued, still seething. "I'm a woman, a person! Didn't you have a family? A mother? A sister? A girlfriend? How would you feel if they were being passed around like...like...like cans of creamed corn?"

The man's mouth opened and closed, as if he were trying to decide on what to say next, yet couldn't quite find the words. "Like I said," he eventually replied, his eyes dancing with amusement. "No offense meant. I wouldn't share you either." His gaze flickered between Alex and me one last time, and then he headed off in the direction we'd come.

"Creamed corn?" Alex asked, raising his brow.

I shrugged. "I was thinking of Eve, holding on to that stupid can. I don't know, it just popped into my head."

Still thinking of Evelyn, of the last thing I'd said to her before she'd left the room, I squeezed my eyes closed. It was a horrible lie born from anger, and I was intensely frustrated with myself.

"I need to find her," I said, opening my eyes. "I need to apologize."

Alex nodded. "We will. She's fighting today. We can head over to the arena soon. But first, I have a present for you."

After taking my hand, he pulled open the tent flap, revealing what seemed to be a small clothing shop. Hangers fitted with dresses and skirts ran across a rope that had been fitted to encircle the entire space. Neatly folded stacks of shirts and pants were piled on miscellaneous end tables and chairs, while pairs of shoes in all colors and sizes were tucked away in every corner.

"Ah! Alex, my boy!" a woman cried out, poking her head out from behind a small, squat dresser. She jumped to her feet and clapped her hands together. "I cleaned them just like you wanted!"

Smirking, Alex pulled me forward. "Lei, this is—"

"Grannie!" the woman practically shouted.

As she stepped out from behind the dresser, I took in her long and colorful shift, which was obviously handmade. It looked like a patchwork quilt turned into a dress, complete with randomly placed buttons and glittering sequins. And an equally colorful scarf had been wrapped haphazardly around her neck amid nearly a dozen necklaces.

She was an older woman, plump but not fat, and if I had to guess I would have figured her to be in her sixties. Her long gray hair was piled neatly on top of her head in a tight bun, showcasing the numerous dangling earrings she was wearing.

Extending an arm in my direction, she wiggled her hand, causing the array of bracelets she wore to shake and jingle. Smiling, I took her hand in mine.

"Everyone calls me Grannie!" she continued excitedly, pumping my arm up and down. "And I have something special just for you!"

Releasing me, she hurried back to the dresser and disappeared behind it. I glanced up at Alex, wondering what on earth he'd done, but he refused to look at me.

"Ta-da!" Grannie sang as she leaped out from behind the dresser, holding in her hands a pair of pink fuzzy slipper boots.

My mouth fell open. Despite Grannie having said she'd cleaned them, they were still dirty and stained, the pink faded to a peachy sort of color. There were obvious holes that I could see, and small patches where the fur was missing entirely. And they were absolutely perfect.

"Oh my God," I breathed, bringing my hand to my mouth. "Oh my God."

"Happy birthday…?" Alex said. "Or Merry Christmas? Whatever," he finished almost shyly.

I glanced from him to Grannie and back to him. "But we didn't bring anything to trade."

"Now, now," Grannie said, thrusting the boots into my hands. "That's all taken care of. You see, I'm a betting woman and I'll be betting on Alex tonight. He's promised me a win, and in return, I've given him a five-finger discount on anything in the shop."

"You heard her," Alex said, still not looking at me. "Go pick some stuff out. For you and Eve."

I gaped at him, shaking my head. "When did you do all this?"

He shrugged his shoulders. "Met Grannie outside the Drunk Tank, got to talking…"

"Come, come!" Grannie urged excitedly. "Let me show you what I've got for a pretty girl like you."

Still smirking, Alex rolled his eyes. "I'll be outside," he said, and moved to turn. I grabbed his arm before he could leave, pulling him back to me. Juggling the slipper boots in one arm, I attempted to hug him with the other.

"Thank you," I whispered, feeling overcome. "I don't know what to say, or what to do."

Running his hand through my hair, he tugged gently, lifting my face. "You can thank me later," he said quietly. "Tonight. After I win that fight." Then he grinned.

"That's four," I said, grinning back. *Or was it three?*

"Four what?" he asked, and I shrugged.

"Never mind."

CHAPTER THIRTY-TWO

Evelyn

"SO YOU WANT to trade, do you, Wildcat?" he asked, his tone languid yet laced with amusement. Leaning back against a brick wall, the man crossed his arms over his chest. His eyes dropped from my face to the can I held, then back up to my face again.

We both knew we weren't talking about food. This was so much more than a simple trade; this was me doing what I'd always done to wash away the pain, the stress, the never-ending disappointments. Using my body, letting others use it as well, to fill the hole, to ease the ache. It was all I'd known for so long now, and I found myself easily slipping back into that role, like an old friend I hadn't seen in some time.

Hey there, how've you been? It's been too long, I've missed you. Let's lose a little more dignity, shall we?

People, like Leisel, thought of me as strong. Brave. Fearless, even. But the truth was that I was just as weak and as fucked up as she was. Maybe even more so.

"What's your name?" I asked.

He smiled slowly, his dark gaze running over me with lustful appreciation, blatant and suffocating.

"Does it matter?" he asked. "How about you call me whatever you want, Wildcat."

Although he was still standing there, his muscular arms folded over his large chest as he smirked at me, his answer almost seemed defensive. Which was ridiculous, that this big hunk of man would feel the need to hide any part of himself from a silly little woman like me.

I rolled my eyes, feigning confidence. "How about I call you whatever your mama named you?"

"All right." He laughed, a deep, throaty bark that sent chills up and down my arms. "They call me E around here."

I frowned. "They?"

He nodded, still smirking. "They," he confirmed, without further elaboration as to who the elusive *they* was.

"They call you E?" I asked, forcing myself to smirk as well. "Seems kind of strange to me. Do *they* not like you very much?"

"Not really," he said. "Not that I give a fuck who likes me or not."

I paused, thinking through my answer before replying. "So, what's your real name?"

"Too many questions," he said, sounding almost irritated. "Why the fuck does my name even matter to you?"

I shrugged, not sure myself why it mattered, or why I'd even asked to begin with. It was just that I'd always asked my sexual partners' names first; it was the only thing I ever asked. Somehow it made the act seem less cheap, made me feel less cheap.

"What's your real name?" I asked again stubbornly, needing to know it before I went any further with this.

He studied me for a moment, his lids somewhat shuttered, before letting out a throaty, annoyed growl. "My name is Adler," he finally said. "It means eagle in German, and they call me E for short. We done with the questions now, Wildcat?"

He didn't wait for my answer. Already pushing himself away from the wall, he landed his hands on my waist and squeezed. His touch, the feel of his big, warm hands on my body, sent a jolt of sexual energy sizzling through me. Lifting them, he rubbed his thumbs against the underside of my breasts while his fingers dug painfully into the skin on my back.

Releasing a breath, I allowed my body to relax, telling myself this is exactly what I needed. Once I did this, I'd feel better, less empty. I'd always felt better after being with Jami. He'd taken away the bad, replacing it with something infinitely preferable—not good, but better than bad.

But E wasn't Jami, and he certainly wasn't Shawn. They'd been good men, kind men, and E was the exact opposite of good or kind. This was dangerous ground I was treading, not knowing E or anything about him, but his hands that were now traveling down my body sent my heart rate skyrocketing.

Like a drug addict who'd been offered a fix, I couldn't resist him. The lure of what he could do for me was too strong; I knew he would numb the unwanted feelings, even if for just a little while.

Spinning me around, reversing our places, he slammed me hard up against the wall. I was reminded of Jami once again, how he'd always done something similar, and a pang of sadness rattled through me.

Because Jami was gone. Shawn was gone. And Leisel blamed me for everything.

It was just me now.

E's mouth had found my neck, trailing hot, wet kisses across my throat and up my chin until his lips finally met mine. Coarse, bushy facial hair tickled against my cheeks while he pushed my lips apart, his tongue slipping inside my mouth. I still couldn't bring myself to touch him, yet he didn't seem to mind. Groping me harshly with experienced hands, he kissed me hard, full of eager tongue and nipping teeth.

"I won't be gentle, Wildcat," he said as he pulled away for a moment, his words as rough and threatening as his hands. Then he bit down on my lip, causing me to gasp while his hands painfully squeezed my breasts, as if to further make his point.

"You're not gonna like me when I'm done," he continued. "But you'll be satisfied."

Pulling away from me, leaving me breathless and full of wanting, he shrugged out of his faded denim jacket and let it fall to the ground. Then he was back, his hands on my waist, squeezing and kneading me as he brought me flush against his waiting erection and ground his hips against mine.

I still hadn't touched him. Beneath all my desire, I was still afraid of this man. He was overly aggressive, dangerous, and didn't strike me as the type to take no for an answer. A small part of me wanted to run from him, but the need I felt was greater, even if it meant lowering myself to this level.

Because feeling anything at all was better than feeling nothing.

His hands returned to my breasts, and with even more force than before, he groped and twisted, squeezing them to the point where I nearly cried out in pain.

I miss Jami.

Leisel doesn't need me anymore.

And Shawn...oh God, my sweet, sweet, Shawn.

Poor, poor, self-pitying me.

Suddenly, I grabbed for E, wrapping my hands around his impossibly thick neck, crushing my mouth to his and kissing him in the same rough and greedy fashion as he'd been kissing me. His hands were everywhere now, exploring, grabbing, taking and taking...

And finally, the noise in my head began to clear, leaving only the here and now, me and E, and—

A siren wailed to life off in the distance, the awful howling so loud, so obnoxious, it ripped me instantly from the quiet place I'd just found. E pulled away from me, looking angry and violent, frustrated sexual aggression radiating from him, making the air around us seem thick and heavy.

"I need to go," he said gruffly as he bent down to grab his jacket.

"What is it? What's that noise?" I asked, realizing that I was suddenly cold, chilled to the bone from his touch. Wrapping my arms around my body, I rubbed my bare biceps, trying to warm myself.

"It's a warning," he said gruffly. "The camp's shutting down. You need to get inside."

Shrugging his jacket up and over his massive shoulders, he turned and began to walk away without even a good-bye. He was quickly enveloped by the crowds of people, nearly lost in the chaos as everyone scrambled to gather their things.

"A warning for what?" I yelled after him.

He abruptly stopped, forcing the surrounding people to find another way around him. "Rotters," he said, turning to look at me. "A horde of them are headed our way." He continued to stare at me, his gaze hard and unwavering. "We'll finish this later, I'll find you," he said, his words a hard promise. Then he turned, the crowd engulfing him once more.

I stood there, still trembling from the aftereffects of E's violent touches, feeling cheap and used despite nothing having actually happened between us. But now I was scared, as well.

A horde of infected were headed this way? I'd heard of hordes before, back in Fredericksville I'd overheard the guards discussing some of the things they'd seen while out scavenging. Large groups of infected roamed the country, growing in numbers as more infected added themselves to their walking collection of horrors.

A wall of death, that was what they'd called it.

"Wildcat, you need to get in here!"

Glancing up toward the voice, I found Dori leaning precariously out of a second-story window, gesturing wildly to me. Realizing that she'd probably seen everything that had transpired between E and me, I felt my cheeks flush with heat.

"My name's Eve," I snapped at her, not wanting to be reminded of E at the moment.

"E said you're Wildcat," she retorted, "and no one argues with E. Now, get in here!" Disappearing from view, she slammed the window shut behind her.

I stood there a moment, still in a daze, not sure exactly what it was that I was supposed to be doing. The camp had grown silent, an eerie quiet befalling the entire place. Slowly, I crept toward the corner, my steps soundless. Stopping at the edge of the building, I watch the stragglers, the remaining people still moving about and gathering their things. Fires were being silently extinguished, food was being boxed and taken away. All around me and up above me, windows were being shut, doors were being locked, and within minutes the place was empty and lifeless.

I was still standing there staring, wondering why everyone was going to such extremes when a heavy fence, wired with electricity, surrounded this entire place. Yet, even the armed guards who always manned the fence had gone. Everyone was just...gone. Everyone except me. I was still standing here, gaping like a moron, when there was an obvious threat approaching.

"Shit," I cursed, willing my legs into motion. I had to get back to Leisel, had to make sure she was inside and safe. Not that she needed me anymore. Not that she wanted me anywhere near her. She'd made her disdain for me painfully obvious with her parting words.

I'd just turned the corner when a hand came down hard on my shoulder, gripping my shirt, the sound of tearing fabric echoing in the silence. Before I could let out a scream, a hand covered my mouth and then I was dragged backward, my feet stumbling underneath me as I was pulled through a doorway and into darkness.

I kicked out in fear, expecting at any second to feel the teeth of an infected sink into my skin, then begin tearing my flesh from my bones.

"Calm down, Wildcat!" a familiar voice admonished me.

I went still, blinking through the darkness, waiting for my vision to adjust. Finally it did, and Dori's face came into sight. Rolling forward in her wheelchair, she flicked her hand in the air, and the hands holding me fell away.

"What the fuck?" I yelled, and almost instantly a hand was clasped over my mouth. I struggled for a moment before realizing that struggling wasn't going to get me anywhere. Another second passed, and the hand released me.

"What the fuck, Dori?" I whispered, glaring first at her, then over my shoulder at the tall man behind me.

Pressing one slender finger to her pursed lips, she grinned wickedly. Jerking her thumb over her shoulder, she began rolling down the hall. I glanced again to the man behind me who offered me a glare in return, showing no sign that he'd allow me to pass anytime soon. Letting out a frustrated sigh, I started after Dori down the hall.

Inside what I was assumed was the Cave was even eerier than the ghost town outside. There were eyes everywhere, peeking out at me from behind partially cracked-open doors, following me as I padded softly after Dori. The entire place smelled, not of garbage or mold, but of sweat and sex. Considering what I'd just been about to do, it was an unwelcome smell, only serving to remind me how low, and how weak, I really was.

"Where are we going?" I whispered.

"My room," she responded simply.

At the end of the hallway we turned left, where two more men were waiting. Dutifully they picked her up, wheelchair and all, and ascended a nearby staircase. I followed lamely after her, still unsure and feeling uneasy as to why I was being forced to remain here.

When we reached the second floor, Dori quietly thanked the men and took control of her chair, wheeling herself along another hallway, this one much narrower and even darker than the first floor. Three doors in, Dori finally wheeled herself to a stop and pulled out a set of keys. Pushing open her door, she gestured for me to enter first. The room was pitch black, the only light coming from a small crack in the dark curtains.

"What do you want?" I asked, not hiding my annoyance.

"Come here, Wildcat," she said, and I could hear the quiet swishing sound of her wheels spinning as she pushed herself toward the window.

Rolling my eyes, I followed her over, watching as she pulled back the curtain and let in the sunlight. "Take a look," she murmured.

Blinking through the brightness, I peered out into the daylight, seeing nothing below but an empty camp, thinking again about how eerie it seemed, this loud and boisterous place suddenly so still. But I was also slightly awed at how quickly and proficiently they'd all worked together to keep this place safe and free from the infection.

"Look up," Dori said, pointing her finger. Lifting my eyes, I followed her finger past the market place, past the fences, and looked out into the wide stretch of empty land surrounding us on all sides.

I saw something dark on the horizon, reminiscent of a storm cloud from far off in the distance. But this wasn't a storm cloud, and it appeared to be moving. My eyes widened in realization as the words *wall of death* lodged in my throat.

"Infected," I murmured, then clasped a hand over my mouth.

"Rotters," Dori said, correcting me. "And yes, it is."

Flustered, I looked down at her as panic rose in my throat. "We can't just sit here and wait. They're coming right for us!"

She shook her head, smiling kindly. "As long as we're silent, as long as they don't see or hear or smell us, they'll pass us by."

"But there's hundreds," I protested, glancing back at the horizon. "Thousands!"

"We've done this before, Wildcat. It's never failed us. We work together to keep them out, to protect one another. We're not as bad as you seem to think."

I knew she was speaking, but words—any words—seemed irrelevant, not when there was a horde of infected headed our way. Far too many for any fence or any number of guns to keep them out.

"I need to get to Leisel!" I shouted, pushing past her, nearly tripping over one of her wheels.

"I can't let you leave here," she replied. "My men won't let you leave, not until the horde passes. And it will pass. You will be safe." Giving me a small smile, she continued. "No one goes outside when a horde is near, it's for everyone's safety."

"But Leisel," I said, feeling tears threaten. "What if she needs me?"

"She doesn't need you, she has her man."

Dori wheeled herself forward, toward a small bed in the far corner of the room. Patting the mattress, she smiled at me. "She's safe with him, and you're safe here with me. Come, lay down, rest a bit."

Deep down, I knew Dori was right. She was only repeating the words I'd been telling myself all day, that Leisel no longer needed me. But I couldn't stop the stomachache that not being with her at a time like this, not being there for her, was causing me.

And then it hit me, a realization that only deepened the empty, queasy sensation in my gut. Maybe Leisel never needed me. Maybe it was me who'd needed her all along.

No. I shook my head. No. She had needed me in the past...and I had needed her. I still needed her. I would always need her.

The only difference was now she had Alex, and I had been placed on the back burner.

With slumping shoulders and tears begging to be freed, I took Dori's offered seat on her bed, and let my head drop into my hands.

"We're all a little broken, Wildcat, it isn't anything to be ashamed over. Just look how broken I am." She laughed, a quiet, tinkling sort of noise. "You don't have to go back to her, or to him. You don't need to subject yourself to her happiness. You can stay here, I'll look after you. We all will. We don't ask much in return, just a bit of your body every now and then to help fill our bellies and keep us clothed."

Sure that at any moment I was going to lose what little remained in my stomach, I lifted my head to look at her. "I'm sorry," I said, my voice trembling. "That's not who I am, I don't do...*that*."

But even I knew a lie when I heard one.

Dori was still smiling at me, a comforting and kind smile, but it was also a knowing one that made me feel exposed and uncomfortable.

"A strong woman knows what she is, Wildcat. And embraces it." She smiled again.

My trembling hands curled into fists as I jumped up from the bed.

Glaring down at her, I shook my head. "No," I said through clenched teeth. "No, that's not who I am. I'll wait here only because I have to, but I won't work here. I won't be a whore for you or for anyone."

Lifting her chin, Dori cocked her head to one side. "You have one man's brand on your wrist, darlin', yet I saw you with E, trading food for sex. Only reason I can reckon you'd be doing that is if your man isn't really your man."

Locking my jaw, I spun away from her and counted to ten before I attempted speaking again. "I'm no one's whore," I gritted out, facing her. "No one's."

"If you believe that," she said, the blatant sarcasm in her tone making me even angrier. "But just remember, you'll have to be the one to tell E that. And he isn't a man to be turned away so easily."

I shook my head. "I'm not afraid of him."

She looked at me with sympathy, as if I was the poor deformed woman in the chair and not her. "You should be," was all she said.

"I've met worse than him, worse than you," I gritted out, though fear was building in my belly. The realization of what I'd almost done, with what kind of man I'd almost done it with, began to dawn on me.

"No, darlin', you haven't. There's never been a man like him before. E is one of a kind."

I opened my mouth to say something, anything, but the words wouldn't come. Closing my mouth, I turned away from her, doing my best to ignore the welling panic rising inside me.

"E is a dangerous man," she said. "He's done things that...well, things that no man should ever have to do. But he'll look after you, and if you're good to him, he'll be good to you. He could do with a good woman like you, and maybe you can tame him, Wildcat. Lord knows we've all tried. He doesn't ask for much..." she said, her voice trailing off into a whisper as her gaze dropped to the floor.

My stomach churned as I watched shame flood her pretty features. What had he done to her?

Bending my knees, I placed my hands on either side of her wheelchair, forcing her to look up at me. "I already told you," I said firmly. "I'm nobody's whore."

CHAPTER THIRTY-THREE

Leisel

"I CAN'T STAY UP here!" I insisted, trying not to shout. "I can't stay up here not knowing whether she's okay or not!"

Leaning over the countertop, staring out at the empty paths below our building, tears were streaming down my cheeks. We'd been ushered, forced actually, back inside our building, and there had been no time to search for Evelyn. Despite all my protests, the armed guards now stationed inside our building's exits refused to let me pass.

I felt Alex's body behind me as he aligned his torso against my back. Not for the first time, his arms came down around my waist, hugging me to him in an attempt to comfort me.

"There is no one out there," he said pointedly. "She's inside another building. She's safe, Lei, I promise you."

"But I never got to apologize," I whispered, then swallowed another sob. "I said horrible things that I didn't even mean, and what if something happens? What if the infected get inside the gates and it's too late?"

"She knows you didn't mean it. She knows you're sorry."

"You don't know that!" My tears began to fall faster, harder, splatting across the stained plastic laminate. "You don't know her like I do."

"You're right, I don't know that," he admitted. "Not for sure, but I have to believe it."

I twisted my body, turning in his arms so we were facing each other. Looking up into his face, I shook my head. "Why do you have to believe it?"

"I just do," he answered, averting his eyes.

I stared up at him in wonderment, seeing something I'd never seen before. There was a sadness in his eyes, in his downturned lips, in the way his shoulders had drawn in.

"Alex?" I whispered, placing my hand on his chest. "Talk to me."

He shook his head, still refusing to look at me, and so I tugged on his shirt. "Alex, you've been there for me, let me be here for you. Talk to me, *please*."

Releasing me, Alex stepped back, then turned away and faced the door. The muscles in his arms and back flexed while he shifted agitatedly from one foot to the other.

"My mom," he said quietly, his voice cracking over the last word. "She didn't come home one day. The infection hadn't reached us yet… or so we'd thought. She'd just gone to a friend's house to check on them, to drop off some food, and then she never came home. My dad and I were freaking out, calling everyone, trying to find her. We drove around for two days looking for her."

Biting down on my bottom lip, I resisted the urge to go to him. I wanted to comfort him, to show him the same sort of support he'd shown me, but I could tell by his body language and his tone of voice that this was a private moment, that I wasn't welcome within it. So, I remained where I was and just listened.

"My dad…he went sorta nuts after that. Everything combined, the shit on the news, the looting, the whole fucking town was panicked, and my dad…without my mom…he just lost it. He started blaming me for crap that wasn't my fault, always yelling at me. He got sick, you know, from not sleeping, not eating, and from being constantly worried about her.

"It was about a week after she'd gone missing when the infection showed up. Everyone was packing up and leaving, and I was trying to get him to do the same. But he wouldn't leave, he kept saying he had to wait there for her, to be there when she came back. I tried to force him, for his own fucking good, but he was a big guy, even bigger than me. We ended up fighting…"

He let out a humorless laugh. "Last time I saw my dad was when I punched him in the face, called him a fool, told him he was stupid for waiting, that mom was already dead. Then I left."

My hand flew to my chest, over my rapidly beating heart, and I swallowed hard. He sounded so young right now, like the nineteen-year-old boy he'd been when everything changed. Gone was the quiet, gruff-spoken man. This was a brokenhearted teenager.

"I ran out of gas eventually. Got lucky, though, ended up getting picked up by a military caravan. They were just handing out guns to anyone, hoping that the more people they armed, the better chance we had."

He turned, facing me with tears in his eyes. "I never went back, Lei. I never saw him again. But I have to fucking believe that he knew I didn't mean what I said, that he knew I loved him."

A choking noise bubbled up in my throat as more tears poured down my cheeks. Unable to refrain from touching him for one more second, I ran forward, slamming my body into his and wrapping my arms around his waist.

"He knew it," I whispered through my tears. "He knew you loved him, I promise you."

Looking down at me, Alex cupped my cheek and tilted my face. Then he bowed his head to mine and kissed me.

Evelyn

"It doesn't matter how much you pace, time won't go any quicker," Dori said, her voice soft and kind. "And stop worrying, everyone will be fine."

Her words should have been soothing, but considering that she'd just tried to convince me to work as a whore by telling me I was already one, her words were anything but. Instead they were annoying and obnoxious, like nails raking shrilly across a blackboard.

Shooting a glance in her direction, I glared at her, but refrained from unleashing the bucket load of profanities that were on the tip of my tongue.

We needed to leave here; I could see that now. This place, these people, the way they lived, it was vile and corrupt, just as bad as Fredericksville had been, if not worse. The only thing that was different was that this place wore their corruption like a badge of honor, whereas Fredericksville hid theirs behind closed doors.

Eventually this place would ruin us. It would change us, harden us to the point where we'd only be concerned with ourselves. It would pry Alex and Leisel apart, Leisel and me apart, all by forcing us to become something we weren't. I refused to let that happen; I might have been broken but I was still worth something. At the very least, I was worth more than a grilled rat.

A creak sounded from behind me and I turned, watching as Dori's bedroom door began to open. My stomach sank as soon as I saw his profile, large and overbearing, the width of him taking up every inch of the doorway.

I stepped back, deeper into the shadows, willing the ground to open up and swallow me whole. He was the very last person I wanted to see, let alone be locked in a dark room with, especially since changing my mind about our little arrangement. Dori's perception of me only convinced me that I wouldn't be trading anything with this man, especially not my body.

"Out." His voice was rough and gravelly, deep and oppressive, brooking no argument.

Dori responded instantly, wheeling herself across the room without question. As the door closed behind her with an audible click, my stomachache only worsened. This wasn't what I'd wanted. This was never what I'd wanted.

"The rotters?" I asked, my words breathless and quivering.

"Almost here," he answered, his black eyes focused on mine.

I could hardly see him, but I could sense the air shift around me as he stepped forward, his large body passing by, his arm brushing against mine and causing me to shiver. The curtains were suddenly yanked open and light flooded the room. It was a welcome feeling, the warm sun on my chilled skin.

He approached me, and when his strong hands fell on my shoulders, I willed myself to remain where I was, to not run screaming out into the hallway and alert the infected to our whereabouts.

Bending down, he pressed a hard kiss on the side of my neck, his coarse beard grating roughly against my skin.

"E," I whispered, shivering again as fear drenched me. "I…I've changed my mind. I don't want to trade with you anymore."

My fear gave way, breaching the hardened walls I had built while talking with Dori. She was right; E was dangerous, and suddenly my fight seemed futile.

His fingers jerked, squeezing my shoulders even harder, causing me to wince. "That ain't an option, Wildcat."

Leisel

"I thought we were waiting?" I mumbled against Alex's persistent mouth. "'Til after your fight…"

I was pressed up against the door, Alex's big, broad body entirely covering mine. His hands were in my hair and my hands were up the back of his shirt, my fingertips digging gently into the smooth skin on his back.

Our one small kiss had escalated rather quickly. Although I was still crying, and Alex was obviously a bit overcome with emotion himself, none of that seemed to matter any longer.

He paused, releasing my mouth, and took a step backward. I slumped against the door, my body overheated and vibrating with excitement.

"There isn't going to be a fight tonight," he said, dropping his gaze down the length of me. "Not with a horde so close by. They won't risk the noise." His eyes looked me over. "And…Lei?"

"Yeah?"

"You look amazing."

I wanted to laugh at that, because I looked far from amazing in my dirty dress and my face all red and puffy from crying. But, *oh God*, the way he was looking at me. It reminded me of the previous night, after I'd been freed from the cage. That hunger, that wanting, it was all back. Watching him watching me, my breaths shortened as my heart began to pound even faster.

In one fluid movement, he'd pulled his shirt up over his head and tossed it aside. Then he was back, pressing his body against mine as he slid my dress straps off my shoulders, then pressed hungry kisses to the skin he'd just bared.

My head lolled off to the right, allowing him better access as his mouth explored my neck. I reveled in the feel of him touching me, kissing me, wanting me in this inexplicably crazy way that he did.

"Lei," he said, my name a mere growl from deep within his throat. His hands fumbled with the hem of my dress and pulled it up, bunching it at my waist, and I helped him along, trying to move the material out of his way while still kissing him.

His kisses—my God, his kisses. I felt so alive beneath his mouth and his hands, so wired, so unlike anything I'd ever experienced before.

Alex's hand slipped into my underwear and then lower, his fingers finding me. In mid-kiss, my body went still, my mouth falling open, my breath freezing in place. I dropped my head back, dropping it lightly against the door, and then he was moving inside me, and all at once my breath released in a whoosh of air that ended in a gasp of pleasure.

As I breathed in, breathed out, my chest heaving, my body trembling, the pressure from Alex's body was the only thing that kept me standing upright. And although I was still standing, I wasn't, not really, not deep inside me. I was falling and then soaring, then falling again.

Through fluttering eyelids I could see him watching me, his eyelids hooded, his lips pressed together in a determined line, and it only heightened my pleasure, knowing that he was watching me, knowing that he was enjoying watching me.

"I dreamed about this," he suddenly said, his voice husky and deep.

I tried to focus on him but his hand was relentless, pulling me out of my weightlessness and back into this moment. To him.

"Hmm?" I mumbled.

"You. This look on your face, because of me. I dreamed about it a hundred times."

A tear slipped free from the corner of my eye, not from sadness, but from being so overcome, so completely mesmerized by him, by us, and by this moment we were locked inside together.

"I wanted you bad, Leisel. From that first day when I arrived in Fredericksville. You dropped off clean clothing and food for all us guys. Ever since then..." His fingers began to move more insistently, as if the memory of that moment spurred him on.

"I was the first woman you'd seen in months," I mumbled breathlessly.

"You were more than that," he said. "You were something beautiful and good in the middle of a goddamn war zone."

This time I only managed a squeaky sort of moan in response, which seemed to be perfectly fine with Alex, considering he was now grinning.

Evelyn

Pulling out from E's grasp, I quickly backed away from him.

"I told you, I'm not trading now." I jutted my chin out, my fists curling into tight balls of defiance. But my knees were shaking, sending trembles rippling up and down my legs.

Taking a step toward me, a grin snaking across his rugged face, E shook his head. "And I told you that ain't an option."

"I don't want your fucking vermin!" I snapped angrily. "I'm worth more than a dead rat!" I took another step backward, my back bumping against the door behind me.

Still watching me, he raised his eyebrows in question. "Where you going, Wildcat? I'm not going to rape you. I ain't never had to rape a woman, and I'm not gonna start now." He laughed loudly, as if the thought of him having to rape a woman was the most ridiculous thing he'd ever heard in his life.

"Well, you're not getting anything from me," I said, and swallowed back the lump in my throat.

"What happened, Wildcat? I thought you were game?" He looked genuinely confused, and perhaps even a little amused by my sudden mood change, as if this was all a game to him. Trading women, sex... it meant nothing.

Reaching out behind me, I fumbled with my hand, searching for the doorknob. "I was," I said tersely. "Until I remembered that I'm worth more than a piece of meat." Finding the doorknob, I turned it just as his eyes flickered from my face to my hand.

He moved quickly for such a large man, reaching me before I had the chance to actually open the door. Slapping my hand off the doorknob, his arms came down to rest on either side of my head.

"I agree," he said, dipping his face down, his mouth on my neck once again. "You're worth a shit ton more than a piece of meat."

A low, throaty growl rumbled forth, then his tongue darted out across my skin. He dragged his tongue up my throat, over my chin toward my mouth, where he licked his way across my lips.

Squeezing my eyes shut, I shuddered beneath him.

"You taste like peaches, Wildcat," he murmured. "Sweet and juicy."

He paused in his wet perusal of my face and lifted his head, his black eyes looking me over. "I can get you whatever it's gonna take." Pressing his hips against me, he rolled them, making sure I knew how hard he was, how much he wanted this—me.

If there was one thing I knew well, it was men. I wouldn't be getting out of this; he wasn't going to let me. But I wouldn't let this happen to me for nothing, for a mere rat.

"I want a truck," I bit out. Thankfully the tremble in my body hadn't yet reached my voice. I sounded strong and sure, the complete opposite of what I was feeling.

Quirking an eyebrow, he smiled slyly at me. "Oh yeah? Why?"

I wanted to snarl at him, to tell him it was none of his business, to tell him he could go to hell for all I cared, but instead I smiled. Two could play at this game.

"Because," I said, "I want me and my friends out of this place."

Leisel

I was still recovering from my orgasm when Alex lifted me off my feet and carried me across the room, then set me down on the mattress. My dress, ruined, torn open from the back, was already hanging half off my body. With one sweep of his hand, what remained of the dress was yanked from my body and thrown across the room.

Seated on his knees between my spread legs, unbuttoning his pants, Alex was still grinning down at me. Giggling, I blushed furiously, not out of embarrassment, but happiness.

"I feel guilty," I suddenly blurted out, my smile slipping away. "There's infected out there, Eve's out there somewhere. We don't know what's going to happen if…" I paused, not wanting to finish my thought. Not wanting to say aloud that we could very well die here, today even, if the horde didn't simply pass by as expected.

"Better to have some happiness before you die, right?" He paused in removing his pants, watching me intently as concern creased his handsome features.

I nodded, although rather listlessly. "I don't want to die," I said softly, and then froze, realizing what I'd just said. It hadn't been all that long ago when I'd been ready to die, ready to just accept my fate and leave this world. I was different now, changed. I didn't want to die, I didn't want to leave, not when my life had finally become my own again. Not when I had two people who needed me now, Evelyn and Alex. How strange it felt to realize you were actually needed, when you'd spent years in stasis, feeling helpless and useless.

"I won't let you die," Alex promised.

Dropping his hands to the mattress on either side of my head, he lowered his face to mine and pressed a soft kiss to my lips. I took his face between my hands, then arched my body, pressing my bare breasts against his chest. Wrapping his arm around my back while still balancing on one hand, Alex maneuvered us both into a sitting position, with me straddling his lap.

We kissed again, a deeply satisfying kiss, long and hard. The smell of him, of me, was all around us now, the heady scent of skin and sweat and bodies pressing together. I found myself unconsciously rocking my hips over his, kissing him more fervently than before.

The ache had returned, the burning in my belly, and excitement snaked up my spine. I wanted more of him, needed more of him, and he seemed to understand this without me having to say a word. Reaching between us, he finished undoing his pants, and somehow—though I had no idea how—managed to wriggle out of them without having to release me. Then he was there, that part of him I was craving so desperately, pressing up against me, then slowly and gently filling me.

Burying my face in the crook of his neck, I squeezed my eyes shut. There was so much, too much that I related to sex, and not all of it was happy memories. But I knew this was different, that this was real and this was good. There was no greed in this bed of ours, no evil lurking behind Alex's handsome features.

"I've got you," he whispered, holding me tightly to him. "I've got you, Lei."

Evelyn

"You'll die out there," E said.

"I'd rather be free," I retorted.

"Free to die?"

"Or to live," I whispered angrily. "Either way, I'll be doing it my way."

He watched me for a minute, clearly deciding if I was worth it to him. "A truck?" he repeated as he grinned at me.

"And gas."

"Done," he said with a shrug. "What else you need, Wildcat? You got a list in that pretty little head of yours?" he said, stroking a hand down my hair, letting my curls fall through his fingers.

I nodded my head. "There's lots of things we'll need."

Throwing his head back, E laughed loud and hard, embarrassing me and making me foolish. He continued laughing, the volume of which made me wonder if the infected outside might hear it. All at once he stopped, his gaze again meeting mine, his features smooth and serious. "Of course there is."

I swallowed again, the lump in my throat stubbornly refusing to go down. "I want weapons, food, water…" One by one I ticked off a survival checklist, all things that Leisel, Alex, and I would need back out in the wild. Part of me hoped he'd refuse me, that he'd laugh at my exorbitant and ridiculous requests; yet another part of me hoped he would agree to my demands, providing us with what we needed in order to be free of this place once and for all. That perhaps if I were able to go back to Leisel with the keys to our freedom in my hand, she would forgive me for my many mistakes.

"Done." He smirked and lifted his hand. His palm landed on my cheek, his fingers running trails up the side of my face and into my hair. Gripping a handful of hair, he forced my head back. "You'll get your truck, Wildcat, when I'm good and ready to give it to you. You done now?"

"How do I know I can trust you?" I whispered.

His smirk turned into a grin. "You don't," he replied. His eyes were expectant now, as if he was waiting for my confirmation, a signal that we'd come to a mutually beneficial agreement, and now he could collect his portion.

I wondered at why it was so important to him, my consent, when we both knew he didn't need it. He was big enough, strong enough, that he could simply take what he wanted and not have to give me anything in return. Was it the brand on my wrist? Was there some sort of punishment that was doled out if you took another man's property? Even if there was, I doubted anyone would go up against a man like E for a woman like me.

Taking a deep breath, I closed my eyes and nodded quickly. No more than a heartbeat had passed before his mouth was on mine, his tongue prying my lips apart as he pushed hungrily into my mouth. Gripping my waistband, he unbuttoned my pants, shoving them down my legs and bringing my underwear with them.

Crudely, he pushed my thighs apart, and then his thick fingers were inside me, pushing and probing, making me gasp at the sudden violent intrusion. He pulled out of the kiss and pressed his forehead against mine, his breath hot and ragged against my face. Grunting, he ground his palm against me, his fingers working faster now, harder.

Biting down on my lower lip, I gripped his shoulders and dug my nails into him, both wanting him to stop and wanting him to continue. I was dizzy, disoriented, my body suddenly a frenzy of want and desire while my mind continued to protest.

One strong arm snaked around my waist, his large hand gripping me as he lifted me off the floor with ease. As he carried me across the room toward the bed, my pants fell from my ankles, and just as soon as he'd set me down he was gripping the neckline of my shirt. With one violent tug, it tore down the center, baring my breasts to him.

Lying there, fully exposed, I watched E as he quickly undressed, pulling his T-shirt up over his head, revealing a stomach packed tight with layers of hard, rippling muscle. Unbuttoning his jeans, he kicked them away, then climbed onto the bed. Situating himself over top of me, he pushed my knees apart and stared down at my nakedness with a salacious grin on his face.

Feeling oddly self-conscious, I attempted to close my legs but his hands were there, stopping me. Pushing them farther apart, he grinned down at me as he moved in, our bodies now touching, his hips aligned with mine.

Leisel

I gasped again, not for the first time, but loud enough that Alex had to use his mouth to muffle the sound. Not an easy feat considering I was lying on my belly, Alex on top of me and buried deep inside.

"Shh," he whispered against my mouth. "I can hear them now. They're all around the gates."

We both fell silent, listening to the odd buzzing noise that came from outside the windows. At first it had sounded like a swarm of mosquitoes circling your head, but the more I listened, muddling through our heavy breathing and pounding hearts, it grew clearer, more distinctive, sounding like something else entirely. A low chorus of groans and growls, too many to distinguish, all droning together and sounding like a low humming noise to the untrained ear.

Beneath Alex, I shivered. They were everywhere now, practically on top of us, and what if they didn't move on? What if they somehow sensed us inside? What if they…

Alex slid free from my body, instantly distracting me from my thoughts, before returning to me slowly and sinking back inside. "Don't think," he said quietly against my earlobe, then kissed me again.

Taking hold of both my wrists, he raised them above my head, using one hand to keep them there while his other traveled down the length of me. Again, his hips retreated, and again they returned.

"I'm going to be so sore," I murmured into the mattress.

We'd already had sex once. Alex hadn't lasted all that long, and after apologizing, had set straight to work on ensuring that I would finish this time. Or he was simply just trying to distract me from what was happening outside. Either way, I wasn't complaining. At least, not yet.

Wiggling my fingers, I beckoned for his hand. He complied, releasing my wrists and sliding his fingers between mine. For a moment I only stared at our wrists, at our matching brands that forever marked me as Alex's, and I found myself smiling, rather liking it there, liking that I belonged *to him*.

With a nudge of his nose, he brushed my hair to one side. His mouth found my neck, and then he was moving again. Slowly at first, the long slide of him in and out of my body forced me to bury my face into the mattress and stifle my cries as pleasure rippled through me. Then faster and faster, his hips worked a breathtaking, heart-pounding pace between my thighs, whipping my entire body into nothing more than a frenzy of need.

Quivering, shaking like a leaf beneath him, I wanted to sob, to scream out in ecstasy. Instead, I bit down on the mattress and let my body scream for me.

My body screamed and screamed until its voice was hoarse, until its insides had been wrung dry, not a drop of moisture remaining.

A little piece of me died that afternoon—the part of me that still cowered in fear at the sight of a fist; the part of me that had wanted to leave this world, too scared and too selfish to realize what I was leaving behind; the part of me that had been forever afraid, my fear making me unwilling to see what was still here, the life that was still right here, even in the midst of all this death. It was gone now, having been whisked away into the ether while my body screamed itself raw in the face of indescribable joy and unimaginable pleasure.

And then I drifted off to sleep, the most peaceful sleep I'd had in the past four years, while held safely within the arms of a good man. A man who loved me.

Evelyn

Gripping my thighs, E angled himself against me, pressing the hard tip of himself just inside my entrance. Releasing my legs, he wrapped his hands around my waist, his fingertips biting angrily into my skin, his grip holding me firmly in place. Then his eyes lifted and met mine, a crude sneer twisted his lips, and with a loud grunt, he thrust himself inside me.

I cried out in pain from the sheer size and savageness of him, attempting to pull away from him until his hand slapped down over my mouth. His weight crushed me, stifling my cries and thwarting my movements.

With one hand clasped firmly over my mouth, the other holding tight to my waist, he slammed into me again and again. It didn't matter how much I tried to buck and twist against him, he simply controlled my thrashing using his own body, keeping me pinned in place no matter what I attempted. In all my life, I had never been fucked like this. He was like a man possessed, as if he was trying to internally brand me with his cock, and make me his forever. The entire time his eyes never left mine, his cruel hard stare burning into me.

Grunting, E flipped me over, pressing his chest against my back as he once again drove himself deep between my thighs. His teeth found my shoulder, biting down, causing me to nearly scream out in pain. Instead, I bit down on the pillow beneath me, knowing there was no point in crying anymore. Everything he did, he was doing it to hurt me. He liked to know that he was in control, that my body was his to use as he pleased.

But the fault was mine; I'd known exactly what I was getting myself involved in. I had been warned by both him and Dori, and yet I had still agreed. The price I'd set—Leisel and Alex's freedom—was too important not to.

But the pain he was causing me, it was more than just physical. With every brutal thrust, with every careless grab and twist of my skin, every biting kiss, and every cry I'd uttered that he'd answered with a grin, he was hurting me in places he shouldn't have been able to reach. He was hurting me straight through to my soul.

Desperate for an escape, I cast about in my mind and remembered the conversation I'd had with Leisel.

"Where do you go?" I had asked. "When you zone out?"

"To the past," she'd said simply. "I go back to the past."

Squeezing my eyes closed, tears leaking from beneath my lids, I did as Leisel would. I went back to the past. I thought of Shawn, of his ruggedly handsome features, the way he'd always tickled me before sex, tickling me until I was laughing and begging him to stop, and then he would kiss me. And his kisses…his kisses had been everything.

And I thought of Jami. His sweet, sinful smile, his skillful hands tearing the pleasure from my drenched and willing body, the beautiful way we'd always moved in sync, skin against skin. It was Jami I was thinking of as E continued to slam his body into mine.

"Wildcat!" E hissed angrily. "Make some damn noise!" Slapping his hand hard across my backside, my body jumped in answer, but I refused to cry out. I refused to allow this man the satisfaction of hearing any more of my pain.

Pulling himself free of me, he flipped me onto my back, and again he buried himself deep inside me. Gripping my jaw, he forced me to look at him once more. "Cry for me, Wildcat," he demanded, glaring down at me.

Looking past him, I focused on nothing, my mind retreating once again to the past. To Jami, and then it was only Jami I saw, only Jami that I felt.

"You stupid whore," E sneered. "You're just a stupid whore no one wants."

Knowing he was only trying to get a rise out of me, that he got off on this, I choked out a bitter laugh. "I'm not a whore," I said, "and I have plenty of people who love me."

And I did. My parents had loved me. Shawn had loved me, Leisel and Thomas had loved me. And Jami, maybe even he had loved me. They were the only ones who mattered, whose opinions of me mattered. Not this man; he didn't matter. He never would.

Cursing, E grabbed a handful of my hair and fisted it tightly. Gripping me like a rider would a horse's reins, he resumed pumping his body into mine. Faster, harder, more painful and angry than before.

I started to laugh then, laughing through my tears and pain, allowing myself to fall even deeper into the oblivion, and closer to Jami.

Leisel

Untangling myself from Alex, I blinked groggily in the semi-darkness, then sat up in bed and glanced around the empty room. Getting to my feet, I headed for the row of windows and peered down below. There was no horde, no black wall of death off in the distance. There were, however, several infected clinging limply to the fence, their bodies black and charred.

Pressing my face against the dirty glass, I attempted to see even farther out and discovered much of the same. Infected, burned to a crisp and all hanging haphazardly from the fence. I had to admit, I was surprised and a little impressed at how easily it had been to hide from the horde, especially inside a camp this size, and with this many people.

Returning to the bed, I took a seat beside Alex. "Hey," I murmured, shaking his arm. "Alex, wake up."

"Hmm…" Reaching around my waist, he smoothed his hand over my stomach, traveling upward until he was cupping my breast, squeezing it while gently thumbing my nipple.

"Again?" he muttered, pressing his hips into my backside.

"No," I admonished, giggling softly. "Stop it. It's nearly dark, and Eve isn't back yet. I think we should go look for her."

Yawning noisily, Alex attempted to push himself into a sitting position using only one hand, the other still firmly attached to my breast. Once sitting, he pulled me closer, nearly into his lap, still kneading and twisting the soft flesh.

Unwittingly, my eyes began to close, my mouth opening in a silent moan. Reaching behind me, I looped my arm around Alex's neck and turned my head, bringing our mouths together.

"I want more," he said, sliding his tongue past my lips.

"So do I," I whispered, gripping his hair and deepening the kiss. I let go, for just a moment, before pulling back. "But we need to find Eve."

With a sigh, he released me, his hands falling away. Blinking, gathering my wits, I rolled off him and out of bed. "You destroyed my dress," I said, picking up the shredded material and wrinkling my nose at it.

Alex grinned at me, a look on his face that I would never tire of seeing, so starkly different from his typical stony expression. "I also got you a ton of new clothes."

"True," I said, already reaching for the bag of clothing Grannie had given me. After digging through it, I pulled free a small pair of men's dark blue Dickies and a black tank top that had been patched over many times with colorful scraps of material. I dressed quickly, then slipped into my new pink slipper boots. I looked ridiculous, but no more ridiculous than anyone else around here.

"Are you coming?" I asked Alex, who'd yet to get up.

Sighing again, he stood up, giving me a full frontal view of his naked body. I took it all in, from head to toe, admiring every perfectly sculpted inch of him.

"If you keep looking at me like that," he said, looking up through his dark lashes and rubbing a hand across his jaw, "we'll never leave this room."

"I can't help it," I whispered, smiling. "You're really nice to look at."

After he pulled a dirty red T-shirt over his head, his eyes found mine. The burning intensity I'd seen in them earlier was back, searing me where I stood. God, this feeling, this incredible mutual attraction… I could have never predicted this turn my life had suddenly taken.

"Come here," he said, his voice deeper than usual.

I took a step forward, my breath hitching in anticipation, when an odd noise from the hallway gave me pause.

I turned sharply, glancing at the door. "Did you hear that? Like crying or something?"

"Yeah," Alex said with a frown, suddenly serious. "Stay here."

After pulling on his pants, he headed for the door, freeing the padlock and gripping the knob. The door swung open, softly hitting against the wall as Alex stepped out into the dimly lit hall.

"Lei!" he called out, his voice panicked. "Come here!"

I ran after him, through the doorway and into the hall. Glancing down, I found Evelyn sitting on the floor, her shirt ripped wide open, her breasts on display, her arms hanging limply at her sides.

From what I could tell she was covered in tiny bruises—her neck, her cheeks, her breasts and arms. Having been well acquainted with them for several years, I knew exactly what they were from. They were fingerprint bruises.

"Eve!" I cried, dropping to my knees. She turned her head, her bloodshot and tear-swollen eyes meeting mine. "Who did this?"

More tears welled in her eyes, spilling over and cascading down her dirty cheeks. "It doesn't matter," she whispered through her choking sobs.

My eyes widened. "It does so matter!" I yelled. I wanted to pull her forward, take her in my arms and hold her, but I wasn't sure that touching her wouldn't hurt her. So I settled for taking her hand, bringing it to my face and pressing a kiss to her palm.

"Who did this?" I repeated, glancing up at Alex. His eyes were still burning, only now there was a different sort of fire within their depths. He wasn't just angry, he was livid.

"It doesn't matter," she said again, drawing my attention back to her. Then she surprised me by suddenly smiling through her tears. "I got us what we need, a truck and supplies." She took a shuddering breath. "We're getting the fuck out of here."

CHAPTER THIRTY-FOUR

Evelyn

THE WATER SLUICED down over my skin, barely lukewarm but feeling scalding hot against my bruises and bite marks. I washed the wounds carefully, wincing every so often. They were healing rapidly, especially after two days of bed rest, Leisel and Alex taking turns waiting on me hand and foot despite my protests.

Even after the horde had passed, for two more days Purgatory had remained silent, no one wanting to risk alerting such a large group of infected to our whereabouts. The clubs had closed and the market was empty; the entire place had remained in stasis until just this morning.

With its awakening we'd had a visitor, a girl in her early teens. At Liv's request, she informed me that I would be fighting in the arena this afternoon. She'd given me a pitying look before taking off down the hallway, leaving me with a sense of foreboding in the pit of my stomach.

Shutting off the water with a sigh, I reached for a nearby towel, wrapped it firmly around my body, and stepped out of the small shower cubicle. Although a metal tub with a pulley system attached to a garden hose could hardly be called a shower, it was the best damn shower I'd had in weeks.

There were a few other women with me, one with two small children, but no one paid anyone else any attention. I stepped around a pile of someone else's clothing and headed for the counter where I'd left my own. After finger combing through my wet, but clean, hair,

I donned one of the new outfits Alex had managed to get for Leisel and me—a pair of faded black cargo pants and a dark blue T-shirt that actually fit me surprisingly well.

Once dressed, I stared at my reflection in one of the many broken mirrors that lined the wall. I looked pale, maybe even sickly, and far skinnier than I'd ever been before. There was something else too, a hollow look to my eyes that I'd never noticed, maybe because it hadn't been there the last time I'd taken a good look at myself. I tried to remember the last time I stared in a mirror, and couldn't. Though I'd taken care of my appearance while in Fredericksville, I'd never just stared at myself. I'd never wanted to, and maybe it was because of this very reason. From the fear of what I'd find.

There had been many times, over the course of the last four years, when I'd felt worthless, useless, little better than something to be used and easily discarded. But I'd refused to admit it out loud, refused to look at myself while I thought those horrible words. But after E, after the way he'd treated me and my body… Forget the brand on my wrist, I actually felt branded now. Branded by E, and branded a whore.

And today was going to be the first time that I would see him since…

He hadn't raped me. I had agreed to it all, and I had no one to blame but myself—not even him. He was purposefully vicious with me, purposefully aggressive and cruel, but I had known he would be. I swallowed thickly, feeling bile creeping up my throat. I shouldn't have been thinking about E, not with my upcoming fight.

"It's just sex," I whispered to my reflection. "It's just sex," I repeated louder, willing myself to feel stronger, glaring at my sad, pathetic reflection.

We'll be out of here soon, I told myself. With a truck, weapons, and food. We'll continue traveling south, continue surviving. Together. As a family.

"Fuck this place," I murmured, and forced myself to smile. I refused to be ashamed of what E had done, of what I'd done. I had a plan, a way to get us out of here, a way to protect Leisel and myself from the madness of this place. And that was all that mattered.

"I'm not a fucking wildcat," I whispered, chuckling darkly. "I'm a goddamn lioness."

I laughed again, a sickly sweet laugh that did nothing but make me feel less like myself and more like a stranger.

"Eve? You in here?" Leisel's soft voice carried across the room, echoing off the cold ceramic tile.

"I'm here," I replied, still staring at my reflection.

As she came up behind me, my eyes flitted to her reflection, watching her gaze graze across the visible bruising on my neck and arms. She hid her reaction well, quickly meeting my eyes with a kind smile. I wanted to laugh, thinking back to how many times I'd done the same to her, hiding the disgust I was feeling for the man who'd hurt her, hiding the pity I felt for her. How quickly our roles had been reversed. Now I was the one who needed the comforting, and Leisel the one offering it.

Leaning in, she wrapped her arms around my middle, resting her chin on my shoulder, still smiling at me. Covering her hands with my own, I returned her smile. She looked so happy, so at peace, and it was a beautiful thing to see. My pain—any pain—was worth it to see that contented flush in her cheeks.

"You know I'm sorry, right?" she said softly. "I didn't mean any of it, not even a little bit."

"I know, you've told me." My eyes again met hers. "A lot." I smiled.

She nodded once and looked away, apparently not wholly convinced that I believed her. She wore her guilt like a badge, visible for all to see, as if she believed that she owed it to me to feel bad. When in truth, it only made me feel worse.

"You ready?" she asked carefully.

She was worried about me, about the fight, about what happened with E, but she was being strong for me, trying to help shoulder my burdens. I appreciated that more than she'd ever know.

"Almost," I said, nodding. Tying my hair up into a tight bun on top of my head, I turned to face Leisel. "Are you sure you want to be there?" I asked her. "I have a feeling it's going to get ugly." *And I don't want you getting upset*, I added silently.

Leisel's lips pulled back in a surprising snarl. "Don't you ever ask me something so stupid again, Evelyn."

I started to smile, a genuine smile, as I reached for her. "I love you, Lei," I whispered, crushing her to me, ignoring the pain it caused my body.

Hugging me back, she squeezed me tighter than she ever had before. "I love you too, Eve."

"Promise?" I asked, choking on my own emotion.

"Promise," she said. "Always."

The makeshift arena was located outside, at the far end of Purgatory's south side, and situated only a couple of dozen yards away from the gate. It was a simple setup, several thin metal poles jutting up from the ground with rope fashioned around them to create a ring of sorts, encircling a small beaten-down stretch of lawn.

Cages of infected, like the ones at the Drunk Tank, were here as well, at least four that I could see as I quickly scanned the area, trying to take in as much as possible as quickly as I could. The infected were wild, riled up and crazy for blood, making the ones at the bar seemed almost subdued. I tried not to look at them, their rotted sallow skin, balding heads, and snapping mouths—even without teeth, all of it only making my churning stomach worse. But I could hear them, above all the yells and catcalls as I entered the arena, their groans of hunger standing out above the rest.

Alex was there among the gathered crowd of spectators, waiting for us. Leisel went to him, slipping her hand in his and smiling up at him while I scanned the large crowd, my nerves kicking into overdrive when my gaze found E. He stuck out, even in a crowd this size, his large frame and thick Mohawk overshadowing nearly everyone else. His face was a mask of calmness, though his dark gaze spoke of death and violence.

Tearing my gaze away from him, I glanced back to Leisel and Alex.

"Don't spill too much blood," Alex said, trying to smile. "Don't want to be slipping all over the place during my fight."

I tried to smile as well, but we both only ended up grimacing at each other, neither of us liking what we had to do.

"Just a few more days," Leisel said, her eyes darting between us. "And we're out of here. Right?"

"Right," Alex said, nodding down at her.

I nodded as well, pulling Leisel in for a quick hug. "Definitely,"

I said, but I didn't share their optimism. I was still at the mercy of E's generosity, and who knew when he'd come through for me.

As I headed toward the makeshift ring, I found E easily among the crowd again. His eyes were still on me, his hard, unwavering gaze seeming to suck the energy straight from my bones, making my arms and legs feel like jelly. Attempting to avert my eyes, I found it difficult, feeling myself unwittingly looking at him over and over again.

The crowd grew more agitated. People shouted as I made my way through them, their arms held high, hands full of food, clothing, or bottles of homemade liquor. A chalkboard had been set up near the fence, where a scruffy-looking man was taking bets, writing down names, odds, and amounts. A caged infected had been placed near him, yet he was oblivious as it growled, rattling its cage as it reached desperately for him.

I reached the ring at the same time Liv did, her pink hair shining even brighter beneath the sun. Her hands were wrapped possessively around another woman's bicep as she dragged her under the rope and shoved her into the ring. She was a bony little thing, my opponent, with a lithe ebony body and raven-black hair. From her mannerisms, I guessed that she was a dirty fighter, probably lacking any real skill. She looked at me, her eyes flashing cold and empty, while Liv smiled a cruel, knowing sort of smile that suggested to me this was going to be anything but a fair fight.

Behind Liv, Jeffers stepped into the ring, his arms spread wide in welcome. He appeared older in the daylight, tougher and meaner as well, his age more apparent in the daylight. The strip of gray in his hair looked almost white, a stark and menacing contrast to his black locks.

"Fighters ready?" he shouted loudly, beckoning us both forward with his fingers.

My opponent and I moved forward until we were toe-to-toe. This close to her, I could see the scars covering her body, hundreds of them crisscrossing her face, neck, and arms, and I began to wonder if I'd misjudged her. She'd quite clearly had her share of fights, and yet here she stood.

"Today for your gambling pleasure we have a new challenger for our reigning champion, *Miiiiiis-ty*!"

At the mention of her name, Misty thrust her clenched fist up into the air. The crowd answered with an unholy roar, chanting her name over and over as well as screaming for my blood.

Misty wasn't paying them any attention, almost as if she couldn't hear them. Her eyes were fixed on nothing in particular; she looked toward the sky, the ground, anywhere but at me or the crowds. Liv, however, was staring at me. Grinning at me, actually.

"Straight from the wild, we have Eve!" Jeffers turned to me with a grin. "Some might even call her a wildcat!"

The crowd roared again, and my stomach turned somersaults at the mention of my nickname. Chancing a glance to where I'd last seen E, I found him still there, his tattooed arms crossed over his chest as he stared at me.

"Fighters!" Jeffers continued. "To your corners!"

As Misty retreated to where Liv was waiting for her, I returned to my corner, ignoring the small stool that had been placed there in favor of searching the crowd behind me for Leisel and Alex. I found them easily, noticing Alex first, pushing his way through the crowd as Leisel hurried after him.

I turned back to the ring, still sensing E's intense gaze on me as the crowd fell silent. It was a deathly sort of silence, like a dark shadow that swallowed up the light, shrouding everything in blackness.

"Ding, ding!" Jeffers bellowed, his deep voice thick with amusement.

The crowd erupted with another ferocious roar, still chanting Misty's name as Misty herself leaped into action and raced across the ring, headed straight for me.

I stepped to the side, just a hairbreadth out of reach from her bony fist, only to come face-to-face with another punch. Her fist caught my left ear and my world went instantly quiet, quickly giving way to a loud ringing that made me cringe and stumble backward. She swung again, this time connecting with my stomach, causing me to fly backward, my body sprawling across the ropes. She joined me there, her fist connecting with my face, then my stomach, her punches relentless, one after the other after the other…

In an attempt to block her, I lifted my arms, managing to thwart merely a few of her punches. I had misread this woman entirely; she was quick and powerful, and brutally efficient.

The pummeling stopped rather abruptly. As I chanced a peek between my raised forearms, I found Misty heading back to her corner to where Liv was waiting for her. Still smiling, Liv winked in my direction, letting me know that she'd won and that I'd lost, making sure I saw the sick satisfaction she gleaned from all this.

As my arms dropped from my face, I watched Liv turn to the crowd, seeking out E, who was now standing directly next to the rope. A silky smile graced Liv's face as she watched him, even though he didn't look her way. She followed his gaze back across the ring to me, her smile gone now, her nostrils flaring angrily, and I realized then that she knew. She knew about E and me; she knew, and she was goddamn jealous.

Staggering back to my corner, I found Leisel and Alex waiting for me. I shook my head slightly, annoyed that my hearing was still spotty; I was only catching a dull hum of the commotion around me.

Gripping my arm, Alex dragged me down onto the stool and began wiping my face with his sleeve. His mouth was moving but I couldn't hear his words, and my vision blurred in and out of focus. Between that and the several dozen punches I'd taken to the gut, I was positive I was going to throw up all over myself at any moment.

But then Leisel was there, pushing Alex out of her way and kneeling down beside me. Taking my face in her hands, she blocked the world out, leaving only her and me. Her mouth, both hard and soft, found mine, pressing a kiss to my lips.

"You promised me, Eve!" she yelled, her voice nearly lost among the shouting. "You promised me we'd always be okay! Don't break your promise!"

Blinking through the blood that trickled down my forehead and into my eyes, I nodded. She was right; I had promised her. I'd promised her that we would always be okay, and I wasn't going to break that promise.

Leisel helped me back to my feet and then she was gone, tugged away by Alex.

I turned to see Jeffers once again standing in the center of the ring. "Ding-ding!" he shouted again with a wicked grin, and my stomach plummeted.

Like a wild animal sprung free from its confines, Misty attacked. No dancing around, no dodging, just another hard-core assault that I wasn't quick enough to dodge. Her fists slammed into me yet again, splitting open my lip, and my mouth filled instantly with blood. Yelping, I dropped to my knees and spun around, missing her second swing.

Grabbing my arms, Misty wrenched me upright and threw me against the ropes. As I hit them, I bounced back, falling into her arms where she promptly kicked my legs out from under me, causing my entire body to slam painfully to the ground. As I lay there, trying to catch my breath, her foot shot out, connecting with my ribs, and what little breath I had all left me in one painful whoosh.

She kicked me again and again, until I could no longer breathe. I was wishing she would end it once and for all, just send that boot of hers straight into my head and end this, but then suddenly she stopped. As I pried open my swollen lids, I found that she was walking away from me.

With a grunt, I rolled onto my stomach, attempting to drag myself across the ground and back to my stool. I'd only managed a few inches when Alex was suddenly there, lifting me off the ground and setting me back down on my stool.

"Eve!" he shouted as he grabbed my chin, forcing me to look at him. I stared at him, though everything was fuzzy and it hurt just to keep my eyes open.

"She's going to kill you! You need to fight back!" he yelled, his features contorting in anger.

"I don't even care," I mumbled, letting my head hang to one side, where I was greeted with Leisel's face. Her beautiful, heartbroken, tear-stained face.

"You promised!" she yelled.

"I can't do this!" I cried out, pushing her hand away as she reached for me. I looked away from her, not wanting to see her pain, her frustration, or her damn pity.

My gaze snagged on E to find him still watching me. His entire face was creased with a frustrated frown, his body taut and rippling with anger. His anger probably stemmed from the fact that I was losing—that he'd bet on me and was going to lose.

"FINAL ROUND!" Jeffers roared. "Ding, ding, motherfucking-*DING*!"

I didn't know how I did it, how I managed to drag my broken body up off that stool and back into the ring. But somehow I did, found some remaining shred of will left inside me, forcing me onward, pushing me to see this thing to the end, even if it meant the end of me.

Gritting my teeth, my guard raised, I waited as Misty came for me, waiting for her fists to once again begin their relentless assault. And as I was waiting, somewhere beneath the roar of the crowd and the humming in my ears, I heard a scream, a loud and shrill ear-piercing scream that splintered my heart. It was Leisel screaming, and my stomach heaved with fear and worry—not for me, but for her.

You promised!

Spitting out a mouthful of blood, I wiped a hand across my eyes and readied my fists. Expressionless, beautiful, her slender body built to inflict pain, Misty ran past me, her small fists curled like solid rocks, waiting to strike. As she circled me, I turned with her, my eyes following her movements when I noticed a flash of light, a glint of something shiny in her fist as the sun touched down on it. I swallowed hard, tasting the metallic tang of my own blood, and realized that Alex was right. She was going to kill me; not beat me to a pulp, but actually end my life.

You promised!

Leisel's words took on a life of their own, imbuing me with the knowledge that she did in fact still need me, despite her having Alex. More than anything, she still wanted me, and I was still worth something. That despite it all, everything that had been done to me, everything I'd allowed to be done to me, I was still worth something to someone. And I refused to let her down again.

My only advantage at this point was knowing how battered I already was and probably looked. As Misty stepped closer, I purposefully made a big show of struggling to catch my breath, staggering as I tried to remain standing upright. And then, as she stepped even closer, readying to swing, I attacked, catching her completely unaware as my fist connected with her face. My knuckles hurt from the impact, but God, it felt good to lash out like this. Despite my blurry eyes and ringing ears, the pain in my stomach and ribs, and the taste of blood in my mouth, it felt good to defend myself.

Surprised, her eyes wide, she stumbled backward, but before she could right herself, I sent my right foot straight into her knee and shoved as hard as I could, sending her sprawling backward.

She crashed to the ground, the back of her head slamming against the dirt. The crowd was suddenly silent as I leaped on top of her, going immediately for the small knife still held tight in her grip. Whereas her hands were battered from our fight, mine were not, and only because of this was I able to wrestle it away from her.

As she continued to struggle beneath me, I kept her pinned tightly between my thighs. I raised the blade high in the air and slammed it down straight into her chest. The crowd was silent now, so quiet that I could hear the tearing of her flesh, the crunching of her bones as the small but deadly knife broke through her chest cavity and slid easily into her heart. Blood gushed around the wound as her eyes rolled back in her head, showing white.

Leaving the knife in her chest, I pushed myself off her, panting hard, and stood to my full height, my entire body trembling with fear and fatigue. The crowd was still silent, their expressions ranging from shock to anger as the onlookers began to realize they'd just lost their golden girl, and with her, whatever bets they'd placed.

Liv was furious. Marching out of the ring, she headed straight for Jeffers, her pink hair whipping around her face like a ball of cotton candy caught in the wind. Immediately, she began yelling at him, though I had no idea what she was saying since my ears were still ringing. But he only shrugged in response, looking helpless in the face of her rage, which led me to think that it wasn't really Jeffers who ran this place, but Liv, the rage behind the muscle.

Their fight ended nearly as soon as it had begun, with Liv slapping Jeffers hard across the face and whirling around to face me. She was glowering, fury and hate pouring from her in thick heavy waves that I could practically feel emanating from across the ring.

Lifting my hand in a halfhearted attempt at a wave, I tried to smile back, but I was far too tired, my features' response as sluggish as my body's. My right knee gave out, and just as my left one was following suit, strong arms hooked around my waist and scooped me off the ground entirely, cradling me against a hard chest. Through blurry eyes, I found Alex's face only inches from my own, his features wrinkled with concern.

"You're all messed up, Eve," he said, frowning down at me. "But you did good out there."

"Lei?" I whispered, my voice hoarse and cracking.

"Right here, Eve," I heard her say, and felt her hand slip into mine. "Right here. Always."

CHAPTER THIRTY-FIVE

Leisel

"PLEASE DON'T DO this," I pleaded, refusing to release Alex's arm. "Please, you saw what almost happened to Eve, and you'll be fighting two men. Two men, Alex! Two!"

Poor Evelyn had half a dozen stitches in her face, courtesy of a man I hoped had been an actual doctor at one point. Although, when I asked him for his credentials, he'd given me a sardonic smile and a loud snort.

Thankfully, legitimate doctor or not, he had an abundance of medication kept under lock and key, along with a dozen armed guards. Two mystery pills and five minutes later, Evelyn was unconscious. Alex had carried her to our room where I'd tried to clean her as best I could using a small bucket of water and a rag, at least managing to get most of the blood off her. After that, I'd simply crawled into bed beside her, and hummed to her while she slept.

Now the sun was setting, the bonfires had been lit, and an even larger crowd had gathered for Alex's fight than had for Evelyn's. Murmurs rippled among the bystanders about the wildcat who had taken down the most fearsome female fighter in Purgatory. If Alex's pending fight wasn't worrisome enough, the thought of Evelyn becoming this place's new source of entertainment was even more so.

If Jeffers and Liv wanted her here to take Misty's place as the reigning champion, then how would we ever leave? And we most definitely wanted to leave. After seeing what had been done to Evelyn, something she still refused to talk about, and after her fight today, no electrical fence, no amount of armed guards could ever convince me to stay here. It was no better than Fredericksville, and these brands on our wrists meant nothing. No one was safe anymore, anywhere. The best we could hope for was to continue heading south, and pray we found someplace safe enough, someplace isolated where we could finally live in peace.

Was I holding out hope that such a place existed? Not really. It seemed too fantastical, a ridiculous fairy tale, but at the very least I had to believe that something better than Purgatory, better than Covey, better than Fredericksville existed. There had to be others like us, people who just wished to live out the rest of their lives in some semblance of normalcy.

Or had everything and everyone actually died alongside the world? If that was the case, maybe this was actually Purgatory, where we were all just waiting to be judged. And if we were killed in the meantime, well then…no skin off God's back if there was one less sinner in a long line of awaited judgments to be doled out.

I almost wished we'd never left the tree stand.

"I'll be fine, Lei," Alex said, sounding exasperated. "Look at them, one's short and fat and the other one just barely hit puberty. He's nothing but skin and bones."

He was right, Mike was tall and skinny and Bryce was carrying around quite the paunch. But it wasn't their sizes I was worried about, it was what weapons they might have concealed on them.

"He'll be right as rain, my dear!" Grannie said, giving Alex a firm slap on his bicep. "And I'll be here to see you through it." She glanced at me, her round, wrinkled face lit up with excitement. "You look stunning, by the way. I knew that color would look wonderful with your fair skin."

Glancing down at my latest Grannie ensemble, stunning wasn't a word I would have used to describe myself. I was wearing a handmade pale pink, short-sleeved shift that barely reached mid-thigh, the material light and flimsy like a bed sheet, which was probably exactly what it had been made from. I'd paired it with a pair of black leggings with holes in the knees, so worn they appeared a faded charcoal gray. Also new were a pair of men's military-issued army boots, a size and a half too big for me. Alex's weapons belt was slung low on my hips, my blade seated firmly at my side.

I looked mismatched at best, like a young girl trying to rebel against societal norms while still attempting to appear cute and feminine. Worse were the looks I'd been getting from the men. Though they said nothing, their expressions suggested I looked like a pretty pink Popsicle they wanted a nice long lick from.

It was an awful feeling, a hundred pairs of eyes on you as if you were nothing more than prize to be won. Back in Fredericksville, no one had so much as glanced my way without purpose, and never to ogle me. But back in Fredericksville, women weren't whores, at least not for the masses. We were simply the whores of the men who'd forced us into marriage.

I didn't know which was worse.

"Stay with her," Alex muttered in Grannie's direction while prying my fingers from his arm. One of Grannie's thick arms wrapped around my waist, a surprisingly strong grip for an older woman.

"I'll be fine!" Alex shouted over the noisy din of the crowd.

Grabbing my face, he pulled me up on my tiptoes and pressed his mouth to mine. His tongue slid between my lips and mine between his, tangling together in a messy, desperate kiss that I didn't want to end. I'd never been a proponent for public displays of affection, yet I couldn't help but worry that Alex was going to fare even worse than Evelyn had. And if that were the case, I wanted him to know how much he meant to me. I wanted to show him.

Too soon, he broke away from me, Grannie still holding tight to my waist as I reached for him. He gave me one last look before shoving through the people in front of us and disappearing into the crowd.

"Let me go!" I shouted, twisting in earnest, trying to free myself. Eventually she did, but it was already too late. As I pushed and shoved through the crush of people who were shoving me right back, by the time I managed to reach the ring, Alex was already inside it, along with Mike and Bryce.

Misty's body had been taken away but her blood still remained, wet and thick as it pooled on the smooth dirt, glinting an ominous red in the flickering firelight. The infected, trapped in their metal cages, were still going wild for the blood and flesh so close to them, yet so far out of their reach.

"Alex!" I shouted, gripping the rope as I was continuously shoved against it. "Alex!"

Either he didn't hear me over the growing noise, or he was refusing to look at me in fear of distraction from the coming fight. Pulling his T-shirt off over his head, he gripped the collar and tore it down the center, continuing to rip the material until he had several strips of cloth that he began wrapping around his hands and knuckles. Neither Mike nor Bryce had done this; they were fully clothed and without protection for their hands, and both were glaring at Alex.

Their angry stares confused me. The last time I'd seen them, they'd been friendly and smiling. We'd saved them from infected, and this was how they repaid us? Had it all been an act? Or was this the act for the fight? For the viewing pleasure of the masses?

I glared around the ring, then focused on Jeffers, deciding that he was to blame. He was the one who had said we owed him—that he'd wanted the score settled.

Stepping inside the ring, Jeffers took his place in the center, his hands raised. All at once, the shouting dropped to a murmur, and then the murmuring to a whisper.

"For your viewing pleasure!" Jeffers's deep, gravelly voice boomed through the silence. "In this corner, two of my best scavengers, Bryce and Mike!"

Grabbing hold of Mike's hand, Bryce thrust their joined fists up into the air, and the audience went wild. Although, unlike the thunderous applause that Misty had received, the crowd seemed less impressed with these two. Amid the cheering there were shouts of ridicule and mockery.

"And in this corner!" Jeffers gestured toward Alex. "Straight from outside the motherfucking gates...a man with not only a claim on one, but TWO women...WILD MAN!"

As the crowd continued to shout and scream, Alex remained still, his gaze solely focused on his opponents. He didn't raise his fist in the air, didn't even turn to acknowledge the crowds. Standing there, his shoulders slightly hunched, his wrapped hands curled into rock-hard fists, he bounced lightly from one foot to the other, and waited.

"Last chance to place your bets!" Jeffers continued. "The payout for this one is gonna be huge!"

"Three cases of my finest!" an older man shouted. "On the wild man!"

"An AK-47 and three boxes of ammo!" another man yelled. "For the wild man!"

"A week of free pussy!" one scantily clad woman called out. "If Bryce and Mike win!"

I tried to drone them out, their greed, their lack of morals, their sick and twisted need to derive pleasure from the pain of others. I stared at Alex, praying that he would come out of this on top, praying that he wouldn't be harmed. Yet, I couldn't help but envision the very worst possible scenario—his death—and without him, the brand on my wrist and Evelyn's meant nothing.

Without Alex, what would happen to us? The possibilities of such a fate were enough to make me shiver despite the heat from the bonfires, chilling me straight through to my bones.

"DING, DING!"

My breath caught in my throat, my body went rigid with fear. Mike rushed forward while Bryce seemed to be taking his time, as if he was waiting for Mike to attack and while Alex was busying fending off Mike, he would strike. Mike never reached Alex, though, as Alex deftly jumped to the side and out of his grasp, then went barreling into Bryce.

Gripping Bryce's neck, Alex sent his fist straight into the older man's face, and just as he was readying to punch him again, Mike jumped onto Alex's back, his arm encircling Alex's neck, and then...

I never did see what happened next. One minute I was watching the fight with bated breath, my heart pounding in my chest, and the next a hand was slapped over my mouth, an arm hooked around my waist, and I was dragged off through the crowd.

I kicked and I screamed, thrashing wildly in an attempt to free myself, but this wasn't Grannie holding me, this was a man, a strong man whose strength was much greater than mine.

This went on for several long, excruciating minutes, me being dragged farther from the fight, and the crowd ignoring me or just plain not noticing as I was hauled off. Once we were away from the gathered masses, the bonfire light waning, I was released and shoved backward.

My back hit a jagged brick wall, the broken cement digging painfully through the thin material of my dress and into my skin. I blinked through the darkness, trying to make out the face of my kidnapper with only the aid of the moonlight.

"You," I whispered breathlessly, recognizing him as the man who'd approached Alex and me outside of Grannie's tent.

He smiled at me, several dimples appearing on his handsome face. "Me," he said, sounding almost proud.

"What are you doing?" I continued whispering, my gaze flitting from left to right, hoping to find someone nearby. But there was no one around this late at night; the market place was empty, everyone either at the fight or the Drunk Tank.

"Your man is gonna die out there," he said, smirking. "Jeffers doesn't allow his men to be bested by any outsider. Figured I'd better stake my claim on you before you're sent to The Cave or put up for auction."

"A-auction?" I asked, my voice shaking as my body shuddered.

"Don't you worry, sweetheart," he said, and I watched, horrified, as his hands dropped to his pants, already working his belt buckle loose. "Be easy enough to cover up that brand and slap a new one on. And don't you worry, I won't share you."

His eyes lifted, meeting mine. In the reflection of the moonlight within them, I could see the sincerity of his madness-fueled promise. He wouldn't share me.

"I'm fucking lonely," he said as he stepped up against me and flattened his body against mine. "I'm sick of whores, sick of having to pay for it, sick of having to share women with every other asshole in this place."

Squeezing my eyes shut, I turned my head away, evading his mouth.

With a sigh, his lips pressed against my cheek and then lower, to my neck. "I had a girlfriend before," he murmured, his teeth grazing the skin along my collarbone. "She was beautiful…I was gonna marry her."

His tongue darted out, licking its way across my neck, pausing every so often to stop and suckle my skin as he ignored my soft whimpers. "Looked a lot like you," he whispered.

Behind me, my nails were digging into the brick as I desperately tried to figure a way out of this.

"You should wait," I stammered. "Wait until you're sure he's dead." It killed me to say it, to even think of Alex dying, but I had to stall him, had to say something to try to save myself from being raped, or worse, from being claimed.

One hand found my breast, his other my backside. Ignoring me, he continued his assault on my neck while his groping became more and more fevered.

"Please," I pleaded. "Please, you need to wait, please...*please*..."

His hands pulled up the hem of my dress and I reacted, grabbing his shoulders and shoving him away. As he took a surprised step backward, I reached for my knife. About to pull it free from its holster, I was suddenly faced with the barrel of a gun.

I froze, letting my hand fall back to my side. Blinking through my gathering tears, I tried to focus blurrily on the man in front of me. "I don't even know your name," I whispered, frantically grasping at straws. "You have to at least tell me your name."

Still holding the gun to my face, he reached forward to pull my knife free and toss it aside. As it clanked against the cement several times, signaling that it was lost to me, my eyes closed, tears of defeat leaking free.

"So pretty," he murmured, using his free hand to brush away the moisture from my cheeks. "Such a good, sweet woman. Don't find that anymore. You're a dying breed, sweetheart."

The gun disappeared as he took his hand away, slipping the weapon into the back of his pants. Again, he pressed his body against mine, and again he went for the hem of my dress.

His movements were quicker now, harsher, as he fumbled to drag my leggings down. When he slid his hand between my thighs, I let out a small cry that he quickly squelched with his mouth.

"No!" I screamed, turning out of his kiss. "No! Please, someone, help me! Help! Help! HELP ME!"

"They can't hear you, sweetheart," he growled, gripping the back of my thighs. With a grunt, he lifted me up off the ground, and then I could feel him, jutting between my thighs, hard and intrusive.

My arms flailed, my hands pushing helplessly at his face, at his shoulders, gripping his hair and pulling as hard as I could, but he wouldn't be deterred. Even when I managed to sink my nails into his cheek and tear them across his skin, he only grunted in pain and continued to push inside me.

The more he pushed, the more I flailed and the louder I screamed. Grabbing hold of anything I could—his arms, his shoulders, his shirt—I pulled and pushed, and screamed, and...

Suddenly I found the handle of his gun jutting from the back of his pants. Gripping it, I pulled it free and lifted it to his head. My hand shaking fiercely, my grip on the gun no better than jelly, I pressed it against his temple.

"Let me go or I'll kill you," I whispered through ragged breaths.

He went instantly still, his body frozen against mine, the part of him he'd managed to inch inside me pulsing angrily in time to his rapid heartbeat.

All at once he dropped me, and I would have gone sprawling face-first to the ground if it weren't for my leggings still wrapped around my ankles, tripping me up, and causing me to fall back against the wall.

Keeping the trembling gun trained on him, I smiled bitterly as tears poured down my cheeks. "Do you know what I did to the last man who raped me?"

He opened his mouth, maybe to apologize, maybe to beg for his life, maybe to say something crude and uncaring. But I would never find out. Utterly unconcerned with what he had to say, I pulled the trigger, blowing a hole through his shoulder. He staggered backward, his eyes wide, his hand reaching for the bleeding wound before falling to his knees.

Still shaking, I aimed again, this time hoping for his heart.

"Lei!"

Alex's voice tore my gaze away from my target. Shirtless, covered in blood spatter from head to toe, Alex stood only a few feet away from me, his chest heaving with anger. He was almost unrecognizable to me, his hair an unruly mess, blood dripping from his short beard, dripping down his chest and arms, and from his clenched fists. His body was trembling, his eyes were wild, crazed even, darting recklessly between me and the man on the ground, looking as if he wanted to rip him to shreds with his bare hands. Looking as if he *could* rip him to shreds with only his bare hands.

Beside him was Jeffers, whose large arm was held out in front of Alex, refusing to let him any farther than where he stood. Next to Jeffers stood Liv, and behind the three of them was a growing mob of people, jumping and shoving as they tried to see past one another.

"Help...me..." the man called out hoarsely, looking up to Jeffers with pleading eyes.

It was Liv who answered. Taking a deliberate step forward, she waved her hand dismissively at my attacker. Then, not bothering to spare him a second glance, she smirked at me. "Finish it." She snarled at me, her tone taunting, her eyebrows arched with intrigue. "Those are our rules."

Shivering now, my teeth chattering, I glanced back toward Alex. Apart from the subtle trembling still racking his body, he was as still as a statue, his wide, wild eyes on me now.

"Finish it!" Liv screamed, startling me. Her tiny features twisted with fury as she thrust her index finger in my direction. "Kill him, you weak little cunt!"

Still shaking, I refocused on the man. His hand was raised now, his mumbled words indistinguishable between his sobs and the pounding of my own heart.

I didn't want to kill him. I didn't want his blood on my hands, but what I wanted and what I felt were two starkly different things. And all I could feel were his hands on me, Lawrence's hands on me, their mouths, their hands, their penises, taking and taking and taking, uncaring that I wasn't willing, that it wasn't something I was giving to them, but it never mattered, they took it anyway.

With an ear-splitting scream, I pulled the trigger, the bullet missing its mark again and sinking into the man's stomach instead. He screamed loudly, his scream fading quickly into a groan, and he slumped even farther to the ground. I pulled the trigger again, hitting him in the leg, and then again, hitting him in the stomach. I continued pulling the trigger, unable to stop, consumed by emotions, even long after the clip was empty and the man had gone deathly still.

I felt a hand on me, on my arm, and I flinched, jerking away and turning the gun on whoever had touched me. It was Alex, I realized belatedly, yet I still couldn't seem to lower my weapon, couldn't seem to stop shaking, couldn't seem to feel anything but the deep-rooted cold that had taken hold of me.

"Lei," he whispered, wrapping his hand around the barrel of the gun. "Lei, look at me."

I did, blinking rapidly, and raised my eyes to his. Gone was the rage I'd seen in them only moments ago, replaced by the genuine gentleness I was familiar with.

"It's me," he said softly. "It's Alex."

I blinked again, trying to see through my tear-filled eyes.

"You're alive…" A fresh wave of tears filled my eyes. "You won the fight."

"I won the fight," he said, pulling the gun free from my hand.

"And your woman just killed one of my men." Jeffers stepped forward, his arms folded across his chest and a calculating smile on his face. "Which means you owe me."

"I don't owe you shit," Alex spat. "I fought your men, I won your fight."

"Let me rephrase," Liv interjected, glancing up at Jeffers. "You don't just owe us, *we fucking own you*."

CHAPTER THIRTY-SIX

Evelyn

IT WAS DARK when I awoke. My eyes opened sluggishly, trying to make sense of the dark shadows all around me. Gradually, with the aid of the moonlight streaming in through the windows, my eyesight adjusted, and with it came the realization of where I was. I was in our room, and I was alone.

My thoughts muddled, my head pounding, I tried to push myself upright in bed, but my body protested as aches and pains flared to life from what seemed like every inch of me. I blinked slowly, trying to remember, trying to recall.

Bringing a hand to my aching chest, my heart suddenly hammering like a runaway train, I gasped. My breath was staggered as I struggled to breathe, to catch a breath without nearly choking on it.

They'd tried to kill me.

Liv and Jeffers and Misty. They'd all wanted me dead.

My stomach lurched, bile rising in my throat. Why were there no good people left in this world? What the hell was wrong with everyone?

I squeezed my eyes closed, forcing back my threatening tears while attempting to steady my breathing. It didn't matter why. None of this mattered. This place, these people, the insane way they lived, none of it mattered because we were leaving. And once we were free of this hell, we would chalk it up to another lesson learned on the road to somewhere safer.

The lesson being we could trust no one. No one but each other.

Swinging my legs over the side of the mattress, my body protesting my every movement, I gently touched my face. Jagged stitches stretched across my left cheek, the skin around them tender and painful to the touch.

Still, it could have been worse. I could have been Misty. I could have been dead.

My thoughts stuttered to a stop. I'd killed her and I didn't feel bad or guilty; I'd simply done what I had to do to stay alive. But shame was another story, and I felt it in spades. The shame of the realization that I was becoming like the people of Purgatory, by selling my body and then killing a fellow survivor without remorse. How easy a transformation it had been, how easy it was to become even more of a monster than I'd already become.

Standing now, I felt woozy, slightly drugged, and parched with thirst. I scanned the room searching for anything edible, my gaze landing on the countertop and all the treasures it held.

My eyes wide, I lurched forward, reaching for the edge to steady myself. There was a veritable bounty of supplies here, and I found myself again searching the room to ensure this was actually our room, that I hadn't been brought elsewhere.

Once positive that this was in fact our room, I turned back to the countertop, perusing the items. There were several handguns, ammunition, blades of all shapes and sizes, short stacks of clothing, jars filled with a yellowish liquid, as well as food, both canned and fresh.

My stomach rumbled and my nostrils flared as the scent of grilled rat wafted up to greet me.

"Rat," I said dryly, staring at the meat I had come to despise so much. "Of course I would get paid in rats."

Regardless of my feelings on the vermin, I grabbed one of the skewers. The meat had grown somewhat cold, yet I tore into it with gusto, swallowing without even chewing. Finished with the rat, I tossed the bones aside and reached for one of the bottles. Unscrewing the cap, I sniffed the contents, and came away coughing. It was a liquor of some sort, though what it was exactly, I had no earthly idea.

Tentatively, I took a sip, wincing as it slid a burning path down my throat. Once I was sure it wouldn't kill me, I took another swallow and then another, and then I was gulping it down with vigor, relishing the burn and the warming sensation flaring to life in my gut.

I was nearly halfway finished with the bottle when I heard noise from the hallway, and a rattling on the door. Reaching for one of the blades on the counter, I gripped it tightly in my fist and waited. When I saw it was Alex who entered, followed by Leisel, I tossed the blade back on the countertop with a relieved sigh.

I rushed toward Leisel, throwing my arms around her and pulling her against me despite the pain it caused me. Only she didn't return the gesture; in fact, she went stiff against me. I pulled back, searching her face. Her mouth was downturned and trembling as she attempted a smile.

"What happened?" I asked, glancing to Alex. Leaning against the closed door, he was looking out across the room, his gaze unfocused.

"Your fight?" I asked, noting the cuts covering Alex's face and fists, and the blood staining nearly every inch of him. "I'm sorry I wasn't there," I stammered, feeling guilty, wondering if that was why Leisel wouldn't hug me back. Did she hate me for this? Was this another item to add to my list?

Without bothering to look at me, Alex merely nodded. Confused, I looked back at Leisel, but she quickly glanced away, her face pale.

"Lei, what's wrong? What happened?"

"Nothing," she whispered. "Nothing happened."

Something was very wrong; I could feel it in my gut. There were two things that Leisel had never been very good at—the first was hiding her true feelings, and the second was lying.

"What happened?" I repeated, my words laced with worry.

Through her lashes, Leisel glanced up at me. "Nothing," she said. "You just focus on getting better."

I scowled at her, flinching as the movement pulled painfully on my stitches. "Nothing?"

She nodded. "Yes, Alex fought and—"

"What did they do?" I interrupted, turning to Alex. "She's a shitty liar, Alex, so one of you better tell me the fucking truth before I go find out—"

Placing a hand on my trembling arm, her features twisted with anxiety, Leisel interrupted me. "A man, he grabbed me—"

"FUCK!" I screamed, whirling away from her. My hands clenched into angry fists, I dropped them heavily on the countertop, making my winnings jump and rattle together. "Fuck them all!" I continued screaming. "Sick, twisted bastards!"

Spinning back around, I thrust a finger into Leisel's face. "Who was it?" I demanded. "You tell me who it was so I can kill him!" I grabbed a knife from the counter, brandishing it in the air.

"He's already dead," Alex said. It was the first time he'd spoken since entering, and his voice was strained, more so than I'd ever heard it before. All at once, some of the anger fueling my rage began to ebb. He was dead, whoever he was. That much was good.

"You killed him," I said, still watching Alex. "Are you in trouble? Does anyone know?"

"I killed him," Leisel said softly. "I shot him. Everyone was there, they all saw."

I blinked at her, staring blankly into her big brown eyes that were surprisingly dry. I was still angry, yet not exactly sure now what to do with my emotions. "Two for two," I said callously, angry that she'd been forced to kill two men now. Men who'd hurt her.

"Yeah," she mumbled, looking away.

"I'm sorry," I hurried to say. "I didn't mean it like that. I'm just sorry you had to… I'm sorry I wasn't there…"

Frustrated, I struggled to find the right words, feeling awful that once again I hadn't protected her, and even worse that someone, another greedy man, had dared hurt her. A building sob burst free from my lips and I quickly covered my mouth, squeezing my eyes shut.

Feeling dizzy again, my newly digested food churning sickly in my stomach, I lurched forward, stumbling my way across the room and dropping down onto the armchair. Holding my head in my hands, I looked down at the floor, noticing for the first time that I was still wearing my sneakers, my blood-stained sneakers. My stomach churned again and I had to fight not to gag, not to sob, not to beat my own self bloody from the unfairness of it all.

"We have bigger problems, Eve," Leisel said, kneeling down beside me. "Because of what I did…killing him."

Lifting my head, I looked her in the eyes. "What?" I snapped. "What the fuck do we have to do now?"

"Whatever Jeffers and Liv want us to do," Alex interjected. He sounded exhausted, but more so, he sounded defeated.

"They're making him fight again," Leisel said. "Tomorrow night.

They're never going to let us leave here, Eve. They're saying we owe them, for killing two of their people."

I jumped up from the chair, anger thrumming through me. "No!" I shouted. "We're not staying here, we're not spending another day here!"

"We don't have a choice." Pushing himself away from the door, Alex shrugged. "Whatever plan you'd worked out, it's shit now. I'd pretty sure no one leaves here unless they're carried out in body bags. They want us to think we have choices, when in reality this place is no better than a prison camp."

Smoke and mirrors, I thought, stewing silently. It had all been an illusion. There was music here, food, entertainment, not for the sake of giving people a sense of the past, but to keep them within the gates, under the control of Jeffers and Liv.

Without looking at either Leisel or me, Alex headed for the mattress and dropped down heavily on it. Rolling onto his side, he faced the wall and his body went utterly still. Leisel glanced between us, her bottom lip disappearing between her teeth, her indecision clear.

"Go to him," I said, grabbing her hand and squeezing, my thoughts aflutter. "I need to go see someone."

The night was still warm, the marketplace empty and silent as I made my way through it. Metal barrels were lit throughout, lighting my way to my destination. Though I was alone, I was armed, a gun tucked into the back of my pants and two blades secured at my hip. I wasn't leaving anything to chance anymore. In fact, I'd never leave anything to chance ever again.

Turning a familiar corner, I found myself somewhat close to the entrance of the camp, but still far enough away that the guards on duty wouldn't notice me. Leaning up against Dori's building, I crossed my arms over my chest and waited, ready to wait all night if I had to.

Time passed slowly, or quickly, I couldn't be sure without a watch. There was really no way to tell time in the dead of night, with everything still and silent, the sky unchanging. Eventually I heard a shuffle, a strong determined gait across the pavement, and a moment later E rounded the corner.

Surprised to see me, he widened his eyes and slowed his steps as a smile curved his lips. "You waiting for me, Wildcat?" he asked smugly.

Moving to come closer, I put my hand up. "Stay where you are," I gritted out, my heart rate spiking.

Pausing, he raised his hands in a defensive gesture. "Don't be like that," he said with a chuckle. "We had fun, didn't we?"

"Fuck you," I snarled.

He laughed again, his tongue darting out to run slowly across his lower lip. "Right here?" he asked, then took a small step forward, his smile growing wider and infinitely more menacing. "Or right here?"

"Again, fuck you," I spat.

"You look a little beat up, you sure you can handle me right now?" He took another small step forward.

My hand went for my gun, whipping it out from behind me and aiming it at his chest. "Take another step, asshole," I growled. "And it'll be your last."

He chuckled again, entirely unfazed by my bravado. "What's a man got to do to catch a break with you, Wildcat?"

Keeping my gun trained on his chest, I didn't respond. There was nothing left to say. He'd gotten what he wanted, and now it was time for him to pay up.

"Where's my truck?" I finally asked. "Where's everything you promised?"

His smile fell away, his dark eyes growing even darker. Sighing heavily, he shoved his hands deep into his pockets. "I've got it," he said.

"Where?" I snapped.

"What's the rush?" He cocked his head to one side. "You got places to be?"

"I'm leaving," I said. "Tomorrow. First thing."

Why I was trusting him with this information, I didn't know. But what choice did I have? If the truck wasn't ready, if he didn't have what he'd promised me, we wouldn't be able to leave. While my winnings had been plentiful, they wouldn't last us for any real length of time.

His dark eyes narrowing, E took another cautious step in my direction. "You sure that's wise? I know what went down tonight, what happened with your girl. According to Jeffers, your man is indebted to him. You try and leave before that debt is paid, it ain't gonna end well for any of you."

He was only three small steps away from me now, his chest only a hairbreadth of a distance from the barrel of my gun. I was nearly trembling at his proximity, and from the unreadable look on his face. This man was a wild card, his dark eyes unreadable, his cryptic words, his carefully calculated actions all pieces of a puzzle that didn't seem to fit together.

"We're leaving," I said, hoping I sounded stronger than I felt. "And I want everything you promised me inside the truck and ready for us by morning."

He grinned. "You giving out orders now?"

"I'm the one with the gun, E," I sneered.

"That won't always be the case, Wildcat. Fact is, it doesn't have to be that way for you anymore."

A moment passed where he only stared at me. Then another as his eyes searched mine, for what I didn't know.

"I could be good to you," he eventually said, all former pretense gone. There was no smug grin, no swagger to his movements. He stood before me a man, nothing more and nothing less. It was surprising and yet…it wasn't.

"I'm not all bad, Wildcat," he continued, his gaze sincere. "At least, I wasn't always this way."

Maybe if this had been our beginning instead of our end, my answer might have been different. But this wasn't the beginning, this was the end, and there was nothing here for me, nothing for me to find with E. And he'd only helped me to see that, to solidify my decision.

"I don't care," I said, shrugging. "We're leaving."

He seemed to expect my answer, his expression unchanging except for his eyes. Flat and dark, yet in the face of my indifference to him and his confession, they'd gone suddenly ablaze. Taking a step back, he nodded.

"You sure I can't change your mind?" he asked coldly, his usual hard exterior firmly back in place.

"Where, E?" I demanded, ignoring his question. "Where is the truck?"

In one swift movement, he'd grabbed hold of the barrel of my gun, wrenching it to the side and bringing my arm with it. Stepping forward, he pressed his chest against me and lowered his head to mine. "What's he have that I don't?" he growled. "What do you see in that little boy that I can't give you?"

I didn't bother to struggle, already knowing that fighting against his strength was futile. Instead, I glared up at him. "He's a good man," I hissed softly.

"He's nothing," E hissed back. "He's young, stupid, doesn't have the guts to do what it takes to get by in this world."

My laugh was soft, yet full of mocking. "He does," I said. "You know he does. You're just jealous that he's better than you, better than you will ever be."

As if I'd burned him, E dropped my arm and immediately backed away. A muscle ticked in his jaw.

"South parking lot," he gritted out. "Dark blue Jeep. Keys are in the glove box. I give you anything better, and it'll be missed."

"What about everything else?" I asked. Keeping my eyes on him, I took a sideways step in the direction I'd come.

Unblinking, his eyes met mine—cold, dark and murderous. "I don't ever go back on a promise. It'll be there come sunup."

Answering him with only a single nod, I turned to go.

"Wildcat?"

I paused, yet didn't look back. "What?"

"How you gonna get through those gates? Past the guards?"

Briefly closing my eyes, I silently cursed myself before turning around to face him. He was right, I had no idea how we were going to get past the armed guards and through the gates, having planned on driving straight through them if it came down to it. Turning, I found E looking rather smug.

"I could help with that. There's another way out of here…" He shrugged, though the gesture was more ominous than any simple shrug could ever hope to be.

"What do you want?" I asked, already knowing and dreading his answer.

Interlacing his fingers, he began individually cracking his knuckles, the sharp sound stark against the silent night, echoing off the wall behind me. "Everything comes at a price, Wildcat. But you already knew that, didn't you?"

He took a step forward, gesturing to the space I'd just vacated. "Right here?" he said.

CHAPTER THIRTY-SEVEN

Leisel

WHAT DID THEY always say about best-laid plans? That they often go astray? Yes, well, then *they* would have been correct.

This whole plan—from leaving Fredericksville until right up to this moment—now seemed to have been doomed from the very beginning, as if every step we'd taken toward progress had simply been another step in the wrong direction. And now the three of us sat here in our dilapidated room, waiting for the minutes to tick by until we could either find freedom once more, or be punished and kept against our will. Yet again.

Our troubled journey so far all seemed to be just a series of mistakes and unfortunate circumstances. Evelyn and myself, Alex and Jami, had run off into the night, fleeing Fredericksville with only the intention of leaving. And Jami had died. A heartbreaking loss for poor Evelyn, something I knew she still hadn't given herself time to properly grieve over.

Then we'd stopped in Covey, a seemingly destroyed and silent ghost town, in hopes of finding food, gas, and shelter, only to end up kidnapped by religious zealots and nearly made a meal out of. And more people had died.

And the man in the cabin, the one with the little girl who'd been bitten. I'd tried to help her, tried to comfort him, yet she'd died anyway, and in his grief the man had disappeared, his fate unknown. But

I could only presume that he was dead now too.

And here, in Purgatory, a place we'd come to in hopes of finding supplies, of finding a way to continue surviving, only to find another version of Fredericksville, another version of Covey, another version of that man in the cabin, losing his daughter…and meeting with only more death.

It was just a continuous onslaught of death lurking in wait at every corner. No matter what we did, we couldn't seem to run fast enough or far enough to escape it.

The pain, the suffering, the struggle, it was never ending, much like the barrage of bullets I'd put into that man the night before, like the number of times I'd driven that blade into Lawrence's body, like the amount of tears I'd shed.

We should have learned by now that nothing was ever easy in this world. Yet, like children, we remained forever hopeful, optimistic that just once something would go right for us.

We were wrong. That was just the way of the world now, and people like us, those who hadn't let go of the old ways, who couldn't let go of the hope that eventually something had to give and change for the better, we had no place here. We were doomed much like the infected were, forever walking the earth, trying to fulfill a need—a hope—that could not be fulfilled. Because there was no good in this world now.

Our belongings were already gathered, our weapons strapped to us, our clothing and food packed neatly in backpacks procured from Grannie, everything ready and waiting for us to flee. And so we waited, sitting silently in our darkened room, just waiting for what was going to happen next.

With the rise of the sun had come a knock on our door. We glanced at one another uneasily, the tension palpable. None of us wanted to open the door, to be the one that let in the crippling disappointment we already knew was waiting for us.

"It could be your friend?" I whispered to Evelyn. "The one you said would meet us at the Jeep?"

Wide-eyed, Evelyn glanced toward the door, her red and swollen nostrils flaring. "No," she whispered back. "He wouldn't have come here."

Another knock sounded, this one louder than the last. Sighing,

Alex pulled his gun from his pants and stepped toward the door. With his hand on the knob, our eyes met, and in them I saw all the things he couldn't say, didn't know how to voice. He was sorry, sorry that he wasn't the man he'd wanted to be for me. Sorry that he hadn't done more to protect me, to protect us all.

I stared back at him, hoping that he could read me as well as I was him. Hoping that he saw my gratitude, that he could see how much I didn't blame him, not for a single thing that had gone wrong. Instead I wanted him to know how thankful I was for him, for everything that he'd done, for the happiness he'd given me by simply being himself.

He hadn't just loved me, he'd freed me. He'd given me back hope, trust, and pride in myself. He'd given me everything that Lawrence had stripped from me in our poisoned marriage. And I loved Alex for that. I loved him for reminding me that not all men were bad, that there were still men like my beloved Thomas alive.

I loved him for helping me to love again.

Alex seemed to understand this, the silent message I was willing him to receive. It seemed to strengthen him, to give him the courage to open the door and once again shoulder whatever burden was handed to us.

As it turned out, it was only a boy, no more than ten years old, with short, scruffy hair and innocent eyes. The boy thrust a piece of paper toward Alex without saying a word, and as soon as Alex grabbed it from him, he took off running down the hall with barely a second glance. Alex unfolded the page, and as he skimmed it quickly, his features pulled tight in annoyance.

"It's for you," he said, looking up at me, both apology and anger written on his face. "You have to work tonight."

"Nobody's working tonight," Evelyn snapped. She glanced from me to Alex. "We're leaving. Are you both ready?" Her look was almost daring us to disagree with her.

Whereas I nodded numbly in response, Alex seemed skeptical. "Who is this guy, Eve? How can you be sure he's going to follow through?"

We'd been over this so many times already, Alex repeatedly questioning Evelyn on who her secret friend was, and Evelyn refusing to give any details. I had my suspicions, mainly that she had traded herself for a vehicle and perhaps a way out of here, but I hadn't voiced them.

Whatever had happened had changed her, the change was written all over her face. She barely kept eye contact, moving away whenever I got too close. Her shame was evident, but I didn't want to press her on the matter. We'd all been through enough, and there would be plenty of time to talk when we were free of this place. *If* we got free of this place.

"I can't be sure," Evelyn answered, sounding exasperated, her expression softening somewhat. "But we'll never know if we don't try, right?" She looked to me for support, knowing that Alex believed that staying alive was the better option than dying while escaping. Anything just to keep me safe.

So many times in the last few years, I'd thought I was going to die, and it terrified me. But now, when I thought about the possibility of being killed for trying to escape, or worse, being forced to stay here and do the bidding of Jeffers and Liv… Faced with the choice between those two options, I wanted out and I *was* ready to die trying. After all, there were far worse fates than death, most of which we'd already lived through.

"We have to try," I said to Alex firmly, reaching out and laying my hand on his forearm. "We can't stay here. I won't stay here."

His eyes closed again briefly, pain washing over his features before he reopened them and focused on me. "Whatever happens, Lei," he said, taking my hand. "It was worth it."

My heart swelled at his words; I wholeheartedly agreed with him. It was worth it, wasn't it? No matter what happened, after years of misery, it had been worth finding even an iota of happiness. It had been worth it to learn there was someone else in the world, other than just Evelyn and me, who hadn't succumbed to the corruption and wickedness everyone else had seemed to. Because the infection ran so much deeper than just turning people into mindless cannibals. It destroyed people's souls.

"I always knew you were a big, fluffy marshmallow, Alex," Evelyn said, attempting to ease the tension. "Big and strong on the outside, but all ooey-gooey in the middle." Her hand touched her stitches subconsciously as she forced a pained smile.

Alex slanted his eyes toward Evelyn. "Are you calling me fat?"

"Yes," she replied, smirking. "Now, get going, fatty."

As was planned, so as not to cause any suspicions on where the three of us were heading with all of our belongings in tow, Alex left first. I was to be next, followed closely by Evelyn. Each of us had our own separate route, but the same destination.

"You know where to go?" Evelyn asked me for what seemed like the hundredth time. "Remember, don't go through the market place, there's too many eyes watching. Too many people we can't trust."

Sighing, I nodded. Though I was anxious, I was more determined than anything else. I was stronger than I had been in years.

"Stop worrying about me," I said. "I can do this." To further prove my point, I patted the weapons belt slung low on my hips, heavy with both a handgun and a blade.

"I'll always worry about you," she said, her bloodshot eyes glossing over. "Always, Lei." She sounded so defeated, and it hurt to see her so broken.

Biting down on my bottom lip so as not to cry, I reached for her hand and shook my head. "It doesn't matter what happens. You made good on your promise to Thomas."

"But I didn't," she whispered. "I didn't do nearly enough."

"I'm still here, aren't I?" I countered, squeezing her hand. "I'm alive, Eve, and that's about the best any of us can ask for anymore."

Her tears spilled over, and despite knowing I had to get moving, I pulled her in for a quick hug, squeezing her tightly to me. "You made me strong, Eve," I whispered, pressing a kiss to her cheek. "You made me want to keep going."

Before my own tears could fall, I pulled out of our hug and turned away, slipping quickly out the door and into the hallway. While trying to keep from looking in a hurry, I kept an agile, yet energetic pace, hoping I didn't seem as anxious as I felt. My bag was slung over my shoulder, some of the clothing that Alex had gotten me and some food all thrown in haphazardly. The bag was heavy, but I acted as if it weighed nothing, not wanting to draw attention to it.

There were only a few people moving about in the building this early in the morning, and those that were around barely gave me a second look as they either entered or exited their own apartments. The stairs were clear as I descended, as was the exit, and then I was outside, making an immediate left, and headed away from the marketplace.

"Leisel! Sweetheart!"

I stopped walking, closing my eyes, sucking in a breath of calming air before turning around. Grannie was hurrying down the pathway, her wide hips shaking back and forth as she waved excitedly in my direction.

"I was hoping to find you before you went to work tonight!" she said breathlessly, coming to a stop before me. Reaching out, she placed her hand on my shoulder and took several deep breaths. "The end of the world isn't meant for old women. It's a wonder I've made it this long!"

I tried to smile at her to hide the spike in my nerves, yet my eyes continued darting left and right as I hoped that no one else of importance had spotted me.

"I have the perfect dress for you to wear tonight," she continued. Straightening up, she smoothed her hands down the front of her shirt. "An old sequined number from the eighties that I've spruced up a bit. Imagine how you'll look up there dancing, the lights catching the sequins!" Letting out a tiny shriek, she clapped her hands together, obviously pleased with herself.

I tried again to smile at her, yet could feel nothing but disgust. Despite her having been kind to us, treating us to clean clothing and such, she was no better than anyone else in Purgatory. She was thriving here, her sewing skills a necessity, so she wasn't subjected to the same sort of cruelty the younger women were. Yet it was that very cruelty she depended on. She enjoyed the fights, made a killing off betting, all while happily supplying ridiculous getups for the dancers and hookers, only ensuring that this ludicrous way of life would continue.

She was part of the problem.

"Thank you," I muttered. "Can't wait to see it."

"No, no!" she exclaimed, reaching for me. "You must come now! I can't wait to show you!"

Swallowing hard, I took a step away from her. "I...um...I can't right now. I have to meet...someone..."

God, I was the absolute worst liar left alive today. Somehow, even surrounded by them, I still couldn't manage to pull it off. And Grannie, despite her penchant for seeming carefree, picked up on this immediately.

"What do you mean?" she asked, her voice hushed, her eyes comically wide. "Someone like...another man?"

"No," I said quickly, bringing my backpack forward, showing her the overstuffed bags. "I'm trading is all."

"Ah," she said, sighing in relief. "Good God, sweetheart, you nearly gave me a heart attack! You've got a good one, you know. Wouldn't want to see him cut you loose and have you end up in the Cave...or worse!"

Yes, I thought dryly, wouldn't want that.

"Give me an hour," I said, slinging my bag back up over my arm. "And I'll come get the dress." Smiling as wide as I could manage, I reached out and touched her hand. "I'm sure it's beautiful."

"All right then," she said, grinning again. Then she lowered her voice to a dramatic whisper. "Happy trading!"

I waited where I was, watching as she walked back in the direction she'd come, her hips swinging as she hummed an out-of-tune melody that I couldn't place. When she was little more than a dark outline in the distance, I turned away, a relieved sigh escaping my lungs as I continued on.

Doing as Evelyn had instructed, I stayed deep within the living quarters, walking between buildings instead of around them, keeping out of the sight line of any of the main buildings. The entire complex was a maze of walkways and buildings, bigger and more labyrinthine than it had seemed when standing on the opposite side of the gates. Several times, I found myself confused and a bit turned around, only to eventually run into old metal signs with arrows directing to the north and south parking lots, from back when the factory had still been in use.

Eventually the shadows thrown by the buildings surrounding me gave way to sunlight. Beyond a widespread lawn, overgrown with wildflowers, weeds, and grass nearly to my knees, was the south parking lot.

Looking left and right, seeing no one other than an elderly man strolling leisurely through the tall grass, I headed out across the lawn. He paid me little mind, busying himself with watching the swarms of bugs hovering over the grass, and smiling to himself.

Once I'd reached the edge of the parking lot, I paused, scanning the rows of vehicles for either Alex or a dark blue Jeep. I found neither, noting that most of the cars in this lot were either missing wheels or windows or both, some having been stripped of their engines and seating compartments. Just as my stomach began to churn with worry, thinking that either I'd gotten myself lost again, or we'd been purposely misled, I thought I spotted someone far off in the distance. Shielding my eyes from the sun, I squinted across the lot, but was unable to be certain who it was without getting closer.

Shouldering my backpack, I hurried forward, quickly weaving around the metal shells until finally I was able to see clearly. And what I saw stopped me cold in my tracks. The frantic beating of my heart skipped, the world around me now frozen as I looked on at the scene unfolding before me with horror.

"No!" I screamed, clasping a hand over my mouth. "NO!"

CHAPTER THIRTY-EIGHT

Evelyn

LEISEL'S SCREAMS ECHOED through the maze of buildings, easily reaching me. My heart stuttered as her cries were abruptly cut off. I dropped my backpack and my feet pounded the ground, the surrounding buildings nothing more than a blur as I sped past them.

Turning the final corner, the dark shadows of the buildings giving way to sunlight and lush grass, I stopped when I saw Leisel off in the distance. This was all my fault, I thought, looking on at the scene before me, my steps now slow and cautious.

Several armed men stood in a circle around my friends. Alex, his arms wrenched backward and secured behind him was being held by one man, while another held a gun to his temple. Leisel had been shoved belly first up against the hood of the Jeep, while the man holding her there was blatantly groping her, grinding his hips against her backside and grinning. And standing in the center of it all, was E.

Slowly, he turned toward me, his gaze finding mine, the grin on his face growing wider with every step I took. Anger and hatred burned hot and thick through my veins, causing my blood to pump furiously, the sound of it beating a fast and heavy tempo in my ears. Pulling my gun from my pants, I brought it forward, ready to shoot my way out of there if I had to.

I stared at E, ignoring Leisel's whimpers, ignoring the gun held to Alex, ignoring everyone until our surroundings seemed to disappear, leaving only E and me.

"What are you doing?" I gritted out between clenched teeth, angry at myself for trusting him.

Chuckling, E spread his arms out wide. "I've changed my mind, Wildcat." He shook his head. "After last night, I know what kind of man you need, and it ain't that." He jerked his chin in Alex's direction.

My fingers jerked around my weapon, and E's eyes flickered to my hand. Lifting his gaze, his grin turned menacing. "You won't be needing that," he said, holding out his hand. "Not if you want your friends to live."

He spoke so nonchalantly, as if he were asking me to share my lunch with him. Not hand over my weapon, the only thing standing between Alex and Leisel either living or dying.

"You bastard," I spat, holding the gun out in offering.

Taking it from me, he shrugged once before tossing it to a man standing behind him. The man caught it with ease and tucked it into his pants.

"We had a deal," I said, my breaths coming in quick, short bursts as I struggled to contain my rage.

"Deals change all the time," he said, his arrogant tone matter-of-fact. "And I have a much better one in mind."

"Fuck him, Eve!" Leisel suddenly screamed, rearing up from beneath her captor. "Fuck him and fuck this whole place!" The man holding her grabbed a fistful of her hair, using it to slam her back down against the hood.

Ignoring her, E continued to watch me. "I think you'll like it," he said. "It benefits everyone. I'll let your friends go, but you're staying here with me." Looking smug, E raised his brow.

"No!" Leisel screamed, the terror in her voice ripping at my heart.

"No, Eve!" Alex shouted.

"And what if I say no?" I asked carefully, keeping my eyes on E.

"Then I kill your man," he replied easily. "Let me make it easy for you, Wildcat. You don't really have a choice here, just the illusion of one. So take my deal—stay with me and your friends can go free."

Placing a hand on my arm, E roughly turned me to face the Jeep. Inside, I could make out several stacks of boxes, though I couldn't see what was in them. "Everything I promised you, they can have," he said.

"Eve, no!" Leisel continued to scream. "You promised! You fucking promised me! We do this together, always together!"

Squeezing my eyes shut, my thoughts drowned out the sound of her cries as I thought back to Thomas—Leisel's husband—and the night that he died. Lying on the floor of my living room, Leisel gripped tightly to his hand, tears streaking down her face while Shawn and I stood solemnly by. Candles flickered all around us, the warm scents of vanilla floating up from them. But even they couldn't hide the scent of Thomas's death that was so close.

He'd looked up to me and Shawn, his bloodshot eyes pleading with us. "Keep her safe," he'd whispered hoarsely. "Promise me, you'll keep her safe for me."

I'd sobbed loudly, my tears streaking down my cheeks. Gripping Shawn's hand tightly, I'd nodded. "I promise," I'd whispered.

"No matter what?"

"No matter what, Thomas, I promise. I'll protect her with my own life."

"It won't ever come to that," Shawn had said, his grief palpable. "I'll protect them both."

Seemingly satisfied, Thomas had turned his gaze back to his wife, whispering things to her that I couldn't make out. Only moments later, his eyes began to cloud over, a gray fog blanketing them. His lungs rattled loudly in his chest as he blinked sluggishly. His grip on Leisel's hand loosened, and as she gasped, clutching him tighter, his eyes rolled back in his head.

"No!" Leisel had sobbed, shaking his arm. "No, Thomas, no!"

While Shawn had pried her off his body, I'd stood there, able to do little more than sob. I had cried for the loss of my friend, for Leisel's devastating loss, for how bleak our futures seemed in that one moment...and every moment that had followed since.

Turning back to E, I swallowed back the lump in my throat and looked him squarely in the eyes. "I'll do it," I said firmly, thinking only of Leisel and Thomas, and of my promise to them.

Despite Leisel's answering sobs, E was smiling, the first genuine smile I'd seen on him, giving me a glimpse of perhaps the man he'd once been. Reaching out to touch my cheek, E ran his fingertips down the side of my face in an almost romantic gesture.

"One more thing," he said, and grabbed my neck, using his hold on me to bring my body flush against his. "A lesson, if you will," he whispered, his breath hot against my ear. Then he tossed me aside, much the same way he'd grabbed me, into the arms of the same man he'd given my gun to.

Shrugging out of his denim jacket, rolling his neck from side to side, E headed toward Alex, his hands clenched into fists. Still being held at gunpoint, Alex showed no emotion as E approached him, meeting him stare for stare.

"You make one move to stop me, Wildcat," E threw over his shoulder. "And I will kill him."

"God, please, no!" Leisel screamed, bucking wildly against the man holding her. "Please don't hurt him!"

Alex squared his shoulders as best he could considering the way he was being held.

"This isn't exactly a fair fight," Alex ground out, his nostrils flaring.

E laughed in response, a bitter, twisted laugh. "This isn't supposed to be fair, boy. This is a lesson to be learned." And then he sent his fist straight into Alex's gut.

Coughing, choking, Alex tried to curl in on himself in an attempt to deflect the barrage of punches E was throwing at him, but it was a useless effort. E continued to hit him like a broken record on repeat, his heavy fist connected with Alex's face, ribs, and stomach over and over again. Blood poured from wounds on his face, purple bruises appearing almost immediately, one eye swelling almost shut, and through it all Leisel was screaming, beating her hands on the roof of the Jeep, yet unable to move.

Once Alex had been beaten into near unconsciousness, his shoulders drooping, blood pouring from his mouth and nose, trailing down his shirt, E gripped a handful of his hair and used it to lift his face.

"You don't come back for her, you hear me?" he said, his tone venomous, promising only more pain. "She's mine. All fucking mine."

Alex blinked up at him through one eye. "Yes," he managed to say between coughing gasps.

Drawing a wad of phlegm from the back of his mouth, E spat in Alex's face and released his head. It fell forward, blood and saliva spattering.

"You see, Wildcat," E said, turning back toward me. "I always protect what's mine."

Taking my face between his bloodied hands, he tipped my head back and pressed a hard kiss on my lips. "Do you see?"

I nodded numbly. "Yes," I said softly. I'd seen it quite clearly, exactly what this "lesson" had been. This hadn't been just a lesson for Alex, or any other man who tried to touch me, this was my lesson. I was owned, body and soul.

E stared at me a moment longer, watching me intently through those black eyes of his, eyes that held so much and yet seemed so empty. His features were hard, his lips pressed tightly into a thin line, and suddenly time seemed to stop altogether. No heat from the sun touched on my skin, no breeze moved through my hair, even Leisel's cries had grown quiet. There was just E, myself, and the soft hum from the electric gates reminding me that that I wouldn't be leaving this prison, not ever. Trapped forever in Purgatory.

Releasing my face, he turned away, then put his fingers to his mouth and whistled loudly. From a ways off, a man appeared from behind a small platform near the gate. Waving to E, he nodded and once again disappeared from view. All at once, the fence's humming ceased.

"Put them in the Jeep," E ordered his men. He turned to Leisel and gave her a sickeningly sweet smile. "You need to hurry on out of here," he told her. "Before anyone gets wind that the gates have been shut down."

"Fuck you," she hissed, struggling against the man dragging her. "I will kill you, I will find a way to kill you, you monster!"

As she was shoved roughly into the driver's seat and Alex the passenger seat, E only laughed at her, turning away from her shouts with a dismissive, sickening smile. The doors were slammed closed, then a set of keys was tossed over the open roof and into Leisel's lap.

"Start it!" one of the men demanded, aiming his gun through the window at Leisel's head. Turning away, she did as she was instructed, and the vehicle roared to life with a healthy rumble.

Slumping back in his seat, Alex attempted picking his head up, his one good eye focusing on me. Placing his hand up against the window, he mouthed the words *I'm sorry* at me.

Nodding, I squeezed my eyes shut, willing my gathering tears not to fall. I took a deep breath and reopened them only to find E staring down at me, his upper lip raised in angry snarl. Grumbling something incoherent, he spun away from me and stalked toward the Jeep. As he gripped the knife he had strapped to his belt, a flash of steel glinting off the sun as he drew it out, I realized what was happening. Screaming at the top of my lungs, I rushed him.

"No!" I screamed, throwing myself at his back, wrapping my hands around his neck, my legs around his waist, trying to force him to stop.

With an angry grunt, E grabbed my arm, yanking me off of him. He threw me down on the ground, making my head hit painfully against the gravel, then wrapped his hand around my throat, pinning me in place.

"What did I say?" he growled menacingly. "What did I fucking tell you?"

Nodding to one of his men, he tossed the knife up in the air. It flew, handle over blade, the short distance between the men, and the man caught it easily. Watching as the man headed toward the Jeep, I gasped for air, finding it hard to breathe, let alone speak with how tightly E had a grip on my throat.

"N-no," I rasped. "Please… He's not…mine."

E's grip on my throat loosened some. "What?" he shouted, his black eyes opening wide. His face was an angry shade of red, his nostrils flaring wildly as his features contorted with fury, and I wondered if I hadn't just made things that much worse.

"He's not mine!" I screamed hoarsely, watching as the man yanked open the passenger door, caught Alex before he could tumble to the ground, and shoved him back upright. "We're not together, E! We never were!"

The man thrust his hand forward, sending the blade into Alex's side. Howling in pain, blood spraying from the wound as the man pulled the blade free, Alex slumped to his side just as Leisel began to scream.

Using his hold on my throat, E pulled me to my feet and glared down at me. His chest heaving, he brought us nose to nose. "You were never with him?" he whispered darkly. "Never?"

Trembling with rage, I shook my head back and forth quickly. "Never," I hissed. "He loves Leisel, you disgusting fuck!"

"Get them out of here!" E bellowed to his men, jerking his chin toward the Jeep. The same man who'd stabbed Alex slammed the passenger door closed, and E turned back to me. "I'll deal with you later," he said, his expression promising nothing but pain.

The thought of Leisel out there unprotected, of Alex injured and possibly dying, and me stuck behind this fence with this madman, spurred me into action. I couldn't stay here, not with him, not without Leisel. Panic and pain driving me, I found myself reaching blindly for the gun holstered at E's hip. Yanking it free, startling him enough to loosen his grip on me, I scrambled backward, firing instantly, aiming for E's heart, his head, anything that would hurt him and stop this madness.

The first shot went wide, my panic enabling E to duck and dodge sideways, and he made a run for one of the broken vehicles. I kept shooting, shooting in all directions, causing his men to scatter.

Shouting sounded all around me as bullets cracked through the air, the noise and chaos bound to alert the rest of the camp that something was wrong. Knowing Leisel and I wouldn't be able to fight off the entire camp, I ducked and ran for the Jeep, throwing open Leisel's door as she scrambled out of my way and into the backseat. Pulling the door shut behind me, I slammed my foot down on the gas, and in a flurry of spinning tires and flying gravel, we shot off across the parking lot.

"Turn the gates back on!" E's angry voice bellowed.

"Leisel!" I screamed, only to find her right next to me, wedged between me and Alex. I tossed her my gun. "The guard at the gate! You need to kill him before he turns the fences back on!"

Gripping the gun, she took hold of the roll bar above our heads and pulled herself upright. Though tears were pouring down her cheeks and her chin was trembling violently, she aimed and pulled the trigger, letting loose a flood of bullets. Her aim was off, not helped by the violent rocking of the quickly moving Jeep.

The guard must have realized his life was in danger, that we were going to hit the gates whether electricity was flowing through them or not, because I wasn't stopping, not a chance in hell. Instead of attempting to turn them back on, he went running in the opposite direction. We flew past him and barreled straight toward the fence.

"Duck!" I screamed, pulling on Leisel just as we hit the gate, our tires spinning only slightly as the Jeep went headfirst into it. Groaning and creaking, the metal tore easily from the ground, the section we hit ripping away from the rest of it, then flying up and over our heads.

Gripping the steering wheel, I turned the Jeep in a wide, tire-squealing arc toward the road. As I spared a glance in my rearview mirror, I saw E running after us, his large form gradually growing smaller and smaller in the distance.

I looked across at Alex, at my poor Leisel cradling his head in her arms and sobbing. His blood was everywhere, covering him and Leisel, and the entire interior of the Jeep. The bitter tang of death hung thickly in the air all around us.

The now-familiar scent that seemed to follow us everywhere.

CHAPTER THIRTY-NINE

Leisel

"HELP ME WITH him!" I cried, unable to bear Alex's weight as he began falling from the open door of the Jeep. Evelyn rushed around the vehicle to my side, and lifted up Alex's arm, slinging it across her shoulders. I did the same, and together we managed to pull him somewhat upright.

"I'm sorry," he mumbled, blood and spit spraying from his lips. "I'm sorry…Lei…"

We'd driven as long as we could, until it had become clear that Alex was losing far too much blood, and we had to stop to try to dress the wound. There had been nothing for miles, just long, empty stretches of wheat fields and overgrown grass. Finally we came to the edge of a small town, where we happened on the shell of a gas station and an old rundown motel situated behind it.

I waited in the Jeep with Alex as Evelyn checked the place out, finding that the rooms had been picked clean long ago. There was no furniture remaining, and the structure was full of rats and insects, but thankfully free from infected.

Using her shoulder to push the already open door even farther open, Evelyn helped me settle Alex onto the dirty carpet. I kicked several cockroaches out of my way before dropping to my knees beside him.

"We shouldn't stop here," Evelyn said, her eyes darting toward the open door. "What if they're following us? We can't be all that far, only a couple miles at best."

I shook my head, unconcerned if they found us, only caring about Alex. He wasn't going to make it, not if we didn't treat the wound. "Let them come," I said bitterly.

Evelyn looked uncertain, but she didn't voice her feelings. "I'm going to see what's in the Jeep," she said, turning away. "See if there's anything we can use for him."

As she hurried out, I gingerly lifted Alex's blood-soaked T-shirt away from his skin. On his bruised and battered abdomen, the small wound was still bleeding profusely. Beneath the blood covering nearly every inch of him, his tanned skin had turned a sickly shade of gray, growing cold to the touch, and his breathing was beginning to slow.

"Oh God," I whispered, my eyes blurring with tears. "Oh God, not again, not again, please, God, not again."

Alex's one good eye opened, focusing on me as he tried to raise his arm. He couldn't seem to manage enough strength to do so, so I gripped his hand and brought it to my face.

"I'm so sorry," I sobbed, my tears falling faster, spilling onto his chest. "I'm so sorry, Alex, I'm so sorry."

"Lei…" he croaked, attempting to turn his head. "You don't… nothing to be sorry… for…"

"Don't try to talk," I mumbled, brushing my hand over his hair, pushing the fallen strands from his eyes. "We're going to get you better, you're going to get better, and everything will be fine."

A single tear that had welled in the corner of his eye slid free down the side of his broken nose. I bent forward and kissed it away, softly kissing his battered cheek, his bloodied chin, and then finally, brushing my lips across his.

I hardly knew him, yet losing him was every bit as painful as losing Thomas was. Alex, the hope he'd given me, the unexpected love, it had brightened my ever-darkening world. Now that small slice of sun that had only just begun to peek through the dark clouds was dimming, fizzling out, leaving me like everything else had.

And it was all my fault. Another consequence. He saved me and because of that, he was dying.

"Worth…it," he struggled to whisper, his breath coming in short puffs against my lips. "You were…worth it."

Pulling away from him as more tears formed, clouding my vision,

I shook my head, knowing full well I wasn't worth it, I wasn't worth this much death and destruction. No one was worth this. "I love you," I cried softly. "I love you, Alex."

I did love him in the sense that he held a place in my heart, one that was solely and irrevocably his and his alone. It might have been a different type of love than what I felt for Thomas or the way I loved Evelyn, but it was love nonetheless.

He tried to smile, wincing as he did. "Take…care…of…" He trailed off, his one eye closing.

Frantic, I dropped his arm and leaned forward, pressing my face against his, searching for his breath. Placing my hand over his heart, I waited breathlessly for it to thump, and sighed in relief when I felt it. Although his breaths were shallow and his heartbeat slow, he was still breathing, and his heart still beat.

My own heart pounding furiously, I fell back on my ankles. I wanted to scream. I wanted to beat my fists on the floor, beat them against my face and my thighs and just scream and scream and scream and scream. It wasn't fair, it wasn't fucking fair. Everything good left in this world was going to be eventually snuffed out altogether, one by one, and not by the infected but at the hands of the selfish, greedy people who'd taken control, who'd turned a worldwide devastation into their own personal playground. Soon there would be nothing decent remaining, only sin or sacrifice, and my only solace was the hope that eventually they'd all kill each other off.

"Move, Lei!" Evelyn shouted, rushing back into the room with her arms full.

Setting down Alex's hand, I scrambled to his other side while she dropped the bundle she was carrying and began to sort through it.

"There's nothing to clean the wound with," she muttered. "Nothing to stitch it with either. I'm going to wrap it as tightly as I can and then bandage it, okay?"

Still crying, I nodded. "What can I do? How can I help?"

She paused in her sorting and looked up at me, her wild eyes suddenly growing soft and sad. Opening her mouth, no sound came out, and she closed it, then licked her lips. As she shook her head slowly, tears began to gather in her eyes. "This is my fault," she said, choking over her words. "This is my fault, all my fault, Lei! It's all my fault!"

She was shaking now, trembling so violently that I stood up, stepping over Alex to drop down beside her. Pulling her quivering body into my arms, I could feel how cold she was despite the heat, nearly as cold as Alex.

"No," I whispered fiercely. "No! Not one single thing that has happened has been your fault! All you've done was fight for us, for me. The actions of others is not your fault, Eve, do you hear me? It's not your fault!"

Pulling away from her, I took her battered face gently in my hands. "Now, please," I begged her. "Please help me save him."

Pressing her lips together, Evelyn squeezed her eyes shut and curled her hands into fists, then shook her head. Reopening her eyes, she swiped the tears from her cheeks and pointed to a pile of clothing. "Help me rip it," she said, her voice sounding stronger. "We need long, thin pieces to tie around him."

Forgetting our grief and our regrets, we busied ourselves with the task at hand, knowing the only thing that mattered at the moment was to try to do something to help Alex. After tearing the clothing into strips and tying them tightly around his abdomen, we continued to bandage him with the remaining suitable articles of clothing. When we were finished, we made a bed of sorts for him using scraps of material for a pillow and his jacket as a blanket.

Afterward, when Evelyn had gone to check the area for threats, I lay down beside him, taking his hand in mine and holding it to my heart. Humming softly, I began to pray. Who or what I was praying to, I no longer knew.

But in the end, all our efforts were wasted. Alex died as the sun was setting, while rays of gold and yellow streamed in through the window, touching every inch of his body. Appearing as if he were glowing, he took his last shuddering breath before going still.

"Thank you," I whispered, kissing his cold lips with my own trembling ones as my tears fell on his cheeks, making it look as if he were crying in his sleep. "Th-thank you for everything."

"Where should we go?" Evelyn asked, her head against the wall, her eyes on the window as she watched the fat and full moon hanging low in the night sky. "Should we still head south? Or west, maybe?"

Seated beside her, my back against the same wall with Alex's head in my lap, I ran my hand through his hair, much like I'd been doing all night. "Does it matter?" I asked.

"No," she answered, sounding listless and far away. "It doesn't."

"I wish we could bury him," I mused, still running my hand through his hair. "Instead of having to just leave him in here."

Several rather bold rats had already begun sniffing around his body, not seeming to mind when I would kick them away. They were waiting, I guessed, for us to leave him here so they could have their meal.

"We could try," Evelyn offered, still staring out the window. "Maybe I could find some rocks for us to dig with."

"That sounds good," I whispered, trailing my knuckles down Alex's scruffy cheek. "We should do that."

We lapsed into silence, Evelyn's gaze still on the moon, and mine on nothing in particular. While Evelyn continued to sniffle, I couldn't seem to cry. It was as if my tears had all but dried up. It was about time, I thought wryly, that I stopped crying every other second.

"Lei?"

"Hmm?"

"Remember what you said to me at my wedding? Right before I was supposed to walk down the aisle?"

My lips attempted to turn upward, wanting to smile, yet I hadn't the strength for it. "Yes," I said. "I remember you were scared out of your mind, and so I told you to put your big-girl panties on and get your ass out there."

"No," she said. "After that, right before you were supposed to walk out there. You looked over your shoulder and smiled at me, remember what you said?"

"I remember."

"You said, 'If you don't walk down that aisle and marry the best thing to ever happen to you, then I'm going to lose the best friend I've ever had. You can't be best friends with your husband's best friend's ex-girlfriend, you know?'"

Evelyn rolled her head toward me, her blue eyes glistening with tears. "I didn't want to lose the best friend I'd ever had," she whispered. "So I put my big-girl panties on and walked down that aisle."

I stared into her eyes and gave her the best smile I could muster.

"I remember," I said. "I also remember what you said to me when I found out I couldn't have children."

Evelyn's eyes closed, more tears spilling out from beneath her lashes. "I said," she replied hoarsely, "that I'd have babies for both of us."

"And Thomas had asked if that meant he got to have sex with you, remember?"

Through her tears, Evelyn smirked. "He was only joking, but I'd never seen you so mad."

I shrugged. "It wasn't funny."

"Lei, it was funny. Even Shawn thought it was funny."

I shook my head. "It wasn't funny."

"It was."

"No." I cleared my throat and glanced down at Alex. Even with only the light of the moon, I could tell that his lips were now blue, his skin a waxy sort of white. Gently, I combed my fingers through his short beard before glancing back up at Evelyn. "In fact, I'm still annoyed with him for that."

"He loved you. He would never have touched another woman."

"That's not the point."

"You're silly."

"I know. And yet, you love me anyway."

Reaching out, Evelyn placed her hand over mine, and together we ran our fingers through Alex's hair.

"Thomas would have liked him," she whispered.

"I know."

Letting my head fall sideways onto her shoulder, I closed my eyes and let out a sigh. "I could've loved him, you know? Not like I loved Thomas, but…I really think I could have."

Pressing a kiss to the top of my head, Evelyn inhaled slowly. "I know."

"I love you, Eve."

"I love you too, Lei."

CHAPTER FORTY

Evelyn

I'D BEEN DREAMING of Shawn. Nothing specific, just another ordinary day in our ordinary life together, lost in the daily humdrum. I dreamed of washing clothes and ironing them, vacuuming the throw rug in our living room, grocery shopping, the feel of his strong arms wrapped around me and the gentle kisses we'd shared. It had all seemed so vivid, so real, that when I awoke, still leaning back against the wall, slumped sideways over Leisel, I sobbed from the loss of the dream, the loss of Shawn, the loss of the woman I'd been.

The sight of the motel room only made my slap back to reality that much harsher—the filthy, blood-soaked carpet beneath me, the dirt-stained walls, the cracked and crumbling ceiling above, and the body of Alex, his once sun-kissed skin now mottled with the bruising appearance of rigor mortis. The smell in the room was awful, the stench of the dead always was, an unforgettable mixture of feces and urine amid the rancid smell of rotting meat. But beneath all the foulness there was always a hint of sweetness, a tinge of fragrant perfume, as if in death, underneath all its ugly glory, lay a sort of beauty trying to claw its way forth.

Worse were the twelve or so rats gathered around his ankles, chuffing and crackling noises coming from them as they chewed happily through his pants.

Pulling away from Leisel, I stood on shaky legs, kicking at them with all the strength I could muster. They squeaked loudly as they were flung across the room, one even going so far as to hiss at me while it scurried across the carpet, disappearing into the tiny bathroom.

Leisel stirred in her sleep, her lips parting as she sucked in a noisy breath, her hand clutching tighter to the grip she still had on Alex's hair. Choking back a threatening sob, I turned away from her, unable to watch her cling to yet another thing she'd lost.

Approaching the window, I touched my face, gently probing my stitches and the tender skin surrounding them. My face was hot, too hot, my cheek burning beneath my fingers. Closing my eyes against the sunlight, I wondered what on earth we were going to do if my wounds became infected. Yet, that was the least of our problems. Where were we going to go? Were we going to make it out there on our own? With no man to protect us?

Did we go back to Purgatory?

Despite my tears, I nearly laughed out loud. Go back to Purgatory? They'd kill us for sure, or worse, enslave us to a lifetime of prostitution. I couldn't even begin to imagine the horrors E would have in store for me.

Opening my eyes, I watched as the sun rose. Another day behind us and the next one beginning, each one worse than the last, becoming harder and harder to keep struggling, though.

The soft humming in my ears and the deathly silence in my heart were all I had left, except for the bittersweet memories of a life I'd never have again. Exhaustion, downright heavy in its intensity, enveloped me. But I was more than just tired; I was excruciatingly exhausted. This world, this life—the misery of it was endless, the constant battle for survival and the hunger, the sadness, all tied up together with so very little happiness woven between. I didn't know how much longer I could carry on like this; the burden of pretense was so thick, so all consuming.

There was nothing left for me here, nothing left for Leisel. There was nowhere to go, nothing we could depend on but each other.

I had failed them all—Shawn and Thomas, Jami and Alex, even Leisel. Their lives, all cut far too short, continually flashed through my mind like an endless fucked-up kaleidoscope of pain and sorrow, and I just wanted to forget it all, wanted to be absorbed by their memories, to be swallowed whole. I wanted to go back to a life I could count on, back to the people I'd loved, to a place where I'd been safe.

A light touch on my arm caused me to jerk in surprise, my heartbeat slowing the moment I realized it was only Leisel. She was filthy, Alex's dried blood covering her clothing and skin, and yet she was still beautiful. Seeing her familiar face, feeling her much-needed touch, reminded me that I still had something left here, something worth facing yet another day of this shit world.

"I'm sorry," I whispered hoarsely, my face crumpling as I tried to stop the flow of tears. "I don't know what's wrong with me."

"You don't have anything to be sorry for," she said softly. Taking my hand, she brought it to her face, pressing a kiss on my knuckles.

"But I don't know what to do..." I choked on another sob as a fresh wave of tears spilled down my cheeks, stinging my wounds.

"We don't need to do anything," she said, shaking her head.

"But we do!" I protested, pulling away from her. Turning to face the room, I gestured wildly. "We can't stay here! And yet, we have nowhere to go! I don't know what to do, Lei! I don't know!"

Leisel appeared in front of me. Placing her hands on my shoulders, she looked into my eyes, her gaze hard. "We bury Alex," she said firmly. "Then we drive. We don't need to do anything more, except drive. We'll keep driving until we're out of gas, and then we'll walk and we'll keep walking until we can't walk anymore. We'll find another place, Eve, we'll find something, and we'll keep going. That's all we need to do."

Her fingers touched the bottom of my chin. "I don't need you to be strong for me; I need you to be strong for you. We're alive today because of you, and I'm grateful for that—for you. There's nothing else we need to be or do except to keep going."

She smiled then, her eyes going soft, shocking me that she had the will to smile after all that had happened.

"Help me bury him, Eve," she whispered. "It's the least we can do after all he's done."

Pressing my lips together, attempting to stop my tears, I nodded. She was right, God, she was right. Alex deserved so much more than anything we could do for him now. He deserved a full life, a family, to have been able to grow old in a world that still had a place for people like him. Good, strong people, people who'd persevered even in the face of adversity, people who were willing to sacrifice themselves for others.

Leisel laid Alex's canvas jacket on top of the mound of dirt covering him and shakily got to her feet. Clasping her hands together, she pressed them against her belly and stared solemnly at the makeshift grave we'd dug. She still hadn't cried.

Together we'd dragged Alex's body from the motel room, a painstaking and miserable task as he was nearly two hundred pounds of foul-smelling dead weight. Then, with only the use of rocks and our blades, and after several backbreaking hours under the sweltering sun, we'd barely managed to dig more than two feet into the earth before realizing it was the best we could do.

Tired and hungry, we'd rolled him into the ground, using our bare hands to cover him with the grass and dirt we'd freed. It wasn't deep enough, not secure enough a grave to keep the animals from getting to him, but at least it was something.

"Should we say something?" I asked quietly. "Like a prayer?"

In Fredericksville, we'd burned our dead. The entire town would gather while Lawrence presided over the service, always saying something kind about the deceased, someone he'd usually barely known. He'd invite others to talk afterward, allowing those who'd known the deceased a moment to reminisce. Yet, it had always felt like some kind of sideshow to me, no real feeling behind it, merely another way for Lawrence to further solidify his place as our leader.

"No," Leisel whispered, her eyes still downcast. "There's nothing to say." She glanced up at me. "But we could sing. He liked music, remember? He missed it."

"What kind of music did he like?"

Leisel shook her head. "I don't know, I never asked." A sob erupted in her throat and she clapped a hand over her mouth, choking it back. "How awful is that?" she whispered, her eyes wide. "I don't even know because I never asked."

Bending down, I placed my hand on top of the dirt and whispered a quick thank-you before rising and going to stand beside Leisel. Looping my arm through hers, I cuddled her close to me. "I don't think it matters, Lei. He'll like anything you sing."

Her bottom lip disappeared beneath her teeth, turning white from the pressure. After a moment she started humming, a familiar tune that made my eyes grow wet.

Clutching her tighter, I hummed along with her; softly at first, until Leisel began singing. And then together we stood there, belting out the lyrics to "The Ballad of Lucy Jordan." It had been her mother's favorite song, a song the woman had played over and over again on her old record player, a glass of gin always in her hand.

It hit me then, I could feel it deep down, the painful realization that this wasn't just Leisel saying good-bye to Alex. This was Leisel saying good-bye to everyone she loved, to everything she'd ever known.

And somehow, knowing that, it made everything seem that much worse.

CHAPTER FORTY-ONE

Leisel

"WE COULD GO back to the cabin," I suggested, pulling another slice of peach free from the mason jar. I swallowed it whole, wiping the residual sticky liquid off on my dirty pants before passing the jar to Evelyn.

Seated beside me on the back of the Jeep, Evelyn pulled her own slice free, popped it into her mouth, and began to chew. "At least he was good for something," she muttered, staring down at the canned fruit. Whoever he'd been, that awful man who'd killed Alex, had at least made good on his word to provide us with supplies. There was fuel, weapons—guns and bullets—clothing, and enough food and water to last us for at least a few weeks.

"Eve," I said, turning to face her. "Who was he? Was he who hurt you?"

She stopped chewing, and still staring down at the peaches, shrugged her shoulders. "Does it matter?"

I didn't respond. She was right; it didn't matter. Not anymore.

"If we head north," she said, then swallowed, "it'll be winter soon. Do you really want to deal with the cold and the snow? On our own? Neither of us knows how to hunt."

"Or chop wood," I added, my shoulders sagging as I turned away. "Or anything at all, really. Never mind, it was a stupid idea."

"No, it wasn't. It was the safest place we've come across so far. If we knew how, we could've fortified it, but I just don't know how."

She sounded so despondent, so empty, so full of regret, that I didn't know what I could say to her to make it better that I hadn't already said. I knew where she was, lost, trapped in a place inside herself, unable to figure a way out, to see anything other than the cause of her pain. I'd been there many, many times before; I'd been ready to die in order to free myself from it. But Evelyn hadn't let me, and I refused to let her fall victim either. I just didn't know how to accomplish that.

"Then we keep going," I finally said. Noticing a shadow of movement, I squinted off into the distance. "Like we'd planned to."

"Maybe we could find a beach," she said, sighing. "Learn how to fish—"

"Eve," I said, interrupting her as I slid off the back of the Jeep. "Over there." I pointed to the road just beyond the gas station where a lone infected was making its slow, shambling way toward us.

Swallowing another bite of peach, Evelyn raised her eyes toward the infected. "We should go," she said, though she made no move to get up. "They'll be more coming, what with all the blood everywhere..." Her eyes glazed over, filling with more tears.

"Eve!" I shouted, slapping my hand against the Jeep. "I know everything sucks right now! Believe me, *I know*! But we can't do this! We can't fall apart now!"

She looked at me through teary eyes, her lips and hands trembling, but said nothing, still not moving.

Letting out a shuddering sigh of frustration, I reached for the gun that had been lying between us. Gripping it, I spun around and marched through the parking lot and toward the infected.

It was an older one, not yet skin and bones but decayed enough that I couldn't tell whether it had been male or female until I was within twenty feet of it. Like so many of the infected, its clothing had been ripped away, exposing its mutilated body. It had been a woman once, its right breast had been nearly chewed off, only dried and clumpy sinew remaining. What was left of her other breast was little more than blackened, sagging, and shriveled skin.

I stopped in the center of the road and raised my gun, pulling the trigger and letting loose a bullet. It just barely grazed its shoulder, and the creature kept coming. I let another bullet fly, this one missing it entirely.

"Dammit!" I shouted. Lifting the gun higher, I squinted as I aimed. A blur of motion to my right had me glancing up, startled, until I realized it was Evelyn running past me, a large serrated blade in her hand. Wide-eyed with shock, I watched as she barreled past me and directly into the infected, shoving it hard and off its feet. It landed on the pavement with a loud crack and then Evelyn jumped on it, straddling it, and sent the sharp tip of her blade into its face.

Lowering my gun, I allowed my arms to fall limply to my side. She was screaming now, stabbing the infected over and over again, in its face, its neck, its chest. Just mindless stabbing accompanied by gut-wrenching screams that made my stomach start to ache.

I'd never seen Evelyn lose control before, not like this, not so completely. It was so utterly heartbreaking it drained all my strength right from me, causing me to drop to my knees in the middle of the road. The gun fell from my weakened grip, clattering to the ground beside me. Tears filled my eyes; fat, sorrow-filled tears, tears I'd thought had all but dried up, but in the face of Evelyn's pain had increased tenfold.

Several long minutes passed during which she continued to scream, stabbing blindly, desperately, until her voice grew hoarse and her screams turned to sobs, the top half of the body beneath her now little more than a mass of unidentifiable gore.

After rising to her feet, she made her way back to me, her entire body trembling violently, her clothing covered in the same blackened sludge all the infected were filled with.

Tears clouding my vision, I blinked up at her, unable to speak, unable to do little more than cry. Awkwardly she reached into her pants pockets, pulling the key to the Jeep free, and with a quivering hand offered it to me.

"You should drive," she whispered.

Having never had a good sense of direction, I didn't have a clue where I was headed or where the hell we even were, especially since all the road signs were either gone or destroyed beyond measure. Regardless, while Evelyn slept fitfully in the passenger seat beside me, I continued to drive aimlessly, through the night and until the sun was just starting to peek through the clouds.

It was only when my eyes were starting to close, exhaustion pulling me under, that I pulled off to the side of the road we were on, just another desolate stretch of highway, empty and devoid of life.

"Eve," I said, rubbing her arm. "Eve…wake up."

Blinking sleepily, Evelyn groaned when the sun shone bright against her newly opened eyes. "Morning," she said with a yawn. She surprised me with a smile, and even more so by how strong she sounded.

"Are you okay?" I asked, brushing a lock of strawberry-blonde hair from her eyes. "Feel better?"

Sitting up in her seat, she surveyed our surroundings with only mild interest before turning back to me. "Yeah," she said, sighing. "I'm sorry about that."

I shook my head, a sad smile on my face. "Nothing to be sorry for," I whispered.

"Where are we?"

I shrugged. "I have no idea. I've been looking for water, someplace for us to clean up a little."

"There's mountains over there," she said, shielding her eyes as she glanced off into the distance. "Probably water too."

I nodded. "Can you drive? I can't keep my eyes open."

Turning back to me, she smiled again. "Yeah. And, Lei?"

"Yeah?"

Taking my hand in hers, she squeezed. "We're going to be okay. I promise."

I didn't know why, maybe it was the peaceful look on her face, or the familiar promise, one she'd made so many times before, or maybe it was the combination of the two. Whatever the reason, I wholly believed her.

We were together, and as long as we had each other, I knew we would be okay.

CHAPTER FORTY-TWO

Evelyn

LOOKING UP THROUGH the open roof of the Jeep, I watched as an eagle glided on the warm breeze above us. It had been following us for a while now, and I couldn't help but think that it was some sort of sign, an auspicious symbol that all was going to be fine. This beautiful giant bird, flying high above us and looking down on the horror that had become of us all, still chose to follow us. Every now and then it emitted a low squawk, as if to announce it was still there, still with us.

Leisel was fast asleep beside me, her face hidden from view beneath a threadbare blanket E had provided us. Though he'd made good on his word to provide us with supplies, my hatred for that man, raging in its intensity, flared to life once again at the thought of him and his vulgar hands. Even now, out in the wide open and far from Purgatory, I could still feel him pressing between my thighs, feel his body pressed against mine. And poor Alex, his entire life ended by one greedy thrust of E's blade. So many evils he'd committed, and he'd never be punished for them. Not when men like him were the hierarchy in the world now.

Shaking away my thoughts of E, I tightened my grip on the steering wheel and focused on only the task at hand. It would do me no good to think of all that had gone wrong so far; my grief and regret had nearly crippled me already. Now I was determined to focus on one thing and one thing only—continued survival for Leisel and me.

I had no idea where we were or where we were headed, only that mountains covered with lush, green forest were springing up all around us from beyond the dusty, unused highways. So far we'd passed several towns but I'd refused to stop, not trusting anything or anyone after so many bitter disappointments. The small groups of infected we passed only reinforced my decision to keep us moving.

As we traveled on, the road grew worse, riddled with broken-down vehicles. The blacktop was ragged with large, vicious splits, nature once again reclaiming what was rightfully hers. Slowing the Jeep, I continued on, driving as carefully as possible over the fissures.

The lack of momentum eventually woke Leisel. Groaning groggily, she lifted her head from beneath the blanket, her eyes finding mine.

"Everything okay?" she asked, stretching.

I nodded. "So far, so good. Still driving. The roads are a mess, though."

Shrugging out of the blanket, she sat up, letting it slide to her feet. "Where are we?"

Laughing, I glanced sideways at her. "I have no idea, but it's pretty, right? And look…" I pointed up through the open roof toward the eagle.

"Oh my God," she whispered, sitting up straighter. "That's amazing."

"It's been following us for about an hour." I grinned at her. "I think it's a good sign."

Leisel smiled, her brown eyes glowing a burnished gold beneath the sun. "I agree, it's definitely a good sign. Although…" Turning back to me, she frowned.

Glancing at her cautiously, I held my smile, refusing to let anything ruin this peaceful moment. "What?"

"You kind of stink," she whispered, wrinkling up her nose. "And I'm pretty sure that's brain matter you have on your shirt."

Looking down on the dried gore encrusting nearly every inch of my clothing, I scowled. "I know," I said with a sigh. "We need to find somewhere to clean up, but"—I glanced sideways at her—"I'm scared to stop."

"I know," she said softly, dropping her gaze. "I am too."

She turned back to stare at the road and we lapsed into silence, just as the eagle above let out another loud squawk. Shielding her eyes, Leisel turned her face toward the sky, watching as it hovered, its great wings outstretched, and her smile began to slowly return. Seeing this, my own smile came back to me, and I refocused on the road with a sigh.

"There's a sign up ahead," Leisel announced, leaning forward to peer out the dirty windshield. "For lodging, I think."

Another mountainside loomed up beside us, giving us a brief reprieve from the sun. Slowing down the Jeep, I pulled up alongside the surprisingly still intact road sign that boasted a variety of fast food restaurants and hotels.

"I don't know," I said, hesitating. "Looks like it was some kind of ski resort town. Towns mean people, and people means—"

"Infected," Leisel finished. "I know. We could drive through, have a look around. If we see any infected, we'll just get back on the highway, right?" She looked at me, her brow lifted in question.

Biting down on the inside of my cheek, I felt my stitches pull, pain shooting up and down the nerves in my face. "Shit," I muttered, knowing I needed to clean and dress my many wounds. If only Alex were here with us, I wouldn't have been so apprehensive. Though the infected were a huge threat, the living were more so, the men especially.

"Eve," Leisel said, touching my arm. "Eventually we're going to have to stop somewhere. We don't have a lot of gas left."

"I know," I whispered, glancing at her. "I just—"

"We'll be okay," she said firmly, giving me a strong smile. "I promise."

Her resolve cemented it. With a brief nod of my head, I pulled the car forward again and back onto the road.

"Since when did you become the voice of reason?" I muttered.

"Since you decided to be the pessimistic one."

Grinning, I looked back at her. "Ready for some skiing?" I joked.

"I hope you brought your snowsuit," she quipped back. "According to the sign, they have the best manufactured snow in the South."

We were both laughing as I turned onto the exit ramp, a strained sort of laughter, but laughter nonetheless.

"I can't believe it," Leisel said, drawing out her words slowly as she glanced around the room in wonderment. "It's...it's virtually untouched."

Much like the rest of the town, the small bed and breakfast we'd chosen to check out was exactly that. Entirely untouched and with no infected to speak of.

We'd chosen this particular building for two reasons. It was a two-story bed and breakfast sitting well off the main drag, on top of a steep ravine, hidden by a thick stand of trees, and it hadn't been looted. In fact, there were no signs of any violence having occurred. Aside from a few broken windows, the layers of dust coating everything within it, and the small forms of wildlife that had made their nests inside, the structure had held up rather nicely. Fully furnished, each of the four bedrooms boasted queen-sized beds, and although filthy, were still made up with their original linens. Towels remained folded neatly on shelves, and several water bottles sat untouched inside the small refrigerators.

Picking up a brochure lying on the dressing table, I skimmed over it. "There's a sightseeing tour at noon today, Lei, down a 'naturally crafted 164-foot ravine bursting with nature and wildlife,'" I said, waving the dusty pamphlet in the air. "I know how much you love that shit."

"We could stay here for a while," she whispered, ignoring my joke. Her eyes filled with tears, and there was a slight tremor in her voice. "Until we figure something else out."

"We should," I agreed. "But before we do that, I need to wash." Gesturing at my clothing, I made a face. The smell of myself was making me feel light-headed and downright queasy. Grabbing a plastic jug full of water from the pile of supplies we'd hauled inside, I headed toward the bathroom.

Not bothering to shut the door behind me, I quickly stripped out of my ruined clothing and inspected myself in the mirror. The cuts on my face looked even worse than they had this morning, swollen and red, fluid leaking from between the stitches.

Grimacing, I closed the stopper in the sink and poured half of the jug of water into the basin. Grabbing a small hand towel from the rack, I shook it free of dust, then dipped it in the water and began the painstaking task of cleaning my wounds.

Hand in hand, we stood by the lone window, watching as the sun began to set on another day. Our bellies were full of peaches, dried rat meat, and complimentary chocolates from the bed and breakfast's office, and the scent of wildflowers blew in through the open window, breezing through my damp hair.

It was a truly perfect moment, and I couldn't help but envision us staying here, maybe even living out the rest of our lives here.

"I'm going to go to bed," Leisel said, pulling away from me with a yawn. She smiled. "If that's okay with you?"

I nodded. I hadn't felt this safe, this secure in our surroundings since we'd left Fredericksville. "While you were cleaning up," I said, "I moved some more of the furniture downstairs. The doors are blocked. If anyone, *anything*, tries to get in, we'll hear it."

As she padded softly over the hardwood floor and slipped into bed, I turned back to the window, wishing the eagle would have followed us here, hoping that, like Leisel and me, it was someplace safe. It was almost surreal, the view of the deep ravine, the dimming sky full of muted shades of pinks and blues. And so peaceful.

This was all we'd wanted. After leaving Fredericksville, this was what we'd hoped for, what we had aimed for. So many people had died just for us to get to this point, so many sacrifices had been made, that it was hard not to be a little morbid about it. But Alex and Jami, Shawn and Thomas, they would have wanted this for us. They'd given their lives to keep us safe, and now we were. And I felt like I'd finally kept good on my promise to Thomas.

I had kept Leisel safe.

A wave of exhaustion tumbled through me, causing me to reach out and grip the windowsill. I blinked several times, my vision doubling and clouding over, yet I didn't want to close my eyes just yet. I wanted to let it all soak in for a little while longer.

"Thank you," I whispered to the sky. "Thank you."

CHAPTER FORTY-THREE

Leisel

I WAS DREAMING OF screaming. Shrill, high-pitched, blood-curdling screaming that was so very familiar to me, it sounded as if it were my own. I searched wildly for it, running through the darkness, tripping over shadows of arms and legs all reaching for me, yet couldn't seem to find anything. Only more darkness and constant screaming.

"Lei! Lei! Wake up!"

More arms grabbed at me, a hand wrapping around my wrist, nails biting into my skin, shaking me furiously.

"Leisel!"

I jolted upright, blinking with confusion at Evelyn's distorted features.

"What?" I cried. "What's wrong?"

"You tell me!" she said. "You woke me up screaming!"

My mouth fell open as I looked around the room, taking in our surroundings. "I...uh..." I managed a sheepish smile. "I'm sorry, I was dreaming."

Shaking her head, her red curls bouncing, she smiled. "It's fine, it was just loud. Are you okay?"

I nodded, then reached up to gingerly touch the angry red wounds on her face. "Are you? These look better than yesterday. They seem to have finally started scabbing."

She made a face. "They hurt like a bitch. The scars are going to be awful."

Lying back down in bed, she pulled the musty bedcovers up to her chin and grinned. "But what good is surviving an apocalypse without the battle scars to prove it?"

"I always thought you were too pretty," I said, laughing as I lay down beside her. Wrapping my arm around her middle, I pulled myself closer.

"Thanks," she scoffed, rolling her eyes even as she turned her face against my chest.

Snuggled against Evelyn's warm body, my eyes began to close. It was astounding how relaxed I was, given everything that had happened. Considering our run of bad luck, it was unreal to find a place such as this one—entirely overlooked. I couldn't imagine that it was going to stay that way forever, but for now this was exactly what we needed. And it was the little things, like finding a slice of safety in a world gone mad, that made the rest of it not seem quite as horrible as it had.

Nearly asleep once again with a silly smile on my face, I heard it, the telltale groaning growl of an infected. My eyes popped open, and I turned my head to find Evelyn looking back at me, her eyes wide.

"Fuck," she mumbled, untangling herself from me. "I knew this was too good to be true."

Yanking the covers off us in a huff, she swung her legs out of bed and strode quickly across the floor toward the window. Pushing open the haphazardly hanging shutters, she peered down below.

"There's two," she whispered, glancing back at me. "They're by the Jeep. Probably heard you screaming, and now they smell the blood."

"If it's only two," I said, feeling guilty for drawing them here, "we can handle two easily."

Rolling myself out of bed, I moved quickly to stand by her side. Like she'd said, there were two shambling around the exterior of the Jeep, wildly turning their heads back and forth and reaching for nothing. Off in the distance, near a thick stand of trees, I noticed more movement.

"There's three," I said, pointing. "Dammit."

"That's a deer, Lei," Evelyn said, narrowing her gaze. And just as she said it, both of the infected noticed the movement. With a growl, they went stumbling off after the deer. It leaped out from behind the tree that had been hiding it and took off running, the infected still following.

"Well," Evelyn said as she turned to me, a smirk on her face. "That solves that."

"What if there are more?" I asked, worried that our arrival here might have disturbed an entire town of infected that we'd somehow missed on our drive through.

"There are going to be infected everywhere," she said. "It's unavoidable. And this is too good of a place to pass up. I think all that really matters is how well we can fortify it."

She pursed her lips together, wincing as the movement pulled on her stitches. Reaching up to touch them, she rolled her eyes and sighed. "Let's go check out the town some more, see what can be salvaged. Finding a drugstore would be great…some painkillers, antibiotics…" She touched her stitches again, grimacing. "Before this gets infected."

The town was quiet. Aside from the water rushing through the nearby gorge, the chirping of small birds, and the sound of our feet as we walked down the center of the road, there was nothing that seemed out of the ordinary. We passed by several lodges, and a lot of vacant lots in between. On the main drag there was little else to be found—a bookstore, a movie theatre, a five-and-dime type shop, a shoe store, and a small department store.

When we didn't find a pharmacy, I gestured to the grocery store we'd passed only minutes ago, and Evelyn made a face. "I could smell that place from across the street," she said. "Ten to one, it's crawling with bugs and rats."

"But they probably had a pharmacy." I shrugged. "It's worth a shot, right?"

"Yeah." She made another face. "I'll just hold my nose, I guess."

Surprisingly, the grocery store wasn't filled with rotting food. Everything had long since rotted, and what hadn't been looted had simply petrified. The smell that remained, though, having probably permeated the walls and floors and everything within reach, was downright awful. Worse than awful. Even holding our noses, I could still taste the stench in the back of my throat.

Side by side, our weapons drawn, we walked cautiously down the dark, empty aisles, the floors covered with sleeping bags, suitcases, even tents.

"We could take some of this stuff," Evelyn suggested quietly. "The clothing, at least."

Grimacing, I shook my head. "I'd rather check the store one block over than try and wash the smell out of these. God, what happened here? Was the entire town camped out here? Where did they all go?"

"Nowhere good, I'm guessing," Evelyn said darkly, kicking a tattered sleeping bag over, revealing a dark stain on the tile beneath it. It was that moment that I noticed the bloody handprints. They were nearly indistinguishable amongst the dirt and dust and stains left from the rotted food, but once I noticed them, it seemed to be all I could see. Handprints, splatters, drag marks, places where blood had pooled heavily.

A sharp *tap-tap* sound had us spinning around, raising our guns, only to find a raccoon standing at the end of the aisle. It stared at us in the dark of the supermarket as all three of us froze in place, its eyes appearing to emit an eerie yellow glow.

"Shoo!" Evelyn shouted, kicking the sleeping bag and startling the creature. It made a *whoop-whoop* noise before skittering backward and disappearing.

"Pharmacy," I said, gesturing with my gun to a sign still hanging from the ceiling. "Though, all things considered…" I looked around at the many makeshift beds. "I'm not holding out much hope there's anything left."

We continued on, passing by more personal belongings, a row of knocked-over shelving, until we reached the far end of the building where a long countertop fitted with Plexiglas windows was labeled PHARMACY. Finding them securely locked, we peered inside. The small room seemed pretty well picked over, but there were still plenty of bottles lining the bottom shelves, along with baskets full of unopened pharmacy bags that remained untouched beneath the cash register.

"What I wouldn't give for one of those to be aspirin," Evelyn whispered, smiling at me. "Fuck antibiotics, I just want some pain relief."

"I think the door to get in is in the back," I said, nodding toward two large rubber doors helpfully marked EMPLOYEES ONLY.

"Great," Evelyn muttered, rolling her eyes. "Just what I want to do, go traipsing through some scary dark storage room."

We stared at each other a moment, as if silently deciding how to proceed. The seconds ticked by while I waited for Evelyn to make up her mind, and I knew the moment she had. Squaring her shoulders, she sniffed imperiously. "If we're going to survive out here, we're going to have to stop being afraid. I'm not afraid. Are you afraid, Lei?"

I was terrified, but it was a different kind of fear than I'd grown accustomed to. It was an adrenaline-pumping, heart-racing sort of fear that didn't so much cripple me as it gave me strength. It wasn't the fear that I was going to die, it was born from the thought of dying. I wanted to live, I wanted to keep going, I wanted to be strong. And in order to do any of that, I had to be terrified; any less was going to get me or Evelyn killed.

"I'm not," I said, grinning. "Not even a little."

Slowly, carefully, we pushed the double doors open, both of us wincing when they let out a loud squeak, loud enough to alert anything that might be back here of our presence. Waiting a moment, listening for any sort of movement and hearing nothing, we proceeded forward. The room wasn't as big as I'd previously thought, and was stacked with empty shipping pallets and piles of folded boxes. Large metal shelving lined the walls, unfortunately empty, and off in the corner sat a small forklift.

"This way," Evelyn whispered. "The door is right up there."

Up ahead of us was a small white door, once again properly labeled PHARMACY – EMPLOYEES ONLY. We crept toward it, constantly checking over our shoulders for anything that might be lurking in the darkness behind us.

Grabbing hold of the doorknob, Evelyn looked at me, her eyes wide. "Please let this be unlocked," she whispered, and turned the knob. The door emitted a soft click, and she grinned. "Jackpot."

I grinned back at her, thinking that finally things seemed to be going our way for once.

Turning back, she pulled the door open slowly, only enough so she could take a look inside. Suddenly it pushed open, startling Evelyn and causing her to release the door and stumble backward. The door swung wide open, hitting the wall, as a skeletal-looking infected, lying on its belly, propelled itself forward, gripping Evelyn's ankle.

With a surprised shout, she started kicking, attempting to dislodge it, and lost her balance. As she tumbled backward, her gun clattering to the floor, the infected gripped both her legs, its snapping jaw full of decaying teeth latching onto her pants.

"Leisel!" she screamed, her legs thrashing wildly as she tried to reach for her fallen weapon. "Shoot it!"

I raised my gun, trying to aim for its head, but my hands were shaking, and fear was causing my vision to blur. I was a horrible shot, and my chances of shooting Evelyn were greater than hitting the infected. As Evelyn screamed louder, I dropped my gun, yanked my blade free from my belt, and rushed forward.

Attached to her thrashing legs, the infected was groaning and growling, flaps of rotted skin flailing from its body like ropes of long hair. Evelyn let out another awful scream just as I sent the tip of my blade into the back of the thing's skull. Everything went suddenly quiet and still as the infected slumped heavily over Evelyn's trembling legs. I yanked my blade free, and Evelyn quickly shoved the infected off her, rolling to her side before jumping to her feet.

"You're bleeding!" I cried, dropping to my knees as I reached for her leg.

She jerked out of my grasp and spun away, giving me her back. She was no longer screaming, but still shaking, trembling violently from her head to her feet.

"Oh God," she whispered hoarsely. "Oh God, oh God, oh God…"

Standing up, I touched her shoulder gently. "You don't get sick from scratches," I whispered. "Not unless there's blood or saliva exchanged. It was an old one, no blood. You're going to be—"

Whipping around, Evelyn raised her tear-filled eyes to mine. My gaze dropped to the leg she presented me with. Bending down and with shaking hands, she lifted the bloody material of her pants, revealing a crescent-shaped wound on her calf, the flesh between nearly torn completely away.

My breath left me in one rapid burst of air, my entire body seeming to deflate all at once. "No," I whispered, shaking my head as tears filled my eyes. "No…no…" My thoughts spun and I raised my blade. "We'll cut it off!" I cried. "Right now!"

Wide-eyed, Evelyn jerked away from me, taking several limping steps backward. "No," she whispered. "No, we can't…"

"We can!" I screamed. "Before it spreads!"

"And then what?" she screamed back, her full-bodied trembling growing worse. "We're not doctors, Lei! I'll bleed out or worse, it will get infected and I'll die anyway!"

"There's still a chance!" I protested, knowing if we did nothing there was no chance. "We can't do nothing!"

"What good will I be to you with one leg, Leisel? And injured for who knows how long. I'll attract infected everywhere we go. I'll get us both killed and you know it!"

My mouth opened, but no sound came forth. I closed it, gritting my teeth together, tears burning hot paths down my suddenly cold cheeks. Turning away from her, I let my blade clatter to the floor as I squeezed my eyes shut and clenched my hands into tight fists.

"No!" I whispered, shaking my head. "No, God, please, no. Don't do this, don't do this to us. I can't be without her. Please, please, God."

"You have to go," Evelyn said, her softly spoken, tear-filled words barely audible. "You have to get in the Jeep and just go. Go back to Purgatory, go back to Fredericksville, just go somewhere. Go, Leisel! You need to go!" she yelled, her voice strangled and pained.

I turned to face her, feeling horrified, shaky, desperate, sick to my stomach—a myriad of emotions, none of which I could pinpoint or focus on. "How dare you!" I cried. "How dare you even suggest that!"

"I want you to live," she whispered, her eyes wide and red-rimmed as tears fell from them. Reaching for me, her fingers wrapped around my wrist, digging into my skin. Squeezing me, she shook my arm. "You need to keep going, Lei," she pleaded. "For me, please, just keep going."

I shook my head frantically, my pounding heart nearly bursting in my chest. "Never," I spat through my tears. "I will never, ever leave you!"

"You have to," she wailed. "You fucking have to!"

Taking a deep breath, I stepped forward and reached for her other hand. Threading my fingers through hers, I tugged her closer to me. "Let's go back to the bed and breakfast," I suggested, my voice shaking. "We'll clean you up. We'll think of something, Eve, we always think of something."

Still crying, Evelyn lifted her eyes to meet mine. I could tell she wanted to say something else, to tell me what I already knew, that there was nothing to do, not for a bite from an infected. To tell me that this was all hopeless. That she was going to die and once she died, she would turn. But instead, she closed her mouth as more tears fell from her eyes, and she simply nodded.

Truth be told, I didn't have a clue what I was going to do. There was only one thing I knew for certain—that I wouldn't leave her here or anywhere, not now, not ever. Especially to die alone. Because without Evelyn it didn't matter anymore, nothing mattered anymore. She was my everything, and there wasn't anyplace else that I'd want to be but right here, with her.

I squeezed my eyes closed. There had to be a way out, there had to be, there was always a way out. Evelyn had proven that to me time and time again. We survived, that was what we did. This couldn't be the end. Not now, not after everything.

But then, I opened my eyes and looked over at her, looked at my beautiful, strong friend with her ruined face, all bruised, bloody, and beaten down. Then my gaze fell to her leg.

She'd been bitten. And as the bitter realization of that truth finally sank deep inside me, it tore to shreds everything it touched on. There was no way out of this. There would be no surviving *this*. No matter what, Evelyn was going to die from the infection that was now burning its way inside her, eating away at every part of her that I loved, and taking away the very last thing that I had left, the only person I loved in this godforsaken world.

Feeling sick, shaking from head to toe, I forced my body to move. Picking up our weapons, I handed Evelyn her gun and she took it from me, staring down numbly at it like she had no idea what it was or what to do with it. I tucked mine into my pants and sheathed my blade with shaking hands, then once again I grabbed her hand and turned us toward the exit doors, pushing blindly through them, not seeing what I was passing by.

My only thoughts were on getting her back to the bed and breakfast, getting her back to our room, cleaned up and tucked in bed. Whatever happened next would happen, but I wasn't going to think on that yet. Because I couldn't. If I thought about it, I'd lose it. And I couldn't lose it, not now, not when Evelyn needed me the most.

"Always together, Eve," I mumbled as I continued to half carry her through the market. "Always."

As we stepped through the broken entranceway, the streets were quiet, seemingly even more so than before, as if the entire town had stilled along with my heart, everything frozen in fear of the doom to come.

We walked slowly down the walkway, Evelyn leaning lightly on me as she limped along. Needing to focus, I tried not to get lost inside my thoughts, tried to stay alert to our surroundings. Yet I couldn't help but think of Thomas and Shawn. How long had they lived after being bitten?

Thomas had been ravaged, bites covering both his arms, his stomach, and his back, large chunks of skin and muscle having been torn from him, and he'd perished rather quickly as a result. But Shawn, just as Evelyn, had been bitten only once, and had lasted three days.

Three days…that was more than likely all the time Evelyn had left. And, God help me, it wasn't nearly enough time for me. Not even close.

"Lei… Stop fussing."

Propped up in bed, the bite on her leg now cleaned and bandaged with gauze I'd pilfered from the first aid kit I'd been lucky enough to find in the bed and breakfast's office, Evelyn wearily waved me away from her. "Just come sit beside me," she said.

I glanced down at her calf, blood already seeping through the fresh bandage, and shook my head. I couldn't just sit, just do nothing. If I did, I knew I was going to lose what little sanity I pulled together while taking care of her. Without that, the edge of the cliff I was precariously hanging on to would crumble, and I would free-fall into a pit of sorrow and grief.

"Leisel?"

I looked up into her bloodshot eyes, noting how flushed she appeared, and the sweat glistening all over her body, all reminiscent of anyone I'd ever watched die from the infection. Swallowing hard, I attempted to school my features, not wanting to give Evelyn the added burden of my own fears, not when she had enough of her own to contend with.

"Please come sit with me," she said, her voice small and afraid. "Please, Lei."

Swallowing again, I nodded quickly and stood, uselessly smoothing the wrinkles in my clothing. Slipping my bottom lip beneath my teeth, I kept my eyes wide and trained on the floor as I slowly made my way to the other side of the bed. I wanted to cry, I wanted to cry my heart out, but I fought the welling emotion inside me, knowing that it would be selfish of me to lose myself.

"Are you thirsty?" I asked as I climbed into bed beside her, careful not to bump against her injured leg. "Hungry, tired, cold—"

"Stop it, Lei," she said, inching herself closer to me.

Her bare arm brushed against mine, her skin a sweaty, sticky, veritable furnace of heat. I couldn't remember if Shawn's fever had progressed this quickly, but I didn't think it had. I remembered him acting normally for a good twenty-four hours before the symptoms began to show. The second day, he'd been riddled with fever, the bloody pustules beginning to form, yet he'd still been coherent. On the third day, he'd fallen into an agitated sleep before slipping away entirely.

It had only been a few hours since Evelyn had been bitten. What did this mean? Would I not even get three horribly lacking days with her?

"It hurts," Evelyn whispered, letting her head fall against my shoulder. "It's almost as if I can feel it spreading. At first it was just the bite that hurt, but now it's my entire leg and my hip too."

I didn't know what to say or do, so instead of speaking I leaned my cheek on top of her head and squeezed my eyes closed, cursing silently when an errant tear slipped free.

"Promise me, Lei," she said, her voice strained with emotion. "Promise me you won't let me turn. That you'll kill me before I become dangerous."

"Shh!" I whispered, turning my body so I could wrap my arm around her middle and bury my face in her neck. "Stop it, Eve! We have time. We don't need to talk about this."

"We do," she protested, trying to free herself from me, but I only clung tighter to her, refusing to let her go, in more ways than one. "If you let me turn, Lei, I could hurt you, and you can't do that to me. If I hurt you, I'll have failed. I promised—"

"Please," I begged as more tears leaked free, my resolve to stay strong slipping away. "I can't talk about this, not yet. Please, Eve, please don't make me."

Letting out a heavy sigh, Evelyn's body went limp in my hold. "Okay," she said softly, sinking into my embrace. Her hand found my back, her grip on my shirt fisting tightly to the material.

"I love you," she whispered. "And I'm glad it was me who was bitten and not you."

Ever the protector, my protector, was Evelyn. Always putting me before herself, doing whatever was necessary to keep me alive and safe. If there was ever a time that I needed to be strong, it was now. To show her the same love she'd always shown me.

"I'll do it," I choked out. "I won't let you turn, I promise you."

CHAPTER FORTY-FOUR

Evelyn

"DO YOU REMEMBER that pretty yellow sundress Shawn bought me for our wedding anniversary?" I asked, then coughed pitifully. Phlegm and blood were building in my chest, clogging my airways and making my breathing sound ragged and crackly while Leisel hummed in my arms, acknowledging my words. "I loved that dress. I wish I still had it," I said softly, my eyes glazing over as I let my thoughts drift back.

I didn't know where the memory had come from, but the image of wearing it, of feeling Shawn's hands wrapped tightly around my waist as we danced, the swish of the soft material on my bare legs…it was almost as if I were there, back at the small bar where we'd celebrated our marriage. I was back in the past when everything in the world was right and good. I could almost hear the music playing, the sound of the acoustic guitar in the background, a gentle strumming, of skin moving down metal as fingers ran along the strings.

"Eve?" Leisel asked, her voice a quiet echo of its true self.

The world was blurry as I drifted along on a cloud of numbness. The excruciating pain that had gripped hold of every part of me had since been replaced as my nerve endings began to die. I could feel them, dying an individual death one by one as the numbness spread further throughout my body. The numbness was a blessing, a small reprieve for such a painful and ugly way to go.

Leisel's hands were on my shoulders, I could sense them, feel her slender fingers pressing gently into my hot flesh. And I was trying, trying so hard to focus on her, struggling to see her face instead of the blur that it now was. Because I wanted to see her one last time. I needed to.

"Eve! No, not yet! I'm not ready!"

She was screaming at me, shaking me now, the soft vibrations of her words dancing across my fevered skin. I was still trying, dear God, I was trying with all my remaining strength to pull back from the impending darkness, to give her more time. Just a few more hours, minutes even. Because this was all happening much too quickly. For her, and for me.

But there was no stopping the infection. It spread like hot acid, burning through my body, infesting and infecting every part of me. I could sense myself slip away, everything that I was and have ever been, and it was terrifying. More terrifying than anything else I'd ever experienced before, and far more terrifying than I had ever thought dying would be.

"Leisel," I managed to say before choking on the phlegm again. My vision momentarily cleared and I could see her face move closer, but the sight of her was heartbreaking.

"I'm so sorry." I sobbed, relinquishing myself to my self-pity, and lifted a hand to her damp cheek.

"I remember," she replied, her voice hoarse. "I remember the dress." Pulling me up and into her arms, she brought me closer until her face was in the crook of my neck.

I knew she was crying, that her tears should be hot and wet against my skin, but I couldn't feel them. All I could feel was the raging panic that barreled through me as my body became something else, something evil and cruel, something that would hurt Leisel without question. The mere thought of me hurting her panicked me, leaving me dizzy and breathless with fear.

"You looked beautiful in that dress, Eve," she whispered. "Shawn always picked pretty dresses for you. He loved you so much." Her words, laced with bitter sadness, trailed off as she began to cry harder.

"I'm sorry, I'm so sorry," I cried again, unable to hear my own words properly, my eardrums feeling punctured and pained. "Forgive me. Please, please, forgive me."

Abruptly Leisel pulled away from me, forcing me into an upright position and holding me there when my body wanted nothing more than to fall limply back onto the bed.

"You stop that right now, Evelyn. I love you and you have nothing to apologize for." Through her waterfall of tears, she leaned forward and pressed a kiss to my forehead. "I'm going to be fine, I promise you. You don't need to worry about me."

"Promise me," I said, my voice hoarse. "Promise me you'll stay here where it's safe. You can live here, Lei. You can survive here. Promise me you'll stay."

A fresh wave of tears cascaded down her cheeks, but she nodded through her tears and attempted a small smile. "I promise," she whispered.

I tried to smile in return, not sure if I managed it since my muscles were no longer responding. But I wanted to smile at the sight of her face, so full of strength and determination, even shrouded in pain. Seeing her this way afforded me a small slice of hope for all that was happening—me dying and having to leave her here alone. It was freeing for me to know that Leisel was strong now, that she'd be able to survive without me.

I remembered Leisel going through each of the five stages of grief when she'd lost her Thomas. And now, with me, she'd done the same, having reached the final stage—acceptance of the situation at hand.

Her denial of the situation had come first, the denial that this was really happening, that I was truly dying and leaving her all alone in this world. Quickly following her denial, she'd become angry, furious even that I *really was* leaving her all alone. Because how could I do that to her? If I loved her, if Thomas had loved her, how the fuck could we all just keep dying and leaving her?

She'd yelled at me as if I had a choice in the matter, as if I were choosing to leave her. As if I could have somehow decided to stay. But I couldn't choose; she'd known that. I was dying, and not only was I dying but I was becoming the very thing that I feared more than death itself. But I couldn't—wouldn't—be angry at her for her erratic emotions, because I actually *was* leaving her all alone. There was nothing I could do about it, and the guilt of that weighed on me heavily, eating away at me worse than any infection possibly could.

Next, she had pleaded with me to let her take my leg, to take both if she had to, as if that would have somehow helped. She'd offered to take me back to Purgatory, thinking that maybe they would help us. Thank God, at the time I'd still been strong enough to laugh at that suggestion. No matter what happened, I would never go back there, and I would never allow Leisel to go back there either.

Because she deserved better than that place, she deserved so much more. She certainly deserved better than this world.

No matter how much she begged and pleaded, I wouldn't relent. And so then the tears came, the sobs and the shrieking, and with them more guilt was piled onto my already aching and fracturing heart. How could I do this to her? She couldn't do this without me. I'd die and then she'd die, and then what would have been the point? What had everyone fought and died for if neither of us was going to make it?

But now, looking into her eyes and seeing such steely determination within them, was like a gift from an unknown force. Not from God, because I no longer believed in God, but maybe something else, definitely something stronger than either of us.

There was no more fear or anger in her features, there was sadness and grief, but beyond that there was strength, and the cold, hard truth of what was coming.

This was it.

My final act.

Our final act.

Together.

"It's time," I whispered, my throat clogged and painfully tight. "I can't—"

Interrupted by coughing, I choked on more blood and phlegm, feeling it splatter across my chin.

"I love you," I said, trying again. "I'm..."

As my entire body went utterly lax, my words trailed off and my vision darkened. A coppery taste filled my mouth, and suddenly I was convulsing, my body violently thrashing in Leisel's arms. Yet I couldn't feel it, not in the sense that it was actually happening to me. It was more as if my body were no longer my own, as if I were no longer inside it but instead looking down at myself, seeing my own body jerking and shuddering, watching as Leisel attempted to hold me down, her sobs growing louder.

I wished I could have told her how much I loved her one last time, how forever grateful I was that I'd had the privilege of being her friend. But more than anything, I wished I could have made her one more promise—the promise that I would see her in the next life, and that I would be waiting for her with Shawn and Thomas. And that until that day, the three of us would be watching over her. Protecting her. Always.

As my convulsions begin to fade, Leisel hugged me one last time before letting me fall heavily down onto the mattress. Pressing her lips to the top of my head, she whispered her final good-bye. It was then that I knew it was time, and strangely enough, I was ready for it. I was heartbroken and devastated to leave her, but I was ready.

I wanted to go home, was desperate even to leave, to go back to before all this happened. I wanted to return to a simpler time full of laughter and love, to when I could still remember the feel of my husband's breath on my cheek. I wanted to stare into his beautiful eyes again, the way they once had looked upon me, so full of life, and not the cloudy, desperate eyes that had haunted my soul for years now. I wanted to slip into my silky yellow dress, feel his warm hands around my waist, hear the sultry riff of the guitar echoing in my ears as we swayed together.

Smiling to myself, I whispered good-bye to my friend, the best friend a woman could ever have, and then I closed my eyes, falling backward into oblivion.

"Forgive me," I heard Leisel say. "Please forgive me."

And then there was nothing more.

CHAPTER FORTY-FIVE

Leisel

I'D NEVER BEEN alone before. Not like this. Not so utterly, completely alone, without another soul in the world to speak with, to laugh with, to share even the simplest and most mundane of things with. As the days turned to weeks and the weeks turned to months, the silence was deafening at times; the echoing of my own footsteps, of my own breathing, sounded hollow and desolate.

Every day I awoke at dawn, washed, pulled my hair into a high ponytail, dressed in one of two pairs of formfitting cargo pants and a tight black T-shirt—outfits I'd begun reserving specifically for pillaging. Then I would make my bed from the night before and set out into the heart of the town to collect whatever resources I could find to bring back to the bed and breakfast. I was fortifying it as best I could, just like Evelyn had wanted us to.

There were more secure buildings, something I'd found during one of my many trips into town, but I couldn't bring myself to leave the bed and breakfast. That wasn't saying the inn didn't have its advantages. It was off the beaten track down a gravel road, set far back atop a steep ravine, and partially hidden behind a smattering of trees. But more than anything, I wanted to stay because it held the memory of Evelyn within its walls, and I wasn't ready to let her go.

First, I boarded up all the first-floor windows and doors, leaving only the service entrance in the back usable. For my own peace of mind, I rigged it with a rather impressive impromptu crossbar, using a block of wood I had mounted to the wall that extended across both sides of the door frame.

I'd left the first floor as it was, broken and in shambles, a mess of furniture and scattered belongings. From the outside looking in, it would seem to anyone or anything passing by just another broken-down structure, and nothing of worth. But on the inside, once you breached the second floor where I'd made my home, it was a veritable fortress.

Next, I'd left only one of the three bedrooms as is, using the rest of the furniture to create a blockade in the stairwell and hallway. Every day it was quite a feat climbing over the mess I'd intentionally made, but it was necessary protection against any sort of intruder. If the noise anyone or anything made while attempting to ascend the stairs didn't wake me, then nothing would.

Even so, I took my safeguards one step farther, creating a fence of sorts, comprised of dozens of ski poles I'd pilfered from the ski lodge. Tying pairs of them together in an X pattern, I set them up all over the inn, the perfect killing tool for a clueless infected, and a somewhat useful deterrent for an unwelcome visitor of the living variety as well.

With the aid of a hand truck from the same supermarket Evelyn had been bitten in, I was able to transport the heavier things back to the bed and breakfast that I wouldn't have had the strength to otherwise. It took long weeks to properly fortify the inn exactly the way I wanted it, in a way that made me feel safe, but it kept me busy. More importantly, it kept my mind off my grief.

Although hard work kept the pain away during the day, nothing could stop my mind from wandering in the dead of night. That was when I missed Evelyn the most, when it was only me and the moonlight, the sweet scent of flowers wafting through the open window on a cool breeze. I ached for her then—the sound of her voice, the glint in her eyes, the way her hand felt when her fingers were intertwined with mine.

But most of all I missed her presence. Just knowing she was there, sleeping beside me, walking next to me; no matter what, she'd always been there.

And now she was gone.

I'd thought about ending it, just letting go. It would be easy to put a bullet in my head, quick and painless. I could be with her again, with

Thomas too. With everyone I'd lost. And a couple of times, during a few very dark nights filled with long bouts of crying and feeling more alone than I ever had before, I almost did just that.

It was the guilt that stopped me each and every time. The many lives that had been lost just so we could reach a safe place like this one. Thomas and Shawn, Alex and Jami, and Evelyn. They had all died trying to survive, trying to ensure we would all survive. How selfish would I have to be to take my own life when they'd given theirs for me to be here, in this very place?

This was all we'd ever wanted. Somewhere untouched, somewhere safe and quiet. Somewhere we could live out our lives in peace. I couldn't waste it, couldn't let it all be for nothing, so I focused instead on the fact that we had all actually made it. Because through me, they had all survived, even if it was only their memory.

So I kept going, kept surviving, and soon the days began to blur together, each one the same as the last. Peaceful and quiet, with the exception of the occasional infected that I always quickly disposed of.

I developed a routine, one I stuck to and could count on. After my walk through town each morning, I'd make myself breakfast, and after breakfast I would read a book from the large collection I'd been slowly amassing. Lunch, I usually spent outside, my legs hanging over the edge of the steep ravine, humming to myself, and every evening, just as the sun was setting, I had my dinner with Evelyn.

With the aid of an actual shovel, I'd buried her close to the bed and breakfast, wrapped in the same comforter she'd died in, near a small grove of trees where the grass and wildflowers grew thick and tall. Her grave sat directly beneath one very large tree, its heavy branches comfortably shading the area, and its thick trunk perfect for leaning against.

"I need to learn how to hunt," I said, wrinkling my nose at the newly opened can of creamed corn. "I swear this stuff has gone bad."

Many times I'd planned on setting up a target practice area, but I was loath to waste my bullets, and even more afraid that the gunshots would alert either any nearby infected or living that happened to be passing by. So I stayed quiet.

Scooping the first spoonful into my mouth, I swallowed it quickly, hurrying to lift my bottle of water to wash down the foul taste.

"God, I miss you, Eve," I said as I set down the can of food and placed my hand upon the small rock. "Everything seems so meaningless without you here."

And it did. All of it, even eating seemed pointless without someone to share the food with. With each passing day I was growing number, but at the same time I was feeling more and more empty. The idea of living became infinitely harder than that of not.

"I just wish—"

An unfamiliar sound silenced me—the crunch of a footfall, the sound of a rock skittering across pavement—and I reached for the gun at my hip. Standing, I ran quickly behind the tree, waiting for what I was sure was an infected to reveal itself. If it was only one or two, I wasn't worried; I could take them out without breaking a sweat. But any more than that...

I'd been purposely starting the Jeep once a day for this very reason, keeping it loaded with supplies, just in case I needed to get out in a hurry. Patting my weapons belt, I breathed a sigh of relief when I found the key hanging beside my knife holster, home to a heavy-duty serrated blade.

"Hello?" a deep voice called out. "Anybody here?"

Surprise welled in my gut, freezing me in place. It wasn't an infected, but a living, breathing person. How many were there? Where they from Purgatory? Had they found me?

As my panic grew, more and more questions arising with each desperate breath I took, the voice called out again.

"I'm not going to hurt you, miss. I'm alone, just passing through, looking for food."

He knew I was here and had seen me, he'd made that clear, so hiding would be futile.

"I'm setting down my gun," he called out. "I promise I'm not going to hurt you. You don't need to be afraid of me."

Peeking out from behind the tree trunk, my gun hand steady and sure, I could make out the blurry sight of a man standing some ways down the road. True to his word, he bent down, allowed his rifle to fall lightly to the ground, before standing tall and raising his hands in the air.

Slowly, holding my gun out in front of me, my other hand wrapped around the hilt of my blade, I came out from behind the tree and made my way toward the road. Scanning the surrounding areas, I searched for any other signs of life and found nothing.

Coming to a stop at the edge of the grass, leaving a good ten feet or so between us, I assessed him cautiously. He was filthy, covered in dirt and grime, as if he hadn't seen a bath or clean clothes in weeks, maybe months. His long brown hair, graying around his temples, was pulled back, becoming dreadlocked, as was his long beard. A large hiker's backpack was seated high on his back, the straps covering his shoulders worn and thin, and a variety of weapons affixed to the pack dangled behind him.

"I'm not going to hurt you," he repeated, his shadowed eyes meeting mine.

I didn't trust him, not for one second. I would never be so stupid to just blindly trust anyone ever again, but there was something about him, something familiar that niggled at my memories. The long ratty brown hair, the scruffy beard, the way his shoulders sagged sadly. Though he was thinner now, not as bulky as I remembered him, and his facial features were somewhat gaunt, darkened, and drawn.

And that was when it hit me, who he was.

"You," I whispered, letting my hand holding the gun fall to my side. I said nothing else, unsure of what to say. How did you a greet a man you hardly knew, a man whose first and only meeting with you had resulted in the death of his daughter?

Cocking his head to one side, he dropped one arm but raised the other to shield the dwindling sun from his eyes. Squinting, he scanned me from head to toe, his eyes widening with surprise when he once again reached my face.

"You," was all he said.

For a moment we just stood there, a mere ten feet from each other, simply staring, until the prolonged silence began to feel somewhat awkward. Clearing my throat, I shifted on my feet and gestured toward my makeshift picnic.

"Hungry?" I asked tentatively. "I have food and water and…" I ran my gaze down his tattered and dirty clothing a second time. "And clean clothes."

His gaze swept the area behind me. "Is it just you?" he asked. "What happened to…" He paused, his eyes again finding mine. A moment passed and his expression shifted, suddenly filled with understanding and compassion.

I shook my head, momentarily averting my eyes. "It's just me now," I said quietly.

Reaching up, he placed his hand on the back of his neck and sighed heavily, his eyes taking on a faraway look. "Lonely life, isn't it? Lonely fucking life." Refocusing on me, he said, "You sure you don't mind company? I'll understand if you don't. Can never be too careful these days. Only need myself some food and a good night's sleep, and I can be on my way."

Fumbling for the right words, struggling to corral my thoughts, I shook my head again. "No," I said hurriedly. "No, it's okay, you can stay as long as you need to. I have a can of creamed corn on hand if you want it."

"Creamed corn?" He wrinkled his nose and gave me a small smile. "Guess beggars can't be choosers, huh?"

I smiled back. "I'm a horrible shot, so hunting has been out of the question."

His eyes widened slightly, and again he did a visual sweep of the area. "Game good around here?"

Nodding in answer, I let out a soft snort. "Not that it matters when you can't shoot it."

Still smiling, he lifted his shoulder and shrugged. "I could teach you. Aiming isn't hard. It's all about your breathing." Suddenly, he held out his hand. "So we got a deal, then? You give me place to stay, and I'll make you the next best gunslinger in the West?"

I didn't know him from a hole in the wall, didn't even know his name, but something innate told me that maybe I could trust him. Perhaps it was the same inkling that told him he could trust us when we came across his cabin in the woods on that awful day.

Stepping forward, I held out my hand. "Deal," I said.

His filthy hand grasped mine, his fingers clasping firmly but gently, and gave me a quick and hearty shake.

"Name's Joshua," he said. "And it's damn good to see a friendly face."

"Leisel," I replied, smiling again. "My name is Leisel."

EPILOGUE

Evelyn

"GRAB ME SOME coffee, babe?" Shawn tore his eyes away from Thomas and their heated discussion over the latest upset regarding their favorite sports team, and quirked a brow at me.

"Who needs coffee when we've got lemonade?" I said as I slipped out of the partially open screen door and onto the porch. Leisel and Thomas's six-month-old black Labrador retriever ran circles around me, nearly tripping me as I attempted tottering over the uneven ground in my three-inch heels.

Wearing my favorite summer dress, long and silky, the shade of the golden sun, my strawberry-blonde curls piled high on top of my head, I was carrying a tray loaded with glasses and a pitcher of lemonade. Setting it down on the table, I pursed my lips together in a sly grin and winked at my husband.

"I spiked it," I said, shrugging my shoulders matter-of-factly.

"Of course you did," Thomas said, laughing as he reached for a glass. "You wouldn't be you if you didn't."

"Thanks, gorgeous," Shawn said, pulling me onto his lap.

Winding my arms around his neck, purposefully letting my hands slip up into his messy brown hair, together we shared a long kiss. I could never get enough of him, and it was the same for him, our passion for each other only increasing with every passing day. Shawn's breath washed over my face as we pulled out of the kiss and I stared into his eyes, smiling softly as I wiped a smudge of my bright red lipstick from his mouth.

"Why do I always get hit when I do that?" I heard Thomas say aloud.

Grinning, I glanced away from my husband, looking across the table at Thomas, who was smiling widely, showcasing the pair of dimples that Leisel adored. His light blue eyes glinting with humor, his ruddy hair glinting golden in the sun, he glanced at the empty seat beside him. "She never lets me kiss her in public."

"But does she let you kiss her when you're alone?" Shawn asked. "Because that's all that matters."

Thomas's grin grew even wider, and a tad bit devilish.

"Well, I guess that answers that," I said, smirking. "Speaking of which...where is Lei? It's not like her to be late."

Thomas shrugged. "She had a few things to do, she can't make it."

Thinking of the chocolate cake I'd made especially for her, I frowned.

"Don't worry, babe," Shawn said, running his hand up my back. "You'll see her again, and then you can ply her with as much of your awful cake as you like."

"Hey!" I shouted, my tone tinged with laughter. "It isn't that bad!"

"It is," Thomas said, nodding gravely. "It really, really is."

Pressing my lips together, trying to stifle my laughter, I shook my head at them both. "You're awful, you know that?" Feigning anger, I folded my arms across my chest and glanced up at the sky.

"Hey," I said, squinting. "Is that an eagle?"

"Looks like it," Shawn said. "Weird, huh? When have we ever seen an eagle around here?"

"Beautiful birds," Thomas murmured, shielding his eyes to watch as it soared through the sky above us.

Snuggling closer to my husband, I couldn't help but wish Leisel were here. She loved little things such as this. She always loved the little things.

"Ooh!" I said, jumping upright. "Give me your cell phone, Tom! We should take a picture for her, so we can show her when she gets here!"

Thomas slid his phone across the table and I quickly lifted it, swiping hurriedly to the camera app, then snapped several pictures before the eagle had flown out of sight.

"Yeah, so, before my beautiful wife interrupted us," Shawn said, his attention back on Thomas. "What I was saying was that it isn't the fault of the owner, it's the fault of the goddamn recruiters! If they'd paid more attention…"

Sighing noisily, I tuned out and untangled myself from Shawn. Standing up, I headed for the house. Once inside, I closed the screen door behind me and glanced around my kitchen, at the chocolate cake sitting beside an opened bottle of vodka, at the sink piled high with dishes from dinner, and at the refrigerator, covered with colorful photographs of friends and family, taken throughout the years, and paused on my favorite one.

It was of Leisel and me, her in a plain white T-shirt and coral cropped pants, me in a black camisole and matching skirt, our arms looped together as we mugged for the camera with wide smiles on our faces.

"I'm covering this cake," I told the photograph sternly. "And I'm saving it for you. You're going to eat every last bite of it when you get here."

Turning, I headed toward the sink, flipped on the radio, and got to work on the pile of dishes, while humming along with the melody of "The Ballad of Lucy Jordan."

Sneak Peek

BENEATH BLOOD AND BONE

Coming later in 2015

CHAPTER ONE

Eagle

MY HEAVY BOOTS stomped angrily over the dry earth, my lungs burning liquid fire in my chest as I headed back toward the gate. Correction, what was left of the gate thanks to her—my wildcat.

I shouldn't have bothered chasing her, I was never going to catch her on foot, and I'd only accomplished looking like a damn fool for trying.

I still wasn't sure what it was about that woman that had gotten under my skin. I wasn't normally the type to bother with anyone, never mind a woman. Maybe her freeness, her unwillingness to be tamed by me or anyone else. Who the fuck knew?

"E, man?" Daniel panted as he jogged up beside me. "Jeffers and Liv want to see you."

Frowning at Daniel, a skinny, ugly, useless son of a bitch, even more useless than a woman without a pussy, I shoved him out of my way and walked on. No one got away from me, no one, nothing, not fucking ever.

"E!" Daniel hurried to catch up with me. "Liv, man, she's pissed."

"So fucking what!" I yelled. Again I pushed him, backward this time, making him fall flat on his ass. Immediately he raised his arms, shielding his face from me. I was well known for my temper, even better known for the many fights I'd fought in Purgatory, never once losing or even coming close to it. Daniel was right to fear me. Almost everyone did.

But not Wildcat...

And definitely not Liv.

"I'm sorry, man," Daniel hurriedly said. "I was just—"

"Following orders," I interrupted. "I fucking get it."

Staring down at him, I felt like ripping into him, tearing his scrawny arms straight from his body and making him eat his own flesh for breakfast. Instead, I looked away and took a deep, not-so-calming breath.

Not only had Daniel never done anything to deserve my wrath, but I was already in deep shit. Jeffers and his woman, Liv, had wanted that pretty boy Wildcat had belonged to. Needed him, actually. There weren't a lot of men left who could fight like he could, and now he was as good as dead. Marcus had done him in with one neat slice-and-dice straight through the liver with a little extra twist to be certain, just like I'd taught him. Wouldn't be a quick death, wasn't going to feel good, that was for sure. I gave him a few hours at the most before he bled out entirely.

A group of men rushed past me cursing, armed with tools to try to fix the mangled gate before any rotters happened to swing by. Off in the distance, I could already hear Liv's shrill voice screeching away at Jeffers. Little pink-haired slut was a demon in bed, but out of bed...it was if the devil himself had gone and possessed a pink-haired, skinny little bitch with a mouth the size of Texas.

As for Jeffers, fuck him. The man was useless now, entirely pussy-whipped by her. He used to be worth a damn, several actually, but now all he was good for was doing her bidding, while I was left to do her bedding.

They were both waiting for me at the edge of the lot, just beyond the newest set of vehicles I'd towed in last week, waiting to get chopped. There were a few other people surrounding them, people I recognized but never had cared enough to meet them, let alone learn their names.

When I reached them, stopping in front of the small group, Liv was staring at me, her eyes narrowed into venomous slits, her too-thin body vibrating with anger. Everyone else was silent, their eyes on anything other than me. Smart people...whoever they were.

"Are you even fucking listening to me?" Liv stepped forward, jabbing a pointy finger into my chest. "Your little act just cost us big-time, asshole."

It never ceased to amaze me how fearless she could be, especially being as small as she was. She was scared of nothing and no one, not even me. I wasn't too sure on the specifics of her story or how'd she come to be here, but whatever kind of hell she'd gone through, it must have been some fucked-up shit. Either that, or she'd just been born one crazy-ass bitch.

Grabbing her finger, I pushed her hard enough that she stumbled backward. She glanced at Jeffers, waiting to see his reaction, though we both knew Jeffers wasn't going to do a damn thing, not against me.

When his eyes finally did rise, his gaze was hard, the way it used to be, the way it had been when we'd first put this place together. From the ground up, just him and me and a small group of survivors had made this place what it was today. Then Liv had come along and took him, his balls, and any last shred of testosterone he'd had, and wrapped it all up in a pretty pink bow around her little finger.

"You let them go!" Liv screamed. "A fighter and two decent pieces of ass! And for what? Because you *liked* one of them? I had plans for them all!"

I shrugged. "I'll fight back what I owe you for the fence."

"Nobody wants to fight you!" Throwing her arms up in the air, she spun away and started stomping off. But not before sending her fist into Jeffers's gut and hissing, "Do something!"

With a sigh, Jeffers took a step forward and opened his mouth to speak.

Smirking, I held up my hand, cutting him off. "Don't you dare lecture me on letting pussy go to my head, you goddamn hypocrite. Not when that bitch has your balls locked up tight inside her skank hole. All I'm gonna say to you is I know I fucked up, and I'll pay you back for that gate."

Pushing past him, I headed straight to the Cave, needing a drink or three and a nice hard fuck in order to put all this bullshit behind me.

When I entered, I found Dori in the back, seated by the bar as usual. Spotting me, she waved happily, a smile curving her lips. She was a striking woman, or at least she had been before the rotters had gotten to her, forcing our sham of a doctor to take her legs. But she was still alive and infection-free, and that was more than most people who'd been bitten could say.

Taking a seat, I held up two fingers, signaling for the man behind the bar to bring me my usual—Dori's homemade concoction. Smelled like shit, tasted even worse, but it did its job in taking me from point A to point B. And I couldn't ever seem to reach point B on my fucking own anymore.

As soon as it was handed to me, I tossed it back and swallowed it all in one gulp, enjoying the burn it ignited inside me, the warmth that swelled in my stomach. Signaling for another, I could still feel Dori's eyes on me, waiting for me to tell her what happened this morning, to give her all the dirty details of what had gone down and why the camp was in such an uproar.

When I didn't, she changed tactics. Rolling her wheelchair across the floor, she parked it next to my seat and placed her tiny hand on my arm.

"The wildcat?" she asked, her voice soft and husky.

"Gone," I replied, swallowing back my second drink. Raising my fingers, I signaled for another.

"For good?"

Snorting, I nodded my head. Of course she was gone for good. Even after her man died, which he would, there was no way she was going to come back here—to me. And two women out there alone, no man to protect them… They'd be eaten up and spat back out before the next nightfall. By rotters, or whoever else happened on them. They were done for.

And it was my fucking fault.

"I don't know," I ground out, hating the guilt I was feeling. Part of me thought I should have gone after them and dragged them back here to safety. But the other part of me, the part of me that liked hearing women cry, the part of me that liked watching my fist obliterate the face of my opponent, the part of me that got off being a king in this cold, dead world, that part of me knew she'd fight me tooth and nail, if not outright kill me, before she'd ever come back here…back to me.

"E," she said, sounding hesitant. "I know you liked her. I know that you wanted her to stay, I did too. She would have been good currency around here. The mousy one too. God knows the men around here love that innocent act."

Turning to Dori, I took her slender face in my hand, squeezing her cheeks until she yelped in pain, pulling her toward me until it was only me keeping her from falling straight out of her chair. I was fully aware of the several men in the room who were now staring at us, waiting to see what was going to happen and probably wondering if they should help Dori. But I already knew none of them would say a word, let alone make a move against me. They weren't that stupid.

"You don't know shit, woman," I spat. "And that wildcat would have been my property. No way would my property have been working in a shithole like this. As for that other one, she's about as innocent as they come these days. Why do you think they wanted to leave? Nobody worth a damn wants to live their lives in a shit pit like this, around people like you."

And me, I added silently.

Beneath my fingers, her chin trembled while her eyes filled up with tears. The sight of her, so weak and pitiful, only made my mood worse. My upper lip curling with disgust, I released her face, thrusting her backward into her chair.

"I thought I was your property," she whispered. "You said before—"

"You had legs then, and I was between them when I said it." Grabbing the drink the bartender brought me, I quickly swallowed it and slammed the glass down on the table. "Now you're just pussy. Nothing more."

Pushing out of my chair, I stalked across the room, grabbing the neck of a tall brunette who'd been hanging off the arm of another man. I'd fucked her before, too many times to count, but I still didn't know her name, and didn't care to ever learn it.

Dragging her up the stairs, I pushed her into the first unlocked door I found, tossed her on the bed, and started undressing. I needed to fuck. I needed to fuck hard and fast, and then I needed to beat the shit out of someone, anyone…so much so I found myself hoping like hell Liv would let me back into the ring. Maybe if I promised to throw a couple of fights…

The fuck did nothing for me. None of these whores did a damn thing for me. The sex was empty and hollow, just the mindless slapping of my body against her used-up one. More than likely she'd fucked twenty guys already this morning, and another fifty would be coming by for more when I was through with her.

Worse, I was still thinking about the wildcat, those sweet red curls, her big blue eyes full of fire, and that tight little body of hers. Even better, how she'd fought me every step of the way, challenged me like no woman had done in far too long. Made me want something I'd thought I was no longer capable of. Made me want something that was no longer possible.

It was good she was gone. I couldn't afford any sort of weakness in this world. Not a single drop. You let that shit spill out of you, and people noticed. And when people noticed, they took advantage.

"Two rats," I yelled as I left the room. Because that was all she was worth to me—two slabs of dead rodent.

As I passed by the bar, buttoning my jeans, Dori was still there, a fresh drink in her hand. Sitting down opposite her, I took her drink and swallowed it down in one wincing gulp.

"You don't mention her ever again, got it?" Glaring at her, I handed her the empty glass.

Nodding, she took the glass and dropped her gaze. "I'm sorry, E."

Another unwanted sliver of guilt snaked its way through me, making my chest uncomfortably tight before coiling uneasily in the pit of my stomach. But instead of apologizing to her like I knew I should have, I got to my feet and muttered, "Know your fucking place, woman."

Exiting the Cave, I found the sun still shining brightly, mocking me from its place up high in the sky where no one could touch it. Because if I could touch it, if I could reach it, I'd beat the holy shit out of it, make sure it never dared to shine again. There was no place for sunlight here. Sunlight was for the living. And no one was living anymore. Speaking of which…

Cracking my knuckles, I surveyed the people passing by me. I needed to beat someone senseless, wrap my hands around their throat and watch as the life began to leave their eyes. I needed to not just feel my strength, but use it. It was all I had left, the only thing that could mirror what actually living had felt like, the only thing that reminded me I was still alive.

My wife had made me feel alive. My kids too. My old job, stripping and rebuilding old cars back to their previous glory, had given me a sense of satisfaction once upon a time. Even Wildcat, she'd given me a tiny slice of something familiar, something I'd been hoping would grow into more.

Two men passing by paused in front of me, a mangy-looking and downright filthy brunette in their grasp. She hung limply between them, her wide gray eyes looking feral as they darted back and forth, taking in her surroundings.

"Found her scavenging out by the turbines," one of the men said, grinning. "The little bitch was eating bugs right off the ground like a damn animal."

"Where do you want her?" the other asked, looking more than ready to get rid of her.

"Ask Jeffers," I said callously. "I don't deal with this shit anymore."

The man slowly shook his head. "Jeffers said otherwise, man. He said all new recruits are coming straight to you. Said it's time you got to keeping yourself busy."

Closing my eyes, I gritted my teeth. Liv, that fucking bitch, wasn't going to let me fight; she was putting me to work like one of her damn minions.

Opening my eyes, I glanced down at the woman, taking in the tattered remains of her clothing, the caked-on dirt covering nearly every inch of her. Her eyes met mine, and though she was obviously dazed from one too many punches to her face, her bloodied nostrils flared as she tried to snarl.

Bending my knees, I dropped down to her level, leaning in close enough to get a hearty whiff of body odor and shit, probably her own. Smart woman...the worse you smelled, the less the rotters noticed you.

"Welcome to Purgatory," I said coldly. "Last stop on the road to hell."

She didn't respond, but neither did she snarl again. She just stared at me, those big wild gray eyes of hers shrewdly assessing me much the way a predator did its prey.

Baring my teeth, I grinned at her. She wasn't going to last here; her type never did. She was too accustomed to the wild, having gone too long without human contact. There was no domesticating those who had given in to the dormant beasts that hide inside us all.

The fence that surrounded us and its gates were the equivalent of a cage, and she'd be climbing and clawing her way out the first chance she got. I would know; I sensed that beast inside me every damn day, constantly trying to rip its way free. Suppression only succeeded in making it worse, the animal within pacing manically back and forth in its small confines.

"Give her to Dori," I said, straightening. "She'll clean her up and put her to work."

"She bites," the second man said, laughing nervously. "Claws, kicks, and spits too. Drew had to hit her a few times just to get her to calm the fuck down. You sure you want her in the Cave?"

"Give her to Dori," I repeated. "Don't make me say it again."

Moving aside, I let the trio pass by me, glancing down at my hands. Caged as I felt, they were all I had left, my hands and the chaos they could cause, the punishment they could bring. The destruction they could rain down on whatever was in my way.

CHAPTER TWO

Autumn

THEIR CALLOUSED HANDS on my arms hurt. I wanted them to let go, to stop squeezing so much. But every time I tried to fight them, the tall one hit me. Best to keep still, to play helpless, useless. That was how I'd survived this long, out here all alone. Play dead, hide, stay away from others, and avoid the biters. Hush, hush, must keep quiet or they'll hear you.

I didn't normally venture so close to people, always keeping my distance from others, dead or alive, but I was so hungry. My traps had been empty for the third day running, the horde of biters that had recently passed through had scared all the animals off, and now I was starving and thirsty, ready to eat anything I could. And so I had gone in search of food, gotten too close to the noisy people who talked too much and still laughed like they hadn't lost everything. Like life was still worth living.

People were bad. Violent. Aggressive. Greedy. They were worse than the biters because other than eating you alive, they didn't want to hurt you, not like the people did. People liked to make you cry; they liked to hurt you, to see you bleed. They kept you alive just to watch you cry and bleed, then laugh while you hurt.

I wasn't going to stay here, and I wasn't going to work here. I was going to kick and scream, to fight and bite anyone who tried to touch me.

The tall one was digging his fingers into my arm, looking down at me with a sick and twisted smile on his face, telling me he was enjoying this, hurting me, teaching me a lesson for hitting him in the face. But I wouldn't have hit him if he hadn't touched me, if he'd just left me alone. I wanted to go home, back to my cave, back to the darkness and the safety.

The men dragged me inside, my feet dragging up the steps since I refused to walk, and they were refusing to be gentle. People weren't gentle anymore; no one was gentle anymore. They used to be, though. I remember how they used to be. But everyone else seemed to have forgotten.

Inside it was cooler, the brightness of the day staying outside where it belonged. I felt better in here with the darkness. My eyes adjusted to the dark quickly and I saw other people, fewer than outside, but still far too many for me to feel comfortable. My heartbeat, already erratic, began to pound harder in my chest. I swallowed hard, my mouth parched and my stomach empty and burning, the few beetles I'd managed to unearth not nearly enough to satisfy me.

It smelled in here. It smelled of something that I remembered, yet something I'd forgotten. I didn't like it—the smells, the people, the noise. It was dangerous, all of it, and would attract the biters. They would come back again, and these people wouldn't be able to hide forever. They'd come and they'd kill, and I didn't want to be here when it happened.

The men came to a stop in the middle of the large room, tables and chairs scattered throughout. People too, all of them staring at me. A woman in a wheelchair loomed before me; she was pretty but her legs were gone. She was blond and thin, and…nearly naked.

Where was I?

"What am I supposed to do with that?" she asked, her soft voice laced with annoyance.

The tall one laughed. "E said to bring her to you. You're supposed to put her to work."

Work. What an odd choice of word considering they'd kidnapped me, dragged me off to their foul place of existence. I wasn't doing any harm to them, wasn't bothering them, yet they'd cornered me, taken me, beaten me.

I wanted to go home.

Home. Was that what I was calling my cave now? Home wasn't

what it used to be. It wasn't a two-bedroom, white brick house with yellow rosebushes lining the driveway and a swing set in the backyard. Home no longer had a pantry and a bathroom, it didn't have a television or a comfy peach sofa with three cream cushions. Home wasn't any of those things anymore. But home, my cave, was safe. Home was something I could trust. Where I belonged. I couldn't trust this place or these people. And I didn't belong here.

The short, fat man was talking now, but I was shaking so hard my teeth were chattering, and I couldn't make out a word of it. I couldn't be here, I couldn't stay here around these awful people, these loud, noisy people. I couldn't be here when the biters came back and killed them all. I wasn't ready to die. Not yet.

"What good is she going to be to me?" the woman shrieked. "She's disgusting! My God, she's growling!"

"Clean her up," the tall one said. "Who knows, there might be a whole lot of good under all that shit." Glancing down at me, he grinned again. "After a week in the Cave, she'll have all that fight fucked right out of her."

My pounding heart stuttered to a stop. Fucked. Fucked. Fucked. What was this place? What were they going to make me do?

No... No, I couldn't be here. I couldn't be here!

"No," the woman said. "You can't leave her here! What in the hell am I supposed to do with her? Why doesn't she speak? Is there something wrong with her?"

"Aw, come on, Dori." The short one groaned, releasing my arm.

My body slouched to the ground, leaving me leaning at an awkward angle. The tall one hadn't let me go, his fingers still curled around my bicep, his nails digging sharply into my skin.

"There's shit going down out there, and we need to get back to it or Liv's going to have a fit if that gate isn't back up. Cut us some slack, would ya?"

The woman sighed, an angry, irritated sigh. "Fine," she snapped, "but only until I speak to E. Put her in one of the back rooms, and lock her up until I can find someone who's willing to clean her."

Gripping the armrests on her wheelchair, she leaned forward as she looked me over. "You try anything," she hissed viciously, "anything at all, and I will cut you. You got that?" Sitting back in her chair, she crossed her arms beneath her breasts and glared at me. "Why can't we leave the crazy ones in the wild?" she muttered. "They don't belong with us."

I wanted to laugh at her, to tell her how stupid she was, thinking that I was the crazy one. They were the crazy ones. Living out in the open like this, playing with biters, being noisy and laughing as if there was still something to laugh about in this world.

"I don't like this," she continued. "I'll never get her stench out of the sheets. I'll have to burn them." Her voice turned shrill. "And sheets are expensive!"

"Sure, sure," the short one said as he reached for my arm again, and it took everything in me to allow him to touch me, to not lash out, to not kick and scream and fight my way free of this place.

I wanted to go back to my cave. I didn't want to be here. I didn't want their hands on me. I didn't want to hear their noisy voices. See their stares. Their anger. Their pity. I didn't want any of it. A hot tear slipped free from the corner of my eye as my panic began to rise.

"I want to go home," I whispered, my throat dry and scratchy, my own voice sounding foreign to my ears.

The woman glanced sharply at me, a flash of sympathy crossing her features. "Don't we all, darlin'?" she replied, easily shrugging away her emotion. "You're better here with us."

I could read her expression—the slight pinching of her nose, the slump of her shoulders—and knew she didn't believe her own words.

"Home is where you stay," she continued. "And this is where you'll stay now. It's safe here. You have nothing to fear from me."

A snarl slipped past my lips, the only sound I could manage to make in the face of her lie. Her cheeks flushed hotly as she realized I could see straight through her, see her for what she really was. A liar. And a bad one at that.

Glancing up at the men, she nodded and jerked her thumb over her shoulder. With a grunt, they began dragging me across the room, my dirty sneakers scuffing across the carpet, lifting the edge of a rug. All eyes were on me, the room quiet save for the sound of my feet snagging on the uneven floorboards and bits of carpet strewn about.

As I was taken down a dark hallway, the air grew considerably warmer, the smells rising in their intensity. Noises came from behind closed doors all around me, familiar noises, groans and moans and cries, not of pain, but of pleasure. I remembered pleasure; even when

I didn't want to remember it, I did. I remembered his handsome young face, the feel of his warm hands, the way his soft mouth would cover mine. I could hear myself crying out, wanting more of him...

"Jesus, she stinks." A naked woman pressed herself against the wall, wrinkling her nose in disgust as I was dragged past her.

"Don't I fucking know it!" the tall one replied, laughing. "But pussy is pussy."

"You're going to hit this?" the short one asked, sounding horrified. "Man, she probably has a hundred fucking diseases."

"I'll hit a hole in the wall," the tall one said. "A knot in a tree, a rip in the mattress, makes no difference to me. Here we are, home sweet home."

We stopped in front of a door, and the short one released me to open it. Gripping me tighter, the tall one pulled me inside. It was dark except for one window that allowed the sunlight in, highlighting the sparse furnishings—a small bed, a dresser, and a chair.

Shoving me forward, the tall one released me, and I fell to the floor in a heap.

"I'll be back once you're cleaned up," he said, and I lifted my head to look at him. Sneering down at me, he touched his cheek where I'd hit him. "You owe me for this, and this." He held up his arm, showing me a bloody bite mark.

The men left, slamming the door shut behind them. A lock clicked into place, the sharp sound echoing loudly through the nearly empty space, sucking all the air out of the room and making it hard for me to breathe. The walls seemed to grow nearer, closing in on me as my heart beat painfully in my chest.

"I want to go home," I whispered to no one.

Only I knew that I was no longer talking about my cave. I was talking about my home made of white brick, the one with two bedrooms, and yellow rosebushes that lined the driveway. My home with the swing set in the backyard. With the pantry and a pretty bathroom, and a TV that I used to watch when I sat on my comfy peach sofa, with the three cream cushions on it. I missed that home. I missed that life.

These people, their noises and their smells, this place, they were making me remember all I had lost.

"I want to go home!" I screamed, slamming my clenched fists down on the floor.

ABOUT THE AUTHORS

Fantastical realm dweller, lover of anything deemed inappropriate, and *USA Today* bestseller Madeline Sheehan is the author of the Holy Trinity Trilogy and the Undeniable Series. Homegrown in Western New York, Madeline resides there with her husband and son where she can usually be found engaging in food fights and video game marathons.

www.madelinesheehan.com
www.facebook.com/MadelinesheehanBooks

THE UNDENIABLE SERIES
Undeniable
Unbeautifully
Unattainable
Unbeloved

THE HOLY TRINITY SERIES
The Soul Mate
My Soul to Take
The Lost Souls

Claire C. Riley is a bestselling British horror writer whose work is best described as the modernization of classic, old-school horror. She fuses multi-genre elements to develop storylines that pay homage to cult classics while still feeling fresh and cutting edge. She writes characters that are realistic, and kills them without mercy. Claire lives in the United Kingdom with her husband, three daughters, and one scruffy dog.

www.clairecriley.com
www.facebook.com/ClaireCRileyAuthor

THE OBSESSION SERIES
Limerence
Limerence 2

THE DEAD SAGA
Odium 1
Odium Origins 1
Odium 2
Odium Origins 2

Made in the USA
Charleston, SC
07 February 2016